Lucy Clare Woolley was born in England of Irish-Polish extrac-
tion. She studied stage management at the Central School of
Speech and Drama in London where she met her husband,
actor James Woolley. She worked in the theatre as an assistant
stage manager and prop maker until the first of her four
children was born. After running a spectacularly unsuccessful
gift shop in Clapham for six years, she became a columnist and
then editor of *Living South* magazine. *Breaking the Trust* is her
second novel. Her first, *Hoping for Hope*, is also published by
Time Warner.

Also by Lucy Clare

Hoping for Hope

Breaking
the Trust

Lucy Clare

timewarner
paperbacks

A *Time Warner* Paperback

First published as a paperback original in Great Britain in 2002
by Time Warner Paperbacks
Reprinted 2004

A CIP catalogue record for this book
is available from the British Library.

ISBN 0 7515 3158 8

Typeset in Berkeley Book by M Rules
Printed and bound in Great Britain
by Clays Ltd, St Ives plc

Time Warner Paperbacks
An imprint of
Time Warner Book Group UK
Brettenham House
Lancaster Place
London WC2E 7EN

www.twbg.co.uk

For the drummers, Kate, Marian and Katherine, with my love

Acknowledgements

To editors Viv Redman from Time Warner Books and Julia Forrest from Edwards Fuglewicz for being so generous with their time, their help and their encouragement. Two wonderful people.

Everyone at Time Warner Books, especially Ursula Mackenzie and Katy Nicholson.

All at Edwards Fuglewicz, especially Helenka Fuglewicz who does so much for me.

Everyone at Dutton, most particularly Carole Baron and Carrie McGinnis.

Derek Orme for the time he spent helping me get right the practicalities of opening a restaurant – and also for reading the manuscript to make sure I'd been listening to him properly.

David Tyrrell for sharing his enormous knowledge of catering.

Tom Furnell the fireman for telling me about fires.

Angela Down for being a perfect reader.

Robert White for his legal advice and for lending me Tymar.

And to Ian Davidson, because he's taught me so much in the last two years.

Thank you.

Chapter One

Mark was in bed with Freddie when his father began to die. The mobile telephone shrieked and Mark leant over, busying through the pile of clothes on the floor. Freddie slipped out of his arm, sighed loudly and turned over on her side.

'Mark Palmer . . . Oh hi. Yes, what? When? How is he?'

Mark was already hopping about on one leg trying to put on his boxer shorts as he spoke on the phone.

'Yup, I'm on my way now. What? . . . No, I'm . . . in . . . er, in Gospel Oak. Just come out of a meeting.'

Freddie turned over and raised an eyebrow at him and Mark shook his head at her. 'Okay, I'll be with you as soon as I can. Tell her I'm coming.'

He threw the little black phone on to the bed and scrabbled around in search of a sock.

'My father's collapsed. Come on, I've got to go.'

Freddie pushed back the duvet and stretched her long legs to the floor. 'Is he bad?'

Mark made a face. 'I wouldn't know. My brother Ralph is a man of few words and they are invariably an order. He's on his way to The Mill.'

'Gospel Oak? Why on earth Gospel Oak?'

Mark, now fully dressed, looked at Freddie – her large, succulent body, half dressed, her long red hair tousled – and he longed to drag her back into bed. She was nearly twenty years younger than he. It's not true that a young mistress makes a middle-aged man feel younger – Mark felt every one of his fifty-two years when he was with Freddie, but he had more fun and he was more relaxed with her than with anyone else.

He shrugged. 'Don't know. I've never been there, but I've always liked the name. Gospel Oak.' He savoured the words. 'John Wesley tub-thumping under an oak tree. It just came out while I was talking and it's a safe distance from Fulham.'

'A word of advice, Mark. On these sort of occasions – selective honesty or, rather, selective lying is the key.' Freddie leant over to tidy the bed and smiled up at Mark. 'There is always a chance that there was a major traffic accident or a bomb at Gospel Oak this afternoon and you would have been caught up in it. You should have told the truth.'

Mark looked mystified. 'What, that I am in a friend's flat, in central London, screwing my young, beautiful mistress?'

'No. That your meeting is in Kensington. You and I are meeting in Kensington. That's a truth.'

'Well, it's been a most productive meeting.' Mark winked at her. 'We must meet again soon.'

'I hope we will.' Freddie smiled at him mischievously. 'Give me a ring, why don't you.'

Mark bent down and kissed her. He made an attempt to help her with the bed, but Freddie waved him away.

'Leave it, I'll tidy up here and lock up. You go. Shouldn't you ring your wife, by the way?'

'Oh shit, yes, I suppose so. I'll do it in the car. Are you sure you're all right with all this?' He gestured at the empty champagne bottle and glasses on the bedside table.

Freddie moved round the bed and put her arms around Mark. 'Of course. Trust me. I'll leave it spotless, promise. Ring me when you can.'

'I will.' He paused for a moment at the bedroom door and said with confidence, 'The Gaffer's done this before. Emphysema, you know. They'll get him on to some oxygen and I'm sure he'll be fine. Nice fuck,' he added laconically.

Titus was in his workshop listening to the afternoon play on the radio when his father began to die. By the time he was dead, Titus had completed the reupholstery of a Queen Anne chair and had begun repairs on a bedhead commissioned by the local museum. He had turned off the radio to answer the phone and now, as he put down the receiver, he absentmindedly pushed the CD button on the stereo. The gravelly voice of Leonard Cohen throbbed round the workshop and he was still sitting motionless on his workbench when Jane came in with two mugs of tea.

'Tea.' She joggled his arm. 'Hey, you. Hello. Tea.'

Titus became aware of his wife's brisk Australian voice beside him and looked up at her.

'My father has died,' he said with a sad formality as he took the tea.

'Oh no. Oh, sweetheart, I'm sorry.' Jane put down her mug and taking Titus's out of his hand hugged him tightly. Cohen's sixties anthem flooded over them.

'When did it happen?'

'This afternoon.'

They stood together in silence.

'So now what?' Jane released Titus and settled herself on the bench beside him. He looked down at her bare feet and found himself counting the red poppy designs on her long skirt. He was waiting to feel something sad, to feel different in some way, but all his feelings seemed to have been suspended.

He shrugged. 'She didn't have time to talk, the others were on their way down. She'll ring me about the funeral and,' he looked at her, 'and she's going to tell them about us.'

Jane drew in her breath. 'Ow. Bad time. Very heavy for them.'

'I suppose this is it. It's all over, isn't it?'

'Why should it be?'

Titus slid off the bench. He clenched his lips together and raised his eyebrows. 'He's dead, so it will be like we never existed. After all, she doesn't have to do anything about me, *us*, if she doesn't want to – not now.'

Jane joined him on the floor and, out of habit, Titus frowned, wishing vaguely that she wouldn't walk barefoot in his workshop.

'That's rubbish. I really don't think she's going to abandon us – she's not that type of person. You know how she feels about you. And the kids.' Jane took Titus's hand. 'And now we've got to tell Summer and Alby everything. We really must.'

'Why must we? Can't we just leave it as it is?'

Jane shook Titus's arm. 'Of course we can't. If *they*'re going to know, so should our kids. I've always thought they should've been told before. Now there's no argument. The secret is out and we've got to tell them the truth.'

Titus shrugged in a hopeless gesture.

'Come on.' Jane took his hand. 'Summer will be home from college in a minute.'

'They'll miss him,' Titus said sadly.

Mark was mistaken. His father was not fine. Not at all. Jack Palmer was already dead by the time Mark arrived at the family house in a small village just outside Tunbridge Wells.

'He's gone, I'm afraid.' Ralph greeted Mark brusquely, his voice choked, holding back unmanly tears. 'Heart attack, very quick, no pain.'

Without thinking first, Mark reached out and squeezed his older brother's arm – an unusually tactile gesture from which Ralph, characteristically, edged away slightly. They rarely exchanged physical expressions of emotion, and Mark's touch was made in an unthinking moment, born of just having spent time with Freddie.

Mark spoke hurriedly to cover the awkwardness between them. 'How's Clattie? Where is she?'

'In the drawing room. Grania's with her. She's bearing up very well in the circumstances.'

Used to his brother's formality, Mark nodded. 'Is there something I should be doing?' he asked diffidently. 'Arrangements and things.'

'All in hand.' Ralph sounded more robust, safer now that he was back to dealing with practical matters. 'He's upstairs, if you want to see him. The undertaker will be here shortly.' He looked at his watch. 'I hope Pippa gets here before he does. She's very late.'

Mark climbed the stairs and went into his father's room. The Gaffer was lying on his bed, fully clothed, eyes closed as though he were still sleeping: his skin had already taken on a waxy patina and his face was empty. Mark looked out of the window and watched the white pigeons on the roof of the outhouses at the bottom of the garden. The bedroom window was closed so he couldn't hear the wind in their wings as the flock took off together in sudden flight, wheeling round the garden in a white cloud. Mark forced himself to look down at the body of his father. He could feel nothing.

Ralph was coming up the stairs as Mark left the bedroom.

'Right,' Ralph said. 'I'd just like another moment on my own . . .' There was genuine pain and grief in his face. 'You better go and see Clattie.'

In the drawing room, their mother was standing, staring at the garden through the floor-length sash windows. The large herbaceous flower beds were full of early spring flowers and wisteria just coming into bud hung heavily over the old stone walls. She was talking as Mark appeared in the doorway.

'Damn, I really needed Jack to strike some camellia cuttings this spring. He was so much better at it than me.'

Ralph's wife rose from the sofa when she saw Mark and kissing him, murmured, 'She's in shock. She keeps saying very strange things.'

Clattie heard her and turned around.

'There is nothing strange about needing some camellia cuttings,' she said patiently.

She tripped across the room to hug Mark. 'Darling boy, I am so sorry.' She held his face in her hands and looked at him earnestly. 'It was a heart attack, just out of the blue. He was fine at lunch, then he went to lie down. I heard him call out. He died at about three o'clock, just as the ambulance arrived. There was nothing they could have done. It was quite quick and I don't think he felt much pain. He would like this. So much better than slowly drowning to death with his emphysema.'

Mark hugged Clattie and felt some of her strength and resilience flow into his stiff, tense body. The first tears began to build up behind his eyes – and they were only for his mother.

Relieved to relinquish the responsibility for her mother-in-law, Grania stood up and offered to make a pot of tea.

'Would you, darling,' Clattie said thankfully. 'Doris is in the kitchen. She insisted on staying on this afternoon – to look after us, she said. She's terribly upset.'

Clattie sat down on the sofa when Grania had left: she patted the seat beside her. 'Come and sit down, darling. Dear Grania. Ralph put her in charge of me when she arrived and she's been so kind and gentle. But,' she drew herself up straight, 'I'm all right. I am not about to fall apart. I have too much to do,' she finished enigmatically.

Mark looked at his mother with affection. She had always been known as Clattie to everyone, including her children. Considerably younger than her husband and now in her mid-seventies, she was like a cheerful exotic bird, pecking and preening about the place. Always energetic and practical, she was surprisingly strong for such a small, delicate-looking woman. Now, as she unsuccessfully tried to tuck a lock of long white hair into the knot tied on the top of her head, her bright blue eyes examined her younger son anxiously. 'The important thing is, are you all right, darling? Is Bella coming?'

Mark had rung his wife on the car phone as he beat his way down the motorway.

'I have to go into a meeting in a minute,' Bella had said impatiently, 'but I'll meet you at The Mill this evening.' Mark could imagine her pulling her Filofax towards her and pencilling the appointment into the time slot marked seven p.m. Bella ran her own PR company with ferocious commitment. 'I'm sure the Gaffer will be fine,' she had added briskly. 'We've had scares like this before.'

'Yes,' Mark said to Clattie now. 'She's coming down after work. She couldn't get away before. Ralph says Pippa's on her way.'

Clattie sighed. 'Poor Pippa, she will be sure to blame herself for not being here. You don't suppose she'll bring anyone from the community with her, do you? It only occurred to me afterwards, but it was too late to ring her back. I don't think I could bear to be prayed over just now.'

Mark and Ralph's sister, Philippa, had been born nine years after Mark. With both boys away at school much of the year, she had had a solitary childhood until she too was sent off to boarding school. As an adult, she had lived an unambitious and single life, moving seamlessly from secretarial college to an office job in a boys' prep school in Bath where she had remained until recently. Prone to sudden enthusiasms, Pippa's life was littered with abandoned fads and hobbies and now, suddenly, aged forty-three, she had become caught up in Christianity and was currently staying at a religious community with, it seemed to her family, a view to reinventing herself as a modern-day nun. No one was quite sure how she had become so involved with this specific group of born-again Christians but her family were disconcerted by this new-found, fierce, evangelical fervour, and Ralph, especially, found his sister's particular brand of Christianity quite unacceptable.

'All this lecturing and "bless you" bit,' he would grumble. 'So bloody presumptuous.'

'This is going to be such a terrible shock for her,' Clattie now went on quietly, fidgeting her fingers over her elegant navy blue skirt. Clattie, with consummate taste, always wore her clothes well.

Mark put out his hand to still hers. 'She knows that the Gaffer was old and had been ill for a long time, so it can't be too much of a shock for her. She'll be sad, particularly that she wasn't here, but it's not really a shock, is it?' Mark was trying to comfort, but he had a growing sense that Clattie's dominant emotion at this moment was, strangely, not so much grief as some sort of apprehension or trepidation.

'And Ralph. I'm worried about Ralph, too,' Clattie said urgently. 'They were so close. This is going to be hard for you all.'

Mark responded briskly. 'We'll be all right. We all knew the Gaffer was a sick man; we'll grieve and then we'll get over it. But you – your life will be very different without him. You must think about yourself as well at this time.'

'I can't,' Clattie said with an odd note of desperation in her voice. 'Not now, I can't.' The front door banged and Clattie rose to her feet. 'That'll be Pippa. I must go and see her.'

Alone in the drawing room, Mark left a brief message on his wife's mobile phone and then sat back on the sofa looking up at the ornate cornicing on the ceiling. The white paint contrasted pleasingly with the duck-egg blue of the walls. The elegant long drawing room at The Mill had been painted in these same colours for as long as he could remember. Nothing ever changed in this particular room. His eyes dropped down to the picture of his father on the mantelpiece. Taken when he was a young man, in his army uniform, Jack stood stiff and proud; it could have been Ralph, they were so alike. And so close. Ralph had been their father's favourite – it was a generally acknowledged fact that Mark could never accept. He was the middle child – the also-ran – who wasn't the favoured eldest son, nor the longed-for daughter, who came so much later.

The haughty expression on the Gaffer's handsome face seemed to glare down at Mark as if he had known then, when the photograph was taken, long before he had had children, that he would, in the future, have one who could never quite manage to please him.

'A chef,' he had bellowed when Mark had told him his

8

ambition. 'A chef? What sort of job is that? You won't make money out of cooking.' But, supported by Clattie, Mark had pursued his own path and now he owned Basil, a successful catering company.

'Glorified servant – a modern-day butler that's all you are,' was the Gaffer's view. 'You should be using your brain.'

Ralph had taken the expected path, joining the family stationery business that Jack had started on leaving the army, and marrying the kind, sensible Grania who had managed to produce the only grandchildren.

Mark had married the exquisitely beautiful Bella whose energy and desire to achieve matched his own. Mark knew it was he who had inherited his father's brains, his ability to think quickly and to manipulate, and he had never grown out of his childish habit of trying to prove that – of seeking his father's approbation. But the Gaffer had not acknowledged Mark's success and now he never would.

Mark turned away from the picture as if unable to meet his father's eye, even in a photograph, and tried to imagine The Mill without him.

Grania brought in a tray of tea. 'The undertaker is here and Pippa has just arrived. Apparently she had an altercation with a lorry on the Malden bypass.' Mark recognised the effort Grania was making not to sound critical of her sister-in-law. Pippa rarely arrived anywhere without some confusion.

Grania unpacked the pile of cups and saucers, looked down at the tray and clicked her tongue.

'Cake. I'll see if there is any.' She left the room again and Mark reflected idly why it was that some people found it so necessary in a crisis to feed those around them.

Pippa, followed by Ralph, came into the drawing room. Her large, strongly defined face showed signs of recent tears.

'Bless you, Mark,' she said in a broken voice as she embraced him and Mark looked at Ralph over her shoulder. Ralph raised his eyebrows and grimaced. Mark gazed at his sister and tried to work out what was different about her. As

Pippa plumped herself into an armchair he realised it was her clothes. For as long as Mark could remember she had worn jeans and a sweatshirt and she'd always used make-up. Now her face was plain and unmade-up and she was wearing a large smock over an ankle-length skirt that billowed around her as she sat forward in the chair. She looked, he thought, like a pregnant bag lady.

'I think the Gaffer should stay here,' she announced imperiously. 'He shouldn't be taken away to some cold mortuary. He should be at home with us, at least for tonight.'

'Clattie and I thought it better not,' Ralph said stiffly, never liking his decisions questioned.

'The brothers and sisters are praying for his soul,' Pippa announced in the sing-song voice that she had recently adopted when talking about the community.

'That is kind of them,' Ralph said with polite irony.

'Everyone sends their blessings. Do you think he had the Lord in his heart when he died?' Pippa looked at her brothers.

Since Jack had not been near a church since he had fallen out with the local vicar in the early fifties, Mark thought it highly unlikely.

It was Ralph who answered curtly. 'I don't think that's any of our business actually, Pippa.'

She looked stricken. 'No, I'm sorry . . . I just hoped . . .' Embarrassed, she swirled to her feet and went out of the room.

'I can't believe that Jesus really demands his disciples to dress as though they've hijacked a ragbag,' observed Ralph.

Grania came in with the cake. 'Tea's all ready. Where's Pippa gone?'

'To administer Jesus to poor Clattie, I imagine.' Ralph threw himself into a chair.

The two men watched Grania dispense tea in silence.

Death creeps into a house, curls itself round a room and makes a hole that has to be filled – even if it's with mindless conversation.

Mark asked after his niece and nephew.

10

'Kit's at last beginning to get into his A-level work,' Grania said, sitting down with her tea, 'and Caitlin is having a fine time at Leeds.'

'Too much so, I would say.' Ralph smiled, and a lightness came back into his eyes as he talked about his precious family. 'I don't know that it's dawned on her yet that she is meant to work at university. What I do know is that it's costing me a fortune.'

Mark turned to Grania. 'And how's the open university course going?'

Grania shook her head. 'So-so. It's a long time since I did anything academic. I'm struggling with Chaucer at the moment.'

Ralph smiled across at his wife. 'She's working harder than all of us.'

The front door banged and Bella arrived in the drawing room, with Pippa and Clattie close behind her.

'I'm a bit late.' Bella sketched a kiss somewhere near Mark's cheek and he could smell her heavy scent. 'I just couldn't get out of the meeting. I saw your message when I came out.'

She adjusted her beautiful face into an expression of sadness. 'I'm so sorry about the Gaffer. Such a shock. I never—'

'Sit down,' interrupted Clattie peremptorily. They all looked up, startled by the ferocity in her normally mild voice. Standing in the middle of the room as though about to address a meeting, she looked pale and strained. She held what looked like a piece of cardboard in her hand and Mark noticed that she was rubbing her forefinger and thumb nervously against the dimpled surface.

'I have something I must tell you . . .' she began quietly and the five of them stared at her expectantly.

'Your father should be standing here doing this.' Her voice gathered strength, becoming, it seemed to Mark, almost belligerent. 'He should have told you a long time ago. I have always urged him to . . . now it is too late and I must do it. And I'm sorry. I am very, very sorry.'

Clattie spoke slowly then, as though she wanted them to

11

understand what she was saying the first time so that she might never have to repeat it.

She told them that they had an older brother. Jack had fathered him in the first year of his and Clattie's marriage. This brother of theirs had a wife and two children and during the last fifty-five years he had been part of Jack and Clattie's lives but, on Jack's insistence, had always been kept apart from the three of them.

'I'm sorry you have to learn all this now. I have also had to tell Titus today that his father has died.'

The mantelpiece clock gave its customary wheezy whirr before it struck the hour. No one moved as the collective initial disbelief was slowly exchanged for shock.

Titus, was Mark's first inconsequential thought. Why Titus? Odd name for a son of the Gaffer's. He instinctively looked at Ralph. His brother's face was blanched pale and the muscles in his clenched jaw rippled. He saw Grania lean over and take his hand. Pippa gasped and held her hands in front of her mouth. Bella, wide-eyed, was staring at Clattie – and Clattie just stood, hopelessly looking at the group sitting in front of her.

Mark realised that he was waiting for Ralph to speak because Ralph always spoke first – that was how it had worked in the family. Jack had believed in what he termed *seniores priores*. Family life had been run rigidly on the eldest taking precedence. Ralph had always got first choice in everything, right down to the first second helpings at meals. Even now Mark could remember, as a young boy, eyeing the dish of roast potatoes, desperately willing there to be enough for him to have another one when it came to his turn.

Pippa and Mark had been conditioned to expect Ralph to take the lead, but now Ralph remained silent. His eyes, deep and dark in his ashen face, fixed on the floor in front of him.

'I don't believe it.' Pippa broke the silence, speaking assuredly. 'It's not true – it can't be.'

'I'm afraid it is, darling.' Clattie's sad voice seemed to come from far away.

12

'Does he know about us?' Mark asked – the first of many questions that were starting to gather in his head.

'Yes.'

'Did you tell him today?'

'No.' Clattie spoke quietly, head bowed as if in shame. 'He and his wife have always known about you.'

Another silence.

'That's not fair.' Pippa's outrage spoke for them all. 'Not when we didn't know about him.'

'That was your father's decision. He was adamant that you should not be told anything about Titus until . . .' Clattie hesitated, 'until later,' she finished inadequately.

'So he's older than I am?' At last Ralph spoke. 'This man is my father's eldest son.' He spelt out the words slowly and savagely.

Funny what matters, Mark thought immediately and then realised it would, of course, be Ralph's first thought. He was also aware that none of them called Titus by name, as if by naming him he would become a real person.

Pippa began crying quietly, tears falling through her fingers as she buried her face in her hands. 'He wouldn't have done such a terrible thing,' she said in a muffled voice. 'Not the Gaffer. He couldn't, I know he couldn't. There must be some mistake.'

It was Grania who stood up and took Clattie's arm and gently led her to the sofa beside Mark.

Clattie waved the piece of cardboard vaguely. 'Here is a photograph of Titus and his family, if you would like to see it,' she muttered, subsiding into the sofa. None of them made any move to look at the photograph.

'No thank you,' Ralph said with a shudder.

Pippa fumbled with her asthma inhaler. 'I feel sick,' she wheezed.

'I don't understand.' The initial numbness that had overcome Mark was beginning to fade and now he was trying to make some sense of it all. 'Why couldn't we know before? Surely it would have been better if we'd just always known . . .?' He petered out, unable to form a coherent sentence.

Clattie spoke carefully as if torn between the truth and disloyalty. 'I thought you should have been told. I wanted you to grow up knowing about Titus. I told your father that children accept things that adults sometimes never can, but he believed he was right – and in the end it was his secret. He always promised he would tell you but, I don't know . . . it was difficult for him to face, perhaps.'

Ralph snorted derisively. 'The Gaffer always faced everything head on.'

Clattie looked up at Ralph. 'Darling, he was a very brave man in lots of ways. But I'm afraid our generation do tend to be a little cowardly when it comes to emotions. It was the way we were brought up by our parents. You see, they believed in the absolute rectitude of adults.' Clattie was momentarily distracted. 'It's almost as though they wanted us to grow up as emotionally impregnable as they appeared to be,' she continued thoughtfully. 'We were encouraged to bottle up our feelings in case of appearing weak and self-indulgent.' She looked at Ralph. 'Your father demanded respect from you children; it was very important to him. I think he was afraid he would lose that respect if he told you about Titus, so he kept putting it off.' She fell silent as if afraid of appearing critical of their father. 'Titus's mother wanted their son to know his father and the Gaffer felt he had a duty to do as she wanted.' Another pause and then Clattie added, 'You all know how strongly the Gaffer felt about fulfilling one's duties and Titus was his son, after all.'

'But I thought he loved *us*,' Pippa said.

'Of course he did, darling. He loved you all and he was so proud of you all.'

Another silence as each child of Jack's registered Clattie's emphasis on the word all. Was she, they wondered, including Titus?

'Where does he live?' Mark asked.

'South London. He's married to Jane. She's an Australian and they have two children.'

There was silence in the room as this information was digested.

Clattie squeezed her hands together on her lap and began talking again. 'Jack knew Titus's mother long before he met me. Shirley was an artist.'

So now this woman had a name and she was a real person. Mark tried to picture her.

'They met at a gallery where she was exhibiting her paintings,' continued Clattie. 'And she introduced him into a bohemian society that was completely strange to him and very exciting. To begin with he was captivated by it all but then Shirley fell in love with him – passionately. He didn't reciprocate her feelings and it became very uncomfortable as he tried to disentangle himself. She adored him – he was the love of her life. When he met me and asked me to marry him, she couldn't understand it and wasn't going to let him go without a fight. She was a very single-minded woman. She came to our wedding dressed in black. I never remembered her being asked, actually, but I do remember having the distinct impression that she had come to give Jack to me as a present. But it turned out that she couldn't leave him alone even after we were married and he was very embarrassed by her constant adoration. Jack tried to protect me from the situation but she would bombard him with letters and telephone calls. I knew nothing about all of this until the poor man had to tell me that Shirley was pregnant. He was abject. He'd had just one weak moment, manipulated by her. I think she was determined to have your father's baby, just to have something of his.'

Clattie paused as if waiting for some response, but no one spoke.

'She gave birth to Titus,' Clattie continued, 'just as I became pregnant with you, Ralph. Jack really had something to fight for then and eventually she agreed to leave him alone. But she made him promise that he would always keep in touch with Titus in some way. And so we always did.'

'Is she still alive?' Mark asked abruptly.

15

Clattie looked at him as if confused by the interruption. 'No, no, she died when Titus was very small. It did cross my mind then that we should offer to take him in and bring him up with you children.'

There was a fierce intake of breath from Ralph.

'But he went to live with Shirley's sister and her husband. They didn't have any children of their own. Jack and I would go and see Titus in London occasionally and when his Alby and Summer were born we saw them too. They were never told he was their grandfather, just that we were old family friends.' Clattie looked worried. 'I suppose Titus will tell them the truth now. That's going to be so hard for them.'

But Clattie's children were not interested in the pain of others.

'They didn't ever come here, did they?' Ralph asked abruptly.

'Yes, they do . . . they did sometimes. Jack grew very fond of the children. But he still couldn't face the idea of you meeting each other. He was most insistent that you were kept apart.'

'I don't understand.' Pippa looked puzzled. 'Any one of us might have turned up one day when they were here, then what would have happened?'

Clattie gave a little frown as though irritated by such a trivial question. 'We would have said that they were friends. Titus and Jane understood that and have been very good about it. I don't suppose it's easy for them—'

'At least they knew the truth,' broke in Pippa. 'If it really is the truth,' she added darkly.

Clattie made no response to Pippa's veiled accusation.

'He would have told you in the end – I'm sure he would – he was just waiting for the best time . . .' Clattie faltered.

Silence descended on the room again.

Ralph stood up and walked to the window, keeping his back to the rest of them. Mark saw Grania watching him anxiously.

'This is stupid.' Ralph spat out the words. 'The woman was obviously an obsessive. How do you know the baby was his? She probably had a string of lovers, any one of whom could

16

have been the father. Why did he let her get away with it? I don't believe it. It's just not possible. I don't understand . . .'

Everyone was watching Ralph's back as he struggled for some sort of comprehension – except Mark who was watching Clattie and who witnessed the sadness in his mother's eyes before she said firmly, 'Shirley insisted Titus was given the name Palmer. He *is* your half-brother and your father acknowledged him as such; he felt he had a commitment to him and later to his children. He had had to make that promise to Shirley so that she would leave us alone, and even after she died he felt he had to keep it. You all know what an honourable man he was.'

Pippa sat in her chair, her face ashen and her lips moving in what Mark could only presume to be silent prayer.

It was Grania who broke the silence and tended to Clattie, whose own children seemed unable to take their thoughts beyond their personal pain.

'I am so sorry, Clattie,' she said quietly. 'It must have been very difficult for you—'

'Oh don't be sorry for me, please,' Clattie said defiantly. 'I . . .' She stopped suddenly and pursed her lips as if to stop words tumbling forth without thought. 'I felt sorry for Jack because he felt so guilty about it. A momentary lack of control with such far-reaching consequences that coloured the rest of his life. Shirley was very beautiful, very determined and very manipulative. Your father didn't stand a chance with her.'

Mark was trying to make sense of the dominant father that he had known being controlled by this woman.

'Does *he* know this story?' he asked.

Clattie knew he meant Titus. 'I expect his aunt Monica would have told him some of it. But it was never talked about in this house. That was the rule. Your father was adamant that it was to be considered past history. He refused to speak about Titus's mother either to him or to me.'

'Did he go to her funeral?' Bella asked curiously.

It seemed to be one question too many for Clattie. 'No,' she said shortly, 'of course he didn't.' She stood up, seeming

17

calmer and stronger, as if she had been set free by this huge disclosure.

'I am so sorry.' She moved her arms in a circular gesture, encompassing the whole room. 'I know this has compounded the shock you're already feeling, but I'm sure you understand why you had to know immediately—'

'He's not coming to the funeral, I hope?' Ralph interrupted harshly.

'If he wants to.' Clattie sounded weary now. 'And the children too.' She looked around at them all. 'I can't make this any better for you and I will answer any questions you have. But now I need a drink – I think we probably all do.' She moved over to the drinks cupboard and poured herself a large whisky. 'Would you all help yourselves. Doris has left some supper for us.' She looked vague. 'I don't know what quite, but we'll eat in about half an hour.'

Pippa rose to her feet. 'I don't think I could eat anything.'

Clattie stretched out her hand in a vague gesture of peace. 'Give yourselves time. We must eat, we must get on. I am going upstairs to change.'

'I'll come with you.' Pippa made for the door, but Clattie interrupted her. 'No, darling, stay down here with the others, please. I shan't be long.'

Pippa slumped back into her chair.

In the silence left behind, the group turned as one to look at Ralph still standing stiffly at the window, but he didn't turn round.

'Bella and I will stay here tonight, of course,' Mark said eventually. He turned to look at Bella who gave a small frown and then nodded reluctantly.

'Clattie will need me,' Pippa pronounced. 'I'll ring the community and tell them I'm not going back, not for some time, anyway. I feel so dreadful that I wasn't here. I just had no idea that the Gaffer—'

'None of us did.' Mark spoke sharply, anxious to cut Pippa short.

18

Ralph turned round and looked at Grania. Mark had never seen such anguish in his brother's face. 'We must get back to Kit and we'll ring Caitlin. They'll be devastated by this.'

Grania acknowledged her husband's command by standing up.

'What about supper though?' she asked. 'Should we not stay?'

'No, we must get home.' Ralph spoke forcibly, as though he feared someone might prevent his flight. 'The others are here, they'll look after Clattie. I'll come back tomorrow, Mark, and we'll sort out the funeral. We must put an announcement in the paper. You'll be here, I assume?' It was as though Ralph had temporarily placed all that he had just heard in some deep recess within his head where it might sink without trace.

Mark brought his thoughts back to his father – he'd almost forgotten that there was a funeral to arrange: the Gaffer's death had now been pushed into the background.

He nodded. 'I've got a big wedding on this Saturday, but the team will cope. I'll ring them from here.' Even at this time, in the midst of high emotion, his natural instinct was to establish his importance in his own field – the competitive habit that he could never break.

'I shall have to go into the office tomorrow morning,' Bella said, also staking her importance, 'but,' she turned to Mark, 'I'll come back in the evening and bring you some clothes.'

He nodded. They were all taking refuge in the mundanity of plan-making.

Ralph and Grania left for their house in south London. Mark felt that Ralph was almost scrabbling to get away from The Mill – to get away from something big and dirty that, for once, he could not quite control. There was a dead look in his eyes as he kissed Clattie goodbye.

Grania sat beside her husband, numbed by the charged silence in the car. Occasionally she turned to look at Ralph's set profile as he concentrated on the driving.

Outside their large house in Camberwell, he turned off the

engine and sat back in his seat. 'You're right. We should have stayed,' he said eventually. 'I'm not in the habit of running away.'

'You're not running away,' Grania said stoutly. 'Shock sometimes means you make hasty decisions.'

Ralph turned to look at her, as though he had only just realised that she was beside him.

'I'm sorry,' he said simply, and Grania didn't know whether to dismiss his need for apology or to ask for what he was sorry.

'I can't really take in what Clattie has said,' he muttered. 'I just can't believe it. Not in our family.'

Grania watched her favourite calico cat wind itself around the lamp post as he waited for the front door to be opened.

'Poor Clattie. She'll be so alone without the Gaffer. So terrible for her. She needs all the support we can give her. We must be there for her.'

Ralph reached out and took his wife's hand. 'You're a very dear person and you're right, of course, we must, but,' in the glow of the street lighting Grania saw Ralph's face contort, 'I wish I wasn't so angry . . . with *everyone*. I can't think of anything else at the moment. It's just filling my head.'

Grania returned the pressure on his hand. 'It's perfectly understandable, darling. It's a terrible shock for all of you and it's bound to take some time to get used to.'

'I don't think I ever will,' Ralph said. 'I really don't. Nothing can be the same again.'

The four of them left at The Mill ate supper in the panelled dining room, sitting silently round the polished table – Jack's chair was left empty at the head of the table and in an unspoken agreement, the subject of the other family was not mentioned. Pippa had insisted on being in charge of the supper, bashing about in the kitchen, noisily preparing extra potatoes and vegetables that no one felt like eating.

Mark had gone in to help her.

'This is all very hard to get my head round,' he said as he peeled carrots. 'I can hardly believe it.'

Pippa had turned to look at him. Don't try to, her eyes begged.

When the meal was served, they all picked at the food.

'I'm afraid I've overcooked the broccoli a bit,' Pippa said. 'Oh no, I've forgotten the bread.' She got to her feet and knocked over her chair. The noise was magnified in the silent room.

'Leave it, darling.' Clattie looked up from her plate. 'We don't need bread tonight.'

'Are you sure?' Pippa looked round the table for confirmation. 'I could go and cut some very easily.' No one answered, and righting her chair she subsided on to it.

Bella suddenly looked up at Mark. 'Where were you this afternoon? I rang the office and Linda said you were out, but she didn't know where.'

'She knew I was quoting for a job in Gospel Oak. A charity function: three-course dinner and a band.' Mark heard himself offering much too much information.

'Oh right. I only wanted Frances Cole's number.'

Mark felt a jolt at Freddie's name.

'Why did you want it?' he asked nonchalantly.

'One of our clients is looking for a designer for their new shop and I couldn't find her number in our book.'

'I thought it was in there,' he murmured. 'She's quite busy with a new shop at the moment. I only know because she's booked Basil for the launch.' Mark was aware that he was still talking too much.

'I'll get the number from you and ring her tomorrow,' Bella said casually, and Mark tried to meet her eye with matching coolness.

Just then Clattie put down her napkin. 'I really think I might go to bed,' she said. 'I am dreadfully tired.'

'Of course you are.' Pippa was already on her feet and moving towards her mother. 'I'll come up with you. We could pray together – you might find that it makes you feel more peaceful. It does me. What about a hot drink? I could make some Ovaltine.'

Mark saw the resigned look in Clattie's eyes as she accepted the offer.

'Don't let Pip keep you up too long. Don't let her be selfish. Be firm with her,' he whispered as she kissed him good night.

'She likes to think she's looking after me and she wants to make up for not being here this afternoon,' Clattie whispered back.

In the drawing room, Mark poured Bella a drink.

'A nightcap,' he said, holding it out to her.

'Thanks. So?' She looked at him and Mark recognised a salacious excitement in her eyes.

'So?' he questioned back, trying to avoid the inevitable discussion that his wife so obviously desired.

'Well, it's not every day one finds a whole family of new relations. I wondered how you were feeling about it.' Bella was irritated by his reticence and Mark was sadly aware that her desire to know how he felt was more prurient than sympathetic.

The trouble was he simply didn't know how he was feeling about it. Everything was still churning around in his head: the Gaffer's death – the space he'd left – then this man, this, this brother that was filling that space. Listening to Clattie's halting voice telling the sad story with no hint of criticism, Mark had thought himself vindicated. He had disliked his father – hated him for demanding perfection – and now it seemed he had the right to hate the Gaffer because it turned out that the great man himself had been flawed. It should have felt like a victory, but somehow it didn't quite.

'I don't want to talk about it at the moment,' he said shortly.

Bella pursed her lips sulkily and opened a magazine.

Much later, when Bella had gone to bed, Mark took his mobile phone into the book room and telephoned Freddie.

'Can you talk?' he asked.

'I'm in the downstairs loo.' Freddie's voice sounded sweet and sleepy. 'Peter's asleep.'

Mark had never met Freddie's husband. He was, she told him, an accountant and economics lecturer and Mark had always imagined him small, efficient and dull.

'How's your father?' she asked.

'He died before I got here.'

'Oh no, Mark, I am so sorry.'

'Actually, something rather strange has happened. It appears that the Gaffer had another family.' There, he had said it. It was not a dream.

'You mean he was a bigamist?'

'No, no, he had an illegitimate son by another woman before Ralph was born. Clattie and the Gaffer have kept up with him and his family, but they've never told us. He knows about us, though.' Something clicked in Mark's mind. Was this what was upsetting him most – that this man had the advantage over him?

'Oh you poor thing,' Freddie said with genuine concern. 'What a terrible shock for you all.'

'Ralph is very angry. He minds that he is not the eldest son. Pippa doesn't want to believe it and Bella thinks it's all rather exciting.'

Mark would have liked to grumble about his heartless wife but Freddie always preferred to avoid Bella as a topic of conversation.

'And how do you feel about it?' She sounded as though she really did care, and bolstered by this the words burst out of Mark's mouth with no warning. 'I hope he doesn't think he's entitled to anything.'

He could hear the frown in Freddie's voice. 'Mark?'

Mark rubbed his hand across his eyes but was unable to drop his line of thought. 'Well, we don't know, do we? You read about this sort of thing in the papers. Illegitimate son claims father's estate. That could happen to us.'

'Presumably your father made a will. I really wouldn't start panicking just yet.' Freddie dismissed the subject. 'What about your poor mother? How's she?'

'Stoical. Quiet. I wish you were here,' he added.

He heard the smile in Freddie's voice. 'I might be a bit unnecessary there just at this moment, don't you think?'

'But I want sex. I want you to make me feel better.' Mark paused and imagined sexy, sympathetic Freddie with her soft pale skin, waiting for him in his bed upstairs instead of Bella, angular, brisk and asleep. Then he remembered. 'Oh yes, by the way, I'd better warn you, Bella says she's going to ring you.'

'Me? Why?' Freddie sounded alarmed.

'Some client needs you, apparently.'

'Oh, oh, I see. Tell her I'm very busy at the moment.'

'I did. Freddie, I need to see you.'

'Ring me when you can. I'm thinking of you.'

'And me you.'

Mark switched off his phone. He heard a rustle behind him, and turning round he saw Clattie at the door. He wondered how long she had been there.

'I thought you were asleep.' Fear of being found out made his voice sharp. 'Are you all right?' he asked more gently.

Clattie moved into the light of the table lamp burning in the corner of the book room. Her thick hair was plaited down her back and her white cotton nightdress and white dressing gown made her look clean and wholesome. As she came near Mark, he could smell the familiar sweet scent of her night cream.

'I couldn't sleep. I came down for a bowl of cereal.' She smiled at him. 'I have to eat something when I can't get to sleep. The times I've forgotten about the burglar alarm and set it off by mistake; it used to drive your father mad.'

Mark knew that his first thought should be concern for Clattie: today her husband had died and tonight would be her first one alone in the bedroom they had shared for well over fifty years. But he had to find out whether she had overheard his telephone conversation.

He waggled his telephone in his hand. 'That was an old friend,' and he waited for a moment to see if his mother responded. She nodded her head vaguely.

Relieved, Mark put his arm round her shoulders. 'Will you be all right, Clattie? You'll be lonely here without the Gaffer. What will you do, do you think?'

'Oh, it's much too early to think anything. But this house will seem very big without him, and when Pippa goes back to her community . . .' Clattie paused thoughtfully. 'We'll see. But you mustn't worry about me. I'm worrying about all of you. Especially Ralph. Family is so important to him and now I'm afraid he'll feel it has been fragmented by this. We can't change anything that has happened, but we must help him to accept it as it is now.' Clattie looked at Mark with an expression that seemed to acknowledge that she and Mark were together in adversity. All his life, Clattie had allied herself to Mark; she always knew when the Gaffer had demanded too much from him, when he was feeling left out and low, and then she would take him under her wing and make them a pair against the rest of the world. But just at that moment he resented this alliance: he wanted parity with his brother – he was, he believed, feeling just as vulnerable as Ralph and he wanted the same concern shown towards him.

'I wish I knew how I felt about it all. I am upset that we were lied to. It wasn't your fault, I understand that,' he said hastily, as Clattie tried to interrupt him. 'It's all the Gaffer's fault. Everything's his fault.'

Clattie knew better than to defend Jack to Mark. 'Try to let the anger go now, darling.'

'The strange thing is, I'm quite curious to meet this man. Just once,' he added firmly. 'But what happens *after* the funeral?' He hesitated, aware that Clattie might not like what he was going to say. 'We don't have to have a relationship with him, do we? I mean, there's no reason for any of us to have anything to do with him, is there, if we don't want to?'

'You must do what you want,' Clattie said firmly. 'I believe that Titus has the same right to mourn his father as you do. If the whole family want to come to the funeral, and I'm sure they will, all three of you will have to make them welcome. What you do afterwards is entirely up to you. I shan't put any pressure on any of you, but I hope to continue my relationship with them all. I owe it to your father. Anyway, they've been part of my life for so long – I'm fond of them.'

Mark wondered at his mother's great strength and her enormous kindness. 'Weren't you angry about it all?'

Clattie was silent for a moment. 'Upset, yes, but there was no point in being angry. Your father had many girlfriends before me. He was over ten years older than me, and,' she gave a little smile, 'actually, I felt rather sorry for Shirley. Poor girl, it couldn't have been good for her and she probably couldn't help her obsession – Jack was a very handsome man. I'm sure she realised that he didn't love her but she got pregnant; whether on purpose or not it was pretty brave even in those days to bring up an illegitimate child. Anyway, abortions weren't easily available fifty-five years ago, so there was nothing to be done about it except accept the situation and support your poor father.'

Clattie moved towards the door, clearly anxious to end the conversation. 'Come on, we should go to bed. It's been a long day for us all.' As she waited for Mark to turn out the lights, she said quietly, 'He's actually a very nice man, is Titus.'

Titus lay silently in bed beside Jane. They each knew the other was awake.

'We are going to the funeral, aren't we?' Jane asked quietly.

Titus moved his legs fretfully under the duvet. 'I suppose we are. We're going to have to meet my brothers and sister and my nephew and niece – those shadowy people who, for all these years, I've not thought of as real. We don't *have* to go, of course.'

'I think we should. Summer and Alby will want to and maybe it'd be good for you to confront these shadows.'

'It's worked all right up to now.'

Jane drew in her breath. 'Right,' she said in disbelief. 'A great big family secret like that – oh very healthy. They're your family. I say get out there and meet them.'

'They're not my family.' Titus sounded scornful. 'I knew they existed, of course, but Aunt Monica always made them so unimportant. The Gaffer was my biological father but Uncle Will was my proper one. The Gaffer was just someone we visited and who, in fact, frequently scared the shit out of me.'

'I don't believe that you weren't curious about the situation, why and how, you know . . .'

Titus shrugged. 'Aunt Monica just treated him and Clattie as people who came on occasional visits, but who were nothing much to do with me. I grew up thinking they weren't that important. Aunt Monica answered any questions I had but in a kind of uninterested way. The fact that I shared the same blood with the Gaffer and his children was just not an issue. I didn't need them, Aunt Monica and Uncle Will were my family. My mum and dad.'

'I've lived in this country for over thirty years and I'm still utterly baffled by the way you Brits behave.' Jane thumped her pillow into a comfortable shape. 'Everything is such a big deal for you, yet no one ever talks properly about anything. You're like your weather, bowed down in some great, grey cloud. And,' her voice became passionate, 'what I really hate is that you drew me into this cloud. And the kids too, that's what's the worst. I've always said we shouldn't have lied to them. Look how they feel now.'

'Summer was okay,' Titus said defensively.

Their daughter had flung herself noisily through the door at tea time, scattering folders and files in the hallway. Titus had seen her eyes fill with tears as they told her about the Gaffer's death and then he had watched them grow round in wonderment as he gently and carefully told her that the Gaffer was her grandfather. Slowly Summer took in the information and worked out the implications.

'So Gaff's family is ours too?' she said slowly. Titus nodded. 'Wow!' Then, almost scornfully, she asked, 'Why didn't you say before? Why couldn't we know Gaff was our grandad? He was your dad,' she looked at him with awe, 'and you never said. His other children have been our aunts and uncles all along – and we've got cousins. You could have told us. It's not that big a deal, is it?'

Titus had tried to explain that it had been her grandfather's secret and one which had to be respected, but he was left with a feeling that Summer was completely confounded by the alien mores of the older generation. Her grief at the Gaffer's death had been temporarily hijacked by pleasurable curiosity at the idea of the set of new relations she had just been given.

'Maybe Summer is okay about it,' Jane admitted, 'but how can you really know what you're doing to your kids? And look at Alby – he is absolutely not okay about it.'

Alby, in Cambridge, had been silent on the other end of the phone. 'I can't get my head round this at all,' he had said eventually. 'Are you seriously telling me that Gaff was our grandfather, your dad? You said your dad died when you were a baby. You lied to us.' It was an accusation. 'What was the point of lying to us, Titus? Why did it have to be such a secret?'

Where Summer's bewilderment had turned rapidly to excitement, Alby's had turned into hurt.

'Are there any more family secrets you've been unable to tell us?' he had asked caustically. 'I mean, we might as well get them all out in the open. Now you've decided to be honest with us at last.'

Titus had put down the phone feeling profoundly guilty, and then profoundly angry that he should have to feel this guilt. This was not his misdeed. He had been forced to dissemble by his father.

'I think Alby will understand why we couldn't tell the truth,' Titus continued now to Jane. 'When he's calmed down and really thought about it.'

'I don't see why he should,' Jane said crossly. 'I'm not sure I would. It's like you've given him a new family—'

'Given him?' Titus was cross too. 'But there is no family.'

'But, Titus, there is. That's the point.' Jane tried to make him think more clearly.

'You know, when Alby was born, the Gaffer seemed so

thrilled with him, his very first grandchild, I thought something might change, that there'd be some concrete recognition of my relationship in the family. But no . . .' Titus's voice turned harsh, 'it seemed not, even when Summer was born. So I forced myself to go back to never thinking about my half-siblings. It was easier not to let them come into my equation. Now the secret is out – everyone knows about each other – yet I have this strange feeling that it's become a bigger secret than it was when they didn't know. I'm afraid that once we've met them all, they might become proper people in our lives, instead of faint rather fuzzy people safely set in an old story.'

Jane took hold of Titus's hand and turned on to her back, staring at the crack of light where the curtains didn't quite meet.

'I keep trying to imagine how they must feel.'

'I don't care how they feel.' After a while Titus's voice came more softly out of the darkness. 'Actually I hated him.'

'I know you did, but he could be very charming.' Jane paused. 'Particularly to women.'

'I don't want his death to make me think about my mother. He never loved her. He was a bastard, but Aunt Monica said my mother loved him passionately. He would never talk about her. It was like I was this son that had materialised out of nowhere. Once when I was . . . I was about eight, I suppose, I asked him something about my mother and he lost his temper, big time, with me: told me never to mention her again in his hearing. What does that do to a child who has no memory of his mother? I still don't understand why I didn't just walk away from the whole thing when I became an adult.'

'He was a pretty forceful man, and he was very fond of Alby and Summer.'

'Why did I let that happen? He need never have known about them. I could have walked then, but I didn't. Why didn't I?' Titus banged the pillow with his fist.

'Because blood is thicker than water?' suggested Jane. 'Look, your father must have felt something for your mother, because he didn't have to make you part of his life like he did.'

'Part of part of his life, you mean. I was kept in a box and brought out at his convenience. And I allowed it to be like that. I was a possession that belonged to him. He probably felt the same about the kids.'

'Don't ever let them hear you say that,' Jane said vigorously. 'I think the old man was genuinely fond of Alby and Summer, and Clattie was always so loving and generous – as though she really was their grandmother, I know she loved them – and you.' Jane faltered as she realised that she had unconsciously fallen into using the past tense. 'I think it's a bloody good thing this is all out in the open. Maybe you can start dealing with it at last.' Jane had a picture of Clattie at The Mill with her children around her – so much unsaid in that family, such a large secret that had been exposed suddenly.

'Poor, poor Clattie though, being left to do the telling after all these years.'

Chapter Two

Mark put a filo pastry canapé in his mouth and ate it thoughtfully. He knew exactly how much it cost to make and this one had way too much expensive filling in it. He hoped that was because his chef had made it specially for him, the boss. He couldn't help thinking that his profit margins would slip radically if every canapé they produced was as full of crabmeat as this one.

He moved around the groups of people in the drawing room, everyone keen to share their memories of his father with him. He rather wished they wouldn't, because he knew they were mourning somebody who wasn't the person they thought he was.

Mark had met Titus. The families had converged outside the church. Introduced by Clattie, speaking in a prosaic voice, the two families had shaken hands formally, suspicious eyes flickering over each other – scrutinising, assessing. Only the younger generation had moved shyly towards each other like animals sniffing each other's scent.

After the funeral in the village church, everyone had walked back to the house. Led by Ralph, keeping his family close around him, the congregation had straggled down the village lane in disparate groups.

Mark had come across Titus in the hall. He appeared to be hesitating.

'We're going to be in the drawing room,' Mark said. Then, without thinking, 'It's that door on the left.'

Titus had responded blandly. 'It's okay. I know where the drawing room is.'

They had looked at each other, both silently staking some sort of claim.

Now Mark glanced across the room at this new brother who was standing apart, watching the little groups of people who were gradually losing their low, mournful voices as the drink kicked in. Titus looked younger than his fifty-five years, much younger than Ralph and probably, Mark thought, even younger than himself. His greying hair was still thick, only slightly receding in the front but much too long at the back. But with a jolt, Mark recognised the similarity between Titus and Ralph. The same aquiline profile and square jaw, inherited from their father. Mark's rounder face was more like Clattie's – it was as though *he* was the odd one out. In his casual jacket over a pair of dark chinos, Titus appeared to Mark to have no gravitas about him. He wasn't wearing a tie, and Mark despised that: the Gaffer deserved a tie at his funeral, surely? He'd always minded about appropriate dress, he had been that sort of man – but obviously Titus wouldn't have known him well enough to realise that.

After the service, Mark had watched Titus and Jane walking towards the graveside. He noticed that they walked closely and easily together and that, although they weren't actually holding hands, they looked as though they should have been. He found himself a little envious; he and Bella rarely walked closely. Jane looked so different from the women familiar to Mark. Clothed in earthy coloured layers of crumpled linen that reached down to her open-toed sandals, he thought she was dressed more for a picnic than for a funeral. Large earrings dangled below her

32

short, spiky hair, and a collection of brightly coloured wooden necklaces hung round her neck.

Catching sight of Ralph across the drawing room, Mark watched him assiduously avoiding the new family – Mark had come to think of it as the 'new family'.

Ralph had been aggressively in charge all day, as though afraid someone would wrest his command away from him, and Grania watched him nervously, worried that his unhappiness and anger might spill over into a typical quick burst of temper.

Pippa was also ignoring the strangers with the happy knack she'd always had of not looking at something that she didn't want to see. Mark was surprised that Pippa, her father's precious baby, wasn't more shattered, not only by his death but also by his legacy. Her initial grief and astonishment had been rapidly converted into a frenzy of activity. Between the death and the funeral she had cooked, cleaned and shopped, anxious to help with everything. He wondered if it was her new-found Christianity that had given her such strength. He watched her now lean over Caitlin and do up the top button of the girl's blouse.

'You shouldn't show so much of your body, Caitlin. You should be more modest,' he heard her say. Caitlin rolled her eyes and when Pippa drifted away, undid the button, and then, defiantly, one extra.

'I've been making an effort with the wife.' Bella came up to Mark, her face alight with an almost happy excitement. 'She's frightfully Australian, a bit jungly, bit intense, and why *has* she come dressed as a totem pole? I said they should come over for dinner one evening.'

Mark frowned at his wife's insensitivity.

Titus munched on a pizza the size of a penny and decided that sunblushed tomatoes were the invention of the devil. He began concocting original canapé ideas in his head, to distract him from thinking how much easier it would have been not to be here. It was noticeable that he and Jane were not being introduced to any family friends, but then they never had been. He had been briefly tempted by the idea of going up to a complete stranger and introducing himself as the illegitimate son of the deceased, but then he thought of Clattie.

He looked at the bank of photographs on the table beside the sofa and then round the room at all of them come to life. The family were almost exactly as he had imagined. Superior. He was watching Ralph and Mark, with a mixture of amusement and growing irritation, as they moved round trying to avoid him. Pippa was dashing about, offering plates of food and stopping occasionally to talk, waving her hands in uncoordinated arcs. Titus watched Grania gliding behind her, efficiently and unobtrusively serving wine and the canapés; he saw her move to take one of the plates from Pippa who immediately held on to it more tightly. Grania moved away with a small smile of defeat. Clattie was hemmed in next to the fireplace by a group of people and Titus saw her looking at him anxiously over their shoulders. He gave her a small smile and a nod. Bella was talking to Jane by the door into the hall. She turned to pick up a crisp without looking at the person holding the dish. Like a claw, her long hand with its painted nails grasped the crisp and held it just in front of her mouth. She was making some point and Titus recognised the look on his wife's face as she gazed silently at Bella. Jane needed rescuing.

Titus began to make his way across the room but Pippa was suddenly in front of him, staring into his face with disconcerting intensity.

'Do you need the loo?' Titus reeled back slightly at this unexpected question. 'Because I can show you where it is.' For a moment, Titus thought she was going to take his arm and bear him off as though he were a child.

'I'm fine, thank you,' he said inadequately, but Pippa was speaking over him.

'That's the trouble with this house, full of funny doors that usually just lead to cupboards. Great for playing sardines when you're young, but very embarrassing for strangers if they're caught opening every door. It would look as though they're prying, don't you think?'

Titus gazed at his half-sister as she gabbled at him as though he really was one of her prying strangers and he wondered if she was slightly deranged. But he noticed that her hands were shaking and he caught a canny look in her eye that made him feel that she was pleading with him to play her game. He felt all his previous pique drain away to be replaced with a sudden and surprising sympathy for Pippa.

'I must get on,' she said briskly. 'So many old friends of the family to catch up with. Lovely service, didn't you think? The family . . . we all spent a lot of effort on getting it just right. Thank you so much for coming.' Titus obediently shook the hand she held out and she turned on her heel and moved away before he had thought of what to say.

He began to move towards Jane and this time it was Clattie who intercepted him. Ostentatiously she put her arm through his.

'I saw you with Pippa.' She looked up at Titus anxiously. 'I don't know what she was saying, but you mustn't mind it. She's always been a great one for talking before thinking.'

'She asked me if I wanted to go to the lavatory,' Titus said, his lips twitching slightly. Clattie raised her eyebrows and Titus couldn't tell if she recognised Pippa's agenda.

'This must be difficult for you,' he added.

'Darling, it's difficult for all of us, but we shall get through this. And your lovely family are doing splendidly.'

Titus wished he could say the same about her family.

Summer parked her gum under the mahogany table in the hall. She would never have done such a heinous thing if Gaff had been alive, but it was his fault; if he hadn't gone and died she wouldn't be at this awful funeral with all these new relations. It was wild, this deal about him being her grandfather. She wished she had known when he was alive because she'd always wanted a grandpa. She had liked Gaff but she would have loved him much more if she had known who he really was – now she could understand why he was so interested in her and Alby. When Titus had told her about Gaff she had been quite excited about meeting his part of the family. At first she had thought it was intriguing and rather romantic to have mystery relations, though she couldn't quite see why she and Alby hadn't known about them all along; she thought Titus seemed to be making a bit of a production number about the whole thing and she couldn't really understand Alby going on and on about being lied to. He was so upset. But then when she was sitting in church with everyone talking about Gaff, she wished she'd always known that he had belonged to her too, and she had felt a bit cross and hurt that Titus had kept the secret for so long. She hated the idea of Gaff not being here any more – it was too late now for him to be her grandfather. She had looked forward to meeting the cousins – she supposed they must be sort of cousins because they shared a grandfather – but here they all were in Gaff and Clattie's house and the mystery family had turned out to be gross, sort of smart and very snotty. Their eyes were hard and cold and Summer could see that the men were politely but firmly avoiding her parents.

The one bright light on the horizon was the boy cousin who was just about the most beautiful thing Summer had ever seen. He had a gentle face and kind eyes, half concealed by a rather old-fashioned flop of fair hair that gave him a definite sleepy, sexy look; Summer thought he was the only one of this lot worth investigating. Alby was talking to the girl and Summer could tell that he was bored, because he kept looking down at his feet and drawing circles with them on the carpet. Caitlin's brown hair was cut stylishly to frame her almost perfect face – pity her beauty was spoilt by the condescending look on her face as she stared snootily at Alby.

Summer thought she had clocked which brother had which wife, even though the four of them looked more or less the same in their stuffy, smart clothes: the women were both dressed in boring little suits and the good-looking one had short, blonde-streaked hairdresser hair; the other had a kind face, surrounded by curly hair and she wore pearl stud earrings. The two men wore dark suits and white shirts with ties that looked as though they were strangling them. Summer was surprised that someone like Clattie should have two such conventional-looking sons and she was a little fazed to notice that Titus and the brother with the stern face looked rather like each other. The sister was a bit odd: she had no make-up on and she wore long thick clothes buttoned up to the neck; she had prayed loudly in church and twisted her body around holding her hands up high in some kind of supplication.

Summer fingered the Gaffer's hunting horn, sitting on the table in front of her. He had taught her and Alby how to blow it when they were very small. She picked up the silver hip flask beside the horn and unscrewed the lid, sniffing the familiar smell of metal and old brandy. An image of herself as a child, pretending Gaff's knee was a horse, became suddenly very clear.

She was sad about Gaff, but somehow his death had become less important than this new family. She looked in the hall mirror, checked the spot on her chin that was threatening to overshadow her lip stud and ran her fingers through her short scarlet hair. She turned around and went into the drawing room, took a deep breath and sashayed up to the beautiful boy standing by the window.

'Hello, Kit cousin,' she said provocatively.

Mark and Ralph stood at the corner table and poured themselves another drink.

'I've just heard one of those children refer to the Gaffer as Gaff,' Ralph muttered angrily. 'That's my children's name for him. Did you know that . . . that incubus brought his family down here at least once every holidays? To our home. I just can't believe it – it's just . . . unbelievable.' He appeared confounded.

'Personally, I think they seem to be irredeemably dull,' Mark said mildly.

'Look at them.' Ralph waved his hand at the room. 'The girl's straight out of a horror film with all that face piercing. And I ask you, Summer. What sort of name is that? You can barely understand the wife with that awful antipodean accent. They're all so . . . so unlike us.' He spat out the words.

Clattie came up to her sons. She was tight-lipped and forbidding, just as she had been when they were naughty as children.

'Please circulate,' she commanded. 'I have not yet seen either of you actually make an effort with Titus and Jane. Kindly try and make this a little easier for us all.'

'I hope they're not going to expect us all to be jolly friends together,' Ralph said furiously.

Clattie gave a strangely cold smile. 'No, I'm sure they won't, considering the way you're behaving towards them at the moment. I'm surprised at your bad manners – both of you. If it makes it easier, be like Pippa and treat them like any other guests. But just be polite. You don't have to see them again until . . . well, I suppose, it would be at my funeral.'

Ralph frowned.

'Clattie,' he said reprovingly.

'However,' she went on, 'you might, if you tried, find that you quite like them. The young seem to be managing to get on.' She drew the men's attention to the group sitting in the window.

'Do all the other people here know about this ludicrous situation?' Ralph asked.

Clattie sighed. 'For what it matters they don't, as far as I'm aware. And . . .' she added with spirit, 'do you know, it really doesn't concern me just at the moment. This is your father's funeral – you two would do well to remember that.' Clattie rarely sounded so peremptory. 'Now, will you kindly both go and talk in a civilised manner to Titus and Jane.'

A small, round man with a shiny bald head arrived beside Clattie. He touched her shoulder in a familiar manner.

'So, these are your two sons?' he said in a friendly voice. Mark immediately understood him to be differentiating between Clattie's sons and the Gaffer's son.

'Gerry, this is Ralph and Mark.' Clattie spoke in a brisk voice. 'Gerry Crockerton. He moved to the village a few months ago. He became your father's favourite chess opponent.'

Mark and Ralph looked blank.

'And he lets me beat him at racing demon.' She looked up at Gerry with a smile.

He returned it affectionately and then turned to Mark and Ralph. 'I've told your mother, anything I can do . . . You mustn't worry about her, all her friends in the village will keep an eye on her.'

Ralph was grimly polite.

'That's very good of you,' he murmured tautly. 'Now, if you'll excuse us, I think we'd better circulate.' He glared at Clattie.

'The way things are going at the moment,' he said to Mark out of the corner of his mouth as they moved across the room, 'we'll probably find out shortly that he is our uncle or something. I'll take the woman – you take the man.'

'Unfortunately, Ralph, he's rather more than a man, he's our brother,' Mark pointed out uncomfortably.

'Not as far as I'm concerned. He's a trespasser,' Ralph said in clipped tones. 'I shall do as Clattie wants and be perfectly civil to him this afternoon and then I never want to clap eyes on him or his grubby little family again.'

Titus had been watching the altercation between Clattie, Mark and Ralph with cynical interest. He could tell that they were talking about him. Mark now came up to him, holding out his hand and speaking formally.

'I think it behoves us to try and get to know each other, even if we never meet again.'

Titus recognised the message in Mark's pompous words.

'Indeed it does,' he said heartily, wondering why he suddenly found it necessary to start talking in as stilted a manner as his brothers.

'I gather you live in south London?' Mark twiddled his empty glass.

'Yes, the rougher end of Norwood.' Titus heard himself being unnecessarily defiant. 'You?'

'Fulham. Parson's Green. Ralph lives your side of the river – Camberwell. Nice area.'

There was a pause in which Titus realised that if they both continued to make a minimum effort at conversation, the silence between them would be a great deal worse than idle chatter. He took a deep breath and began to talk.

'I'm in furniture restoration. Jane, my wife, runs a playgroup. Our daughter, Summer, lives with us and is taking her A levels at the local college and our son, Alby, is at Cambridge.'

'At the university?'

Titus, irritated by the incredulous note in Mark's voice, answered sharply, 'Yes, doing English and modern politics. Final year.'

He was slightly mollified by Mark's small apologetic smile in acknowledgement of his prejudice.

'Good for him. Bella and I don't have any children; never really got around to it. We've always been career fiends, my wife and I.'

Titus asked of what careers Mark and his wife were both such fiends and listened politely to a list of his and Bella's achievements. Mark stopped suddenly.

'This is a very peculiar situation, isn't it?' he said abruptly, as though the idea had just occurred to him.

Surprised by the change of tack, Titus agreed. 'It is. Very. Difficult for us all and especially for Clattie. I've always held the view that it would have been better for us to meet with the Gaffer alive and here.' He watched Mark blench involuntarily at his use of his father's familiar name, and he regained his composure with an effort.

'Absolutely,' Mark replied. 'It's come as a bit of a shock to all of us, as you may imagine. I mean, you knew about us, but we had no idea about you. I'm sure you can understand how upset and hurt we feel.'

'Of course.' Titus was unwilling to let Mark be the only

victim and he startled himself by his sudden competitiveness. 'But then we've had to live as the second-best relations for all these years. We felt, you know, always kept apart, a bit like pariahs.'

Jane had arrived at Titus's side as he was talking, and she slipped her arm through his.

'No photographs, you see.' She smiled politely at Mark. 'There have never been any photographs of Titus and the children in this house—'

Titus joggled his wife's arm warningly. 'Janey.'

She looked at him defiantly and continued speaking.

'Our children's relationship with their grandfather was based on lies. They should have grown up knowing who he was. Instead they were periodically paraded for your father's benefit and at his convenience. Isn't that right, Titus?'

Titus half nodded and half shrugged.

Jane's usually still, gentle mouth worked itself into odd shapes and Titus realised that she had clearly been upset and was making a heroic effort not to cry. She continued jerkily, looking at Mark, her accent becoming more marked in her distress.

'I've been talking to your brother, who seems unable to disguise his view that we are some sort of vulgar rabble that have emerged out of the woodwork.'

'I'm sorry if my brother has upset you,' Mark said politely. 'He is particularly unhappy about the situation. Ralph has always taken his role as the eldest son of the family very seriously. It has come as something of a shock to him to find that he is not actually the eldest son.'

Jane, calmer now, shrugged and said disparagingly, 'Well, if that is the most important thing for him, he must deal with it, I suppose. This is no one's fault, no one that's here anyway. Your father,' she glared at them both, 'if he had had the guts, could have confronted this problem early on in your lives and avoided all this unpleasantness.'

Titus and Mark found themselves in the curious situation of

cleaving together in a spontaneous and unfamiliar defence of their father. They both spoke at once.

'He had every intention of telling us,' Mark said stiffly.

'He probably didn't expect to die so suddenly,' Titus said.

Jane lifted her hands in submission. 'Yes, yes, I'm sorry. What do I know? I've never understood the situation, all the deceit and whatever, it's . . .' words failed her. 'Anyway, it's nothing to do with me.' She glanced behind her at the group of children still talking by the window. 'If you'll excuse me, I think I'll go and join the kids – they seem to have a more open and giving take on this situation.' She turned on her heels and left the two men.

'I'm sorry about that.' Titus heard himself quietly apologising for his wife.

'I'm sorry about Ralph. He's obviously upset her. The thing is, he was always my father's favourite. He's taken it rather badly.'

A silence, heavy as a jackboot, fell between the two men.

'Well . . .' Mark became flustered '. . . he was in our bit of the family, anyway.'

Titus cast around in his head to find a blander topic of conversation that would get them both out of the mire in which they found themselves.

'So you have a catering company? Do you cater locally much?' There was, he felt, something about this occasion that was making his choice of words most eccentric.

Mark picked up on the question gratefully. 'We cover most of London and the Home Counties and, in fact, at the moment we're picking up a lot of business your way, south of the river. It's become such an affluent area.'

Titus nodded. 'The area's certainly changed a lot in the last twenty years.' He wanted to add, and not necessarily for the better, thanks to the newcomers in their four-wheel drives who can afford caterers . . .

'People are moving further out,' Mark rolled on. 'Your area's full of big houses, and their owners have nice big parties. I'm always looking to expand. I imagine you're the same.'

'Well.' Titus shrugged. 'The influx of the wealthy into the

area has helped me. I do occasional restoration work for the large companies, but most of my jobs come by local word of mouth – usually upholstery, which is pretty run of the mill, but I've never regretted binning the architecture degree.' He watched Mark register what he was saying, wishing he could stop the streak of competitiveness that he was bringing out in him.

'I never attempted a degree. Went straight into the catering trade. Apprentice chef.'

Somehow, Titus thought, that still sounded superior. For his own sanity he changed the conversation.

'Talking of up and coming areas, I've just come into possession of some empty premises near us. There's a bit of an ongoing family debate about it: Alby thinks we should turn it into a decent flat, Summer says it would make a good party venue and Jane wants a playgroup there. Personally, I want to be a bit philanthropic with it, do something that benefits the whole community as well as us. I had this idea of creating small work units for local artists. Make it into a sort of local market place – a community thing.'

Mark felt his business antennae begin to hum. Someone with empty premises and only a hazy idea of what to do with them? This was the stuff of which his dreams were made.

'Large place, is it?' he asked casually.

Titus nodded. 'Yes, it's quite big. My uncle had it as a shop originally, then he leased it as warehouse space. The tenancy's just terminated, but the place is very run down, so we're going to have to sell it. It's been great fun dreaming up ideas, though.'

'Where is it exactly?'

'You probably wouldn't know it. Squarey Street. It's a small run-down shopping parade. It's just a thoroughfare to our main high street nowadays.'

'Interesting.' Mark continued to play it casual. 'Difficult to find places like that at the moment. You wouldn't have any trouble selling, I imagine.'

'I'm sure I won't.' Titus hesitated. 'I still can't help wondering if there isn't some sort of opportunity there for me to do something different. You know what it's like once you pass fifty and the kids are grown up, you start wondering whether you can't change your life a bit. Stop working so hard and do something that brings in enough money without the stress and the long hours.'

Mark nodded attentively. He had no idea what Titus was talking about. His driving ambition thrived on long hours and stress.

Titus made a dismissive gesture. 'But we'll probably sell and we'll be able to pay off the mortgage and take a long holiday in Australia.'

Mark waited two beats and then spoke as though the thought had just occurred to him. 'Could you get A3 use for the place? Would it make a good restaurant, do you think?'

'Yes, yes, I suppose it might. Jane and I don't eat out a lot, but when we do there isn't much choice around us: a Chinese, quite a good Italian that's just opened—'

'Italian?' Mark couldn't disguise his eagerness. 'You always know an area's coming up when the Italians move in. A new restaurant there might be very lucrative.'

'Obviously I want to make some money on the place,' Titus said, 'but I'd have to think about who I sold it to. I think it should be something for the good of the community. I'd particularly like to encourage creativity, which is why I liked the idea of the work units and giving opportunities to struggling crafts people.'

Mark controlled his irritation. What a pea-brained philosophy this man had – and what a waste of potential. Mark pressed home his point once more.

'I always think a decent restaurant is very good for a community, brings everyone together, you know.'

'Only for the people who can afford to eat out,' Titus replied tartly.

Mark was becoming dispirited – this man couldn't see an opportunity if he tripped over it.

'Well, whatever you decide, I'd be very interested in looking round the place,' he said, smoothly taking out his wallet and handing Titus a card. 'Here's my card. Give me a call if you're up for it.'

Titus took the card with a wry grimace.

'Funny to be handed a business card by a stranger who also turns out to be your brother,' he said.

Mark did not respond. He always kept business a completely separate and contained area.

'So, what A levels are you taking?' Summer asked Kit.

'Geography, French and English,' Kit said. 'You?'

'English, art and DT. I really wanted to take French, but I only got a D at GCSE.'

'I'm lucky with French. We've got a house in France and go there most holidays.' Kit regretted saying it as soon as he saw Summer raise one eyebrow and her lip curl.

'Oh I say, how handy,' she said sarcastically.

Kit blushed and shuffled his feet.

'Yes . . . well, it's very small . . . more a sort of gite thing really,' he mumbled. 'Where are you doing A levels?'

'College. What about you?'

Kit regretted this line of conversation as well. Unwillingly, he named his smart south London private school.

'My school used to beat up some of your lot on the bus,' Summer said in a friendly voice. 'But I couldn't wait to leave. I'm hoping to go on to art school.'

She fumbled in a pocket and brought out a packet of cigarettes. 'Clattie always lets me smoke in the conservatory.' She offered one to Kit. 'Want one?' Kit nodded his head and hoped she hadn't noticed that he had instinctively looked around to see if his parents were watching.

'Come on then, let's go.'

Kit looked at this vision of loveliness beside him and testosterone galloped around his body, ending up, rather embarrassingly, as a lump in his trousers.

45

He attempted an offhand shrug. 'Yeah, whatever.'

'This is all rather strange, isn't it?' Alby said politely to Caitlin.

'Yes, it is,' Caitlin said shortly.

'I always thought Jane and Titus never had any secrets from us.' Alby immediately regretted displaying his grievance.

But Caitlin changed the subject.

'Have you always called your parents by their Christian names?' she asked curiously.

'Yes, always.'

'How odd.'

'Never really thought about it.'

They subsided into silence, both staring out across the room.

On the way to the funeral, Jane had suggested that Summer and Alby make an effort with their new relations. 'It would just make it easier for everyone,' she had said.

Alby forced himself to try again. 'What are you going to do when you leave uni?'

Caitlin shrugged. 'Don't know. Get a job I suppose. I'd like to go abroad.'

'Oh yes. Where?'

'Anywhere really.' Caitlin shifted her weight from one foot to the other.

The silence grew between them.

Alby made one last effort. 'I want to work in films.'

'Oh right.' Caitlin turned and stared out of the window.

Alby admitted defeat and went to find comparative normality with his sister.

Left isolated by the window, Caitlin was peeved that it was Alby, not she, who had terminated their stiff little conversation. She went off to find her mother.

'The boy's really nerdy and Kit's hooked up with the girl,' she said crossly when she found Grania in the dining room putting dirty glasses on a tray. 'They've disappeared off together somewhere.'

Her mother looked up at Caitlin, her sweet face crossed with anxiety. 'Cate, darling, are you all right?'

Caitlin shrugged. 'I don't like them,' she said petulantly. 'They're nothing to do with us.'

Grania put down the glasses in her hand and spoke seriously. 'Look, it's a really peculiar situation, I know it is. And I know Dad is dreadfully upset, but it's up to us to help him through it. And we can't do that by matching his anger.'

Caitlin made to interrupt but Grania went on. 'I'm not saying you have to make best friends with them or anything like that. I'm just pointing out that it's not really your hurt, it's Dad's and Pippa's and Mark's. It's a great shock for them and they need time to adjust and it's up to the rest of us to try and help them by keeping things in perspective. Just try for Dad's sake.'

'I hate seeing him so . . . so sad and angry. It's not fair. And Gaff was our grandfather. Kit's and mine.'

'He was their grandfather too, but they never knew that when he was alive. I don't suppose that makes them very happy either.' Grania hugged her daughter before giving her a tray of glasses. 'Don't worry about Dad, darling. He's grieving for Gaff now, like we all are, but he'll be all right, honestly he will.'

Grania took her tray into the kitchen, thinking about Caitlin. She and Ralph had always been particularly close but Grania wasn't sure whether the hurt her daughter was feeling was mostly for herself or for her father.

Bella was sitting on the table by the Aga, noisily eating an apple and waiting for the kettle to boil. Grania began stacking the glasses into the dishwasher.

'This has been quite a day,' Bella said cheerfully. 'Honestly, who would have thought it of the Gaffer – and kept it a secret for all these years, I still can't believe it, it's all so . . . I don't know, unlikely somehow.'

'I think it's all awful.' Grania shuddered. 'It's made everyone so unhappy – them and us.'

47

'Well, I don't suppose they'll feature very heavily in our lives.'

'And poor Clattie,' Grania murmured, 'having to keep the secret and then left to tell us.' She unbent from the dishwasher and gazed at the plate in her hands. 'And having to accept another woman's child like that. Particularly when you've got your own children.'

Bella spoke through a large mouthful of apple. 'I wouldn't know about that. I'm just thankful I've never had any children. I couldn't bear all that emotion and all that responsibility.' She spoke abrasively, as though defending her position. 'It's bad enough getting older without the extra responsibility of children. You know I'm going to be fifty next year,' she said suddenly. She shuddered. 'God, that sounds so middle-aged.'

Grania looked at her sister-in-law and wondered whether it was not having children that made Bella looked so unlined – so polished and pressed.

'Being fifty's not nearly so bad as you think it's going to be,' she said with a small smile. 'Believe me, I've been there. Anyway, there's nothing you can do about it.'

'Except fight the frontiers of decrepitude in the gym and not give in to grey cardigans.' Bella aimed her apple core at the dustbin and slid off the table. 'So, how does Ralph feel about all this then?' she asked as she began making the tea.

'He varies from being terribly quiet and sad to being incandescent with fury. I can't seem to get near him at all. I know he's grieving but the last few days at home have been hell. He's devastated and he won't acknowledge that the Gaffer had anything to do with the situation. He blames Titus, and Titus's mother, even Clattie in a funny sort of way – anybody really so long as it's not the Gaffer. What about Mark?'

'Oh, Mark had a rather more complicated relationship with the Gaffer. You married the golden boy, I married the one who thinks he was fucked up by his father. No, I don't think there's much grief there. Just worry that he'll be inheriting less money. You know what Mark's like, completely venal.'

48

Grania dried her hands and began to put out cups and saucers on a tray.

'What do you think of them?' she asked.

'Muesli sandal brigade,' Bella said dismissively. 'Probably vegetarians, definitely socialists and unutterably dreary. Not our sort of people at all and,' she groaned, 'I've gone and asked them to dinner.'

'I think they're quite decent people and I feel almost as sorry for them as I do for our side of the family.'

'Grania.' Bella made a face at her sister-in-law. 'You're being Pollyanna again.'

'I'm not. I'm just saying this must be pretty traumatic for them too and that perhaps we should make an effort.'

Bella took the kettle off the boil and began to make the tea. 'Actually, I only invited them round to annoy Mark.'

Titus drove his family back to London. He could see from Jane's pale face that she was feeling as drained and tense as he was. He rested his hand on her knee.

'Thanks for that. For your support.'

She turned to look at him. 'I don't think anything we do could ever be as awful as that. It was much worse than I imagined. Still, we managed, it's over and maybe you were right about not getting involved. We don't ever have to see them again if you don't want to.'

'*They*'re not going to make the effort, that's for sure.' Titus's voice was expressionless.

'Except Bella did throw out an invitation to dinner. She's a bit in-your-face.'

'She won't follow it up,' Titus said confidently. He remembered Mark's card sitting in his pocket. 'Mark was professing interest in the warehouse, but I think it was just a case of desperately looking as though he had something to say to me.'

'We all had to do that, just for Clattie's sake.'

Titus spoke gruffly. 'I think it was pretty obvious that none of us could care less about each other.' He negotiated the car on to the South Circular, barely thinking about what he was doing. He was feeling strangely confused about the day.

Jane looked out of the car window and watched the bleak outskirts of London roll past her. She was very glad that she didn't have to live in Swanley and she suddenly wanted to be back under an Australian sun where people she knew did care about each other.

'Actually,' Titus said, 'I quite liked Pippa. She offered to show me to the bog, like I was a little boy that might wet his pants. She was perfectly polite but absolutely refused to see me as anything other than an anonymous guest. I thought she was as dotty as a sock at first, but I think she was just handling it her way.'

'I talked to Grania a bit.' Jane leant forward and took some chewing gum out of the glove compartment. 'She's doing an open university degree and she wants to move to the country. I thought she was the only one who was okay, but I can't see what's she doing with Ralph. I think he's a monster. In fact, I'm with you now – let's have nothing more to do with them.'

Titus squeezed her knee and they lapsed into exhausted silence.

In the back of the car, Summer was talking to Alby in a low voice.

'I quite enjoyed today.'

Alby frowned at his sister. 'I don't think you were meant to, Summer.'

A look of genuine sadness crossed Summer's face. 'No, not Gaff. I hate that. I meant meeting the cousins and watching their parents thinking of something short and polite to say to us.'

'I actually don't really want to talk about it, Summer.' Alby turned on his Walkman and turned to stare moodily out of the car window.

'That Caitlin is a snotty little cow,' Summer murmured, 'but Kit is definitely okay.'

*

There was a feeling of anticlimax at The Mill. Left to themselves, the family's conversation was desultory; everyone fearful that they, or someone else, might inadvertently bring up the one topic that was in the forefront of their minds.

And no one quite wanted to make the leap into what normal life would be without Jack. Ralph and Mark poured drinks that no one wanted after an afternoon of drinking. Grania and Pippa fussed about with supper that no one wanted to eat. Kit and Caitlin were invited to go into the book room and watch television – an invitation they accepted with alacrity.

In the drawing room Clattie lay back on the sofa with her eyes closed, while Mark and Ralph had an inconsequential conversation about road works on the motorway.

'Why do men always resort to journey conversations?' Clattie, eyes still closed, said to Bella beside her on the sofa. Bella put aside the magazine she was flicking through.

'I know,' she agreed. 'Extraordinary, isn't it? I've known Mark arrive at a dinner party and spend half an hour discussing routes when we've usually only just gone half a mile across London.'

Pippa arrived at the door in a stripy apron. 'Which would everyone prefer: cauliflower or cabbage? Grania has no view and I can do either or both. Just say.'

'I'm really not hungry,' Bella said in a bored voice, picking up her magazine again.

Clattie struggled to open her eyes. 'Whichever is easier, darling, but don't cook a lot, we've all eaten much too much of Mark's food.' She smiled gratefully at Mark. Pippa banged out again.

'She'll have another asthma attack if she doesn't calm down,' Clattie said. 'I wonder if she's got her puffer with her.'

'What are her plans?' asked Ralph. 'Is she going back to the community?'

Clattie struggled to an upright position and spoke wearily. 'I imagine so, but I think she feels she has to stay and look after me for a while. I've told her I shall be fine, but you know how she worries.'

Part of Clattie wanted everyone to go away as soon as possible so that she could start the process of learning to live without her husband. The longer her family stayed with her, the more remote she could feel real life becoming – it was, she thought, like waiting for a child to contract whooping cough: the fear and dread beforehand was far worse than the actual arrival. She felt that once she was on her own she could start finding things to do; she could be busy and, more importantly, be relieved of the heavy weight of responsibility for her children's grief and confusion.

'I've suggested that she stays here another week.' Clattie smiled affectionately. 'I expect I can manage one more week of being looked after.'

Ralph and Mark sat on in the drawing room after everyone had gone to bed.

'Wilkinson is sending out copies of the Gaffer's will in the next few days,' Ralph said, pouring two large brandies. 'Apparently the Gaffer specified that no one should see it until after the funeral.'

'That sounds ominous.' Mark felt his stomach lurch in panic. 'I suppose this involves Titus in some way.'

Ralph looked at his brother sourly, as though by mentioning the man by name, Mark had breached some protocol. 'I don't know. I suppose it's likely he will be mentioned in the will and he will have to be paid off accordingly. At least then life can return to normal for us all. Like it was.'

Mark leant back in his chair in a studied, casual manner. 'I hope he doesn't think he's entitled to anything much. We don't want him contesting the will or anything.'

Ralph's lips tightened slightly. 'I imagine the Gaffer made appropriate arrangements, Mark, and we will see that his wishes are carried out, and as soon as possible so that we can put an end to all this. I would hate to think that we didn't behave in a strictly fair way.'

Mark retreated sulkily in the wake of his brother's obvious

reproach. Ralph had always held great store by fairness without ever realising that his younger brother believed that he had never been treated fairly – certainly not by the person who counted.

That night Mark lay in bed beside Bella fretting that, because of Titus, there might not be enough of his father's money left to finance his great dream – an ambition that had been his heart's desire ever since he was a trainee chef. An ambition that, since his father's death, he had begun to believe he could realise very soon. His own restaurant.

Chapter Three

*F*reddie leant on the bar, waggled her empty glass and smiled ingratiatingly at the busy young barmaid, who studiously avoided her eye.

'Sorry I'm late.' Mark came up beside her and winked at the barmaid who immediately scurried over to serve them. With detached amusement Freddie watched the two of them flirting.

'Where have you been anyway?' she asked when they had moved to a small table. 'I've been here for hours.'

'You have time to be here for hours. You don't work.'

Happy to allow her husband to finance the two of them, Freddie seemed to accept the few commercial design jobs she did each year merely to underwrite her social life – a philosophy that Mark found alien, naughty and very beguiling.

'So where have you been?' Freddie persisted. 'You're looking remarkably pleased with yourself.'

'I've been driving down Squarey Street.'

'That's good, is it?'

'Squarey Street. Titus's premises. I told you about it.'

Freddie nodded.

'It's a prime place,' Mark continued enthusiastically. 'Places like that don't come on the market that often—'

'Hang on, but it isn't on the market, is it?'

'No, it isn't, but that's the place I want. A restaurant there would be a certainty, I know it would. I could do so much with it.'

'Except that it belongs to someone else and, anyway, it costs a fortune to open a restaurant and you don't have one of those.' Freddie stood up. 'Mark, if I don't eat something, I'll be too pissed to drive home. I'm going to order tacos. Do you want some?'

'Whatever.' Mark was drawing on the back of a paper napkin.

'Look, I want to show you,' he said, when Freddie returned from the bar with another round of drinks. 'This is the front, it's big, it would make an inviting window for passers-by. It's difficult to see how big it is inside and I couldn't get round the back, which was a bugger—'

'Mark,' Freddie interrupted him, ready now to change the subject, 'even if you found the right premises, you don't have the right money.'

Mark looked at her triumphantly. 'Ah but I will have, won't I? Some money, anyway. From my father's will.'

Two plates of food were put down in front of them. Freddie looked at her watch surreptitiously. Peter was not a possessive husband, but she was always careful never to stretch him too far.

Mark talked on. 'He hasn't a clue what to do with the place, that's obvious. All that crap about putting something back into the community – he's not going to make money going down that road. He wants to sell it and I've got to make sure that he sells it to me or, much better, persuade him to lease it to me. Less outlay for me and regular rent for him. I can make the place work, I know I can.'

'Of course,' Freddie said thoughtfully, 'he may not want to get involved with you, given the circumstances.'

Mark looked blank. 'What circumstances?'

'The family thing?'

'Oh, I don't think that will have any bearing . . .' He waved the thought away with a dismissive gesture. 'This is purely business – nothing more. I don't consider him family anyway.'

When Mark received the executor's letter about his father's will the next morning, he read it through twice before the contents sank in. Steadfastly, over the last week, he had forced himself not to put a figure on his expectations. Now with nothing staring up at him from the paper in front of him, he felt first outraged, then panicky and finally beaten and wretched. He handed the letter to Bella.

'Bloody hell!' she exclaimed. 'Nothing? That's so unfair. What was the Gaffer thinking of? You need that money now, just like Titus.'

'Clattie's got to live on something, but I thought she'd got a bit of money of her own.' Mark spoke in a dull voice trying to reason with the shock he'd just sustained. 'I can see what the Gaffer was doing. This is a sort of pay-off for Titus, so that he can never ask for anything else, so he needs no reason to have contact with us.' He shrugged as he watched his dreams tumble down. 'We'll just have to wait for ours.'

'And that'll be seriously depleted if Clattie needs looking after for any length of time when she's older,' Bella complained. 'I don't suppose Titus will be first in line to contribute to her care.'

Mark felt guilty that his wife had echoed his own thoughts. 'No restaurant now, then,' he said gloomily. 'I couldn't raise enough serious capital for a lease, let alone to buy the place.'

'There is a way round this, Mark, there must be,' Bella said with determination. 'If you can get Titus to sell it to you, you can bloody well find the money. It's out there for you: backers, banks, another mortgage, I don't know, but you can do it. It's a good investment, you know it is. Don't let your father grind you into the ground from beyond the grave.' Bella was pushing all the right buttons. It was a long time since

Mark had seen his wife that feisty and it really rather turned him on.

Titus waved the executor's letter at Jane.

'Told you. We've been bought off – this is goodbye.' He sounded resigned. 'Everything has gone to Clattie, except for a small trust for each of the kids and this to me. The rest of his estate will be divided between the others on Clattie's death. This is my directive to disappear back into my hole and never be seen again.'

'Well, actually you're wrong,' Jane said, waving back at him the letter that she had been reading. 'This is a letter to us from Clattie. She says she must leave it up to all of us as to whether we keep in contact, but that she hopes we will continue our relationship with her as it was. She also hopes that you understand about the will. Apparently the Gaffer wanted you to have your share now so as to prevent any chance of fighting between you all after Clattie had died.'

'Right. I'm paid off early, so that I can't make trouble.' Mortification and hurt were beginning to build up inside Titus.

'Come on. It's nothing to do with you making trouble. It just makes sense. No chance of squabbles. Though I wonder how the others will feel about it,' Jane added thoughtfully. 'They might have been expecting something.' She took the letter from Titus and her eyes widened.

'Shh-it. Two hundred thousand? We could all go to Australia several times over on that. And get rid of the mortgage. This is a lot of money, Titus.'

'Not necessarily,' Titus protested, the words out of his mouth in an instant. 'We don't know how much his estate is worth. If I've got this much, you can be sure the others will have a lot more later. The Gaffer will have seen to that. The others are bound to get much more than me in the end. I mean, look what The Mill must be worth.'

Jane glared at her husband as though he were speaking another language.

'He-llo,' she said fiercely. 'Where the hell is this coming from, Titus? Am I hearing a bit of greed here? Acquisitiveness?' Her voice rose as she looked at him in disgust. 'You've just got your hands on a large building and now you've got a fuck-off amount of money. And you're beefing about what everyone else inherits? I don't think so, Titus. Take the money, thank you very much. Sell the warehouse, pay off our mortgage, put some aside for Summer's uni or art school and let's go to Australia for a long holiday and then decide what we do next. Stop worrying about not getting what you're due. I don't understand it, especially when you didn't expect anything in the first place.'

Titus had startled himself by his strong feeling of being hard done by, of being a victim. But listening to Jane's tirade, he felt his sanity begin to return. He stood up and hugged his wife, holding on to her tightly to feel safe.

'Janey, sweetheart, you're right. I'm sorry. I don't know what that was about. It's gone, I promise. I'm very lucky to have this.' He put the letter back into the brown envelope and hid it away under the bills and the junk mail. 'And much, much luckier to have you,' he said as he kissed Jane on her lips.

'. . . so I've suggested to Jane, dinner next Tuesday. That's okay with you, isn't it?' Bella thumped around the kitchen making her own breakfast, impatiently pushing Mark's cereal bowl out of her way. The casual tone of her voice belied the familiar combative glint in her eyes as she looked at Mark to make sure she had his attention.

'You should have discussed it with me first,' Mark said, retrieving his bowl and pouring milk into it. 'We really don't want to get involved with them on a social level like this.'

Bella stopped what she was doing. 'Excuse me, I thought you wanted to get your hands on his property?'

Mark wrinkled his nose in disgust at his wife's crudeness.

'It's out of the question now, isn't it? I haven't got any investment potential.'

'So you're giving up?' Bella glared at her husband.

'No, I'm being realistic.'

'There's got to be a way round this. And we're going to get Titus, before he turns the place into an organic garden centre or something. Or sells it to someone else.'

'It's just not feasible. Not at the moment.'

Bella sighed at her husband's uncharacteristic reticence. 'I'm trying to help you here, Mark,' she said patiently. 'I've invited them to dinner so that you can find out more about the place.'

Mark studied his wife as she leant against the sink, sipping her coffee. She was right of course, much as he hated the idea, something informal like a dinner party might well be just the thing. Bella had decided to play the supportive wife and he was grateful for this departure – it had been a long time since she had taken any interest in his business.

'Anyway,' she went on, spoiling it immediately, 'I think it's intriguing – he's your long-lost brother. And they live so close.'

'Hardly long-lost. I didn't even know he existed, let alone that he was lost – and lots of people live near by but we don't ask them to supper.' Mark was holding on to his temper with difficulty.

'Clattie was rather pleased when I rang for their number. I thinks she wants us all to be cosy together.'

'You didn't tell her why you want to invite them to supper?' Alarm bells began to ring in Mark's head.

Bella looked injured. 'Of course I didn't. I just said I thought it might be a nice thing to do. For the sake of the unity of the family.'

Mark raised his eyebrows, reluctantly admiring his wife's guile.

'So,' she went on briskly, 'if you bring in a starter, I'll do some sort of fish dish.'

'I thought you'd decided they were vegetarian.'

'She didn't say so. Don't vegetarians usually mention it when they accept a dinner invitation? Anyway, I always think fish is halfway between meat and vegetable.'

Wondering on what premise Bella based this particular piece of wisdom, Mark got up and gave in.

'I suppose we'll have to have them then, if you've already invited them,' he said in a tired voice, putting his bowl in the dishwasher, 'but I can't see what good it will do.'

'Think about it. I know you'll come up with something.' Bella picked up her briefcase and kissed him on the lips.

Mark recognised the gleam of ambition in his wife's eye – it mirrored the one that was, unfortunately, growing in his own eye.

'Jane, we can't. I don't want to.' Titus was rarely irritated with his wife. 'I can't believe that they really want to see us and I certainly don't care if I never clap eyes on any of them again. I reckon it's Bella being meddlesome, she looked the sort. Why on earth didn't you say no?' He looked at her amazement and then grinned. 'It's not a word you normally have a problem with.'

Jane, sitting at the kitchen table cutting out brightly coloured paper shapes for her playgroup children, smiled guiltily over her reading spectacles.

'Oh don't. I know. I'm really, really sorry. She sort of steam-rollered me; said how thrilled Clattie was that she was ringing me and that we were going to get together. I did refuse several dates, honestly I did, but it began to get ridiculous, she just kept coming up with other ones. In the end I accepted the original date. I was pathetic.'

It was unusual for Jane to be so vulnerable. Titus went and sat beside her, putting his arm round her shoulders and squeezing her to him.

'I'd probably have had the same problem,' he said, kissing the top of her head.

Jane made a face. 'Let me try and cancel it,' she said decisively. 'I don't want to go. I'll say we're going to Australia that day.'

They sat in thoughtful silence for a while, Jane snuggled comfortably into his shoulder.

'No,' Titus said suddenly. 'We should go. I didn't think Mark and Bella liked us particularly, but they obviously didn't hate us like Ralph did. I didn't really like them, but I'm probably judging too hastily. If they're prepared to make friendly overtures to us, we should respond. We'll go.'

'Where? Can I come?' Summer poked her head round the kitchen door.

'Supper with Mark and Bella,' Jane said, getting up and putting on the kettle. 'They've asked us next week.'

'Great. I like having new rellies,' Summer said cheerfully. 'I want to get to know them.'

Her mother frowned at her. 'I don't think you were included in the invitation.'

'Oh charming.' Summer flounced out of the room.

'It might be quite interesting, to find out what they're really like,' Jane said, pouring water into the teapot.

Titus, sitting back in his chair watching Jane's breasts move as she reached up to a cupboard, wondered if curiosity was primarily a female trait.

Bella was cutting up monkfish in the kitchen when Mark came home. The place had the airless, evening sultriness of a London house with a long, hot day trapped inside it. The sound of *Carmina Burana* came loudly from the CD player in the sitting room and the table on the terrace had been laid with all the best silver and plates. The house was full of garden flowers and smelt of hot bread, coffee and rose petals. Mark recognised his wife's particular form of superior set-dressing: she was running a PR exercise and Mark was very grateful to her. This was Bella at her best and she was right to have insisted on this dinner party. He had been thinking and Bella was right, there *was* an opportunity here, tantalisingly just around the corner but a possibility, and he wanted to hook it in. If Titus and everything he came with, was the price that had to be paid, so be it. Mark was torn between avarice and unease.

Bella poked the trays of food Mark had put on the table. 'Greek salad? Not over original.' She sounded resigned. 'But I suppose that'll go with monkfish, will it?'

She clicked around the kitchen on her high heels while Mark, a glass of whisky in his hand, sat on the table, swinging his legs and resisting the temptation to take over the cooking. Bella was only an average cook, but he was determined not to appear that he cared if Titus were to think he'd cooked it. Probably thinks macaroni cheese made with parmesan is gourmet, he thought cruelly.

He watched Bella slice a heap of red peppers. Her gold bracelet falling over her hand caught the sun shining low through the window. He had given it to her nine years ago on their eighth wedding anniversary; he remembered choosing it himself, probably the last time he had ever spent time choosing a present for Bella. They had married when they were in their early thirties and each had felt then that they had met their soul mate; both were trying to get their own business off the ground and they had shared ambition, a love of money and a voracious sexual appetite fuelled by the excitement of success and power. In those early days, Mark had been faithful – more or less. Neither he nor Bella had wanted to be tied down by children – they had been a single-minded couple dedicated to their careers. But nowadays, Mark reflected, all they seemed to share was their living space and the occasional expensive holiday. He and Bella were like two concentric circles buzzing around, only touching each other briefly as they spun off into the space that was their work. Sex was still good, on the rare occasions that Bella felt like it, and there were odd moments of companionship between them, but lately he had begun to wonder if in Freddie he had perhaps found the first of his affairs that could have a future.

'So,' Bella said, picking up her glass and looking at him over the top, 'have you come up with plan B yet?'

Mark made a face. 'I'm working on it. I've done some ballpark figures and I would definitely need a partner. I can't raise enough to go it entirely on my own. I don't want to jeopardise Basil Catering. Ideally I'd like a couple of people to come into a restaurant company with me, but finding them might be difficult.'

Bella checked the potatoes on the hob and then sat down beside him. 'Well, we know who does have the money, don't we?'

'Titus, you mean? Oh yes, he's got the money now. Thanks to

the Gaffer.' Mark made no effort to disguise the bitterness in his voice.

Bella looked thoughtful. 'In my experience, you invariably get what you set out to get, Mark. You've been looking for restaurant premises like these for ages, he's got them. QED.'

'The timing is so bad,' Mark grumbled. 'I don't know the man. And I don't know what his plans are for the premises – in fact, I don't think he even knows that—'

'Sell him the restaurant idea then,' Bella interrupted. 'When he's hooked into that, get him to part with some of his money. You can't raise enough on your own, but he doesn't need to know that. It's all in how you put it to him. Offer him a partnership. He could be a sleeping partner and you can make the place work for him.'

'Bella, that's ridiculous, I can't get into bed with a man I've only met once—'

Bella got up and fussed over a saucepan. 'You're about to meet him for a second time.' She pointed her wooden spoon at him. 'Like you said, this is too good an opportunity not to try and go for it. You can be very persuasive, Mark. Just don't look too eager – you don't want him to think he's in control. I suggest you try and keep the conversation general this evening. Pick non-controversial subjects to begin with.'

'You mean like families?' Mark said sarcastically.

Both Mark and Titus were anxious not to get bogged down in a family discussion, and the subject of Clattie and how she was coping was an easy option to get them through the initial conversation over drinks served in the small walled garden.

'I think she's beginning to come to terms with being on her own,' Mark said. 'We all ring her every day but lately she's taken to hurrying us off the phone, which I think is a good sign. Pippa has been persuaded to go back to finish her six months at the community and whether she'll elect to stay on is anyone's guess.' He raised an eyebrow. 'My sister is convinced that she is indispensable to everyone.'

63

Bella and Jane played their parts well that evening. By sustaining light conversation and exchanging trivial information they evaluated and assessed each other and gradually it became clear to them both that they had little in common and didn't like each other very much. In stark contrast, Mark and Titus held stiff little conversations that petered out after a few minutes; they touched on such subjects as local transport, football and the unseasonably warm weather and found out absolutely nothing about each other.

Titus, watching the two women, thought how well they were getting on and he wondered if women had some genetic skill that enabled them to perform so fluently in such hazardous situations.

'This is very good,' Jane said, moving her head enquiringly between Mark and Bella. 'Which of you is the cook at home then?'

Mark pointed to Bella. 'We share on the whole, but she is this evening.'

'Mark is very restrained about criticising my efforts in the kitchen,' Bella laughed, 'but he does like to cook sometimes and of course his meals are always far superior to mine.'

'It's monkfish, isn't it?' Titus said. 'It's good. Lovely firm fish, you can do so much with it. I've done the Two Fat Ladies' recipe of monkfish with anchovies. Do you know it?'

Mark caught his wife's eye and read the warning message in it. *Don't say what you feel about the Two Fat Ladies*.

He smiled. 'Actually, I'll tell you a better way of doing monkfish and that's with sesame seeds, scallops and champagne. I'll give you the recipe.'

Titus caught his wife's eye and read the warning message in it. *Don't say that we don't go in for expensive ingredients because we've never been rich enough and, anyway, we're not middle-class food snobs*.

Titus smiled at Mark. 'Yeah, I'd be interested to try that; sounds good.'

'So you're a bit of a gourmet, are you?' Mark asked.

'No I wouldn't say that, but I'm into simple ingredients, preferably organic and never from a bloody supermarket. I hate supermarkets.' Titus talked passionately on a subject close to his heart. 'They're destroying local communities, putting small shops and markets out of business. Disgusting great conglomerates steam-rollering over real people.'

'But real people find supermarkets convenient,' argued Bella.

'People are so lazy and no one cares any more. They get in their great big cars, polluting the air, and fill up their baskets with all that packaging that's got to be dumped somewhere. And the worst thing is it's all crap, tasteless food full of hormones and antiseptics.'

'Now there I do agree with you,' said Mark.

So, as it turned out, it was the subject of food that saved the dinner party from troubled silences. They all breathed a sigh of relief as the conversation began to revolve more naturally and easily around the table.

At the end of the evening, Mark and Titus ended up in the hall together, waiting for Bella and Jane to emerge from the sitting room where Bella had been looking for a book for Jane.

'Women always swap books, don't they?' Titus observed.

'It must be some form of cementing a friendship, I suppose.' Mark wasn't concentrating. He was about to broach the important subject.

'We didn't get to talk about your new premises at dinner,' he started diffidently, 'but I would be interested in having a look at them. I've been investigating similar properties recently and I'd like to get an idea about your area. I don't know it at all.'

'Any time,' Titus said airily. 'It was you who suggested a restaurant, wasn't it?'

Mark nodded noncommittally.

'Oddly enough,' Titus continued, 'a couple of local friends have suggested the same thing. We do need a good place to eat round us, it's true.' He shook his head. 'But it's much too big a project for me.'

'Not necessarily, I'd have thought.' Mark spoke slowly as though he were thinking on the hoof. 'It depends, of course, where your interest lies, in the building or the restaurant. Didn't you say you trained as an architect?'

Titus shook his head dismissively. 'I did, many years ago, but I never graduated. I realised I preferred more practical work – that's how I got into the restoration business. Anyway, no. I'm selling the place. And if a restaurateur buys it, that'd be good.'

'Still,' Mark persisted, 'it seems a pity to sell it without thinking carefully about all the possibilities.'

Jane and Bella arrived in the hall before Mark could overplay his hand and in the general mêlée of goodbyes and thank yous, Mark extracted from Titus a specific invitation to visit the warehouse.

'That really wasn't too bad, was it?' Titus stretched his legs in the passenger seat and yawned. 'It was a bit sticky to start with but I thought we all got on rather well in the end.'

Jane threaded the car through the line of traffic on Wandsworth Bridge roundabout, bit hard on her lip and didn't answer.

'You and Bella were okay, weren't you? Talking about books and things . . .'

'She's okay,' Jane lied cautiously. 'A bit hard-bitten for my liking, and actually we don't have the same taste in books. Not at all. But, yes, we got through the evening.'

'Mark's coming to see the warehouse. He's been looking at similar properties, apparently, and wants to compare them with something in this area.'

Jane parked the car outside their house and turned off the engine.

'You bet he does,' she said, turning in her seat to look at Titus. 'I can tell you, this evening was not just a friendly overture from your newly found brother and his wife, not at all. Mark is an ambitious entrepreneur who has designs on your premises.'

'I don't think he has. Not particularly on this one.'

'Yes, Titus, he has. I got the line from Bella when we were looking for books. It was oh-so casual, of course, but the message was crystal clear. It's a natural progression for him, you see – owning a catering company then expanding into the "restaurant business". And now his new brother has the perfect premises. *Very* convenient.'

'He's not the only person who's suggested a restaurant.'

'No, Titus,' Jane persisted gently, 'but he's the only one suggesting *his* restaurant.'

'But all these people could be right. It might be just what our area needs.' Titus banged gently on the dashboard with his hand. 'It'd be good for the community. It's not such a bad idea, you know.'

'Hang on here. We are going to sell. Aren't we?'

'Of course, but if I could get A3 restaurant use first, we'd get a better price for it. Or, more lucratively,' Titus's eyes lit up, 'we sell a lease. That way we have an income from the place.'

'And you'd be happy leasing it to Mark, is that right?'

'I'm sure he'd want to buy it outright – he's obviously rolling in money. But if he wanted a lease, he's got experience in the catering business. He'd be a reliable tenant.'

'And you'd trust Mark, would you?' Jane was wishing that this conversation was not happening.

'Better the devil you know.'

'He may well be a devil, and you don't know him.'

'He's my new brother. He's blood.' Titus smiled, teasing her now, but Jane was past seeing the funny side of anything.

'My point exactly,' she said through gritted teeth, hoping that it was Mark's ridiculously fine claret that was making Titus so charitable and so unperspicacious.

'I think that passed off very well,' Mark said as he and Bella stacked the dishwasher. 'Apparently some friends of his have also suggested a restaurant.'

Bella was dismantling her stage set. She replaced the bunch

of garden flowers in the middle of the table with an expensive florist creation.

'You don't want to let this get away from you,' she warned. 'The friends might want to run a restaurant there and you don't want to be bumped out of the deal. You've got to get in there fast.'

Mark sighed. 'Bel, even if I did what you suggest, and Titus came in as a partner, I'm still looking at heavy borrowing for my share. I've really got to consider this carefully.'

'What about Ralph? Wouldn't he be interested in coming in on this?'

Mark made a face. 'Shouldn't think so, you've seen how he is about Titus. But I have thought about touching him for a loan. I reckon the family business owes me that facility at least. You know,' Mark continued, 'I'm beginning to think that if he wasn't who he was, I might quite like Titus. I think they're a friendly couple, probably nice people really.'

Bella looked at him quizzically. The drink may have made Mark sentimental but she had been drinking designer water for most of the evening and she thought that Titus and Jane were, without exception, the dreariest couple she had ever had the misfortune to meet.

Mark parked half across a private drive. He had checked that the owner of the drive could, albeit with patient manoeuvring, get his car on to his property. Judging by the state of the house, he probably wouldn't have a very big car anyway. The only other option was to park outside a rough-looking estate and he wasn't prepared to risk his car ending up with no wheels at all. As he turned into the road leading to Squarey Street, he noticed, with pleasure, the terraces of grander, double-fronted houses. He also passed a legitimately parked old red Volvo full of dust sheets and tools.

The door of the warehouse was unlocked. Mark pushed it open and walked into a large dark space filled with pallets and metal shelving.

'Oh hi.' Titus emerged from a dark corner and surprised Mark by shaking his hand as though he was a client.

'Did you find somewhere to park? They've got the high street up this week, and I'm afraid it's hellish.'

Mark began to wander round the building. 'Good size. What business was your uncle in?'

'Hardware. When he died, Aunt Monica closed the business and kept the freehold. Recently it's been storage for the bed shop round the corner. Aunt Monica and Uncle Will brought me up. She was my mother's sister.' Titus wanted to establish that Mark's family was not the only one to whom Titus belonged. 'It needs a lot doing to it, as you can see,' he added.

'Good space though.' Mark prodded a few walls with his car keys, looking, he hoped, knowledgeable. 'Pretty sound too, by the looks of it.' Then he remembered that Titus had architectural experience and would probably know more than he about the fabric of a building. 'Of course, you'd know better than me,' he deferred quickly.

'No, you're right, it is. And it could be turned into any sort of space really. It needs light let in at the back, but that shouldn't be too difficult.'

'Quite coincidentally . . .' Mark began lying casually, 'I had to ring up the planning people the other day. I'm thinking about moving the Basil Catering kitchens south of the river – cheaper rents. We got on to the subject of restaurant use – I can't remember how – anyway, they seemed to think that there is very little problem around here at the moment. The council is looking to upgrade the town centres. A3 use is a good way of making an area more upmarket.'

'Really.' Titus sounded cool. 'Well, that's interesting.'

A silence fell between them.

Mark had to strike a happy balance between instilling enthusiasm for the idea in Titus without pricing himself out of the market by overselling the obvious financial potential of the premises.

'If you were to go down that avenue, of course, this place

would lend itself very well to a restaurant.' He looked questioningly at Titus, waiting for some sign to continue.

Titus nodded. 'Yes, I think it would.'

'Well,' Mark began. 'Let me see. You could have a small bar here with a simple but good menu.' He moved near the door and spread out his arms. 'That would appeal to the young, the ones with disposable income, I mean.' Unaware of Titus's wincing, he continued lavishly, 'You might even get some morning coffee trade. Then, in the back, you could have a smart restaurant: tablecloths, à la carte, proper waitresses, that sort of thing. It will appeal to the young married couples round here. It could be open all day – breakfast to midnight. Of course, good kitchen space is paramount, but, look . . .' Mark swept to the back. 'Great area here for kitchen, storage and lavatories – it's perfect. You could make this a very exciting restaurant and bar.' He subtly emphasised the word 'you'.

'Yeah, it could work, I suppose,' Titus said slowly. 'For someone prepared to make the capital investment.'

'It would be a winner, I'm sure.'

'Well,' Titus appeared to be winding up the conversation, 'I'm not rushing into anything at the moment. I'm fortunate to be in a position where there's no great hurry to decide.'

It was Mark's turn to wince. He thought there *was* a hurry – the place could be up and running in time for Christmas. He chose his words carefully.

'November would be an ideal time to open – catch the Christmas trade.'

'Are you prepared to make me an offer for the freehold?' Titus asked suddenly.

Mark backtracked rapidly. Buying the freehold was now out of the question – leasehold could still be a possibility.

'Well, I'd need to know it had restaurant use. And there are quite a few other places around here that are worth considering.'

Mark was being very careful. He had a suspicion that Titus was interested in a restaurant, but he couldn't afford to let him run away with the idea. He had to lock into Titus and make sure he didn't just sell it on – or suddenly go into partnership with someone else.

'You know,' he went on casually, 'if you were to go down the restaurant route, it would be great to get yourself involved in the transformation. Use your architectural experience.'

'I think it'd be too big a project for me.' Titus shook his head thoughtfully.

'Well, I'd be interested to know what you do with the place.' Mark paused, uncertain how much to offer. 'I might be interested in helping with the project . . . in some way.' Mark was trying to sound noncommittal, keen to keep off specifics at the moment, knowing that it was always a mistake to corner your quarry until you were sure of a kill.

'Yeah, thanks,' said Titus. 'You've given me quite a lot to think about.'

'Keep in touch.' Mark shook Titus's hand heartily to underline their professional relationship. 'There's a lot of money in a good restaurant. And,' he added, suddenly remembering Titus's previous philanthropic ideas for the building, 'as you said, it's just what this area needs: good food but not expensive – a decent meeting place for the whole . . .' Mark used a word that was quite alien to him, but one he knew would please Titus, 'community.'

Kit came out of the school gates with a group of other sixth formers. He was deep in an earnest conversation with his friend Ed about the merits of attending Sixth Form Society that evening. They had just about decided on giving it a miss and going off to the pub when Kit felt a tap on his shoulder.

'Kit cousin.'

He swung round and came face to face with Summer's laughing face.

'Thought I'd come and meet you at your snotty school – help you cross the road and that.'

Kit could see Ed casting an appreciative look over what appeared to be his cousin's near naked body. His eyes were

71

greedily taking in the tiny crop top and the long bare legs barely covered by a short skirt. The ring in her belly button glinted in the centre of her slim, brown torso.

'Hi, I'm Ed,' he said.

'Summer.' She nodded towards Kit. 'His new-found cousin.'

'Oh right.'

'So, what shall we do now?' Summer asked.

Kit pulled himself together.

'We were just deciding whether to go to Sixth Form Society,' he said stupidly.

Ed raised one eyebrow in disgust.

'No, we weren't,' he said quickly. 'We were just deciding to go to the pub.'

'Great. Good call.' Summer started walking. 'I'm up for that.'

The three of them walked off down the road.

'This is a bit of a coincidence,' Kit said, still reeling from the vision of Summer appearing out of nowhere. He hoped that at least some of the lower sixth had seen them together.

'Not really, I've been waiting for you. I waited yesterday but you never appeared.'

'Yesterday? I think I went to play football yesterday. A few of us get together on Thursdays and kick a ball about, y'know—'

'Hey, do you ever go to the Brass Bar on a Monday?' Ed had obviously decided that if he didn't inject something more vibrant into the conversation immediately, Kit would send this sensational girl screaming for her train home.

'Yeah, I do – great place,' Summer said. 'Did you get to see that amazing guy who used to play with some band in the sixties? Can't remember his name, my dad knew it. He even came to the gig with me.'

Kit whistled. 'Bloody hell! You wouldn't catch my dad in a place like that.'

In the pub, Ed elected to go to the bar and Kit and Summer ordered lager.

'So what are you doing tonight?' Summer asked.

Kit shrugged. 'Dunno. Going home, I suppose.'

'On a Friday night?' Summer said contemptuously. 'I don't think so. There's a bit of a party going near me. Want to come?'

'Okay,' Kit said recklessly. 'Why not?'

'Your mate can come too, if he wants.'

'Oh, he'll want,' Kit said with a glimmer of a smile.

Summer mirrored back the smile.

'Thought he might,' she said.

'So you two are sort of cousins, then?' Ed said, when he came back with the drinks.

'We only have the same grandfather,' Kit said, 'not the same grandmother.'

'But you both have the same great-grandparents on one side though, don't you?' Ed persisted. 'That must make you sort of cousins.'

'Suppose,' Summer said vaguely to him. She turned to Kit and said wistfully, 'I wish I'd known all these years. About everything.' Her face brightened a little. 'Did Gaff used to teach you to play croquet?'

'Did he ever!' Kit had found a subject about which he could speak without stumbling. 'Did he used to draw you diagrams of all the manoeuvres and then make you learn them?'

'A rush is a roquet hit firmly,' Summer recited in a deep voice. 'Line up the ball with the help of your foot . . .' Kit joined in and they finished together '. . . halve the angle and aim for that spot.'

'We should have a game one day,' Summer said.

Kit was about to agree, then he thought of his father.

'I doubt it,' he said gloomily. 'My dad isn't very happy about all of you. We're not even allowed to mention you at the moment. I don't suppose we'll ever be playing happy families together at Clattie's.'

'Alby and I love Clattie.' Summer's light, sassy voice turned wistful. 'I hope we can still see her sometimes.'

'I wish I could suddenly find new relations out of nowhere,' Ed said enviously. 'My family is *so* gross.'

But Summer and Kit were not listening: they were talking about their grandfather again.

'He'd get furious if he thought that you were mumbling, do you remember?'

'Did he used to tell you the story about how he broke his nose hunting? And did he make it click when you wiggled it?'

Ed gave up trying to join in and stared at Summer with an expression of deferential lustfulness on his face.

The party turned out to be a surprisingly mellow affair. In a large terraced house in East Dulwich, a group of students sat around listening to music and drinking wine and beer.

On the strength of meeting this intriguing and very cool cousin of Kit's, Ed had hoped for lines of coke and a bit of group sex at the very least. It was, as he pointed out to Summer, disappointingly quiet.

'You private school kids are always much wilder than us lot,' Summer said loftily. 'It's because you're so repressed in your posh little lives.' She handed him a large spliff. 'Here,' she said, not unkindly. 'Have some puff and shut up.'

Ed spent the evening watching Summer come on to Kit and, infuriatingly for Ed, Kit failing to take advantage of the situation; he seemed perfectly happy just to be talking to her and Ed thought what a terrible waste of such a mega chick.

'Blew that one then didn't you, mate?' Ed said, as they shared a minicab back to Camberwell.

Kit looked at his friend blankly. 'What?'

'Summer.'

'Oh, she's great. I really like her.'

'She's hot for you. I was watching her.'

Kit frowned at Ed. 'Get real. She's my cousin.'

'Only a half one,' Ed said cheerfully, 'and, anyway, I think you're allowed to shag your cousin, aren't you?'

Chapter Four

Jane barged into the workshop. 'I've just met Patsy Crane in the newsagent and she says you never turned up yesterday to estimate for her wardrobe. And,' she picked up Titus's mobile phone and shook it at him, 'apparently you never answer this because there are two agitated messages on the home phone from Mrs Morahan. She needs her dining-room chairs in two weeks at the latest. A christening or something.'

Titus looked up from a chair that was viced into his workbench. Jane, usually so phlegmatic, sounded agitated.

'Shit, I'm sorry. I completely forgot about Patsy. But here, look, the chairs are nearly finished.'

'Well, tell Mrs Morahan that, would you please.' Jane stood in front of Titus, hands on her hips.

'I will, I promise.'

'Titus, sweetheart,' Jane began in an ominously reasonable voice, 'you must talk to me properly. Your head is just not here at the moment and Palmer's Restoration seems to be last on your list of priorities.'

Titus's head was full of restaurant at the moment. The idea

had been growing daily ever since Mark had so graphically unfolded his vision in the warehouse. When he had suggested that Titus design the interior, Titus had rejected the plan out of hand. But slowly, over the past couple of weeks, the idea had begun to ferment and now, if he passed a restaurant, he would note the space, the light and the choice of fixtures and fittings, and a few days ago he had pulled out his old drawing board and sketched some drawings of the place.

'I know what you're doing, Titus,' Jane was hovering over him, 'and at the moment it's freaking me out. We need to talk.'

Titus put down his chisel, took Jane's hand and led her to a stool next to his drawing board. 'You're right, I'm sorry. We do need to talk.'

'I've got a very bad feeling about all of this.' Jane sat down gracelessly and began fiddling with a roll of upholstery webbing.

'Look, Mark started me thinking—'

'Oh Mark, bloody Mark. If he wants a restaurant, just sell him the place.'

Titus sat down opposite her and took a deep breath. How he put this to Jane would maybe affect the rest of their lives.

'I will. Sell it or lease it to someone, anyway. That's not the issue. It's the design and build bit I'm interested in. Making it work as a space. I'm just trying out a few ideas, see if I can do it.' He spoke slowly, keeping it as low key as he could. 'It's a challenge.'

'But you don't know anything about designing a restaurant,' Jane argued. 'I understand that it's a challenge, but, come on, you've got absolutely no experience.'

'Look.' Titus, encouraged by Jane's discursive tone of voice, attempted to sell her the idea of what he wanted to do more than anything else. 'Give me some credit here. I wouldn't be getting this far,' he gestured to the drawings in front of him, 'if I hadn't already done a lot of research.'

'What sort of research?'

76

Titus took a deep breath and told the truth. 'I've had a meeting with Geoff Turner. You know Geoff, he designed that coffee house on the corner of the high street.'

'I know Geoff. His youngest daughter's at the playgroup,' Jane said coolly, looking sideways at Titus.

'Well, with his help I've worked out some figures and a projected time scale for the building works. I've got a list of local builders that Geoff uses and he's offered to work as a part-time consultant . . . if this came to fruition, of course,' Titus added hurriedly.

'You've achieved quite a lot in just over a week,' observed Jane, still chilly. 'It sounds as though you've decided to do this already. Without even talking to me. I thought we were in this together.'

'I haven't decided. And I would have talked to you when I was sure it was even halfway possible. I haven't even heard about A3 use yet.'

'Titus. We were going to sell the place as it is. I know we all had ideas of what we could do there – not one of them was a restaurant, by the way – but I thought we were just having a bit of fun. We'd decided to sell. Now you're changing the goal posts without even discussing it with me.'

Titus sighed. He had never wanted to hurt Jane but clearly he had.

'No, not necessarily, but first I wanted to see if it could work. So that we could make a measured decision.'

Jane laughed unkindly. 'Measured decision? You do talk crap, Titus. Look, just be straight with me, okay? You really want to do this, don't you?'

Titus nodded. 'I think I do. I'm sure it would work. And the prospect of designing the place . . . well, it's just very exciting. It feels like a new life. I haven't felt so motivated for years.'

Jane looked around the dingy workshop and then back at Titus. She stared into his face, now becoming creased at the corners. His deep-set eyes were clear and sparkly. She picked up his hand that was resting on her knee – beautiful long hands, slightly calloused, one dark, bruised nail – such dear, familiar hands.

'Are you telling me you're fed up with all this?' She gestured round the workshop. 'You could have said.'

'I'm not fed up exactly. I just realise that I'm in a rut. It's the same old stuff, and I'm starting to wonder if this is it. If this is me until I'm too old to do anything else.' Titus looked at her, clearly waiting for her to show some understanding of his feelings.

Jane fiddled with his hand still in her lap. She thought of how often her circle of women friends discussed their futures. They were all over fifty and the What Next? subject had replaced the education- and car-parking conversations of their forties. Jane watched her friends, listened to them: so many of them were restless, unsettled and ultimately destructive. They were bored and dissatisfied with their lives; they wanted something different, but often couldn't be clear what to change. Why should these feelings be exclusive to women? Why shouldn't men feel the same? It disturbed Jane that she had been so busy being content with her life she'd failed to notice that Titus was not keeping step with her. Now he had found a change that he wanted to make and she could let him make it. She nodded her head gently.

'So, how are we going to pay for this?' she asked. 'Won't it cost a lot to fit out?'

Titus silently acknowledged her gift by taking her hand up to his lips and kissing it gently.

'It will. But we could use some of the Gaffer's legacy, that's the beauty of it.'

Jane breathed in sharply. 'Titus, that is so risky, surely? Supposing the work goes way over budget? Or we can't sell it? We might end up with no safety money at all and what do we do then? For the first time in our lives we've got enough money; we can stop scrabbling around to pay the bills. We could treat ourselves. Go to Australia.'

'It won't use all the money, no way. And it's a good investment.' Titus's face was alight with enthusiasm. 'We'll sell the place at a profit. We'll be able to go to Australia, I promise.'

'What about paying off the mortgage?' Jane wailed.

'We're going to do that, but we'll just do it later, when we sell. Of course we should look into leasing it. We'd get three times more than we've been getting from the bed company. Thirty thousand a year would pay the mortgage and then some.'

'To Mark? Lease it to Mark?'

'Maybe, I don't know. But he's obviously got the money and he's interested for sure.'

'Hang on, Titus.' Jane let go of his hand, got to her feet and started pacing the floor. 'Let's just think about this. If you leased the building to Mark, that will make you his landlord, and he'll be your tenant. Titus, he's your *brother*. That could end up being a very embarrassing situation.'

But Titus could see no correlation between business and relationships. 'He's okay, really he is. This would be purely business. I don't even think of him as my brother.'

Jane considered that a formidable thought. She stopped her pacing and stood beside Titus.

'I think you *should* think of him as your brother,' she said fiercely, 'and be aware that, on the whole, family and business should be kept apart.'

Titus shrugged his shoulders in a gesture of compromise. 'Sweetheart. If we don't want Mark to have it when it's finished, that's fine. And if you want us to sell outright, that's fine too. I assure you we won't have any trouble selling it.' He looked earnestly at Jane. 'I just want to build this restaurant. I don't mind what happens after that. We knew we were going to sell the place. This is a sensible way to use the money, to make more in the end.'

'But it is different. This restaurant is, I don't know . . .' Jane couldn't explain the knot of uncertainty and distrust that was growing steadily tighter inside her '. . . bigger than us,' she finished lamely.

*

It was rather like chasing a woman, Mark realised – and he had always been good at that. He kept his distance for a week or so, hoping that Titus was absorbing the vision that he had drawn for him at the warehouse. Then, at the optimum moment, Mark telephoned Titus.

'Just wondering how you were getting on with plans for Squarey Street,' he said breezily. 'Only, funnily enough, a mate of mine, who lives near you, was talking about your place.' Mark was lying glibly. 'He'd heard rumours that it's been bought by one of the big supermarket boys for a high-street shop. I said that I knew you and I thought it highly unlikely.'

Titus laughed. 'You wonder where these rumours come from, don't you? This one's not true anyway. Certainly not.'

'I thought not,' Mark agreed and began to terminate the conversation. 'Well, I just said I'd check. All of you are well, I hope?'

'Yes, we're fine. Actually . . .' Mark heard Titus hesitate for a moment down the phone and he held his breath, 'Jane and I have decided to go with the restaurant idea.'

Mark clenched his fist and breathed, 'Yes'.

'I'm going to do it myself and then sell it,' Titus went on. 'I've applied for a provisional liquor licence and I've put in an application for A3 planning permission.'

Mark's euphoria evaporated. 'Already got a design?' he said nervously. 'That's pretty quick work.'

'It's a draft plan. If the whole thing's a non-starter, I can ditch it without feeling I've wasted too much time on it.'

'I'd be interested to see the plans,' Mark began modestly. 'Give you any help I can.' He took a deep breath and stopped pussy-footing around. 'I'll be honest with you, Titus, I'm seriously interested in the place. It's just what I've been looking for.'

'I'll bear that in mind,' Titus sounded businesslike and non-committal, 'when I put it on the market.'

Mark replaced the receiver with a thoughtful frown on his face. He was not in a position to buy the restaurant.

*

'It looks great,' Freddie said enthusiastically. 'Lots of potential. He should make a tidy profit when it's finished.'

Freddie and Mark were sitting in her car which was parked in Squarey Street. Mark had waited until it was dark to show her the place; he was anxious not to be seen hovering around.

'I've got to stop him from selling.' Mark stared at his dream, which seemed to be frustratingly unattainable. 'I can't raise the finance to buy so I really want a lease from him based on the shell, with a rent-free period until I start trading. I reckon I could fit this place out quite basically, quite reasonably and pretty quickly. Unfortunately, I seem to have unleashed a wild enthusiasm in the stupid man and he's intent on doing all this on his own. And you know what architects are like; ploddy old women usually, who do everything very slowly and always by the book.'

'Excuse me, some of my best lovers were architects.' Freddie poked her finger into Mark's thigh.

'More information than I need to know,' he said, tugging at her hair. 'At the moment he's definitely saying he wants to sell,' he went on seriously. 'They're the sort of people who would probably use the money to hitchhike round the world or something. No, I've got to get in there and be part of the project. I need to be on the spot to persuade him to lease, then I can get first hit at it.'

'Okay.' Freddie rested her elbows on the steering wheel. 'So where are you planning to get the money to pay for all this? Are you going to sell Basil Catering?'

'No. Anyway, it wouldn't fetch enough. I'm thinking bank loan and remortgage the house. I want to set up a separate restaurant company.'

'You need a partner.'

'Exactly. Interested?'

'Me? I'm much too young to be tied down,' Freddie said lightly.

'Rub it in, why don't you.' Mark squeezed her hand. 'Anyway, I'd expect my partner to work and you only play.'

'When I have a job I work,' Freddie protested. 'I just do the jobs I like. So, who've you got in mind as a partner?'

'Titus.'

Freddie turned to Mark. In the glare of the sodium street-light, he could see the astonishment in her face.

'Titus? Titus? You're not serious?'

'Why not? You know my situation. I would need a partner with reliable money. Titus has had his inheritance from the Gaffer and he owns the bloody building. Think how useful it would be to have a partner who was also the landlord.'

'And also your eldest brother who your family has only just found out about.'

But Mark could see no correlation between business and relationships.

'Family has nothing to do with it. This is business. It's an ideal arrangement. Obviously he'll be a sleeping partner, he knows about design but he knows nothing about the restaurant business. He won't want to be involved in the running of the place. Once he's designed and built it – with input from me – and once I'm trading, he'll collect his no doubt substantial rent, have a few free meals and drinks to show off to his local friends, then get back to his cushion covers or whatever he does. It would work for us both.'

'And how do you think the rest of your family will feel about this business marriage?' enquired Freddie.

'What the fuck do you think you're doing?' Ralph spluttered, drops of red wine splashing on to the white tablecloth. 'Have you lost all sense of . . . loyalty?'

Mark and Ralph were having lunch at a restaurant in town. The two brothers invited each other out periodically to make them feel that they had an acceptable fraternal relationship and, if it had been a boozy lunch, they would part with a rare feeling of mutual affection.

It had been Mark's turn to choose the restaurant and this was one he had earmarked for the purposes of research.

Ralph had wanted to talk about Clattie first. 'I worry about her rattling around in that big house all on her own,' he started. 'Pippa does nothing but ring me from her nunnery to say how worried she is too, but not, it seems, enough to go home. I suppose she might take the veil and we'll never see her again.'

'I don't think modern-day communities like that are enclosed, nor do they insist on hair shirts and shaved heads,' Mark responded mildly.

'Pippa has her own mental hair shirt, anyway. She always has. Do you remember when she came to help Grania with Caitlin when Kit was born? God, did she fuss and worry over us all, rushing around doing things about the house that didn't need doing, reorganising cupboards, turning out the cellar and breaking things. It was chaos. She made so much more work for Grania, we had to send her home in the end.'

Ralph laughed at the memory – and it was the last time he laughed at lunch because it was then that Mark had told him about his plan to lease the restaurant from Titus.

'We don't want anything more to do with that lot. I thought *that* was understood,' Ralph said, tapping his finger angrily on the table.

'He's got the perfect premises,' Mark said patiently. 'It's always been my game plan to own a restaurant in the right place – now these premises appear to have fallen into my lap out of the blue.'

'At much too great a price, I assure you.'

'I might as well make use of the place. He hasn't a clue about anything. He's interested in the design and build, but that's all. I want him to give me a lease. I really can't let this excellent opportunity slip through my fingers; it just doesn't make good business sense.'

Mark watched Ralph struggle with his outrage. 'If you've really got to have it, why not offer to buy the freehold outright?'

'I can't afford to buy anything, thanks to the Gaffer's skew-eyed will.' Mark made no effort to keep the resentment out of his voice.

'I think it was fair,' Ralph said shortly. 'This way, the man can make no demands on us and Clattie will be secure for the rest of her life.'

'I thought she had money of her own,' interrupted Mark.

'She has, but I think she'll continue living at The Mill, certainly for the moment, and that takes some upkeep. In fact, it's Pippa who might feel hardly done by, if anyone.' Ralph was admonishing his brother. 'I don't suppose she earns, or rather earned all that much when she was working and I doubt she's a great saver, so if she wanted to buy her own place she probably wouldn't have the money.'

'I had hoped to do this on my own.' Mark, anxious to bring the subject back to himself, spoke more loudly than he intended. Ralph looked up from his meal. 'But I can't. The financial commitment I would have to take on is just not tenable—'

'I hope you're not going to ask me—' Ralph started warningly.

'No,' Mark answered stiffly. 'I was just going on to say that the obvious answer is to form a partnership in a new company for the restaurant.'

Ralph placed his knife and fork neatly on his plate. 'And you surely weren't thinking of suggesting that I might be interested . . .?'

If Mark had entertained any thoughts of assistance from his brother or the family firm, they were now unequivocally dispatched. He felt the familiar surge of bullishness rise up inside him.

'Certainly not,' he said in a proud voice. And with an equally familiar desire to hit out spitefully, he said with almost childish triumph, 'My only option is to offer Titus the partnership. After all, he's the one with the money now.'

Ralph's face closed up with pain. He spoke slowly, obviously trying to control his temper.

'I don't understand you, Mark. You appear to have gone quite insane. I thought we all agreed that once the Gaffer's will had been paid off we could forget the man ever existed. It was obviously what the Gaffer had in mind when he drew up the will and we should abide by his wishes.' He frowned at Mark. 'But you, it seems, are determined to prolong the relationship for your own ends.'

'It's a business opportunity. The Gaffer would have understood that,' Mark persisted.

'I was staggered that you suggested leasing premises off him.' Ralph ignored his brother's interruption. 'But now I know that you intend to go into partnership with him, I'm just reeling with your . . . perfidiousness. I warn you, I can't give you any support on this. I want nothing, nothing to do with that man or anything that belongs to him. I'm sorry, Mark. I understand you think this is a good business opportunity and it might well be but, as far as I'm concerned, in this case there is something much larger at stake and I'm surprised that you can . . . prostitute yourself like this.' Ralph took a swig of wine and Mark noticed his hand was gripping the glass tightly. Dark silence fell between the two brothers as they concentrated on their food, unable to break the deadlock.

'I meant what I said, but I apologise for being so vehement about it,' Ralph said eventually.

'I'm sorry you feel this way,' mumbled Mark, never one to find apologising easy, 'but I think you're being irrational.'

There was a fleeting flash of sympathy in Ralph's eyes as he said, 'We'll have to agree to differ then. I can't stop you doing anything, but I do suggest you think very carefully before you act. You don't know what can of worms you'll be opening and you'll hurt a lot of people.' He put down his knife and fork in a final gesture. 'End of subject. No further discussion. Now, I gather you're coming down to The Mill this weekend as well?' Mark nodded. 'That's great. I think it's good for Clattie to have us all together now and then. Kit's playing football, so he won't be there. Pippa is coming over on Saturday, bringing a friend from the community apparently. I do hope they're not planning on group worship.' Ralph raised his eyebrows and Mark, his temper slowly returning, smiled back reluctantly.

'Clattie will keep calling this weekend a family weekend. She makes it sound like a Tampax commercial. I checked that she hadn't done anything silly like invite the other lot. I think her loyalty to them is quite misplaced, but she seems to think that she still has a duty to them.'

'We had them to supper recently,' Mark said stubbornly. 'You know, they're very ordinary people, harmless – slightly dull even. Really, Ralph, they're not the ogres you're making them out to be.'

'I'm not interested in them,' Ralph said dismissively. 'At least Clattie seems to have got the message that *we* are not prepared to play happy families with them.' He glared at Mark briefly. 'Well, the rest of us aren't, anyway.'

Clattie was learning to be alone. She was grateful that her children were concerned for her, but she rather wished that if they were going to ring they might do it at different times of the day rather than every evening; because it was the evenings that she was trying to get used to. She was putting in place a routine that filled the time when she and Jack would sit down for a drink together. The house seemed larger than it had ever been, and as darkness fell every noise was magnified in the silence of the shadowy rooms. She did miss Jack's presence. She didn't miss the young, arrogant Jack, nor the demanding, testy, patriarchal Jack – she missed the man that Jack had latterly become in his illness. This ill and vulnerable Jack had, curiously, developed an unexpected and almost childish desire to please her. Did he, Clattie wondered now, have a premonition that he was going to leave her imminently with their family in such disorder and confusion?

There were days in her grieving when Clattie was angry with Jack, a bubbling, uncontrollable anger that had lain dormant for all their married life; yet there were times when she felt, in some confused, loyal way, that she wanted to protect Jack's memory for his children's sake. Ralph refused to speak of Titus, but was unable to disguise the darkness inside him, and Clattie had watched Pippa at the funeral mentally wiping her hands of the situation. Only Mark appeared to have extended a tentative hand of friendship. The subject of Titus was too new for discussion, so Clattie had no real way of knowing quite how her three children were coping. She had had years to accept the situation, silently and uncomplainingly doing what was expected of her, but now her emotions were churning up and down, scrambling inside her, changing every day, so that she couldn't quite place how she was feeling.

Over the last few weeks Clattie had been trying to make the house her own. She cleared out Jack's clothes and rearranged furniture to make the rooms in The Mill look different. When she came upon the dusty bundles of letters at the back of Jack's desk, she sat turning them over in her hands for some time. She knew what they were immediately – Jack and Shirley's letters. His had been returned by Shirley's sister when Shirley died and she had no idea that Jack had kept them all those years in such an uncharacteristically sentimental gesture. She knew what they said, she had no need to read them again, and she knew that Titus should have them. Someday. She couldn't let him have them now – not yet, it was too soon for her to give up their secrets. Clattie tucked away the letters in the desk and raged at her husband's cowardice. 'Thank you for leaving me with this,' she said out loud to the piles of his shoes she was bagging up, 'and for the final indignity – clearing up your mess.'

She had been thinking about Titus a great deal. Must the secret go on and must she manage it alone? To continue to see Titus without her children's knowledge, strangely, after all these years of secrecy, seemed even more dishonest and disloyal than it had before his existence was known. It would be like managing a lover – a secret from her own children. Yet to see Titus and his family openly would upset and hurt her family. She needed Jack back to sort out the pain he had caused. She wanted to believe that this whole thing was not the fault of anyone left behind, but she couldn't help feeling that it was she who had been remiss all this time. She realised, with helpless clarity, that she was taking on the guilt that Jack should have been suffering, yet she couldn't stop herself.

'I can't force Jack's children to talk to each other or to me,' she said to Gerry, as they shared supper in the garden one evening. 'It must be up to them, so I've decided on a policy of letting them find their own level – like you do with dogs.'

And it was Clattie's new dog that greeted the family when they arrived for the weekend.

'What on earth is that?' Ralph looked down in astonishment at an elderly Staffordshire bull terrier wheezing around his legs in the hall.

'Gerry – you met him at the funeral – thought I needed company, so he gave him to me,' Clattie said. 'He's a rescue dog.'

'Hardly worth rescuing, I'd have thought,' remarked Ralph.

The dog, minus an ear, was badly scarred and had a round body like a battered, brown leather pouffe.

'He's called Razor, unfortunately,' Clattie said apologetically. 'I know, quite dreadful, but I can hardly change his name to Rover – he's much too old.'

Razor turned out to be rather a blessing – he provided a constant topic of conversation that was neither controversial nor sad. This was the first time the family had been at The Mill together since Jack's death and they were all conscious of the large space he had left.

Pippa arrived on Saturday morning with a young man whom she introduced as Meredith, one of the elders of the community.

Ralph, studying the man's youthful face and unkempt hair, was moved to wonder, *sotto voce*, how much younger an elder could be. Clattie frowned at him.

'We couldn't miss Agape last night,' Pippa explained. 'That's our monthly love feast, you see.'

Ralph rolled his eyes.

Meredith went round the whole family shaking hands. 'How do you do. Bless you,' he said shyly to each one.

Clattie and Grania had laid lunch in the dining room but Pippa reorganised it outside, under the old cedar tree.

'It's such a lovely day, seems to be a pity to be inside,' she said bossily and then looked anxiously at them all. 'Well, is that all right with everyone? Are you sure? I mean, do say if you don't want to.'

'Might I say a simple grace, Mrs Palmer, before we eat?' Meredith asked politely.

Ralph flashed a pained look round the table before casting down his eyes and folding his hands together in a parody of Christopher Robin saying his prayers.

'I'm watching the cricket this afternoon,' Ralph announced before the family's tentative amens had died away. 'Do you like cricket, Meredith?'

Meredith smiled politely. 'I'm afraid we don't really go in for competitive games in our community, Ralph.' He pronounced the 'l' in Ralph.

'We are all equal in the eyes of the Lord,' Pippa said sanctimoniously.

'Well, I wish he'd made the Australian team as equally lousy as ours then,' Ralph said gloomily. 'They're slaughtering us at the moment.'

'So, Ralph is settling in front of the television this afternoon.' Clattie spoke quickly. 'What are the rest of us going to do?'

Bella, always bored and restless in the country, suggested to Grania that they went shopping in Tunbridge Wells.

'What about you, Pippa?' asked Grania.

Clattie watched Pippa look up eagerly at the prospect of a shopping trip and then remember her duties as a hostess – and as a daughter.

'Are you going, Clattie?'

Clattie shook her head, 'No. Shopping on a Saturday afternoon fills me with horror. I'll stay here and take Razor for a walk.'

'We'll come with you,' announced Pippa, looking questioningly at Meredith, who nodded his approval.

Neither cricket nor shopping held any allure for Mark, so he elected to go on the walk.

'Where shall we go?' Pippa asked as they gathered in the hall. She looked anxiously at Clattie. 'Where would you like?'

'I don't mind, darling. We should think of one that Meredith might enjoy.' Clattie looked instinctively at Meredith's feet, shod in socks and sandals. 'Not too muddy perhaps.'

Pippa looked worried. 'What about you, Mark? You like the scarecrow walk, don't you, but it is muddy.'

'Yes, but I'm easy. I don't mind, I really don't,' Mark said patiently.

'What about up past the churchyard?' Clattie suggested.

Pippa thought, head on one side. 'No, I don't think so. We can't do a circle on that walk and you like doing circles, don't you, Mark? Where do you think, Meredith?'

'How can he have a view?' Mark pointed out irritably. 'He's never been here before.'

'I want us all to enjoy the walk.'

'We will, if you'd just choose somewhere to go and we could get going,' Mark said, bored now by the preamble.

Ralph came through the wide hall with a cup of coffee and a newspaper in his hands.

'Haven't you lot gone yet?'

'We can't decide on the best walk.' Pippa appealed to him.

'The ridge,' Ralph said immediately.

'That's a long way and it's very uphill.' Pippa cast an anxious glance at Clattie.

'Go halfway then.' Ralph disappeared into the book room.

'Turning back always seems so . . . hopeless, somehow.' Pippa sighed.

Mark couldn't bear it any longer. 'Come on. I'll make the decision.' Pippa looked at him gratefully. 'We'll go down Jelly's Lane and cut across to Mill Lane.'

'Good,' approved Pippa. 'That's a nice walk.' She paused and looked round at Clattie and Meredith. 'Are you sure everyone's happy with that?'

Clattie and Mark soon lagged behind Meredith and Pippa who set off at a brisk pace, deep in conversation. Grateful that they didn't have to keep up, mother and son slowed their pace even more and sauntered along the lane in the warm sunshine. Razor bumbled beside them, nose down in the hedgerow, his scraggy tail beating round in a circle.

'What's the deal with Meredith?' Mark asked. 'Is he a boyfriend?'

'I gather not. He's just befriended Pippa.' Clattie pulled absent-mindedly at the vegetation along the verge. 'He's her mentor.'

'Is she going to stay at the community?'

'She says she'd like to but she's worried about me being on my own. I've told her I'm not a dependent old woman yet and she must do what she believes is best for her, so she's thinking about it. If she wants to join the community, I expect she will.'

'Yes,' agreed Mark. 'Pippa generally does what she wants in the end, despite her outward concern for everyone else.'

Clattie threw him a look.

'Rather like your father,' she said drily. 'Anyway, if she does join, I hope it's the right thing for her.'

'She'll have a whole community to look after and worry about,' Mark said glibly. 'She'll be in her element.'

Clattie looked at him earnestly. 'But she needs looking after too. She always has and I'm not just saying that because she's the youngest. All that worrying about people and organising them, it's disguising her own need to be looked after.'

Mark, who had never bothered to delve into his sister's psyche, spoke dismissively. 'She'll be fine.'

'The thing is,' Clattie talked on as though Mark hadn't spoken, 'when you lose both your parents, that's the time you have to accept you really are an adult, and when you lose a husband or a wife, you realise that death is also going to happen to you, sooner rather than later, probably. It makes you think – of what has happened and also what *hasn't* happened in your life. And you want the people you love, and who you're going to

91

leave behind, to be settled and on track. Of course Titus coming into your lives has disturbed and upset you all. It couldn't not, could it?' Clattie gave a huge sigh. 'But I can't see any way of me making it better for you. I know you're all adult and you've got to sort it out for yourselves. I feel completely helpless. I'm worried about Ralph, he's so angry, and I don't think Pippa has given herself enough time to mourn your father. They were very close and yet she seems to have shut everything away.' Clattie tucked her arm into Mark's. 'I was pleased though when Bella rang for Titus's number. It seemed normal.'

'They came to supper with us—'

'Did that go all right?'

'Yes. Well, I must be honest.' Mark spoke diffidently. 'There was a bit of an ulterior motive there. You see, I'm interested in these premises he's got.'

'Oh yes, from his aunt. I knew about them.'

Mark found himself momentarily disconcerted by the knowledge his mother had of Titus. In London, alone with Bella, Mark could think of Titus only in business terms, but here, in the middle of his family, the situation became disturbed and displaced and it was not quite so easy to divorce business from brother.

'There is a small possibility that I might be able to persuade him to let me open a restaurant there.' He waited for Clattie's reaction.

'A restaurant,' she said thoughtfully. 'That sounds exciting. Won't that entail a big investment?'

'It will. I'd need to borrow a substantial amount . . .'

Clattie stopped on a small bridge over a fast-running brook, traditionally the place where, as children, they had played Poohsticks. Almost automatically, she picked up two twigs and threw them over the bridge. As one they moved across the bridge and leant over the stone wall, gazing down at the dark water below them. Clattie contemplated the little sticks making their jagged way through the stones in the brook.

'I wish I could help you,' Clattie said eventually.

Mark made a small gesture of denial. 'I wasn't thinking of—'

'The thing is, I don't know what I'm going to do,' continued Clattie. 'I don't know whether I shall stay at The Mill . . . I haven't made any definite decisions, of course. It's all so new and recent. It's a big house just for me, but it's so familiar. Sometimes, you know, I think I can hear your voices when you were children. It's as though there's a bit of you all still here, locked in. And I love the garden, but it's so much work . . . I just don't know.' She looked up at him with a worried expression. 'Everything is in a state of flux at the moment, it's all so uncertain and I'm determined not to be a burden on you children.'

Mark squeezed her arm.

'You know you would never be a burden to us,' he said abstractedly. 'Actually,' his voice became more brisk, 'I haven't spoken to Titus yet, but I am thinking of suggesting that he and I do the restaurant as partners.' He looked at his mother to see her reaction.

Clattie beamed at him. 'Good heavens. Darling, what a simply splendid idea. I said they were a nice family, didn't I?'

Mark was silent; he was far away in his head composing a letter to Titus.

Occasionally Clattie would have a mental aberration and, in her sons' opinion, asking Gerry for drinks before dinner on Saturday evening was one of them. He arrived promptly at six, bearing a large bunch of flowers from his garden and greeted them all affably as though they were old friends. Ralph, just down from his bath, poured out the drinks in ill humour.

'Why him?' he groaned at Mark quietly. 'And tonight. It's bad enough having to cope with Merrylegs. Speaking of whom . . .'

'Do you have anything soft?' Meredith wandered up to them.

'I'm sure we do somewhere,' Ralph answered doubtfully, as though Meredith had asked for something rare and exotic. 'Grania's in the kitchen, she'll sort you out.'

On the other side of the room, Clattie burst out in laughter. Gerry was telling a funny story to the women grouped around him.

'At least he makes Clattie laugh,' Mark said. 'And he's been digging the garden for her.'

'Making himself indispensable, no doubt,' said Ralph with a sniff.

'Where's Meredith?' Pippa came up to them.

'Getting himself a drink in the kitchen.'

'He's a very encouraging man,' she said cryptically. 'They all are at the community. I'm learning a lot. They're teaching me obedience.'

'I see. Well, I wish them every success then,' Ralph said caustically.

Pippa threw him a hurt look. 'I mean obedience to God,' she explained. 'Do you think I should feed the dog? I don't think Clattie's done it.'

'Why not?' Mark said.

'Actually it makes me very wheezy.' Pippa waved her puffer. 'I've had to use this twice already today. Should we invite Gerry to stay for supper, do you think?' Pippa looked at her brothers for guidance.

'No.' Ralph was definite.

'Right. Okay. There probably wouldn't have been enough meat to go round, anyway.' Pippa bumped into the drinks table as she went.

'Do you think the community could teach her to be less clumsy as well?' Ralph enquired.

He handed Mark a drink and cleared his throat.

'Look, Mark,' he began slowly, 'I wanted to say . . . well, I wanted to clear the air after the other day . . . our conversation at lunch. I know you think I'm unreasonable but—'

'I called you irrational, actually,' Mark interrupted smoothly, his lips tightly pursed. 'In either case we don't need to discuss it again.' He moved swiftly to the centre of the room, away from his brother before the conversation could take root.

Gerry headed over towards the drinks table and Ralph was captive.

'So what do you think of Razor then?' he asked, bending down to pat the dog. 'I thought he'd be good company for Clattie.'

'It was very thoughtful of you,' said Ralph politely.

'I'm very fond of your mother. I can't bear her being sad. In fact . . .' he added confidentially, 'I wanted to ask you what you think of my whisking her off for a little holiday later in the year – got a friend with a house in Tuscany. I think Clattie could do with a good break.'

Ralph was put out by Gerry.

'I can't stand this proprietorial stance he takes with Clattie,' he grumbled quietly to Grania, as Gerry was taking his leave. 'She's got us to look after her, she doesn't need him around all the time.'

'He's a nice man.' Grania began clearing the drinks tray. 'And he lives near by. She needs friends as well as family.'

'As long as he hasn't got an eye on taking the Gaffer's place,' muttered Ralph darkly.

Pippa appeared beside them and took the tray out of Grania's hands. 'Let me do this. You've done most of the supper. I've added some more wine to your gravy. Isn't Gerry kind?' she added. 'Razor's a brilliant idea even though I'm allergic to him.'

Ralph was still twitchy during dinner.

'You think television is the invention of the devil I expect, do you?' he suddenly demanded of Meredith, who gave a small smile and answered calmly, 'Devil's a bit of a strong word, but I think it's a very bad influence on the world, yes.' His spectacles glinted in the candlelight.

'It certainly is,' Mark said. 'It's full of crap, never anything decent on.'

'It is an instrument of mammon rather than of the Lord.' Meredith, ignoring Mark, spoke to Ralph. 'Encouraging thoughtless consumerism. It's just one of the temptations of the outside world.'

'Does your Lord require you never to enjoy yourselves?' Ralph asked.

'We do enjoy ourselves,' Pippa answered quickly. 'We have great fun doing the chores together. We talk, we pray and we sing together every evening, sometimes we dance for the Lord.'

'Heavens, that does sound fun.' Ralph avoided Clattie's eye, as she shook her head warningly from the other end of the table.

'The idea of convents and monasteries as a powerhouse of prayer has always appealed to me.' Grania, the peacemaker, entered the discussion.

'If anyone needs a good PR company it's the Church of England,' Bella drawled. 'If they employed me, I bet I could get people flooding in.'

Pippa looked at Meredith and some sign appeared to pass between them.

'Actually,' Pippa said, 'now might be the moment to tell you that I've decided to stay at the community. In fact, I'm going to be baptised in a few weeks' time.'

There was a momentary silence as Pippa's family digested the information.

'Darling, I am pleased.' Clattie wanted to ask Pippa if she was absolutely sure, but she felt it would be impolite in front of Meredith.

Pippa turned to her mother with a satisfied smile.

'I'm glad you're pleased because so am I. If you're sure you can manage without me?' An anxious expression crossed her face. 'I can drive over at any time, if you need me. It's not far.' The words began tumbling happily from Pippa. 'And you can visit me, come to some services, see how we worship. I feel this is the right thing for me. Actually,' she looked round bashfully, 'I'd really like it if you all came to my baptism.'

Another silence and then a murmur of acceptance passed round the table. 'I want you all to experience the joyfulness of the sisters and brothers,' Pippa went on with a beatific smile. 'We're always praying that our families and friends can hear the Word and find the truth, aren't we?' She turned to Meredith who gave her an encouraging smile. 'We want you to be just as *joyful* in your lives,' Pippa reiterated, holding out her arms in an expansive gesture.

'I already have quite enough joyfulness in my life without your help, thank you very much,' Ralph said dourly.

'Pudding.' Clattie rose swiftly to her feet. 'Grania has made us a pudding. I can't wait to try it.'

Mark had an idea. He offered to help Pippa cook the Sunday lunch. His sister was one of the few people who never deferred to him as a chef. When she was in charge of The Mill kitchen, she was king, so although Mark was longing to rescue the roast beef from being murdered he had to accept the more humble job of peeling potatoes.

'Have you thought about inviting Titus and Jane to the community thing?' he asked casually.

'Who?' Pippa wheeled round, her face set in a blank expression.

'Titus and Jane. I wondered whether you might be going to invite them to your christening.'

'Baptism. It's called a baptism. And why should I?'

'It might be a good way of bringing us together.'

Pippa still looked blank and Mark, recognising his sister's stonewalling, tried a different tack. 'Actually, you'd be doing me a favour. You see, I've got a business proposition to make to him and I want to play it informally to begin with. It would be helpful to meet him at something like this.'

'What about Clattie and Ralph? What would they think?' Pippa fiddled nervously with the pile of cutlery in front of her.

'Ralph needn't talk to them if he doesn't want to, and Clattie would like us to be friends, you know she would.'

'That's what they are, isn't it really? Just family friends. Not even very good ones.'

Mark recognised Pippa's need to cement her notion. She had chosen the position she felt comfortable with and now she needed Mark's collusion.

'Absolutely,' he agreed. 'Just acquaintances who could be very useful to me. It would be helpful if you'd send them an invitation. I'd be so grateful,' he wheedled.

Clattie stood on the steps outside the house and watched her family leave. She waved until the lights of the last car disappeared round the corner of the lane and her shoulders drooped as she sank her hands into the comforting pockets of her cardigan. It had been lovely to have them for the weekend, but it had left her dreadfully weary. Clattie's pleasure that Pippa had found happiness was tempered by guilt at her relief that Pippa was not coming home to live. Since Jack had died, she had been so tired that all her energy had been taken up with getting through each day, and the possibility of Pippa coming home was a prospect, she now realised, she had been dreading. On her own, Clattie felt, she could begin to regroup and grow again.

'You are sure this is what you want?' she had asked Pippa quietly after dinner.

'Absolutely,' Pippa had said stoutly. 'Do you remember when I was little I wanted to be a nun? I used to dress up in your old black cloak with a white tea towel on my head. The Gaffer used to tease me, said I looked like a moorhen. I used to learn great chunks of the Bible, remember? I've thought a lot about that while I've been away and maybe I've always had a sort of calling. I love the community life and the people. I'm going to help run the community's craft shop and do some secretarial work in the office. The filing system badly needs reorganising.' She had looked at Clattie. 'Honestly, I shall be very happy. You mustn't worry about me. Will you be all right? I want you to promise me to ring if you need me for anything. I'll come immediately.'

Clattie was about to turn back into the quiet house when Razor's claws clicked on the York stone of the path and he gave a throaty bark of welcome. Gerry emerged from the little side gate of the sunken garden and Clattie smiled at the man who so recently and so quickly had become such a good companion – a kind of gift for the end bit of her life. He and Jack would sit hunched over the old baize card table while Clattie read her book on the sofa; the whole house would be uncomplicated and peaceful as though Gerry had a sedating effect on them all. He was gentle, kindly, thoughtful and he cared for her – just because she was who she was.

'Saw the cars leave,' he said, joining her on the steps. He put his arm round her shoulders. 'How about sympathy, support and scrambled eggs at my kitchen table?' He looked carefully at her washed-out face. 'And a large dry martini too, by the looks of it.'

Clattie looked up at him with a soft smile and patted his hand resting on her shoulder. 'That would be just lovely,' she said gratefully.

Titus read the letter twice before he took in its contents.

'You might have trouble with this one, Janey,' he said with a broad grin. 'Pippa has invited us to her baptism.'

Jane looked up from her post. 'What? I'm sorry, her what?'

Titus threw the letter across the table. 'Read it. For some extraordinary reason the woman is getting baptised and even more strangely she's invited us to the ceremony.'

Jane read the short letter written in neat schoolgirl handwriting.

'Bloody hell.' She handed back the letter with a laugh. 'The prospect of witnessing Pippa's baptism almost outweighs the awfulness of being with the rest of them.'

'I think we should go,' Titus said.

Jane looked at him in surprise. 'Why?'

'Well, why not? They're obviously making an effort to include us. At least,' he added, his eyes narrowing slightly, 'we can be sure that Pippa doesn't have designs on our warehouse.'

Jane heard the point that Titus was making but she didn't rise. Since she had agreed to Titus's plans for a restaurant, he had worked hard to clear the backlog in the workshop – he needed to please her, to thank her for letting him do what he wanted. But Jane couldn't shake off her nagging uneasiness about the family situation. Now their roles had reversed, and she was finding it hard to disguise her mistrust and dislike of Titus's half-siblings. Nowadays Australia seemed further away than ever.

'Come to think of it,' she said, making an effort to smile, 'the warehouse would make rather a good church.'

'Clattie's probably suggested she ask us. We should go for her sake.'

And that settled it.

As Jane wrote the acceptance note, she realised that the decision had been made. The 'other' Palmers, as she always thought of them, had become a tangible part of their life. She remembered the fun she and Titus and the children had had thinking up their dreams for the warehouse, even while knowing that they would probably, in the end, sell it. She blamed the *other* Palmers for turning their ideas for Aunt Monica's legacy from the initial charitable ones into something quite different. Something, Jane felt, that was potentially big, brash and greedy.

When she returned from the postbox, she found herself looking up capitalism in the dictionary – 'the condition of possessing capital or the economic system which generates and gives power to capitalists'.

Jane wished that somebody else's Aunt Monica had owned the building in Squarey Street.

The letter from Mark arrived a few days later in the afternoon post, while Jane was still at the playgroup. Titus read it as he walked to his workshop and then sat at his drawing board in deep thought.

Mark was suggesting that Titus might like to consider the idea of a partnership in a restaurant company. He set out the proposal in a fluid way, ending by suggesting a meeting between the two of them at a mutually convenient date.

Titus looked at the work on his drawing board. In his spare time he had been honing his original designs for the restaurant, and on the evenings that Jane was out, he would spend hours poring over the plans, and imagining his creation come to life; and just sometimes he pictured himself, front of house, as host and owner.

Titus kept the letter secret from Jane while he thought about its contents. For three days he turned over the idea in his head. When he gave Jane the letter to read, his heart sank at the apprehension in her eyes.

'You're not serious? A partnership – with *him*?'

'I do think it's worth discussing, yes.'

'Just tell me when exactly you decided to become a restaurateur?' snapped Jane.

'I didn't decide anything. I haven't done anything yet. I'm discussing it with you now.' Jane made no reply. 'I've had time to think while I've been doing this.' He gestured towards the drawing board. 'I'm interested in food, I like the idea of feeding people—'

'Oh please. What a load of crap. We're talking a full-blown restaurant here, not spaghetti carbonara in our kitchen.' Jane took a deep breath and carried on more calmly. 'You talked about being bored, in a rut, and I understand that. I can see this is a challenge that you need and I'm with you one hundred per cent. We agreed you would convert the warehouse and then we'd sell it. But,' she stared fiercely at Titus, 'now you want more. You're like the fisherman's wife in Grimms'. You'll keep wanting more and more and then one day you'll end up with nothing—'

'Be fair, Janey,' Titus interrupted, 'and credit me with some intelligence. I'm not going to rush in without making sure – talking to the accountant, the lawyer—'

'I'm thinking that would now be all of the Gaffer's money going into this? Plus some?'

'No.' Titus spoke firmly. 'If the whole project was to come out as more than the inheritance, I promise I wouldn't go ahead. Look, Janey, you bollocked me a while ago for being greedy about the Gaffer's will, and you were right. We're bloody lucky to have what we've got. This time last year there was no legacy and we were managing to survive. I'm not going to give up Palmer's Restoration. That's the joy of this proposal. I'd have a partner so I can keep on with this place.' He thumped the work-bench beside him. 'I wouldn't want to give this up.'

'But we were going to pay off the mortgage. What about paying for Summer's college . . .' Australia hung silently between them.

'We'll make a good return on our investment—'

'You hope.'

'Yes, it's a risk. Everything in business is a risk. But we'll always have the security of the rent coming in, particularly as I would be a partner in the company paying us rent. I promise you, we will have the money for the things you want to do—'

'But not now, though.'

'No-o. But much more money later. More trips to Australia.'

'You can't let the workshop go under, Titus. We can't afford to live just on my salary while we're waiting to make our fortune.' Jane couldn't keep the sarcasm out of her voice, but Titus believed that Jane's storm was weakening.

'I'm not going to do this without your support. If you don't even want me to explore the idea, that's fine.' He spoke bravely, but truly. 'I don't want us to quarrel over it, I really don't, and I'm not going to do anything without you by my side.'

The two of them looked at each other in silent contempla-tion, waiting for the ground to give between them. They knew each other so well. Titus had been right: Jane's feeling of losing control and becoming isolated from him, her upset and panic were all beginning to diminish a little. Titus was so sure, so eager. How could she not give him what he was asking for? This man she loved so much and who apparently had been having a mid-life crisis without her realising. He had made her so happy. How could she not make him happy now? Jane folded up her plans for Australia and said piteously, 'But why does it have to be Mark?'

'Because he's there. Mark knows what he's doing. I've checked up on his company. It's solvent, well thought of. He's got the catering experience and he's up for it. Let me meet him and find out what exactly he's got in mind. I promise I'm not going to do anything that will jeopardise the family's security. I won't let us become penniless.'

Funnily enough, just at the moment, the money was not what Jane was primarily concerned about.

Chapter Five

*I*t was Grania's turn to host the book-club meeting and this month the four men and four women in the group were discussing her choice: *Adam Bede*.

'Why this book particularly?' someone asked.

'Because it's such a bucolic novel,' Grania answered without hesitation. 'The descriptions of the country, the peacefulness of pastoral life, just makes me want to be there. In fact, I wasn't so interested in the story,' she added honestly. 'I just absorbed the scenery and it did my soul a lot of good. And it made me want to get out of London more than ever,' she finished vehemently.

'You sound as though you're on the move,' one of the women said with amusement.

'I'd like to have gone years ago, but you know schools and things . . .' Grania replied with a sigh. 'We were always going to move when Kit left school. I was going to have my hens and my ducks and Ralph was going to have his sweeping lawn to mow. Only now my father-in-law has died and everything has suddenly become a bit up in the air . . .'

The men in the group moved the discussion back to the

book but Grania had become distracted. The fall-out from the Gaffer's death had changed everything. Before he had died, she and Ralph had begun looking at houses in that vague sort of way that people do who have no specific place in mind. Grania fancied the sea. Ralph wanted to be near enough to London to work part-time in his office. They had discussed converted barns, walled gardens, thatched roofs, but these slow-forming contented country-house conversations had been terminated abruptly by Ralph.

'Our plans are going to have to go on hold for a bit,' he had decreed. 'We've got to concentrate on Clattie now; see how she gets on living alone at The Mill, before we can even consider moving. She's not thinking clearly just now, that's obvious.'

'It'll take her time to adjust to the Gaffer's death.' Grania had tried to placate him, but Ralph had scoffed back at her.

'That doesn't seem to be a problem at the moment. You know she's not coming at half term?'

He had looked at Grania as though it was in some way her fault that Clattie had refused the invitation to stay in France.

Ralph was feeling marginalised by Clattie and Mark's toleration of Titus's family and Grania could almost feel his panic. He was retreating into himself, snarling at everyone like a terrier protecting its kennel from marauders. And that was obviously how he saw Titus – as a marauder. Titus had taken away his role as eldest son.

'I've always been the eldest Palmer boy. Now the Gaffer is gone, *I* am head of the family.'

Grania was worried for Ralph; she could see him becoming increasingly paranoid about Titus and his family. She hated seeing him so unhappy, but she also felt guilty that her concern for him was tempered by vexation. The Gaffer's past had arrived in their own present and now their life must, apparently, go on hold. She knew her feelings to be unworthy, but she couldn't get rid of them. Grania sighed heavily and forced her thoughts back to *Adam Bede* and wished she was sitting peacefully on a village green in a bonnet.

'Is Kit taking his As this year?' One or two of the women stayed behind to help Grania clear the coffee cups.

'No, next year,' Grania replied. 'It's a real rite of passage, isn't it? When your last child leaves school. It opens up all kinds of new vistas. I'm looking forward to new starts, new life. Time for me and Ralph.' She could hear herself sounding more positive than she felt. She didn't admit that her confidence in this new life had begun to drain away under the strain of the disclosure of the Palmer family secret.

Kit was spending every free moment with Summer and when he wasn't with her he was discussing her with Ed.

'Go for it, mate,' was Ed's advice. 'She's up for it, I can tell you.'

'She's a good friend, that's all,' Kit insisted, 'and my dad would kill me if he knew we were hanging out together.'

'I reckon she's worth the risk. You should take the initiative. Get her pissed and go for it.'

Kit had become adept at sliding unobtrusively out of school and meeting Summer in McDonald's or the pub. He went to her college and sat around in the canteen, relishing the free, easy adult atmosphere and wishing that he had fought more strongly to leave school after his GCSEs, the previous summer. The two of them spent much of their time watching videos in the grubby house in East Dulwich rented by Summer's friends. With its perpetually moving population of students, casually dropping in and out, the easy ambience there was a relief from the highly charged atmosphere that now prevailed at home.

'Don't you want to live here all the time?' he asked Summer curiously.

'I'm happy at home. I get on all right with my family, it's cheaper and I've always got a choice, haven't I? Veg out there or veg out here.'

Kit thought he would do anything to live away from his family at the moment and he was envious of Summer's ability to be so unencumbered.

He was also becoming increasingly aware of wanting to touch her breasts.

Sitting opposite Summer, one afternoon, he was looking at them constricted in a tight T-shirt when she asked him back to her house.

'Do your parents know . . .' Kit chose his words carefully, 'that we're friends?'

'No, but they'd be cool about it.'

'My dad wouldn't be. No way.'

Summer shrugged. 'We've been invited to your aunt's . . . christening or something. Weird!' Summer thought for a moment. 'I suppose she's a bit my aunt too, come to think of it.'

'Are you going?'

'Yup. Titus thinks we should. Jane's trying to get a cold off one of her playgroup kids, so she doesn't have to come. Alby's doing his finals so he won't be there and, anyway, he's freaked out by the family thing. He's really pissed off at Titus lying to us about Gaff. But I'm definitely coming.'

'Dad's got a three-line whip on us. Supporting the family must come before anything else.' Kit made a face and then added nervously, 'We shouldn't look too friendly though. We don't want anyone finding out about us.' He experienced a moment of panic: 'us' sounded a bit heavy, he hadn't meant to say us, meaning they were *together*, and now he didn't know how to unsay it without making too much of an issue of it. Summer rescued him from his discomfiture. 'We should be allowed to be friends. God, we're related, we're cousins.'

Kit then found himself, contrarily, cast down at Summer's assumption that they were nothing more than friendly cousins.

'Yeah right,' he said quickly, 'but Dad . . . he's just obsessed.'

Summer leant back against the sofa and casually stretched her arms behind her head. Where Ed would have drawn his own conclusions at the body language, Kit only slavered meekly.

'Did you know that Mark's been to see my dad? Got him into the idea of a restaurant. Titus is really boring – he spends all his time drawing. Jane really hated the idea of a restaurant at first but she's cool now and when it's finished they're going to sell it and we're all going to Australia to see Grandma. Yes.' Summer punched the air with her fist and Kit watched her breasts make a satisfactory movement under her T-shirt.

'So,' she looked across at him, 'I'll see you at Pippa's thing then.' She cast her dancing eyes downwards in mock subservience. 'I will of course be behaving in an appropriately fitting manner – as one of the Palmer family.'

Kit already knew Summer well enough to be concerned that her behaviour might not conform to his family's idea of appropriate.

Pippa's community turned out to be accommodated in a large imposing Queen Anne country house surrounded by mature gardens and set in rolling parkland. The interior of the old building, in order to institutionalise it, had been vandalised with woodchip wallpaper, linoleum and dead-coloured beige paint. Cheap utilitarian tables and chairs replaced the heavy polished furniture that a house of such beauty would normally merit and the overhead lighting was harsh and unforgiving. Children's drawings, paintings and tapestries, all with biblical texts written on them in wobbly writing, hung on the wall and there was an all-pervading, evil smell of cooked cabbage.

'Bit like school, isn't it?' Pippa said with a wheezy giggle when she met the family in the hall. 'But the people make up for the decor, I promise you,' she added, her eyes alight with happiness. She led them through a vegetable garden, past a hen run and a field full of llamas and goats, into a large barn that had been converted into a church with heavy wooden crosses on the walls. To one side was a tank of water set into the floor. Pippa seated her family and then picked up the edge of her long skirt and showed it to Clattie.

'Look, I've sewn little pieces of lead into the hem so that my skirt won't billow up.'

Clattie looked alarmed. 'You're getting into the water?'

'Just for a moment, total immersion, of course, total cleansing.'

'I hope you don't get cold, darling,' Clattie said.

'I'll be fine. Now, are you all comfortable?' She surveyed her family with an approving nod. 'Have you got everything you need?' She glanced at her watch and then at Mark. 'He said they were coming, but they're not here yet. They'll have to sit in the back now.'

They all knew who Pippa meant by he. Ralph took a loud breath as if in pain. 'Anyway,' Pippa went on, ignoring the hostility coming from her elder brother, 'I must go and get ready. Are you *sure* you're all comfortable? See you after the service. Bless you. Oh, have you all got the song books?' Pippa dragged herself away from ministering to her family and they watched her disappear through the curtains at the end of the barn.

'Do we know how long this is going to last?' Bella whispered to Grania, who shrugged and shook her head.

'You know Clattie didn't come to France with us?' Ralph spoke out of the corner of his mouth to Mark. 'Apparently she'd rather go off with this Gerry to Italy in September. I really don't think it's a very suitable thing to do.'

Mark looked across at Clattie, sitting quietly in her chair, reading the service sheet. She looked very composed and very controlled.

'She'll be fine. I think Gerry seems a genuine friend.'

'The jury's still out on that one,' Ralph snapped in a whisper.

'What do you keep turning round for, Kit?' Caitlin asked curiously.

After the long service the exhausted congregation were ushered towards the house.

'Dreadful music. I've always thought the devil has all the best tunes,' Ralph said balefully. 'I don't know how God got left with such dirges.'

Bella laughed and Clattie frowned at them both.

Trestle tables laden with plates of cakes and sandwiches were set out in a long room of imposing proportions. A large urn bubbled in one corner, on a table covered in thick white cups and saucers.

As he came into the room, Ralph was approached by Meredith, and Mark watched from a distance as Meredith talked earnestly right into his brother's face. Mark was reminded of the horse they'd had when they were little; when she was rattled by something she would show her teeth and toss her head. Now Ralph had that same fragile, nervy look as Meredith's conversation obviously became more animated and intense.

There was a sudden hiatus at the back of the room and the six newly baptised men and women filed in to enthusiastic clapping from the rest of the community who then all fell voraciously upon the food, piling their plates high. Watching them scrabble round the table and move away holding their booty protectively to their chests, Mark wondered abstractedly whether they normally got enough to eat. Then he caught sight of Titus moving towards a door to the garden and, pausing only to pick up a cup of tea, he followed him out.

Jane was debating risking a sausage roll. They looked thick and greasy, but she was bored and boredom always made her hungry.

'They don't look as though they've been made with a very light touch, do they?' Grania stood beside her.

'No,' agreed Jane. 'Apparently they're completely organic here, so one of the inmates was telling me. You'd think there'd be piles of healthy food, wouldn't you? I don't think I can face another paste sandwich. I haven't eaten paste since my mum put it in my lunch pail when I was a kid.'

Grania gazed out of the window in front of them. 'I keep looking at the kids and wondering what sort of life they have here.'

The two women watched a group of children playing with a ball on the grass.

'They seem perfectly happy,' Jane said. 'It's what they're used to, I suppose, but it's hard not to judge them by our standards.' Worried that she sounded sanctimonious, she added hurriedly, 'I mean, it's a bit odd really. I'm the first person to disapprove of endless television and violent video games and yet, here I am, feeling sorry for this lot because they're not allowed the twentieth-century entertainment that I so despise.'

'I know exactly what you mean.' Grania smiled. Jane smiled back at her.

They rather liked each other.

'This is pretty frightful, isn't it?' Bella loomed up to them. 'They will all try and evangelise at you. Quite frankly, I'd be happy to get down on my knees and pray if there was a chance of getting a strong gin and tonic.' She grinned at them conspiratorially.

Grania looked at her watch. 'I should think we can leave soon, can't we? Who's taking Clattie home? Where is she anyway?'

'She's talking to Big Daddy, the man who took the service. And I think we're taking her home, but I've lost Mark. He's completely disappeared.' Bella settled her jacket lapels, her varnished nails matching her elegant Schiaparelli-pink suit. She stood out like a beautiful butterfly among the sombre, dun-coloured clothes of the community.

'I'm going to find Ralph.' Grania put down her cup. 'I think Caitlin wants to get the train back to Leeds this evening and I promised her we'd go to IKEA on the way home.'

Bella and Jane watched her thread her way through the room.

'Honestly, Grania just lets her children run her life for her,' Bella said contemptuously. 'She lives for them. By the way,' she turned to Jane, 'Mark was hoping to see your husband here today. He's keen to discuss this restaurant idea. Titus could learn a lot from Mark. He started Basil Catering with next to nothing, you know.'

'Really,' Jane murmured.

'Yes, and it's doing really well,' Bella cooed. 'The chef is very good, but Mark likes to do a bit of cheffing himself every now and then – keep his hand in. He's a wonderful cook, loves doing it.' There was genuine admiration in Bella's voice. 'He understands everything about food – the whole caboodle. And you need experience in the catering trade to run a restaurant. Usually the ones that go bust in the first year are owned by people who think it's easy to open a restaurant. It's a cut-throat business, I can tell you.'

'I'm sure. Running any business is not easy,' Jane answered politely.

'Running a playgroup is quite a different kettle of fish. It could hardly be seen as the cutting edge of commerce, could it?' Bella laughed light-heartedly. 'Frankly, I think you're an absolute saint to be able to cope with a load of dribbling kids all day.'

Jane and Bella looked at one another. They really didn't like each other at all.

Mark found Titus sitting on a bench in the garden, his head bent over a small heap of tobacco he was rolling untidily in liquorice paper. He looked up when Mark approached.

'Hi.' He grinned. 'I'm hiding from Jane.' He gestured with the hand holding the roll-up. 'She doesn't like me doing this. I've given up really; just occasionally I still fancy one. Do you?'

For a moment Mark wondered what he was being offered. He shook his head. 'No, I never have. Asthma in the family.'

There was a pause between the two men. Family was a difficult word between them.

Mark sat down beside Titus. 'D'you mind if I join you? I wanted to talk to you. You got my letter?'

Titus fumbled with the cigarette and tobacco fell out. 'Shit, I'm out of practice.' He started rolling again, head down, concentrating on the task.

'Yes, I did,' he said. 'I was going to ring you.'

Mark waited patiently for Titus to light his cigarette. 'Interested?' he asked casually.

'Maybe.'

Mark was aware that he had clenched his hands. He spread them out on his knees.

112

'I'd certainly like to talk the idea through with you,' Titus said, breathing smoke out slowly.

'Any time you like.'

The two men danced round each other, like swaying snakes, both waiting to strike, yet not wanting to appear too eager too soon.

'I'm attracted by the idea.' Titus's cigarette had gone out. He relit it awkwardly.

'Right, so perhaps we should meet up next week, have a bit of a chat?' suggested Mark.

Neither of them were prepared to admit at this stage that they were depending on the other. Each had something the other wanted – Titus the premises, Mark the experience – and both needed the other's money. Mark was uncomfortably aware that there were plenty of people around wanting to run restaurants, it was the suitable premises that were difficult to find. He had initiated the game plan with his letter, but he was determined not to appear desperate. Titus was trying to stay cool and curb his natural enthusiasm.

He gave up on his recalcitrant cigarette and threw it on the ground. 'Yeah, that would be good.'

Mark took out his diary. 'Shall we make a date now then?'

Kit was enjoying his afternoon hugely, and it had absolutely nothing to do with his aunt Pippa's baptism.

While he was in France he had thought about Summer constantly and now here she was as brilliant as ever in a surprisingly demure skirt and shirt that only seemed to make her look even more sexy.

As soon as they had arrived at the house after the service, she had sidled up to him and whispered, 'C'mon. Get a plate of food and meet me where the cars are parked. Bring an empty cup with you.'

Now they were sitting in the back seat of her father's car, which smelt of wood glue and sawdust, drinking vodka out of thick white teacups.

Summer was rolling a spliff beside him.

'Put a tape on,' she ordered. 'There's Ben Harper somewhere.'

Kit had never heard of Ben Harper, but certainly wasn't going to admit to it. He pushed through to the front of the car and fossicked through a pile of tapes, all without cases and in a dusty condition that would have sent his father into a complete wobbly.

He found the tape and put it in – gentle black music filled the car and he sat back beside Summer. She handed him the spliff.

'There you go. It's good stuff – take it easy.'

Kit looked out of the window and hoped that the car was parked far enough away from the house and his father's car.

Half an hour later, he couldn't really have cared less. The vodka and dope had combined to put him in a curious mellow condition of passive recklessness. The landscape outside the car had taken on a wavery effect and inside the car Summer smelt hot and sweet – he thought that perhaps this was the nearest he would ever get to paradise.

'I wonder what it would have been like if we had known each other when we were kids?' he mused.

'Let's not talk about family. I'm sick of it,' Summer said crossly.

Afterwards, Kit wasn't sure who had first kissed whom – which of them had first moved closer to touch the other. Summer's mouth seemed large and inviting, and her breasts looked ready for him to explore. Everything about her felt just as Kit had imagined it would. He wasn't sure he was in a fit state to do anything more, and this time he was not required to because there was a loud knocking on the window and his elder sister was glaring into the car, making wind-the-window-down gestures.

'We're going home. Dad's looking for you. He'd better not find you here.'

Summer unwrapped herself from Kit and started doing up her shirt buttons.

'Hello, Caitlin,' she said cheerily.

Caitlin nodded cursorily at her and then turned back to Kit. 'Mum and Dad are saying goodbye to Pippa. Come on. I want to catch a train. We've got to go.'

'I'll see you then.' Summer grinned at Kit as he clambered out of the car.

The fresh air hit him in the chest and his knees buckled. He had to blink to make the trees around him stand still.

'Bloody hell, Kit.' Caitlin took him by the arm. 'You've got to be a bit more together when you see Dad. You stink of dope. Come on, let's take the long way back.' She marched him through the line of cars and then round the parkland surrounding the garden.

'Dad'll go mental if he catches you snogging her. Anyway, she's related to you.'

'I like her,' Kit mumbled. 'We're mates.'

'Pretty matey mates then. You'd better pretend you're ill. Food poisoning or something. And, for God's sake, don't be sick on the way home.'

Kit was beginning to feel better, his head was readjusting itself, becoming less fluffy. He looked at Caitlin. 'Don't say anything, please.'

She made a silly face at him. 'C'mon, what do you think I am? Of course I won't. You've got to be careful you don't get caught though, Kit. Dad's spooked enough already.'

But Kit wasn't listening to his sister, he was thinking about seeing Ed on Monday and telling him that he was right. Summer was hot. He giggled to himself foolishly – a hot Summer, in fact.

Clattie sat in the back of the car as Mark drove skilfully fast through the Home Counties. She was turning over the day in her mind. She hoped Pippa was doing the right thing. 'Pippa will be in her element here,' Ralph had said as they were leaving. 'She'll be head girl in a couple of weeks, I should think.'

Pippa had looked happy enough as she kissed her mother goodbye. 'I'll probably be over next week, so save up any heavy

115

jobs for me, won't you? Just don't tire yourself out. I can come back whenever you want.' But Clattie was not so sure Pippa could.

'We don't really encourage the sisters and brothers to rush home all the time,' Meredith had told Clattie in a friendly voice with just a hint of steel in it. 'Pippa's commitment is to the Lord and to the community now. And, of course,' he added, 'her car will be put into the house pool so it won't be readily available for her.' Clattie rested her head against the back of the seat and wondered a little anxiously how Pippa would respond to the novelty of such unexpected discipline.

In the front of the car Mark was answering his wife in monosyllables. His mind was on his forthcoming meeting with Titus. He was cautiously optimistic. No, in fact he'd go further than that – he was pretty sure they were in business. He must move quickly to raise the finance and get the deal signed. So now, as he pounded down the motorway, he was trying to work out the partnership agreement that he hoped he and Titus would shortly be forging.

Titus was also silent on the way home. He was wondering if Jack's death and the subsequent meeting of Mark was some divine grand plan and that this restaurant had always been his destiny. No, he was getting carried away – too much spirituality for one day. He glanced at Jane, sitting beside him, her head resting on her hand against the window, eyes closed. Dear, generous Jane who, despite her misgivings about his new family, was prepared to support him in his newly found dream. He must make her believe in its success and make her understand that this was purely a business arrangement with Mark and would have no effect on all the family stuff. Titus wriggled in the driving seat to ease the pressure on his back and indulged his imagination by planning the colour scheme of his new restaurant.

*

In Ralph's car, Mozart was booming out of the CD player and Kit was trying hard not to be sick.

Pippa rubbed cream on to the little patches of eczema that were beginning to appear on the inside of her elbows. She had had such a happy day, but she was feeling a bit anxious about Ralph. She hadn't meant to upset him by inviting Titus. She'd only wanted to please Mark because it seemed so important to him. She'd spoken to them briefly at the end of the day when she'd introduced them to Meredith as friends of the family. But she should have considered Ralph's feelings. He hadn't gone on about it, just said as he was leaving, 'I really don't think we should make a habit of including them in private family occasions in future, Pippa.' And she had apologised without exacerbating the situation by mentioning Mark's part in their invitation.

Her new room mate, Sister Joyce, came in from the bathroom. Now a permanent member of the community, Pippa had been moved from the visitors' wing into this bedroom and she was rather looking forward to sharing a room again – the companionable feeling of knowing someone was in the dark with you; listening to their breathing; able to call out and hear their voice.

'We must keep this room tidy,' Sister Joyce said nicely, but with a disapproving glance at Pippa's clothes that were strewn around her bed. 'It's an important discipline. An ordered room for an ordered mind.'

'Oh gosh, yes, I'm sorry.' Pippa picked up the clothes. 'I'm awfully untidy. I always have been.' She cast her eyes down obediently. 'But I shall make it one of my journeys.' She got into bed and then clambered out again when she saw Joyce kneeling by her bed to pray.

Clattie was relieved that Mark and Bella declined to stay when they delivered her home. Mark turned on the lights for her and Bella went to the lavatory and then she was alone and it was blissfully quiet. It was past ten o'clock and Clattie felt tired and cramped – all she wanted was to go to bed with some hot milk and cereal. The telephone rang.

'Saw the car come in.' Gerry's comfortable voice floated down the phone. 'Wondered whether you'd like me to bring Razor round. He's been missing you.'

A nice, warm, meaty-smelling dog curled up in the crook of her knee was just what Clattie wanted.

'Oh, would you? Thank you.'

'I'll be round in a tick.'

Razor threw himself at his mistress as though they had been parted for weeks.

'How did it go?' asked Gerry.

'Fine, rather a sweet service I thought. Long though. Pippa looked very happy.'

'And the opposing families?'

Clattie sighed. 'I saw Grania and Bella talking to Jane. I don't know about Mark. Pip just treats them like distant friends and Ralph, of course, wouldn't go near them.'

'You know what we men are like. We take an awful long time to get over things.' Gerry consoled her with a smile. 'Give him time. You said he and his father were close; he obviously feels very hurt and betrayed by him.'

'Hurt, yes. And betrayed, but not by his father. He behaves as though it's the rest of us who've betrayed him. He's just going into himself. I want to pinch him hard,' she said spiritedly. 'I did that once when he was a little boy and his favourite kitten died. He just wouldn't cry and he got paler and paler. I couldn't bear it all in there, so I pinched him really hard and made him cry.'

'Something'll unblock him eventually, I'm sure.'

'But he looks so strained,' cried Clattie.

Gerry took her arm. 'You go to bed, you look exhausted. And tomorrow we're going to plan our holiday. No argument.'

Mark told Bella about his conversation with Titus as they drove home from The Mill.

'He's interested. I'm pretty sure it's a goer. So now I've got to move fast to put the money in place. Hey.' He glanced at her and joggled her arm. 'Are you listening? It's good news.'

Bella heard what Mark said but she wasn't listening. She was thinking – as she had been a good deal in the last few months. She couldn't say when the first tentacles of insecurity had begun to grip her deep inside, when she suddenly began to feel as though she were deteriorating, slowly and relentlessly. It could have been in the gym when she looked into the mirror and saw the almost imperceptible sagging around her breasts and knees; it could have been one evening after a heavy day when she took off her make-up and saw the beginnings of stringy dewlaps round her neck; and it could have been the gradual realisation that she was stuck in some sort of groove from which she saw no way out. Her business was a success but she felt like a dinosaur in her own company. She was employing girls who were herself twenty-five years ago, except by the time they were thirty they'd left to have babies. Recently Bella, strangely, had found herself wondering if she should have had babies after all. Perhaps they would have made her life a little less one-dimensional.

And then there was Mark. Bella was quite sure he'd started an affair again. It'd been some time since the last one, but she recognised the signs. He had taken to being either very specific about what he'd been doing or alternatively very vague. Bella knew exactly what the girl would be like: blonde, twenty, decorative, dim, and she would probably last a couple of months, maybe six if she could manage an occasional sentence with a verb in it. In the past Bella had always been confident that Mark would get bored and that she would be able to haul him back to her and she didn't doubt it now. Did she? No, not really. It was a bad time in her life for Mark to be doing this, and she'd been formulating an idea that would, she was sure, hook him back quickly and firmly. He would owe her, be tied to her in the one way that he understood – financially. And he would be grateful. She was going to offer to take the pressure off him and service his loans. She knew it would be a good investment, both financially and emotionally.

Bella had already worked out the agreement in her head and now was the time to make the offer.

'That's an excellent idea,' he said, when she'd finished. 'Yes, if you could just see me through the initial start-up period. Thank you,' he added, almost as an afterthought. 'I would really appreciate that.' They had stopped at traffic lights and he put his hand on her knee and squeezed it. 'The bank manager will too, no doubt,' he said with a laugh. 'It's good—'

'One other thing, Mark,' Bella interrupted him, nettled by his calm acceptance of her offer. 'No interest on the repayment, but I want fifteen per cent of your profits when the restaurant starts making money.'

'That's going to be difficult. I've got a partner—'

'No, Mark. Your profits. What *you* take out of the business. I want fifteen per cent of profits for at least five years or, if you sell before then, fifteen per cent of sale price.'

Mark stared at her. He looked arrogant and confident.

'Five per cent,' he said.

'Ten. Take it or leave it and you're on your own.'

There was a pause. The traffic lights turned to green. Mark snorted with laughter. 'Go on then. I'd expect nothing less than a hard bargain from you.'

Bella thought she could hear admiration in his voice.

Mark and Titus met in Mark's office. Basil Catering was in a small, thriving commercial estate off the Fulham Road and Titus stood for a moment outside the building watching, through the window, a chef working in the kitchen. He noted a van parked outside with the name of the company, Basil Catering, Party Designers, written in smart green on the side. Titus wondered why you needed to design a party. Didn't you just *have* parties?

He rang on the bell and was greeted as an expected and honoured guest by a young blonde girl with a cut-glass accent, wearing a business-like overall. Her fingernails were long enough to strip wallpaper.

'Oh h-i. Come in,' she twanged.

'Come through, Titus.' Mark appeared in a doorway. 'Thanks, Caroline. Chef wants you back at the carrots.' Caroline sighed theatrically and disappeared through a door. Mark raised his eyebrows. 'Sexy waitress, but hopeless in the kitchen. Still, she's shagging Chef, so she likes to hang around and make herself useful.'

Titus smiled in vague collusion.

'I'd like to show you my operation before we get down to business,' said Mark, smoothly opening a door.

He took Titus round the kitchen, explaining how orders and deliveries were operated and showing Titus how professional and experienced he was. Titus peered through the kitchen door at steamy pans of food bubbling on the cookers, listening attentively to Mark. They finished the tour in Mark's office with two cups of excellent cappuccino.

'I was rather dreading Saturday, but it wasn't too bad, was it?' Mark began.

Titus's head was in the future, not the past and he looked momentarily blank.

'Oh Pippa, yes.' He was about to say that they were surprised to be asked, but then thought better of it. 'I brought you these to look at.' He unrolled his drawings and Mark moved the things off his desk so that they could be spread out.

'Great. Let's see.'

Mark had confided in Freddie that he thought Titus might favour something along the lines of cosy kitsch, but she had reprimanded him for stereotyping.

'Just because he doesn't do suit and tie, doesn't mean he's a purple-and-silver-star merchant,' she said severely.

And she was right. Titus's vision was all clean, clear lines, understated design of steel, glass and blond wood, using top quality materials. Mark was impressed. He cautiously made a few practical recommendations, careful though not to let Titus run away with his personal dream. He was painfully aware that

Titus had the design *and* the premises and was not tied into Mark at all, at the moment. Titus could rent out his vision to someone else, or even risk doing it alone at any time. Mark's priority was to establish himself as vital to this operation. He picked up a plastic file and handed it to Titus.

'These are some figures I've been working on. Typed up by Caroline, I'm afraid, so the spelling may be a little eccentric. Of course I haven't included the cost of building works.'

'I've got those.' Titus handed Mark a similar file and there was silence as both men read.

Mark looked up first. 'So, what do you think? Worth a discussion?'

'Yeah. It's a big commitment from us both—'

'I've over-estimated some of the start-up costs,' Mark said confidently. 'We'll be able to spread the bills and defer payments along the way. And, of course, there's the terms of the lease?' He smiled pleasantly at Titus. Much would depend on the rent that Titus as the freeholder would demand.

'Of course.' Titus was noncommittal. He gathered up the papers and shuffled them into a neat pile. 'I'll take these, if I may. Talk to my accountant and get back to you.'

Mark had to know. 'But you're interested – in principle?'

Titus relaxed and grinned. 'I certainly am. I'll be in touch as soon as possible.'

Both men stood up and Mark held out his hand.

'I'll firm up these figures then and contact a company agent with a view to forming a company. What do you think? We should get the preliminaries in place. It'll save time, when we hear from planning and, of course, if we decide to commit to this.' His words hung for a moment.

Titus nodded his head slowly. 'Yeah, I suppose we might as well get on with it.'

Mark's sentiments exactly.

The council's planning officer had implied to Titus that the committee would look favourably on the restaurant scheme, particularly since he had submitted a revised and more comprehensive design.

Mark and Titus attended a residents' meeting held in a local scout hut. Jane, slipping nervously into the back of the hall once it had started, recognised quite a few people: there were at least two lots of parents whose children went to the playgroup.

The meeting started calmly with several people asking practical questions and showing interest in the project. Most of the residents seemed to be in favour of the restaurant, including, vitally, the two young couples who lived in the flats above. The meeting appeared to be nearing a conclusion when a young man in a smart suit and a careful accent, stood up and began to speak in a clipped, irate voice. 'We already have a problem with parking. This . . . bar will just make it worse.'

'But most of you have your own driveways,' Mark argued.

'My wife and I live opposite this proposed nightmare.' The man locked eyes with Mark, and gestured to a young, pregnant woman by his side. 'We are Paul and Millie Woods and we are firmly against this proposal. We shall be kept awake all night, we shall have drunks throwing up in our garden and it will obviously have some impact on house prices.'

'This is a restaurant and bar, aimed at people like you who want a quiet, smart place to eat.' Mark spoke slowly. 'It's not intended solely as a drinking place.'

Paul Woods strode up to the restaurant plan tacked on to the wall. 'It says here a bar area.' He jabbed his finger at the paper.

'For people who might like a quiet drink with the choice of a light, well-cooked meal.' Mark spoke smoothly in an authoritative and convincing manner; nevertheless, Jane, sitting at the back, cringed, bitterly hating the aggravation. Titus, in his favourite old leather jacket and looking scruffy compared to the elegantly suited Mark beside him, spoke up quietly.

'Actually, picking up on your earlier point, Mr Woods, I think you'll find that a good restaurant in the locale only enhances house prices.'

Jane wondered when he had found that out.

'The parade is run down, as I'm sure we all agree,' Titus went on. 'It is full of empty premises. We want to create a community restaurant, somewhere where everyone can come, whatever their age and bank balance.' He was speaking passionately now. 'We want this to be a central meeting place. Nowadays, we all live in our little boxes and worry about our neighbours encroaching on us. A restaurant could bring back the spirit of community living again. This is your restaurant – a restaurant for the people, a centre for all of us who live here. We want your input—'

Jane caught sight of the expression on Mark's face as Titus was speaking and it was at once glaringly apparent to her: Titus's vision of a restaurant for the people was clearly not a vision shared by Mark and he wanted Titus to stop talking.

'If we go ahead with this project, it will encourage other decent businesses to open,' Mark butted in.

'I'm not saying that we couldn't do with some proper shops,' Paul argued. 'But something like this, with all the extra people and rubbish it will attract, is absolutely unacceptable to the residents of this area. And may I ask where you live?' he demanded.

'My brother,' Mark motioned towards Titus, 'has lived in this area for years.'

'But where do *you* live?' Paul batted back.

'Fulham.'

'Ah.' Paul sounded triumphant. 'So you're quite happy to come over here and destroy our quality of life and bring down our property prices. Go and open your restaurant in Fulham if you're so keen.'

'We have restaurants and bars cropping up around us all the time,' Mark responded, 'and we welcome them as a valuable amenity. This area is obviously beginning to come up and a good restaurant can only help it in its journey upwards.' He spoke in such superior tones that Jane could sense a collective intake of breath from the people in the room.

'Mr Palmer.' Paul spoke in reasoned tones, but was clearly not prepared to give up easily. 'I'm the first person to welcome rising house prices but we don't need your restaurant to improve this area, thank you very much. I'm sorry, but I intend fighting you all the way on this.'

An informal vote was taken at the end of the meeting and the result was largely in favour of a restaurant in Squarey Street.

Despite a small local campaign run by Paul Woods, the council's planning committee also came down in favour of the restaurant.

Two weeks later Grania was on her hands and knees cleaning out the oven when Ralph answered the telephone. She heard his voice grow cold as he began speaking in curt monosyllables. 'Right. I see. Yes. Oh. Really.'

Grania strained to listen, then she heard a note of finality in Ralph's voice. 'It's your choice, of course, nothing to do with me, Mark. But you know my feelings on the subject. Thank you for telling me.' Grania heard him put the receiver down sharply.

He came into the kitchen and she was shocked by the ashen look on his face.

'That was Mark.' He began to wander around the kitchen, silently picking up pieces of crockery and realigning them in neat rows. Grania sat back on her heels.

'What did he want?' She tried to inject some cheerfulness into her voice.

'Planning permission for the restaurant has gone through.' Grania's heart sank. 'They're forming a company – *together*.' Ralph almost spat out the word.

Grania sought desperately for some words of comfort that might dispel the grey tension on her husband's face.

'Well, it's Mark's decision, and you just have to walk away from it.'

'Oh, I will, believe me.' Ralph sat down with a thump and rested his elbows on the table, rubbing and squeezing his hands together. Grania got to her feet and sat opposite him. She stretched out and took his hands to still their ceaseless movements.

'Ralph, my darling—'

'I just can't believe that Mark would take up with him just as though he were some ordinary man.'

'He is an ordinary man, darling.'

'No, he's not, he's an interloper. I am not going to accept him as my father's child, nor as anything else.' Ralph looked at Grania, his eyes pleading with her. 'Can't you see that? I want him to go away. I want to forget about him. He and his mother have caused so much unhappiness in my family already. The Gaffer was a good man, a loyal husband and a marvellous father. He didn't deserve to have some neurotic woman as a lifelong burden or a child who might not even be his. I, personally, don't think he ever wanted us to know about Titus, whatever Clattie says. He would have told us if he had. He never shirked his duty like that, he played fair with everyone in his life.'

'He did leave Titus money in his will,' Grania pointed out.

'But he didn't name him as his son in the will, did he? We didn't have to know who he was.'

Grania's eyes were wet as she watched Ralph's face twist in unhappiness; his eyes, though, remained dry.

'I simply do not understand my family.' He sounded genuinely perplexed. 'Clattie persists in acknowledging them as part of us; Pippa doesn't seem to care. I mean, what was she doing inviting them to her ridiculous christening? Mark wants this restaurant and he'll walk right over everyone's feelings to get it. He's selfish and thoughtless; he doesn't care about anything or anybody—'

'I don't think that's true,' Grania cut in.

'Well, it was brave of him to ring me and tell me,' Ralph said, always fair, 'when he knew perfectly well how I would feel about it.' His eyes darkened. 'I'm sorry to keep saying this, but I would prefer this family, at least, not to have truck with any of them. I hope that's clear.'

Kit, cleaning his football boots in the scullery next door,

heard his father's stentorian voice and the message seemed very clear to him.

Mark suggested that the new restaurant company be called Tymar. Tymar stood for Take Your Money And Run and was Mark and Freddie's private joke, cooked up one afternoon in bed. Mark shared the joke with Titus who laughed uncertainly and wisely decided not to share the joke with Jane.

Over the next month the two men held a series of meetings with each other and with their own accountants and lawyers. The financial side had been formalised to the satisfaction of both parties. Each man would put the same amount of money into the business. With Bella's offer behind him, Mark was confident about his investment. Titus's share was covered by his legacy from the Gaffer, with only a very little to spare. In consultation with his accountant and solicitor, he agreed to a fifteen-year lease on the premises between himself and Tymar with a rent-free period until the first day of trading.

Then Mark instigated a discussion on the day-to-day running of the restaurant. 'We need to have clear leadership. I think the staff need to know who they are responsible to and we must ensure there are no confusing signals. We'll obviously install a manager and we should advertise immediately and interview as soon as possible. He or she will be in charge, of course, but I suggest, to begin with, for simplicity's sake, that I take responsibility for working closely with them.' Mark looked across at Titus to affirm his agreement. Titus was nodding thoughtfully. 'Obviously you and I will make all major decisions together and we'll keep in close contact,' Mark went on, 'but the little everyday things I think we can leave to the manager under my auspices, if that's agreeable to you? Might as well make use of my catering experience, don't you think?'

Titus thought. 'Ye-es, that makes sense,' he said slowly. 'Obviously I want to be closely involved—'

'Absolutely,' Mark chipped in. 'That goes without saying. We're talking me being there just to troubleshoot the small, dull problems. We'll naturally have regular directors' meetings. To keep us both up to speed.'

'Weekly, I'm assuming.'

'Mmm. I don't think they need to be that frequent. We've both got other businesses to run. I reckon once a month with the profit and loss accounts in front of us will be fine. We get in a good manager and all we should have to do in the end are the fun bits like choosing wine and checking the chef's menus. And collecting the vast profits, I hope,' he added with a broad grin.

By September the contractors had started work in the warehouse, transforming it from a dark, oily cavern into something light, low ceilinged, smelling of new wood, fresh plastering and plumbers' blow-lamps.

'I have an interior designer friend,' Mark said, 'who specialises in fitting out shops and businesses. We might get her in further down the line – just for another eye on the final fit-out, you know.'

'Why not,' Titus agreed.

'Up to you, of course. We've agreed that you're in charge of the building.'

One more decision remained to be taken and that was the name of their new restaurant. Mark and Titus drew up a shortlist and had a convivial discussion, making each other laugh with ludicrous suggestions.

'Let's just call it Palmer's,' Mark said eventually. 'It's short, snappy and very classy.'

Titus bit his lip at the word classy, but agreed that Palmer's was the best name that they had come up with.

Mark doodled the name on a piece of paper – Palmer's.

'Yup. I think we've got it.'

Taking the paper from him, Titus looked at the word and tried to work out what was wrong with it. Then it came to him.

'It should be Palmers'.' He reached out for the paper and rewrote the word. 'The apostrophe should be after the "s" because there are two Palmers who own it.' He looked at Mark steadily, defying him to disagree.

There was a short, awkward silence.

'What about Palmers with no apostrophe at all,' Mark suggested and the moment of disagreement passed into an uneasy agreement.

The common goal of Palmers was gradually drawing the brothers together, and although they didn't quite behave as friends they were beginning to behave as partners.

'I had lunch with Mark today.' Dan Seagrove, Mark's oldest friend, poked his head round his dressing-room door and looked at his wife sitting at the dressing-table mirror, prodding at her stiff, saloned hair with a comb. 'He was telling me about this restaurant of his.'

Lizzie Seagrove made a pretty face into the mirror.

'God knows it'll be nice to have somewhere different to eat – even if it is south of the river. You could take your clients there. Knowing Mark, it will be a stylish place with good food.'

Dan, resplendent in dinner jacket, emerged completely from next door.

'I suggested to Mark that he hang some of your little watercolours in the restaurant. He quite liked the idea of selling art work and I bet they'd sell rather well,' he grinned at his wife, 'especially to the really pissed.'

Lizzie, who was now painting her nails, turned round and threw a hairbrush at him. 'Don't be so horrid. Whenever I find a new interest you do nothing but mock it. Do you think he'll give us discount on our meals?'

'Shouldn't think so, after all, it's not just him, is it? He's got a partner.'

'Of course. It's his bastard brother who's his partner. I'd forgotten that. Bella says he and his wife are the dullest thing on God's earth.'

'Mark reckons he'll pretty much take a back seat when it's open. Apparently, he's never been near the food business before and he's got his own furniture company or something. Bit of a lefty, by all accounts.'

The room was suddenly rocked by a deep base thudding of drums.

'Oh, do go and tell Max to shut up.' Lizzie picked up her glass of wine with her fingers delicately outstretched. 'The neighbours will start complaining again.' She gazed with admiration at her reflection in the mirror. 'I think I'll offer Mark my little green watering-can series for the restaurant,' she murmured to herself.

Jane and her friend, Natasha, were clearing up after the afternoon session of the playgroup.

'I walked down Squarey Street at the weekend,' Natasha said as she threw plastic bricks into a red bucket. 'It looks as though your restaurant's beginning to come together.'

Natasha worked with Jane at the playgroup and, as fellow Australians, they had, over the years, become good friends – an important link with home for each other.

'It's not mine, it's Titus's,' Jane said.

'Well, it must be quite exciting.'

'I suppose so.'

'Oi!' Natasha exclaimed loudly to attract Jane's attention. 'What? Are you not? Excited?'

Jane finished covering the sand tray and plumped herself down on a chair. 'Oh, Nash. I don't know. I really wish I wanted this as much as Titus did.'

'It should do well. God knows there aren't that many decent places to eat out round here.'

'It's not the money, it's the people involved. They're dire.'

Natasha looked across at her friend sitting hunched, miserably, on the tiny child's chair. 'They can't be that bad – they're Titus's family.'

'Oh, they can be. They're a cold, snobby lot. Mark, the partner, is pretty single-minded. He wanted that place and he's made bloody sure he's got it. Titus doesn't see any of it, of course. He's just like a little boy with a new train set.'

'Well, we all know adults are just bigger versions of children.'

130

Natasha tapped the bucket of bricks with her foot. 'And it doesn't take them much to revert – especially men.'

'You can't get a sensible word out of him at the moment,' Jane continued glumly, 'unless it's about RSJs and uplighting. Alby's travelling in India at the moment, Summer's never around, so it's just me to listen to him. It's doing my head in.'

'I can see that.' Natasha was sympathetic; then her voice bubbled. 'Still, just think how rich you might end up. And you can eat out any night you want. Not bad I say.'

'I don't want to eat out every night, I want to go home. I haven't been back for nine years, and I last saw my mum three years ago. I want Titus and me to go, maybe take the kids, and have a proper extended holiday. I just want to go home.'

'Me too,' agreed Natasha. 'Can I come in your suitcase?'

'The thing is, I can't possibly go at the moment; all the money's gone into this restaurant.' Still seated, Jane began piling up sheets of paper in a lacklustre fashion. 'And now Titus seems to have abandoned his real job. There's still some unfinished work to do, but he's not doing it and the new clients have stopped ringing up because he never answers the phone. We're living on my salary and it's not enough.'

'He said he'd come and mend my banisters. That was a few months ago.'

Jane got to her feet and made a face at Natasha. 'You'll be lucky. Not before Palmers restaurant opens anyway. I tell you, once it has opened Titus has got to get back into real life and into Palmer's Restoration; start thinking about something other than the restaurant. Do you know, yesterday we went to an art exhibition – we haven't been to one for ages and I was really looking forward to it. Something we could do together. They were great pictures – big modern swirly abstracts – but what do you know, they were ideal for the restaurant, so I was left on my own for ages while he struck up some deal with the artist. I am sick of it. It's all . . . I don't know, like big business. I really wish Aunt Monica had left him a little cottage in Suffolk instead

131

of a property,' she smiled wryly at Natasha, 'that is apparently so full of commercial potential.'

Clattie lay on a chaise longue under a still fiery Tuscan sun. Gerry slept under his panama hat in the shadow of a twisted olive tree. They had been in these positions for most of the last five days and she was already a deep brown all over and feeling more rested than she had for years.

Holidays with Jack had never been like this; he had always wanted to be by the sea, the rougher and colder the better. Holidays with Jack were on the east coast of England or Scotland in shrivelling cold. Long walks collecting wood for camp fires, interminable games of Halma that he always won, and the children always cold and dribbling. Here, in this peaceful brown Italian farmhouse, with the valley stretching down below them, thick in undergrowth, Clattie felt as though she was slowly unfurling from an embryonic position in which she had lain for a hundred years.

Gerry stirred and lifted up the rim of his panama to look at her.

'Cup of Earl Grey?'

Clattie swung her legs over the chaise longue, but Gerry was ahead of her. 'Stay there, I'll do it.'

Clattie was enjoying the novelty of being cared for. Gerry left her to do what she wanted. Each morning he would come into her bedroom with a cup of tea and leave it by her bedside – it was up to her whether she felt like opening her eyes and acknowledging him. If she did, he would sit on the bedroom armchair, sipping his tea, and they would talk about the day ahead, the shopping they would do, the food they would eat, the walk they would take – easy things, things that didn't make her anxious.

Slowly the panic she had felt when Jack died was beginning to subside. The switchback into which her emotions seemed to have got locked was flattening out and she was starting to think more clearly. Her sin of omission and the guilt for *her* part in perpetuating Jack's secret was still with her and would, she thought, always be there. But, here in this brief and agreeable holiday in the sun, far away from England and the family, she had time for herself – to unravel her previous existence, take from it what she wanted and move on into the future.

Chapter Six

The structural alterations to the warehouse in Squarey Street were almost completed despite Paul Woods, who had been dropping by at regular intervals to complain about the noise, the dust and anything else on the list he carried around with him. Mark dealt with him rather as he might a wasp buzzing around his breakfast table, getting into the marmalade, and batted him away in a lordly manner, but Titus was more conciliatory and he made constant efforts to placate the man. Then a drainage problem was found. It involved the property adjoining the restaurant and was more serious than was first supposed: the party wall needed to be renewed and the shop owner next door was cantankerous and unhelpful. Titus's time was taken up in negotiations with plumbers and the water company, so it turned out to be Mark who interviewed prospective managers on his own.

Greg, a young man in his early thirties, arrived at the interview in a well cut tweed jacket and an insouciant confidence that immediately appealed to Mark. In the first few minutes of the interview the two men found that they shared a love for playing cricket and watching rugby. They came from similar backgrounds and Mark found that not only were Greg's credentials and references impeccable but also that he had, many years after Hugh, been to the same prep school.

When Mark took Greg round to the restaurant to meet Titus after the second interview, it was a *fait accompli*; the job was already Greg's. After the restaurant tour, Greg and Mark went to the pub. Titus was too tied up with the drainage problem to join them – even had Mark thought to invite him.

Bella, dropping into the restaurant one afternoon, found Titus sealing and polishing the underside of the long wooden bar.

'Hi.' He rose to his feet to greet her in a friendly fashion. 'What do you think?'

'About what?'

'The building? The colour? The bar? The look of the place?'

Bella didn't pick up the caustic note in Titus's voice.

'Oh yes. Fine, very nice,' she replied, patronising him. 'I need to see Mark. Where is he?'

Titus shrugged. 'Dunno, haven't seen him today. Probably at Basil.'

'Oh right.' Bella was casual. 'I was just passing. I forgot he said he was there today.'

She turned and left as rapidly as she had arrived. She drove back to her office almost relieved to have her suspicions confirmed.

The drainage was sorted, the structural building phase completed and phase two – the fitting out – was rolling. Mark had been in charge of choosing and ordering the kitchen equipment and Titus the restaurant furniture. Both men were pleased with the result.

'I'd like this designer friend of mine to have a look round,' Mark said demurely to Titus. 'I think I mentioned her before. She might have some ideas about the final fripperies. You know, the feminine touch.'

Freddie, Mark and Titus met at the restaurant. Mark introduced them.

'Frances Cole. Titus . . . Palmer.'

Freddie noticed Mark stumble over the surname as she stepped forward to shake Titus's hand.

'Do call me Freddie.' She was struck by his kindly, open face and took an instant liking to him. 'This place is really, really great,' she said, meeting Titus's eye. 'It's clear . . . refreshing. I love it.'

'I think we're pleased with it.' Titus looked at Mark. 'Aren't we, Mark?'

'We certainly are. Can't wait to open now. Just a few ends to tie up. By the way, I've got some pictures in the car that are going to look good.' Mark disappeared through the door and Freddie drifted off to wander round the building.

'They're wonderful, so roomy,' she said when she emerged from inspecting the lavatories. 'Loos are really important and the Ladies is invariably cramped, with ghastly lighting, and if you try and put on make-up in them you come out with a bright orange face.'

Titus was laughing with her when Mark came back with a bundle of pictures and laid them on a table still padded in cardboard.

'Here are some great pictures. A friend of mine does them. We hang them here, put a price on them and Lizzie gives us commission if she sells any.'

Freddie and Titus looked in awe at the pictures laid out in front of them.

'They're very nicely executed,' Freddie said eventually. 'Colourful.'

'Appropriate too because they've all got gardens around here and she'll paint houses and gardens to order.'

Titus moved over to his briefcase and pulled out some photographs.

'Actually, I went to a show just the other day,' he said, laying out the photographs beside the paintings, 'and I saw these abstracts. They're big and bold and would fill these walls brilliantly. Same deal too, we'd get a bit of commission from the art gallery.'

'Now they *are* good,' Freddie said definitely. 'What do you think, Mark?'

'Yes, they're fine. But these are better for us – as a local restaurant.' Mark and Titus looked at each other.

'But I think these are a better size for our space,' Titus argued and Freddie could hear a combative note in his soft voice.

She looked at the two men and wondered if this was the first time they had manipulated themselves into a position of openly disagreeing.

Titus turned to Freddie. 'You're the interior designer,' he said with a smile. 'What do you think?'

'Those,' Freddie said without hesitation, pointing to the abstracts. 'Without a doubt.' She heard Mark draw in his breath beside her and turned to him. 'Think about it, Mark. This is a great space. You don't want to spoil it by filling the walls with ditzy geranium and watering-can pictures. You need big, bold, strong colours. These, honestly, are the ones.' She made a small conciliatory face at him. 'You asked for my professional advice and that's it,' she finished.

There was a moment's silence, then Freddie thought of something else. 'And,' she looked at Mark, 'your commission will be much higher on these. I should think they go for quite a price.' She looked at Titus, who nodded in agreement.

'Well, I'll be guided by you, I suppose,' Mark said sulkily, beginning to pile up the pictures. 'We should talk about plants as well while you're here; what greenery to have and where.'

Mark took the pictures out to his car and when he got back Freddie and Titus were up the other end of the restaurant in deep consultation. They seemed to be sharing some sort of joke. Freddie patted Titus's shoulder. 'Don't be silly, Titus, yucca plants would prick everyone's bottom as they passed. No, we want palms, great big sexy wavy palms.' She gestured expansively towards a corner of the restaurant.

'You and Titus seemed to hit it off pretty well,' Mark said peevishly. He and Freddie were back in their usual meeting place. Mark was now permanently pumped up with the heady prospect of success, and sex had been lavish and satisfactory.

137

They lay together listening to the early evening traffic rolling by under the window of the Kensington flat.

'Yes, he's a nice man.' Freddie shifted herself into a comfortable place under Mark's arm.

'Was it really necessary to flirt with him in quite such a dedicated manner?'

Freddie propped herself on her elbow and studied Mark. 'I beg your pardon?'

'Well, really. You were. You were batting your eyelashes at him like Miss Piggy.'

Freddie snorted with laughter. 'Oh *please*. Is this because I liked Titus's pictures better than your friend's nauseous little watering-cans? They wouldn't have done, you know. Apart from their toxic colours, they were way too small for those big walls.'

'No.' Mark was still huffy. 'Nothing to do with that, although I don't think they're that bad.'

'They are, trust me. Anyway, I thought you said Titus was in charge of restaurant design.'

'Now you're defending him,' Mark sniffed.

Freddie, still laughing, groped him between his legs.

'No, I don't fancy Titus if that's what's worrying you. I just liked him. I fancy you. You're my best friend. My fucking friend, in fact, so don't push it, otherwise I won't take you out to lunch next week, I'll take Titus instead.' She paused and grinned at Mark. 'I'm joking. Hello, humourless Mark.'

Mark reluctantly allowed himself to be appeased. 'Okay, sorry. Where are we going?'

'That place just down the road from here. Café Raisin. I did the other restaurant in Hampstead for them and they're so pleased, I've got a free meal – anything we want.'

Mark looked interested. 'Good. I'm interested in that place. They've got a forecourt, haven't they? They've made good use of the space. Will the owner be there? I think we should apply for use of our forecourt at Palmers. We could get at least eight tables out there—'

'Shut up, Mark.' Freddie rolled over on top of him. 'I'm sick of listening to you go on about that bloody restaurant. You don't think about anything else. I might as well be at home with my husband, listening to him wittering on about his economics students. Just concentrate on me for a moment, will you . . .'

Titus looked around for Jane. Carefully carrying two polystyrene cups of coffee he scanned the airport benches until he found her. She was sitting disconsolately in front of the departure boards watching Australian destinations come up. Melbourne, Sydney, Canberra, Perth, the cities of her home country rolled up and she wanted to be travelling to any one of them. It was early in the morning and the two of them were meeting Alby back from three months in India. Outside, the sky was gradually becoming lighter as inside the airport slowly came to life; the staff of Smith's were raising the grilles and cutting open the piles of newspapers, travellers wandered around with trolleys laden with luggage, faces already lined with jet-lag before they'd even set foot on a plane. Titus plumped himself down beside Jane and handed her a cup.

'We will go. I promise, very soon.'

'My mum's getting frailer, you know,' Jane said miserably.

'Look, if there was an emergency you could go at any time, if you had to. We would just have to borrow the money.'

'I don't want to go in an emergency. I want us all to be together in Australia once more before Summer and Alby go off and do their own things.'

'This time next year at the very latest. That's a promise. Just as soon as the restaurant is on its feet and some money's coming in.'

'Oh yes, the restaurant.' Jane grunted into her cup. 'Of course.'

Titus rested his elbows on his knees as he sipped his coffee. 'Talking of the restaurant, I've been thinking: we ought to invite Mark and Bella to supper.'

'Oh God. Must we? Why?'

'Well, they had us.'

'Mark wanted the warehouse then,' Jane pointed out. 'He's got it now.'

'I think it would be a nice gesture.' Titus ignored Jane's remark. 'Nothing special, you know.'

'Oh, whatever,' Jane said wearily. She turned her attention to the arrivals board. 'Alby's landed, luggage in hall. Come on.'

Alby, stumbling through from customs with a torn rucksack hung with a pair of broken sandals, was tired, stubbly, grubby and smelly. Jane flung her arms around him.

'So, how's it all going at home?' Alby asked when he'd eventually stopped talking about India and they were stuck in a traffic jam on Hammersmith flyover.

'Good—' Jane started.

'The restaurant's coming on well. The builders should be out in a couple of weeks,' Titus burst through Jane. 'It's looking very good . . . isn't it, Janey?' He cast a look at Jane, who nodded. 'I can't wait for you to see it. Everything's come together, just a few problems but overall it's been very smooth. I'm really pleased with the bar – my design – and the floor looks great . . .'

Jane swivelled round in the front seat and smiled at Alby.

'Your dad has not stopped talking about this place for the past three months, he is absolutely relentless . . . I'm glad you're home. Now *you* can do some listening duties. All you have to do is nod a lot and look enthusiastic. You'll get the hang of it pretty quickly.'

If Titus or Alby heard the rancour in Jane's voice neither made any comment.

Titus and Alby were unpacking the car outside the house.

'Titus.' Alby stood on the pavement. Titus, head in the open boot, heard the urgency in his son's voice and looked up, a duty-free bag dangling from his hand.

'Look, Titus,' Alby began awkwardly. 'I just want to say . . . The thing is, I've been thinking,' his voice gathered speed, 'about the family thing, the Gaffer and all that. I was really hacked off about it, all those lies, y'know. I thought you were always straight with us, always told us the truth.' He paused and looked at Titus.

'I didn't really have a choice,' mumbled Titus. He couldn't read the expression on his son's face.

'Yeah, I can see that now,' Alby said, without any of the contempt that Titus expected. 'I, like, blamed you for all that shit; gave you a bit of a hard time. But I've been sorting it while I was away, and it's cool. I know it wasn't your fault and not really *your* lie. Maybe in those sort of circumstances it's okay to lie to your kids.' He clapped his hand on his father's shoulder in an embarrassed gesture.

But Titus, returning the gesture, knew inside him that it was never okay to lie to your kids.

Kit and Summer had finally made it into bed.

And it was in a bed, not on a sofa, not a fumble in someone's garden, not in the back of a van, but in a proper bed. Summer contrived for it to be convenient for Kit to stay over in the student house after another party, and by some happy coincidence – which in reality involved Summer's organising and paying for her friend's taxi to north London to stay the night at her boyfriend's flat – there was an empty bedroom.

Kit, aware of Summer's agenda, had spent the evening nervously tokeing on large spliffs on the principle that alcohol was not a reliable aphrodisiac. He wanted to do this very much, but he had only done it once before and he had made a complete mess of it. Whenever he came across the girl he could feel a sweaty blush of shame spread across him.

He wanted it to be different with Summer. He lived and breathed her – why she should want to be with him baffled him and he waited daily for her to slip out of his life as rapidly as she had slipped into it.

'Tell Ed to piss off home, why don't you,' Summer whispered into his neck as they sat on the low sofa surrounded by a forest of dancing legs.

Ed was a bit of a maverick in Kit and Summer's relationship. Always looking for sex and never finding it, he regularly resorted to behaving like their chaperone – as though he believed that some of Summer's slinky sexual aura might rub off on him.

'Are you ready to split?' Ed bounced up to Kit and Summer. 'I could order a cab.'

'I think I'm going to hang around here for a bit,' Kit said awkwardly.

'Oh, okay, I'll go and get another drink.'

'Actually, Ed, I might like to stay over, y'know.'

Light dawned across Ed's cheerful face. 'Oh. Oh right. Go for your life then.'

Kit woke up in a tangle of navy blue duvet and wondered for a moment why he wasn't in his own bed. He looked at Summer with her head under a pillow and her long body spreadeagled beside him and he wanted to do it all over again. This time it had been brilliant. Excellent. He had been more sure and she had been less sure than he'd imagined they'd be; he was surprised how tentative she had been to begin with – so different from her outdoor persona. They had groped and bumbled around and Summer had looked up at him, vulnerable and shy, and he had, all at once, felt wonderfully in charge and confident. All night they explored and experimented and now, this morning, Kit knew that he would die for the magnificent girl lying next to him. Summer emerged from under the pillow and, still lying on her stomach, twisted her head round to look at Kit.

'Hello.' She grinned at him. He suddenly felt his daytime awkwardness return and he didn't dare stretch out his hand and stroke her brown arm as he wanted to. He stared at her silently and moved his head slightly, then caught sight of the clock on the bedside table.

'Oh shit.' He shot out of bed. 'Look at the time. Shit, shit, shit. I've only got a bloody mock French test in half an hour.'

'Skip it.' Summer lay on her back and watched as Kit rummaged through the clothes abandoned on the floor.

'I can't, this is bloody school, remember.'

'So?'

'Well, they get on your back, don't they, if you blag. So we don't very often.'

Summer moved on to her side and let the duvet slip below her perfect breasts.

'You do now,' she said seductively. 'And then I'll make pancakes for breakfast.'

The offer was too good for Kit.

In the second week, Gerry and Clattie's holiday took on a different sort of energy. As if slowly emerging from a long hibernation, they began, a little further each time, to venture beyond the garden. Gradually whole days were spent exploring the glorious Italian countryside. They walked with awe around duomos that looked as though they were made from dolly mixtures; they found brown-baked villages with tiny shops like larders, pungent with the smell of good things to eat. They wandered together through the fields of harvested sunflowers, and then up into the hills to find deserted farmhouses slowly crumbling into the valleys below. They crept into small quiet churches, where incense filled all their senses, and were silenced by the power of the shrines. And then they would drink an inordinate amount of wine and grappa. Gerry was an amiable companion, undemanding and anxious to please her every hour of the day, and Clattie felt released, as though, one by one, the elastic bands that had kept her so tight together were snapping and letting her out of a box.

Every evening they sat round the table talking through the deep Italian darkness while the insects dropped from the rattan roof into the candles on the table.

'May I ask you something very personal,' Gerry said gently one evening, 'now that your face is round and brown and not pinched any more?'

'Of course you may.' Clattie stretched luxuriously against the creaky wicker chair.

'Did you really love Jack?'

Clattie was silent.

'I was very angry when my wife died,' Gerry said eventually, trying to draw her out. 'In a strange way, I was angry with her to begin with. When I felt strong enough to let out the happy memories we had, the anger disappeared.'

'You don't always marry the right person,' Clattie started haltingly, 'but, in a way, knowing that from the start makes the marriage easier. Easier than finding out halfway, I imagine. The problem with Jack was that he was an obsessive: obsessive about everything, right down to the exact angle he laid his slippers beside his bed and what time his meals should be served. He used to line everything up neatly and he had little rituals, like the order in which he undressed, and touching the top of the garden gate whenever he went through it. Ralph does the same, you know. Jack was obsessed by people too. I mean, he quarrelled with the local vicar and he would never speak to him again. Of course, I constantly gave in to him. I allowed myself to be bullied into doing what he wanted, so I just fed his obsessions and they got worse. What I *should* have done was to find ways he could capitulate without losing face. He was a very proud man. He needed me to look after him but he wouldn't give me any room to expand. He never demanded or expected any passion from me. Which was good in a way,' she added prosaically, 'because I don't think I've ever had any passion in me. I don't really understand it,' she finished on a forlorn note.

'Passion is thoroughly overrated, in my view,' Gerry said, stretching out his hand to cover hers. 'It leads to all sorts of trouble. You, Clattie my dear, have something much better. You have a great capacity for love. You are the kindest, most caring person I have ever met. You're honest. You're a good person.'

'No, I'm not,' Clattie said quickly. 'You don't know me.'

'I know I care for you very much.'

They sat quietly, listening to the cicadas fizzing around them.

'I know you do,' Clattie said eventually. She placed her other hand on top of his – his hand sandwiched safely between hers.

'I'm not deserting my children,' Clattie started speaking slowly. 'I'd never do that. But I really would like to get on with *my* life now. What's left of it. I just want everyone else to deal with their own lives and leave me to be me.' She looked across at Gerry. 'Do you understand that? Does it sound so selfish?' He shook his head gently. Clattie was quiet for a moment, then she said shyly, 'I'd like us to sleep together tonight. If that's all right with you?'

Very slowly, Gerry removed his hand, catching one of hers and keeping it tucked into his as he gently pulled her upright and led her up the stone stairs.

'You're looking thunderous,' Bella remarked when Mark came into the kitchen. 'Not had a good day?'

'You could say so.' Mark banged around the kitchen, pouring himself a drink. 'One of the Basil waitresses has been nicking on the job.'

'Yes, I'd love a drink too, thanks for asking.' Bella put down the papers she had been reading at the kitchen table. 'So what happened?'

'We had a big job on, private house and marquee affair and we were short of staff. I was busy so I stupidly let Caroline take charge of hiring extra staff.'

'Caroline's nothing more than a glorified waitress herself,' Bella said.

'I know, but I was busy with Palmers, wasn't I? There's so much to do there and I didn't have time to phone around for staff. I gave Caroline the list of our regulars and left her to it. She exhausted the regulars and God knows where she found this one, but it helped itself to a selection of valuable goodies from the client's house. I've had the police round all morning, and this afternoon an unpleasant interview with Mrs Irvine. Let's just say, she won't be using Basil Catering again.'

Bella pointedly moved Mark's whisky glass to one side and took a bottle of wine out of the fridge.

'Well, I have to say, you've been spending so much time on that restaurant I'm not surprised things are slipping at Basil. You haven't been there, and you've left it all up to Caroline and the chef. You want to get in there and start repairing the damage.'

'Oh, I intend to. Just as soon as Palmers is open and trading. It's important we get this right; this is going to be the greatest and most successful restaurant south of the river.' Mark's voice became more cheerful. 'Did I tell you, I've managed to get one of the Sundays to come and review it? I'm hoping we'll get some—'

'Yes, Mark.' Bella sat down again with her glass of wine. 'You have. And you've told me about the new cocktail menu you and Greg have dreamed up and the T-shirts the staff are going to wear.' She struggled to keep her voice even. She was imagining Mark's bimbo listening dewy-eyed and admiringly to his boring monologues about the restaurant and she refused to have herself contrasted unfavourably. Bella had done this before; she was no lightweight in the game. Do a bit of pandering to Mark, match him intellectually and emotionally, and the bit of fluff would soon be tossed aside like all the others.

'The thing is, Mark,' she couldn't resist saying pointedly, 'you've just got too much in your life at the moment. You've got to give up something.' She fixed him with a beady look and hoped that he recognised the message in her words.

Mark gave no sign. 'By the way,' he said casually, 'Jane and Titus have invited us to supper next Tuesday.'

Oh God, must we? Bella thought. 'Okay,' she said aloud. 'I suppose we'd better keep in with our partner.'

Jane was also dreading the dinner party.

'An Aga. How lovely – you must be a real cook,' Bella exclaimed when they arrived, thus putting a status to the meal which Jane knew it would not achieve. Sitting round the table in the kitchen, Titus and Mark had launched immediately into restaurant talk while Jane and Bella rapidly exhausted most non-controversial subjects.

A few months ago, Jane thought gloomily, Titus would have noticed the conversational stickiness up the other end of the table, but now he just poured wine for himself and Mark as they discussed cheese suppliers.

'So what about the opening party?' Bella interrupted the men loudly. 'You need to open with a big bang.'

'All in hand,' Mark responded airily and Jane watched her husband's eyes widen slightly in surprise.

'I'm working towards a start date at the end of October. I want the staff to have worked themselves in, ready for the Christmas period.'

Jane looked at Titus and wondered if he had registered Mark's use of 'I'. From across the table his outline seemed wavery behind the candles, as though he had two different faces.

Jane had been to see the old warehouse in Squarey Street several times and had watched it grow from a cavernous dark space into a light, bright place with another character altogether. She was proud of the work Titus had done and she knew that he wanted her to love Palmers as much as he did. But she wished that the two of them could walk away from it when it was finished. She couldn't shake off the feeling that the restaurant was just too big and grown-up for people like themselves. Every day at the playgroup she would watch the children and breathe in the clean, clear air of innocence and simplicity and wish yet again that life hadn't changed in this way.

'I thought October the thirty-first might be a fun day for the official opening.' Mark addressed Titus. 'If you agree, of course. Hallowe'en. We could make a theme of it.'

'A party at Palmers will be a brilliant opportunity to invite all those friends we owe who are just too boring to invite to dinner parties.' Bella looked at Jane, who silently wondered why one should bother to have friends who were too boring to invite to supper. 'And I've got a few clients who should be invited too,' Bella went on.

'We're not having a repeat of the Basil party,' Mark interrupted tetchily. 'I'm not filling my restaurant with all your free-loading friends. There are a couple of Basil clients that it would be tactical to invite but I'm not in the market for supplying a free PR exercise to all your clients.'

The atmosphere turned acrimonious.

'I'm only trying to help.' Bella tossed her head. 'You need a theatrical first night with the press there, photographers and as many celebs as you can muster.'

'I know perfectly well how to run an opening party, thank you very much.'

Mark and Bella glared at each other across the table and Jane caught Titus's eye. He raised his eyebrows and Jane suddenly felt comforted. So they could still speak silently; surely they would never get like Mark and Bella . . . would they?

Titus and Mark sat down the next day to organise the guest list for the opening party.

'Ask who you like,' Mark said generously. 'Particularly anyone you think will use the place regularly.'

'We should invite the Woods,' Titus suggested.

'The Woods? That fussy bugger. Why?' Mark was baffled.

'Politic. Good for community and neighbourly relations. Anyway, he seems to have stopped complaining recently.'

'Whatever you like. I don't mind. I've found a photographer for the party, did I say?'

'Will Ralph come?' The question was out before Titus could think about it.

'I'll invite him, but I doubt it. Curmudgeonly sod.' Mark kept his voice light.

It was only much later that Titus realised that both he and Mark would have liked Ralph to be there – as if to give his seal of approval to their venture.

Pippa received her invitation at breakfast and found herself folding it up and putting it into her pocket as though it were a piece of contraband. After four months in the community as a fully fledged sister, things were not easy for her and sometimes, alone at night, listening to Joyce breathing heavily in her sleep in the next door bed, Pippa wondered if the Lord really meant her to be there at all. It was only at the services that she felt she really belonged; the singing and praying made her feel happy and near to God. At first she'd loved the camaraderie and the friendship round the table every evening at supper. She'd thought she was fitting in well: the office work was easy – once she had set up a system that was manageable – and she enjoyed working in the shop. That had needed some rearrangement as well. In the house, most of the community seemed to appreciate her energy and willingness for domestic work and when she had misunderstood instructions or took it upon herself to change something, the brothers and sisters had been patient and kind with her.

So it came as a shock when Meredith pointed out at a house meeting that her tendency to rush into things, her belief that she was always right, her tactlessness and – and this hurt Pippa the most – her dedication to self were all personal faults that she should work on with the help of the Lord. He even suggested that her asthma was born entirely from needing to be the centre of attention. It was then that Pippa's confidence began to dwindle away and her asthma and eczema became worse as she began to have difficulty conforming to the subservience of living in a community. For all the emphasis put on love, Pippa was finding her new home a surprisingly chilly and cheerless place, both emotionally and physically. She remembered dreary winter weekend walks taken at boarding school. Walking down country lanes, she would peer enviously through cottage windows at warm, cosy people sitting in big armchairs by roaring fires. She had always longed to be curled up in any one of them rather than be returning to the bare, uncomfortable school common room with its hard chairs and brash overhead lights. Here too there was no physical warmth, no comfort, and Pippa had never realised quite how much one could yearn for something as fundamental as a table lamp.

Worse still, she was beginning to feel captured and claustrophobic.

She had removed her car without permission twice from the community car pool to visit Clattie at The Mill.

'Disobedience, Pippa,' Meredith had said severely, 'is probably the hardest of your sins to overcome. And humility the hardest thing to learn.' Pippa felt she was being treated like a child.

'But you are a child,' Meredith had pointed out. 'You're a child of the Lord.'

Pippa had never felt so undermined or so sinful in her life; and the more she tried to please her brothers and sisters the more she got it wrong. Resentment was beginning to burn like a slow fire inside her, and she found herself yearning for the comfort of her mother, surprised to find quite how insecure and anchorless she felt while Clattie was away in Italy.

'Look.' She handed Joyce the invitation as they were getting ready for bed. 'I've been invited to my brother's restaurant opening. Am I really going to have to ask permission to take my own car to that?'

Joyce looked over the invitation and handed it back. 'I wouldn't even bother to ask. You won't be allowed to go at all. It's a party.'

'But it's my family.'

'Here we believe that Jesus and all his true believers are our family.'

Pippa looked at her room mate.

'Actually,' she said loftily, 'you can have more than one family. Believe me, I know.'

The steel band in the corner thrummed out a tribal rhythm. Waiters and waitresses wove their way round the crowded room with trays of food, their hips undulating slightly to the beat, avoiding the hollowed-out pumpkins dotted around on tables. The dull roar of people talking rose to accommodate the music, and beside the band some of the younger ones were beginning to dance.

Mark moved from group to group, collecting compliments which he accepted almost demurely while inside his heart was leaping with excitement. This was his dream come true and he wished that the Gaffer could have been here to witness his success. He wished Ralph was here too. Fuck you, big brother, he thought triumphantly. Watch me make a success of this, and weep.

To have a vision that comes even halfway to reality is a heady experience for anyone and Titus had a bubble of excitement inside him that had been fizzing all evening. Everyone loved his restaurant; he listened to snatches of conversation –

'This is brilliant. Should do very well.'

'Love all the glass and the steel.'

'Very sophisticated. Just what we need round here.'

'A local architect designed it, apparently.'

And Titus just could not stop smiling.

Jane met Grania in the cloakroom. Grania seemed pleased to see her.

'You must be very proud of Titus. I think it looks fabulous; it's so beautiful and sophisticated and I'm sure it'll be a wonderful success. He must have worked so hard.'

Jane could have said that Titus had worked so hard that the rest of his life seemed to have been put on hold. She could have said that, personally, she thought it was a yuppie trap – just that little bit too beautiful and sophisticated for *real* people. She could have said that she was fed up with the whole enterprise and that she was looking forward to life getting back to normal.

'Yes, I think it will be,' she said instead.

Titus was talking to one of his neighbours when he caught Mark's eye across the room. Mark beckoned him over.

'Wanted you to meet some good friends of ours. Dan Seagrove and his wife Lizzie. Lizzie's an artist. It was her work that we looked at with a view to hanging in here.' Mark's tone was jovial, but Titus recognised the point that he was making.

'I'm sorry we couldn't use them.' Titus looked at Lizzie. 'They're great pictures, the colours are wonderfully vibrant.' He could hear himself overdoing it. 'They were just a little small for these big walls.' Lizzie made no response. 'If you've got some larger work,' he went on desperately, 'I'd love to see it sometime. I plan to change the artwork in here every few months or so.'

Lizzie Seagrove smiled graciously at Titus as though granting him the forgiveness that she felt sure he had been seeking. 'Actually, I'm working on a series of large canvases at the moment. "Scenes on the Common", I've titled it. I think you'll find they'll be very suitable for here.'

'It really is a super place,' Dan murmured. 'Absolutely super. You've always had a good nose for a commercial opportunity, Mark. Should be a great success judging by this turnout.'

Mark sketched an awkward, half-hearted gesture to include Titus.

'This is the man with the opportunity,' he said cordially, 'but I think we're going to make good partners, eh, Titus?'

Titus nodded.

'They always say you should keep business in the family, don't they?' Lizzie drawled.

Bella buzzed round the room — networking. She was in her element here, searching out the useful people, flitting from group to group, giving each person her undivided attention for as long as it took to impress them with the restaurant, with Mark and with herself. She glanced contemptuously at Titus and Jane standing around stolidly in a group of their friends. They had no idea how to court the clients, they were just passengers on this boat.

'Hi, Frances.' Bella smiled at the woman edging past her in the crowd around them.

'Oh hello. Isn't this great? Haven't Mark and Titus done well with the place?'

Bella smiled her agreement. She cast her eyes critically over Freddie's voluptuous body encased in a low-cut deep purple velvet dress that clashed exotically with her red hair which was piled up and fastened with shiny silver clips. This woman needed a course of evening primrose oil, a diet and a gym pretty urgently, Bella thought. Otherwise she'd be past redemption by the time she was forty and she couldn't be far off that age by the look of her.

'Mark says you've been terribly helpful with the decor and everything,' Bella said graciously.

Freddie waved a hand vaguely. 'God no. It was mostly Titus. I just did a bit of tweaking with the plants and things. Must go and find my husband . . . lovely to see you.' She disappeared into the crowd.

Clattie arrived at Bella's side and gave her a kiss.

'I think this is splendid,' she said. 'Such a grown-up place,' she added with a smile.

'Sophisticated, you mean? Yes, it is,' Bella agreed.

'I was thinking,' Clattie went on, 'how nice it would be if we had a girls' lunch here one day. What do you think?'

'Lovely,' Bella murmured. 'The three of us don't get together very often and I haven't seen anything of Grania recently.'

'I thought we'd do it on a Friday, in a couple of weeks. The four of us,' Clattie said solidly. 'Jane can usually get a Friday off.'

'What a triumph. I'm very impressed.' Gerry came up beside Mark and Titus who were talking to a journalist from a local magazine. 'Thank you for inviting me.'

He held out his hand to Titus.

'You must be Titus. Gerry Crockerton, I don't think we met at Jack's funeral. I'm a friend of Clattie's. She tells me you're the architect. Wonderful place, so modern.'

Titus murmured his thanks and Gerry turned to Mark.

'Doesn't your mother look well? Our holiday did her good, I think.'

'Yes, she seems to have had a very enjoyable time,' Mark said politely. 'And it's very helpful of you to bring her up for this,' he added, as though Gerry was a minicab.

'Absolutely my pleasure. We're having a fine time.' There was just a nuance, Titus noticed, on the word we.

'Good, good.' Mark turned back to the journalist, excluding Titus and Gerry.

'I've been talking to your son Alby.' Gerry smiled at Titus. 'What a very nice boy he is.'

'We think so,' Titus said with a grin.

'I know Clattie does as well. She's very fond of you all and proud of you.' Gerry spoke so confidently of Clattie's feelings, it seemed to Titus that he was behaving almost like one of the family.

Later in the evening, Freddie met Mark outside the cloakrooms.

'I haven't met your husband yet,' Mark said with a flirtatious grin.

'Do you need to?' Freddie grinned back.

'We've got a few things in common, I suppose.'

'Not a lot, believe me. He's a nice young man.'

Mark laughed. 'You wouldn't love me if I was nice.'

'Who says I love you?'

'I do.'

Freddie raised her eyebrows enigmatically. She could see from his glittering eyes that Mark was highly charged, not from drink, but from success, and their sparring conversation was a prelude to some game of Mark's. It was a game that at the moment she was prepared to play.

'Very sexy loos,' Freddie said, laughing up at him. 'All that blue marble, very enticing.'

This evening, Mark felt invincible and the sense of power was making him lecherous. He surreptitiously caressed her bottom as he pushed her back towards the cloakroom. 'May I entice you in then?'

'Ladies or Gents?'

'The disabled, I think.'

He pushed her backwards into the empty cubicle, his fingers scrabbling up her dress. 'I've always wanted to screw in a restaurant lavatory, especially one that belongs to me.'

Freddie recognised that Mark was not thinking about her as he swiftly took her against the wall. This was a power fuck and she accepted it as such with equanimity.

A few minutes later Mark emerged from the cloakrooms, followed, after a short interval, by Freddie. Several pairs of eyes noted them.

Kit was watching Summer in front of him writhing to the Caribbean music. He ran his eyes down her surprisingly elegant black strappy dress and thought lustfully of the body underneath that he now knew by memory. He wished his family weren't around, but Summer seemed not to care. The music slowed down and she took his hand and yanked him towards her.

'Chill, it's okay,' she whispered as she rested her hands lightly on his shoulders. 'They're all too pissed to notice us.'

Grania propped herself up against the bar and wished that Ralph had come with her and Kit. He had been calm and firm when she had suggested that he was making a big statement by not coming.

'I *am* making a big statement,' he said. 'I'm making it quite clear how traitorous I believe Mark has been.' He'd smiled bitterly and said, 'Who would have thought my family could be so complicated? But you must go if you want to,' he'd added.

Caitlin was in Leeds, but Kit had seemed very keen to come and Grania felt that she should be here if only to prevent the sibling rift becoming too wide ever to close.

'I'm sorry.' A pregnant woman knocked her arm as she hoisted herself on to the next door stool. She smiled at Grania. 'I'm a bit cumbersome at the moment.'

'When's it due?' Grania asked politely.

155

'Christmas Day, poor little mite. Which means it'll probably be just after Christmas. First babies are always late, aren't they?'

Grania nodded. 'Usually.'

'I'm Millie Woods.' She held out her hand for Grania to shake.

'Grania Palmer.'

'Ahh, Palmer. Then you'll know I'm married to the neighbour from hell.'

Mystified, Grania put her head on one side. 'No. I'm not really involved in the restaurant. I'm married to Mark's elder brother.'

'Oh, I see.' Millie lowered her voice. 'It's my husband. He's really cross about this restaurant. Personally, I think it's brilliant. The parade has been almost derelict for years and this place has been empty for ages. Now Palmers has opened, we might get some more decent shops round here.'

'Is he here?' Grania asked.

'Paul? Oh no, and I should go home before he gets back from work.' Milly raised her eyes. 'It's probably kinder if he doesn't know I've been here. He got a bit obsessed by the whole thing, took it as a personal affront. You know what men are like, never let things go. Complete tunnel vision.'

Natasha tugged at Jane's arm. 'Well, I'm having fun. I've been watching the family . . .'

Jane thought how family had become such a loaded word in the last six months.

'Clattie's lovely, you're right,' Natasha declared, and then confidentially, 'and so is that rather sweet man who follows her around so protectively. I think he's in love with her. I'm pretty sure Mark's having an affair with that red-headed woman and I think, but I'm not sure, that his wife, who is seriously scary, has clocked him with her. The other wife is obviously longing to go home.' Natasha kissed Jane on both cheeks. 'Which is where I'm going. Home. Good luck with that lot. Oh, and by the way . . .'

she whispered in Jane's ear, 'Summer and that boy she's dancing with really fancy the pants off each other.'

Titus looked at his watch. It was getting late; everyone seemed to have had too much to drink and no one was ready to leave. The champagne had flowed round the room in an endless circle and Titus wondered how much it was costing the company. The band played louder; the tables, piled with empty plates and glasses and burnt-out pumpkins, were pushed back against the wall as more and more people lost their party inhibitions and began to dance. Titus bumped into his friend Geoff Turner.

'I've been looking for you.'

'Just arrived, sorry. Late, I'm afraid. Had a meeting. Going well, is it?'

Titus nodded. 'They seem to like what they see.' He handed Geoff a drink off a passing tray. 'I really appreciate all your help. I couldn't have designed this without being able to run to you for advice.'

'Next one, I'll charge a proper fee,' Geoff said with a grin at Jane, who had appeared beside them.

'Next one I reckon I can do on my own. I've had a real learning curve with this place.'

'Not the next one quite yet, please.' Jane purposefully kept her voice light as she turned to Geoff. 'Titus has got a backlog as long as a train at home to get to grips with. He's been neglecting our real business for far too long.'

If Titus heard the message in his wife's words he made no acknowledgement of it.

Later, as the party began to break up and he watched the guests slowly making their way out he caught sight of Mark by the glass doors, with Bella by his side as consort, bidding farewell to the guests, smiling and nodding his thanks for their praise. Hemmed in at the bar by members of the band and the line of guests waiting to leave, Titus wanted to force his way through, to stand beside Mark and stake his position, but he couldn't get there. And he felt, for that moment, not part of

157

Palmers at all. He looked down at his glass and noticed that the fizz had gone from his champagne.

There was a small hiatus in the front of the restaurant as the line of people trying to get out stood back to allow someone to come in.

Pippa came through the doors wearing a thick coat. Wheezing heavily and her face flushed, puffed up and sweaty, she clutched her inhaler, holding it near her face. She stood for a moment, facing the sea of people all turned to stare at her.

'I'm awfully sorry but I think I've lost the Lord,' she said breathlessly.

Chapter Seven

Pippa's entrance at the end of the party succeeded in finally clearing the restaurant of all the guests except family. She sank on to a chair and her face became greyer as she struggled for breath.

Titus, on the other side of the room, watched, embarrassed and useless, as Pippa's family gathered around her. Clattie threw off her overcoat and crouched beside her daughter.

'Pippa.' She spoke calmly and clearly. 'Listen to me. Breathe. Think of running water and breathe slowly. Come on . . . in, out.' She breathed along with Pippa.

'She certainly picked her moment to lose something as large as the Lord,' Bella said irritably.

Grania, arriving with a glass of water, frowned at her. 'She can't help an asthma attack, Bella.'

'She could have had it at home,' Mark muttered crossly. 'I didn't think she was coming. I've booked a table for a family dinner round the corner.' He stumped over to the bar to dismiss the restaurant staff.

'I'm so sorry,' moaned Pippa through her wheezes. 'The train was delayed . . . I was rushing . . . to . . . get . . . here. So . . . sorry.'

'Stop trying to talk.' Clattie looked worried. 'This is a bad attack. I think we should take her to hospital. She needs to be on a ventilator.'

Titus looked across the room at Jane and they made a silent and mutual decision. They would leave; they were not part of this. But before Titus and his family could get home, they had to negotiate saying goodbye to the family thronged around Pippa. Titus had a strong sense that, engrossed in their own drama, they had closed ranks and he felt excluded, as though *his* family were no more than unwelcome visitors, left behind by mistake. The two families had only ever been together with other people around them and now Titus had to make his exit without the security of a bustle around them. He felt disadvantaged, as though he was being pushed out of his own restaurant, and it made him feel awkward and put about.

Jane signalled across to Summer and Alby who were sitting by the bar with Kit, watching silently. They slid off the high stools and Jane noticed Summer give Kit a gentle squeeze on his arm as she stood up.

'Look, I think we'll shoot off now . . .' Titus began uncertainly into the air, conscious that no one was paying any attention to him.

Mark, murmuring to Greg, didn't bother to look up. Bella appeared to stare through him, and Grania and Clattie remained bowed over Pippa's prone figure.

Titus stayed where he was, needing some sort of farewell before he could move.

Gerry stepped forward, looking relieved to have something to do.

'It's a wonderful restaurant, Titus,' he said gravely, 'and it's been a wonderful party. Thank you very much. I'm quite sure that you and Mark will do very well with it.'

They shook hands for a fraction longer than was necessary, each man grateful to have been rescued by the other.

'Go and say goodbye to Mark,' Jane murmured in Titus's ear as she also shook hands with Gerry. 'We'll see you outside.'

Titus looked at Summer and Alby who were hovering uncertainly on the outside of the circle round the table. They were, he realised, waiting for him to be first past the group round the table. Shaken out of his hesitancy, he gestured them to follow Jane out of the door, and stubbornly, refusing to be seen slinking out of his own restaurant, he moved beside Mark.

'Right, Mark. I'll see you in the morning.'

Mark looked up at Titus and spoke to him briefly as though he was being bothered with something trivial.

'What? Oh right, yes well, I'll certainly be dropping in tomorrow,' he said offhandedly.

'We should be here,' Titus said coldly, stung by Mark's cavalier tone. 'First day of trading. I'll want to see how it's going.'

'Quite.' Mark still sounded indifferent. 'Though Greg's got it pretty much under control.'

'See you tomorrow then. I hope Pippa's okay.' Titus followed his family out of the door.

'Well, that was like parachuting into a minefield.' Jane flung herself on to their bed and covered her eyes with her arm.

Titus, undressing slowly, sat on the bedroom armchair. 'I don't know, I thought it went all right. Until Pippa arrived, that is. Poor thing.'

Jane slid to an upright position against the pillows. 'Did you see Mark's face? He was furious she'd spoilt his evening. Something about dinner booked for the family. Not for us though, interestingly.' She gave Titus a knowing stare.

'Mark and I have a business relationship,' Titus responded defensively. 'That's all it is. It's nothing to do with anything else.'

Jane hit her forehead with the palm of her hand. 'God, why are men so *stupid*. Titus, you cannot divorce business from family in these circumstances.' She spoke in a more measured voice. 'Believe me, it's impossible and *they* are certainly not doing it. Don't you see? By not acknowledging the family connection you're both making as big a deal of it as if you were. And, by the way, I think Summer is having a thing with Kit.'

'Oh. Well that's okay, isn't it?'

Jane looked at Titus in astonishment. 'Well, it's not ideal, is it? You think everyone is going to be thrilled if Summer and Kit—'

'No, not thrilled, but it might help ease things between the families.'

'Like Romeo and Juliet did, you mean?'

'I don't think it'll come to murder and suicide.' Titus gave a hopeful laugh.

Jane was not laughing. 'Look at the big picture, Titus. You have tied us up financially with them.' She spat out the words. 'And, now, if I'm right about Summer and Kit . . . well, I just think it's all wrong.'

'It's going to be all right, Janey,' Titus wheedled. 'Look at this evening. You can tell that Palmers is going to be a great success. And I've been thinking of things to make it even better—'

'Titus.' Jane's voice was sharp and full of warning. 'I thought now that Palmers is open, Palmer's Restoration was going to get your full attention. You promised, Titus. You said our life would get back to normal once the restaurant had started trading. And now it is, and we're going to get the rent, we can begin to think about the things we were planning to do before all this happened.'

'We can. Eventually. But Mark and I can't afford to take our eye off the ball. It's early days.'

Jane winced. Titus was even beginning to sound like Mark.

'Before we start thinking about ways of spending the money,' Titus continued, 'we've got to make sure the restaurant is really going to take off. I've got a list of suggestions I need to discuss with Mark.'

Jane was bitterly offended by Titus's implication that her haste in thinking about the money was unseemly.

'I thought we'd agreed all this. I said, if you remember, that I didn't want you as involved and tied up with the place once it got going. And,' she added darkly, 'I have a feeling your brother Mark might feel the same.'

So Palmers was open for business and, whether from curiosity or need, the local residents began to crowd in immediately. The restaurant attracted the new breed of middle-class home-owners who were moving further south from the more affluent areas of London: young executives looking for flats to make chic and trendy, and families needing larger houses with bigger gardens. The less well off, who'd lived in the area before its gentrification, thought the place too smart and yuppie for them. So the morning customers were au pairs drinking coffee, relieved to have deposited their tiresome charges at school. They sat around smoking and laughing and snatches of their different languages hung suspended in the air. Lunchtime was business-suited men and women, mobile phones lined up on the table, shuffling through documents and trying not to stare at relaxed mothers round the larger tables, surrounded by prams and pushchairs, breast-feeding their babies under their shirts. The elderly of the area tried Palmers for tea-time, but they were looking for copper kettles, cucumber sandwiches, cream cakes and a proper pot of tea and, disappointed, they did not return. Five-thirty to seven-thirty became a quiet time in the restaurant and Greg, the manager, suggested a Happy Hour: he called it Greg's Un-happy Hour as a joke and young professionals and students dropped in on their way home to take the opportunity of half-price drinks. The more financially sound stayed on for dinner, joined by young married couples, grateful to leave their children in the care of au pairs and babysitters.

This new eating place was a bit of a novelty in the area so, for the time being, the Italian eating place was abandoned and Palmers – the restaurant – looked set to be a happy success. Palmers – the family – on the other hand, was less of a certainty.

Mark, empowered by the success of his venture, was still feeling invincible. Which is why he was confident that he could sort out the problems that were beginning to appear in Basil Catering.

'It's entirely my fault that revenue has fallen,' he said breezily to his accountant who had called a meeting with him. 'I dropped the balls a bit while I was setting up Palmers. Haven't had time to push for orders and that trouble with the waitress thieving has had an impact on the business. Unfortunately the client was local and rather high profile. I think word must have got around. I see what you're saying and I've got it in hand. I need to concentrate on the PR side and start building up the client base again. Leave it with me.'

This cocoon of arrogant invulnerability also prevented Mark from noticing that there was something changed about his wife.

If Bella was to explain exactly how she was feeling at the moment, she would have said it was like when she was a child at the seaside; she would build herself a sandcastle, it would be a well-defended fortress, unbreachable, and she would feel clever, secure and triumphant at her success. But when she wasn't looking, the sea would begin to trickle in through the sides of her castle, gradually wearing down the secure walls, making her feel vulnerable and uneasy.

Her life was leaking. She had seen Freddie and Mark emerge from the lavatories at the Palmers' party. The official photographer had caught them on camera, talking, their bodies close up, familiar with each other. And Bella had watched Mark fill Freddie's empty glass and Freddie, in conversation with someone else, had not even turned to look at him or thank him. With a shock that belted through her, Bella had realised then, that Mark and Freddie were a couple. It was Freddie who was the blonde twenty-year-old bimbo that Bella had imagined – except she wasn't: she was confident and intelligent – not beautiful but, much more dangerously, she was young, but not too young. For the first time, Bella found herself threatened; her fortress was in danger of being breached. Her immediate thought in the shock and panic was to confront Mark: rage at him, hit him, give him ultimatums. But, helped by the distraction of Pippa's entrance and the ensuing events, Bella's mind had time to work logically. This was the big one – Frances Cole, Freddie. Bella knew she had to keep her head; deal with the situation rather as she would a problem that arose in the office. But her innate conviction in her own power had been ebbing away slowly and now she was scared of failure. So she kept her secret huddled miserably to herself until she had decided what to do.

'Jane knows about us,' Summer said lazily as she lay against Kit on the sofa in a local wine bar, 'so now you can come round to mine any time.'

Kit experienced a sick sinking feeling in his stomach. 'Shit, that's not good. How did she find out?'

Summer twisted round and looked up at him with her big brown eyes.

'Someone checked us out together at the party, apparently, and so she asked me about it.'

'Why did you tell her?' Kit looked down at her in amazement.

Summer shrugged. 'What's the point in lying? It's okay, she's cool about it.'

In fact Jane had said, 'Do be careful, Summer. I don't know how far this has gone or is going, but please be aware that your father's half-brother's son would not be my choice of boyfriend for you.'

'You don't know him,' Summer had protested.

'Just think of his family. They're a toxic lot.'

Summer thought it was most unlike Jane to be so uncharitable. 'Kit's not like that at all. He's okay. It's not his fault his family are wankers.'

'No, I suppose not,' Jane had sighed. 'You can't help the family you're dealt, but I wish they would realise that.'

'Well,' Kit said now, squeezing Summer's arm to get her attention. 'I can't risk my dad finding out, he'd go completely ballistic. But I don't need to come to yours. Can't we just hang out here?'

'Whatever,' Summer said carelessly.

*

Titus was feeling deflated and a little dispirited. After the work and excitement of getting the restaurant open, he found Palmer's Restoration quiet and dull. He realised, with shame, that he had subconsciously been thinking that he had left this sort of work behind him. He wanted to be there in the restaurant every day to watch it at work and to receive the plaudits. Logically, he had known his role in Palmers would diminish once it had opened. He had agreed with Mark's division of labour and he had also accepted the fact that, because there was no space for an office at the restaurant, the new company would use Basil Catering offices. The problem with this arrangement, largely unforeseen by Titus, was that Palmers' office was most definitely on Mark's territory and Fulham was too far to drop into comfortably. He was also aware that Jane was covertly watching him to assure herself that the restaurant was taking a back seat in their lives. Titus took to ringing Mark regularly.

'Greg's doing an excellent job,' Mark assured Titus. 'It's better for him if we let him find his feet without breathing down his neck. We'll have our meeting in a couple of weeks, shall we?'

So, with no specific reason for calling regularly into the restaurant, Titus was beginning to feel as though there was not much evidence that he was part owner of it.

'Let's have dinner at Palmers,' he suggested to Jane one morning.

'Yeah, okay,' Jane said equably. 'I'll book it.'

There was a new waiter greeting and seating when they arrived. He looked through the book. 'I'm sorry, sir, we don't seem to have a record of your booking.'

Jane read the book upside down. 'Yes, you do.' She stabbed at the book with her finger. 'Look. Palmer, eight o'clock.'

The waiter smiled confidently. He had not been wrong after all.

'The owner is called Palmer. That will be Mark's table.'

Pippa had been in bed at The Mill for over a week. She'd been put on a ventilator in the A&E department of a south London hospital and Gerry and Clattie had been able to drive her home later that night.

'I'm sorry to be such a nuisance,' she had said to Clattie as they went upstairs in the early hours of the morning when Gerry had seen them safely into the house. 'I'll be fine tomorrow. Up and about, ready to help you.'

But the next day she lay in bed, breathing more easily but pale, bog-eyed and listless. And for the next week she stayed there complaining of chest pains and headaches. Clattie called the family doctor.

'Her chest is clear,' he said. 'Knowing Pippa, I think this may be more mental than physical. I should just allow her to do what she wants. Take each day as it comes.'

Pippa clearly had no intention of returning to the community.

'It wasn't for me,' she said simply. 'I thought it was, but it wasn't. I should never have gone.' She looked at her mother, her expression full of remorse. 'I shouldn't have left you. Not when you needed me. I feel so bad about that. As soon as I'm better, I'll be able to look after you. I'll get a part-time job locally, so I can be here for you.'

Clattie sat in the chair beside Pippa's bed and at once felt bound and constricted. The web she had broken out of, in the hot Italian countryside, seemed to be spinning around her again.

'Your friend Joyce keeps ringing,' she said cautiously. 'She's very keen to speak to you.'

'I can't speak to her,' Pippa sighed. 'I didn't tell her I was going. I just slipped out.'

'I'm sure she'll forgive you for that.' Clattie saw Pippa shake her head doubtfully and continued crisply, 'I always understood forgiveness to be one of the fundamentals of Christianity; it's one of the things that sets it apart from other religions.'

Clattie was starting to prepare for Christmas, but in the light of Pippa's arrival she was beginning to regret insisting that Christmas should be at The Mill as it always had been. Jack had demanded that the family should never deviate from the traditional Christmas that they had celebrated since time immemorial. So every year, Clattie had worked herself almost to a standstill to ensure that the whole ritual was followed slavishly, from the family's arrival on Christmas Eve to the final disbandment of the party three days later – everything had to be done just as Jack's mother had done it for him and his brothers. Clattie had thought it important to do the same this year, but she hadn't reckoned with Pippa settled in upstairs, silently and inexorably sapping energy from the house and from Clattie herself.

'What about all her stuff she's left at the community?' Ralph demanded of Clattie when he and Grania came down for the weekend.

'She says she doesn't want any of it. It's only clothes—'

'Oh God, those ghastly weeds they wear.' Ralph was disparaging. 'They're certainly expendable. What about the car, though? I don't see why the community should end up with one of our cars.'

'I'll deal with it after Christmas,' Pippa said dully, when Clattie asked her.

Ralph also tried with Pippa.

'I think it's time you got up, Pip,' he suggested when he visited her bedroom. 'You're not really that ill.' He looked down at his whey-faced sister sitting up in bed and he softened his tone. 'You've got to get up and face life, you know, like we've all had to do.'

'I get an asthma attack every time I get up and go downstairs,' Pippa answered defensively.

'You can't stay up here for ever. We all need to stick together and support each other. Think about Clattie, she needs your company desperately. She's missing the Gaffer so much and she's very unhappy. Think about her.'

But when Ralph went downstairs, Gerry was sitting in his father's chair by the fire talking to Clattie and Grania. Grania was laughing and Clattie's face in the firelight looked round and smiley. For a moment, Ralph felt outside their circle of warmth.

*

On Sunday, Ralph and Grania walked back from church, the long way round, through the village.

'I'm worried about Clattie,' Ralph said.

'Why?' Grania asked. 'I think she's doing terribly well.'

'I don't like the idea of Clattie living at The Mill alone.'

'But Pippa's here at home with her.'

'Well, she is now. But for how long? You know what she's like. Anyway, at the moment, lying up in her bedroom, she's no company at all. Who can Clattie talk to?'

'There's Gerry. He seems such a nice man – a real friend.'

Had Grania not been walking with her head down, she would have seen her husband purse his lips.

'The Mill's a very big house. Too big for Clattie to manage on her own. She's very lonely, I know she is.' Ralph paused for a moment, as if searching for the right words. 'She loves living there and I'm sure she doesn't want to leave it. So I've come to the conclusion we should suggest taking over the house. I imagine it would be quite easy to make a flat for Clattie, possibly building out from the back scullery incorporating the conservatory—'

'Hold on, Ralph.' Grania broke into her husband's vision. 'We've never ever thought of living at The Mill.'

'It's the country, isn't it?' Ralph sounded defensive. Grania, looking up at his face, could see in his eyes that he was uncomfortable, but determined, about what he was saying. 'You must see how things have changed,' he continued. 'She'd never admit it, because she can be so stubborn, but I'm quite sure Clattie feels very vulnerable alone at The Mill. She's getting older and she's easy prey for anyone walking into her life and taking it over.'

Grania frowned. 'Nonsense. Clattie is an independent, energetic woman at the moment. I really think we should let her get on with living her life and wait for her to tell us what she wants. She might eventually like to live somewhere smaller than The Mill. Something easier to manage.'

'Oh, she'd hate that,' Ralph said dismissively. 'She's always lived in big houses. I shall pick the right moment, of course, but I intend to make it clear that we're prepared to come and look after her. We'll be able to keep an eye on who's coming and going and, apart from anything else, we don't want The Mill to go out of the family.' And suddenly Ralph's meaning became crystal clear to Grania. They would move into The Mill only to keep obtruders out of it.

'Titus, Greg here. Sorry to bother you, mate. Could you come over? We've got a bit of a problem with the women's bogs — water seems to be coming up through the floor.'

It was a cold and foggy Sunday evening. Jane was at the cinema with Natasha and Titus was slumped in front of a trashy television programme with no desire to take off his slippers and go out.

'Have you rung a plumber?' he asked.

Greg seemed surprised. 'No. Mark told me to contact you in the event of any building emergency.'

'Right.' Titus kept a lid on his irritation with difficulty. 'I'm not actually a builder or a plumber,' he pointed out acidly. 'I'll come and look at it, but I don't know whether I can do anything.'

He rang Mark before he left the house, but he was out and when Titus tried his mobile it was switched off.

Titus did find the problem and helped by Greg he managed to solve it.

'Well done,' said Mark when Titus got hold of him the next day. 'Excellent. Useful having you on the team; I told Greg to get in touch with you in that sort of situation. I hope that was okay. Seemed sensible, I don't know anything about plumbing or electricity.'

'I think it was just luck I could deal with that particular flood—'

'Well, thank you anyway. I must go. This is a very busy time for me.'

'About our meeting,' Titus said firmly. 'Shall we make a date?'

'Absolutely,' Mark responded buoyantly. 'I haven't got my diary on me. Can I ring you when I'm in the office?'

'That was Clattie confirming our girls' lunch tomorrow at Palmers.' Jane came back into the kitchen where Titus was cooking the supper. She grimaced. 'I'm only going for Clattie's sake. By the way, do we have to send Christmas cards to all of them?' She gestured towards the pile of half-finished home-made cards on the sideboard.

'Not Ralph, I think.' Titus brandished his knife in a stabbing gesture. 'He'd probably have a ceremonial burning. But send one to Mark and Bella.'

Jane made a face. 'I can just see what sport she would have with one of my cruddy handmade cards.'

'They're beautiful. Infinitely nicer than anything you can buy. Anyway,' Titus added, 'if we send them a card, it might jog Mark's memory that he's got a partner and one that's not just there to deal with building emergencies.'

'I thought you two were going to meet soon?'

'We're meant to be, but Mark's very busy. I suppose this time of year is one of the prime times for caterers.' Titus put down his knife and looked at Jane. 'Maybe we should have a Christmas party. Ask them to it and then I could really pin him down.'

'Give us a break.' Jane threw her dish cloth at him. 'Social occasions involving your family have not been an unmitigated success so far, have they?'

There was an air of expectation, of suppressed excitement in Palmers. Outside it was cold and grey, people walked past in thick coats, whipped up by the wind and laden with parcels. Although it was only early December, Christmas decorations were already up, organised by Greg, minimal and tasteful, and taped carols and church music played quietly in the background.

Jane arrived late on purpose. It was typical, she thought churlishly, that the other Palmers would arrive even later. Greg

171

showed her to the table and she buried herself in a newspaper.

'Hello.' Grania appeared by her side. 'God, it's Christmas here already and I haven't done a thing yet.' She looked round the restaurant. 'The others are late, I suppose. They always are. It's a family failing.'

There was a pause as the two women entered a danger zone.

'Look, there's something I want to say—' Grania began to speak, her soft face looking earnestly up at Jane.

'Hi.' Bella was suddenly between them, jangling her car keys in her hand. 'I'm a bit late – had trouble getting away from a meeting.'

Grania stood up ready to kiss her, but Bella immediately sat down, slipping off her coat. 'I should be at a book launch actually, but Clattie was so insistent.' She barely looked at Jane before turning to Grania. 'I've just been discussing holidays with my staff. When are you going down to The Mill? I'm closing the office on the twenty-third and I don't think there's a Basil booking on Christmas Eve this year. I don't know what Mark's doing about this place. I imagine it'll close on Christmas Eve so that we'll be able to get down in good time.'

Grania wondered whether her sister-in-law had chosen to discuss these arrangements now in order to exclude Jane. Embarrassed, she answered quickly. 'I've told Clattie that I'll go down the day before Christmas Eve to help with everything.'

Jane listened to the exchange with the fixed smile of someone who finds themselves in the midst of a personal conversation.

'Let's order some drink, for goodness' sake.' Bella called across the restaurant, 'Greg, can we have a bottle of house wine.' She turned to Jane as an afterthought, 'White all right with you? Grania and I usually drink white during the day and Clattie only ever drinks gin at lunch.'

Bella's expression was confrontational as she looked at Jane who was fighting an overpowering desire to get up and leave.

As if tuned in to Jane's feelings, Grania turned to her. 'How are Summer and Alby? Is Alby back for Christmas? He went away, didn't he?'

Jane joined in gratefully. 'Yes, he went off in the summer for a few months doing the usual India and Nepal trek. He decided to have his gap year after university. Now he's hanging around applying for film school and working in a local pub. It's great having him at home.'

'Cate's back for the holidays soon and of course she's bringing back everything she owns. She's only home for a month but it seems she simply can't live without her duvet and her stereo. I'll be pounding up the motorway to Leeds—'

'Here, you two earth mothers,' Bella interrupted. 'Have something to drink. Do you know who was in here last week apparently?' Bella poured the wine and named a well-known actor. 'He's a local boy and he came in with a large party and spent all evening here.' She was already bored and beginning to wish that she had gone to the book launch after all. But Mark had been keen for her to come to the lunch.

'Maybe you could get it through to Jane,' he'd said, 'that everything at Palmers is under control and that her husband should get on with his own business like I am, and stop ringing me up all the time. I'll make sure Greg knows it's a complimentary lunch,' he added. 'He'll give you something to sign, but don't make it obvious that it's a freebie otherwise Jane and Titus will be constantly entertaining all their friends for free.'

Clattie arrived in a bustle carrying John Lewis bags.

'I'm so, so sorry I'm late. I couldn't get a taxi.' She kissed Grania and Bella and then moved round the table to kiss Jane. 'Oh good, you've ordered something to drink. I'm longing for a gin and tonic. I'm quite exhausted, Christmas shopping is much more restful in the country, but then I suppose that's because there's nothing you want to buy there.' She sorted her bags under the table and looked round with an anxious expression on her pretty face. 'Now, let's have a really good lunch. This is on me.'

Clattie had tried hard to get there first. She studied the three women around the table. Jane looked dejected, Grania nervous and Bella aggrieved.

Greg brought the menus and there was silence as the four women examined them.

'The calves' liver is very good,' announced Bella. 'Have you tried it yet, Jane?'

'No, I haven't, but I've only eaten here once. This is building up to a very busy time for me, nativity plays, glueing and sticking, Christmas parties. I'm longing for the end of term, then I can unwind properly.'

Grania glanced up from her menu and gave Jane a smile in empathy. 'I miss having small children around at Christmas. Their excitement is so infectious.'

'I never knew when Christmas *was* when I was a child.' Bella surprisingly joined in the conversation. 'I could never work out when you *started* having a happy Christmas. Everyone was so hassled beforehand and always so nice on Christmas Day, but then on Boxing Day they went back to being themselves and it was as though Christmas had never happened.'

Jane thought how sad that sounded.

'Back home,' she said, her eyes softening at the thought, 'Christmas was never such a big deal. It was just one day on the beach with a barbecue for most people, then it was completely over. I'd like to take my kids back to experience Christmas in the sun one day.'

'Well, I think Christmas is thoroughly over-rated,' Bella said flatly and then, as though she had become too intimate, she rustled her menu and pushed Jane out the only way she could. 'I must speak to Mark about putting some different salads on this. Caesar salad is just too unimaginative.'

Grania felt the need to divert the conversation. 'How's Pippa?' she asked Clattie.

'Not so good. There doesn't seem much wrong with her physically although her asthma's worse than it's been for some years. She lies in bed most of the day, listening to the wireless.' Clattie gave an anxious smile. 'It's very unlike her to be so inactive. I quite miss her banging around the house, dropping things.'

*

Their food arrived and Bella took the opportunity to order another bottle of wine and more gin for Clattie. Clattie let her take charge and wondered why she looked so pale and was being quite so brittle.

Jane looked with awe at the plate put down in front of her – a great tower of exotic vegetables topped off with yellow sweet potato crisps and drizzled with balsamic vinegar.

Grania smiled across at her. 'I'd love to make something like that at home but I know I'd make a real hash of it.'

Jane took a bite. 'It's very good. Titus does most of the cooking in our house. He loves experimenting.'

'I only married Mark for his culinary skills.' Bella poked at her salad. 'But we're both so busy we don't have time to do anything much in the kitchen except eat left-overs from Basil Catering.'

The conversation stuck with food. As a topic for the four women to discuss, it was not perfect, but it was safer than most.

Clattie only half joined in the conversation. She had become painfully aware since she'd returned from her holiday that the feeling of remoteness that had so relaxed her in Italy had been purely transient. Nothing had changed in the family. Ralph's enmity was still there, colouring the lives around him. It saddened Clattie that he'd boycotted the opening party. She had had some half-formed thought that the women of this ailing family could be the ones to heal it and she was hoping this meal would bring the three of them into some sort of relationship.

Grania was wishing that she and Jane were on their own so that they could get to know each other better without Bella in the way.

Bella and Jane were wishing the same thing. They both wanted not to be there.

They all refused pudding, despite the waiter's enthusiastic reading from his pad. Bella got out a small gold-edged Smythson notebook and began writing.

'Just a reminder for Mark,' she said, looking up when she had finished and snapping her pen shut. 'I really think it would be better if the puddings were included in the general menu.'

Jane pursed her lips in recognition of Bella's little game and Clattie jumped into the silence. 'How's Summer getting on at college? She tells me she's going to try for art school.'

Bella's mobile rang and she answered it, speaking in short, sharp sentences while looking at her watch. She clicked her phone off and said with an air of relief, 'I've got to get back to the office. I'm sorry to break up the party, Clattie.'

She remembered about the bill and said in a low voice to Clattie, 'I'll just sign the bill on my way out, so you don't have to worry about that.'

'It's all right, darling, I shall deal with it.' Clattie, looking up in surprise, spoke brusquely. 'You just get back to work.'

Bella left with a distinct feeling that the others were rather relieved to see her go. The lunch party had been a strain for her. Like most things at the moment. Keeping up an appearance of strength had been hard; patronising Jane had not given her much pleasure in the end – it had been a pyrrhic victory and she was left with a strangely nasty taste in her mouth. As she drove back to the office, she couldn't shake a vision of the three women settling down to easy conversation now that she had gone. It made Bella feel uncomfortably left out.

'Let's have another drink,' Clattie said when Bella had swept off. 'My train doesn't go till five and I wouldn't mind a brandy.'

Clattie watched Bella leave with mixed feelings. Bella had seemed tense and nervy. She looked tired and stressed and her deliberate provocation seemed to be coming from some barely controlled inner rage. Yet Clattie felt that she had glimpsed some sort of sadness in Bella's eyes.

'Mark and Bella are always so busy.' Clattie sighed. 'Sometimes I wonder when they ever have time to see each other.'

Natasha's remark about Mark and another woman floated into Jane's head.

'I never had a proper career,' Grania said meditatively, 'and I

176

really don't regret it at all. I enjoyed being at home with the children but now I'm really rather looking forward to them going off on their own, leaving Ralph and me with time together.'

'I don't know.' Jane smiled at Grania. 'The thing is, children are always coming home and they expect their home and their parents to be exactly as they left them. Never mind that you might be moving on in their absence. There's no one more set in their ways than young adults.'

Grania laughed. 'No, you're quite right.'

'You're still planning on moving to the country, aren't you?' Clattie asked.

'Well, yes, we were . . . but . . .' Grania faltered, unable to be completely honest. 'Ralph seems to have gone off that idea at the moment.'

'He's not being particularly easy just now, is he?' Clattie sounded so sympathetic, Grania could feel the tears beginning to burn behind her eyes.

'No, not really.'

It was a relief to both Jane and Grania that Clattie had openly acknowledged the enormous barrier that stood between the two of them being friends.

Grania turned to Jane. The disloyalty she felt talking about Ralph was outweighed by the relief of being able to share some of her unhappiness.

'I'm afraid Ralph is still taking all this very hard. He misses his father, of course, but he just can't accept Titus. He's feeling marginalised: Mark having this place with Titus has really upset him and he thinks Pippa doesn't seem to be bothered about it all. I don't think he knows who to blame, so he's blaming us all.' Grania looked apologetically between Jane and Clattie. 'He's in some sort of denial and I think he feels that if he acknowledges you and Titus, you'll exist and then there'll be a tie between us all.'

Jane thought of Kit and Summer and her heart went out to Grania. Another secret that would cause pain and disruption.

'It must be so hard for you,' she said inadequately.

What she really wanted to say was that it wasn't easy for them either and that Ralph's denial was, in some silent way, affecting her family as well. She wanted to point out that the restaurant had changed their lives; that she feared that Titus would never be content with what he had had before it came into being. She wanted to say that she hated being barely tolerated by this new family; hated Bella's obvious hostility, Mark's cynical machinations to get his hands on the warehouse and Pippa's indifference. She really wanted to say that now she had met them she desperately wished the family had been kept secret for ever.

But she said none of this out loud.

Grania said to Jane, 'I should love to hear about your family, Jane. We know so little about you . . .' She hesitated and looked at Clattie, momentarily embarrassed by the unwitting implication of her mother-in-law's part in the concealment. 'When did you come over to England?'

'About thirty years ago and I met Titus at a party twenty-eight years ago this month . . .'

Grania and Jane began to talk, exchanging their histories and gradually becoming friends – if only for a lunchtime.

Clattie eventually looked at her watch. 'I must go. I need to get my train. Gerry is meeting me.'

'It's nice for you to have Gerry as a friend,' Grania said comfortably.

'Yes, it is. He's such a dear man.' The way Clattie's face softened and her eyes darkened, made Jane wonder if there was another family secret being kept.

Clattie called for the bill. 'By the way,' she looked at Jane, 'you will all come down for the day after New Year as usual, won't you?' She looked apologetically at them both and said, 'When the others have gone.' She paused for a moment and then said boldly, 'I'm afraid at the moment it still has to be like that, but I hope not for ever.'

'We do seem to be the social outcasts,' Jane said sombrely.

Grania stretched out her hand. 'It's a horrible situation,' she said with feeling. 'I wish we could all be together at The Mill. I'd love the children to get to know each other. After all, they are cousins.'

Clattie paid the bill, despite Greg's insistence that it was taken care of.

'Don't be silly. If I can't support my son's venture, I don't know what I can do.'

Grania offered to drive Clattie to the station, but Clattie was determined to take a taxi. 'We must do this again,' Clattie said, clambering into the minicab.

Grania and Jane smiled at each other in agreement.

'It would be nice to keep in touch,' Grania said shyly.

'Yes. Yes, it would,' Jane responded with genuine feeling.

Yet neither woman made that social leap of asking for the other's telephone number.

Grania saw Kit and Summer while she was sitting in her car at the traffic lights. The afternoon play on the radio was coming to a climactic end as she gazed idly at the people, heads down against the swirling wind, going in and out of the Underground station. A young couple were entwined against a nearby doorway. Grania watched them vaguely, her mind wandering through the past couple of hours. The lights changed and the car in front of hers stalled. Grania concentrated as she manoeuvred round it, but she missed the green light and now she was almost beside the loving couple in the doorway. Like the slow development of a photograph, a picture was gradually forming in her head, and as the couple broke away from each other, holding hands until the last minute, Grania saw the boy turn towards the station. Although she must have recognised him subconsciously, it was still a surprise when she saw it was Kit. She only felt shock when she turned her head round and saw that the girl was Summer. And there was no doubting the relationship between them. The lights changed and someone hooted at her from behind. She lurched forward in the wrong gear and by the time she looked back Kit had disappeared down the station stairs.

*

Clattie let herself into The Mill, dumped her parcels, shed her overcoat, and called up the stairs with her usual whistle.

'I'm home.'

There was no reply and Clattie went upstairs. Pippa's bed was empty, the bedclothes pushed back.

'Pippa.' Clattie checked the empty bathroom and felt a bump of panic. 'Pippa.' She moved down the stairs, looked into the drawing room and finding it empty she went into the book room. Pippa was sitting on the floor in front of the wood stove. Beside her were two drawers of loose photographs and a pile of family photograph albums. She looked up as Clattie came in.

'Didn't you hear me calling?' Clattie demanded crossly and then immediately changed her voice as she saw Pippa's tearstained face. 'Oh, darling, I'm sorry.' She crossed the room and sat down beside her daughter.

'Look, here's Mousie.' Pippa handed Clattie a faded photograph of a pony. She turned the photo over and read the back. Mousie, Seldon Gymkhana 1965. 'Do you remember how cross the Gaffer used to get?' Pippa went on. 'He was horrid to Mark about riding and Mark did so hate it. Gaffer would make him get back on every time he fell off. And Mousie used to bite him.'

Clattie remembered the frequent and often traumatic scenes between the young Mark and his father.

'Your father was a very good horseman. He wanted all of you to be too.'

'I expect I was just lucky,' Pippa said. 'I always liked horses and riding – and,' she added perspicaciously, 'I was the only daughter and the youngest. He was always nice to me.' She smiled weakly. 'I suppose, if I'm honest, I was a bit spoilt.'

'Yes, I'm afraid you were a little. He was so pleased to have a daughter.'

'I liked him spoiling me; it made me feel safe.' Pippa seemed almost to be talking to herself. 'While he was alive, I could be a child.' Tears began to roll down her cheeks again. 'The awful thing is, I think I'm crying for me.'

'That's all right. It's what you do when you mourn,' explained

Clattie. 'You're sad for yourself that a person you love is no longer there for you.'

Pippa rustled through the pile of photographs and picked out one of the Gaffer sitting in a garden chair, his face obscured by a garden hat. Her shoulders began to shake and she held the photo against her body as the sobs shuddered out of her.

Clattie knelt down and put her arms around her, cradling her in her arms. She welcomed her daughter's tears – they had been a long time coming. She had begun to think that Christianity had completely deodorised her daughter's emotions.

'I loved the Gaffer because I know he loved me. I'm so lonely without him.'

Clattie's immediate thought was shockingly selfish. And I was so lonely *with* him.

Titus and Mark eventually had their meeting at Palmers just before Christmas. Mark handed Titus a sheet of paper.

'The monthly profit and loss accounts. Don't read too much into them. As I'm sure you know from your own experience, the first few months of any business are usually up and down. We started well – a bit disappointing in the last couple of weeks, I must admit, but to be expected. We're working ourselves into a routine. Greg's proving a good man but it takes time for advertising and word of mouth to kick in.' Mark was obviously in a hurry.

'So what are we doing about opening over Christmas?' Titus asked.

Mark looked at him in surprise, almost as though Titus had asked an inappropriately personal question.

'We're closing on the twenty-third for the week, reopening for New Year's Eve. Bella and I go down to The Mill on Christmas Eve for a few days and then on to friends in Wiltshire and back for New Year.'

'I'm here between Christmas and New Year,' Titus offered.

Mark looked slightly bemused, as if trying to work out the relevance of Titus's remark. 'I'm happy to put in some hours if it means we can stay open,' Titus went on.

'Oh, it's just not worth opening between Christmas and New Year. We'd have to pay staff.' Mark paused. 'I mean, what do you think? All business is usually put on hold in that week.'

Titus capitulated. 'Yeah, you're right, I suppose. Most of London shuts down then.'

'Greg's got it all under control.' Mark spoke smoothly. 'He and the assistant manager will sort out the shifts between them.'

'Assistant manager?' Titus didn't know they had one.

'Yes. Athene.' Mark made a face. 'Hell, I'm sorry, Titus, I meant to ring you about that or at least send you a memo, but I've been so busy I've got behind with everything. Anyway, Athene's the best waitress we have and we wanted to make sure she stayed, so Greg suggested making her his assistant.'

'I see. I would like to have been consulted.'

'Of course. *Mea culpa*. Won't happen again. In fact I'll tell you now, while I remember, we should change the menus after Christmas. Obviously want your input. Now,' Mark raised his glass in a conversation-terminating gesture, 'if we're finished here . . .? Happy Christmas and here's to a very lucrative new year for us both.'

The point that Titus wanted to make to Mark was in danger of being hijacked by Christmas spirit.

'This menu change, we'll discuss it at the next meeting then?'

'That has to be a separate meeting, because obviously Chef and Greg need to be involved. I'll ring you about that one.'

And with that Titus had to be satisfied. At least to be going on with.

Mark glanced at his watch, drained his glass and stood up. 'I must go.' He paused for a moment. 'Actually, I've been meaning to ask you, do you play cricket?'

Titus shook his head. 'Nope, sorry. I'm not really much of a sportsman. Used to chew the sleeves of my jersey during PE at school.'

'Oh. That's a shame,' Mark said. 'Greg and I are starting a restaurant eleven. You could have joined us.'

*

'So I won't see you for at least two weeks then,' Kit said miserably to Summer. 'We're off skiing for a week straight after Christmas.'

'Oh super,' Summer said sarcastically. 'Do we have a skiing house too?'

'No, we don't, and don't be like that. I'd much rather be here with you.'

'Well, why don't you say you don't want to go?'

'I can't, it's been booked since last year. We always go at this time.'

Summer and Kit were in the pub. Their last meeting before Christmas. Kit had given Summer her present – a silver bracelet, bought on the advice of Ed's sister – Summer had given Kit a mobile phone that he could see no way of disguising from his parents. They knew he didn't have that sort of money. Questions would be asked.

'Wow,' he said when he opened it. 'These are really expensive, you shouldn't have.'

'Unlike you, little rich boy with no cash,' Summer said with a smile, 'I have a Saturday job and I earn money. And, anyway, it's crap not being able to ring you.' She rustled in her bag. 'I've got something else for you too.' She brought out a piece of paper and handed it to Kit. It was a voucher for an appointment at a tattoo parlour. 'We're going to have matching tattoos done when you get back.'

Kit looked down at the piece of paper in dismay. If a mobile phone was complicated to explain, a tattoo would be much more controversial.

'I think we should have them on our shoulders,' Summer said. 'I'm going to design us something really fab and groovy.'

Kit looked across at Summer – her dark eyes shining and her glossy lips smiling – and he thought that it didn't really matter. He would have his whole body tattooed for her if that was what she wanted.

'Shit, I wish you were spending Christmas with us,' he said. 'It'll be so boring, especially without Gaff.'

Summer dangled her bottle of lager by its neck. 'Yeah, it would be good, wouldn't it? What's it like spending Christmas at The Mill? I bet Clattie makes a brilliant Christmas.' She spoke enviously.

Kit shrugged. 'It's okay, but it's always the same, very traditional. We have Christmas dinner in the evening and everyone dresses up. Gaff always insists – insisted – on a toast before we pulled the crackers. He was most particular about that and it was always the same toast: "Absent friends". I never really understood it.'

'Hey, maybe that was us. Absent friends?' Summer sounded hopeful.

'Yeah, maybe it was. Who knows. Anyway, we were never allowed to stay up for dinner until we'd had our eighth birthday.'

Summer grimaced. 'Eh? Why not? That doesn't sound very fair.'

Kit shrugged. 'No, but it's always been like that. Under eight, you went to bed with a present. Actually, I preferred it to staying up to begin with. I hated having to dress smart for dinner and sit there for hours. It's quite fun now, though.'

'So what do you do all day if you don't have lunch?'

'I don't know, usual stuff. Open stockings, go to church – Dad and Pippa make us do that – go for a walk and at tea-time we light the candles on the tree and open our presents. I suppose it's all right.' Kit turned gloomy. 'But it would be better if you were there.'

Summer wanted to be there too. She had this rather upsetting feeling that she was missing out on something much more fun and to which, in a way, she now felt she had a definite right.

'Well,' she said in an aggrieved voice, putting on her coat, 'I hope you have a good time. And skiing. I'll see you when you get back to London.'

Kit sensed Summer's change of mood and stood up.

'Hey.' He took her hand. 'What's the matter?'

Summer struggled for a moment and then gave Kit a small

smile. 'Forget it. I'll just be bored without you, that's all. Anyway,' she tapped the bag Kit was holding, 'at least we can phone each other now. It's the same network as me, so calls are cheap.'

Kit couldn't bear to let her leave. The next couple of weeks stretched out drearily in front of him.

'Don't go yet, it's early,' he said desperately. 'Have another drink, or let's go somewhere.'

Summer smiled mischievously at him. 'You could come home with me, if you like. I'm sure Jane and Titus would love to see you.'

'That's not what I meant.'

Summer took pity on him, her good humour almost completely restored.

'Come on. The house is empty. Everyone's gone back home for Christmas and I've got the keys.' She dangled them in front of Kit. 'We can be completely on our own.'

Later that night, back in her own bed, Summer lay awake in the darkness. She couldn't get the picture of Christmas at The Mill out of her head. Drawing on every image of Christmas she could think of, she imagined that it would be just like Christmas in a book: thick snow outside the windows, carol singers at the door, holly boughs along the mantelpieces, candles all over the house, the long dining-room table piled high with crackers and sweetmeats. *Absent friends*. Summer felt left out. She wanted to be there and it made her wonder if her father used to feel the same when he was a little boy and not part of the Palmer family.

Chapter Eight

There is a certain security in tradition, but when tradition becomes superfluous to requirements, or inappropriate, security can turn into a kind of imprisonment. Christmas at The Mill — and everyone was wishing they were somewhere else. There was, among the whole family, a distinct air of going through the motions.

The Mill had been transformed into Christmas: thick branches of holly and fir framed every picture, candles glowed on richly polished furniture and there were heavy scents of pine, cooking pastry, cinnamon and warm wine in the air. In the drawing room, Razor sat below the large tree, his eyes mesmerised by the twinkling decorations in its branches. The Mill was dressed, ready for the festive season as it always had been.

Pippa entered into the preparations with a renewed energy: shopping, cooking and decorating the house at a frenetic pace. It was as if, with the help of the photographs, she had cried her grief in and then out again — acknowledged and accepted her father's death and had now let him go.

Clattie was feeling very responsible for this Christmas. She wanted to make it the same as usual, but she knew it was impossible and she wished she had never embarked on this herculean task.

'Don't expect too much,' advised Gerry, who was going, as he always did, to a cousin in Norfolk for his Christmas. 'The first Christmas without someone is always the worst.'

Grania was sitting on the floor in their bedroom stuffing the children's stockings. Ralph thought they were too old for stockings, but Grania couldn't quite bring herself to stop them. Someone banged on the door.

'Don't come in. Secrets,' she shouted. Secrets. She'd always hated secrets and now there was another one. One big secret had fostered so many little ones. Yesterday, before everyone arrived, Grania had come upon Clattie and Gerry in the drawing room. There was an almost childlike softness in Clattie's eyes as she unwrapped a book that Gerry had just handed to her and Grania had watched her smile at him and he return the affection with his eyes. Grania was left in little doubt as to their feelings for each other. Here was a new secret that she must keep to protect Ralph. His son and Titus's daughter now and his mother replacing the Gaffer with another man – the ultimate betrayal of his father, the conspiracy he believed in, would be proved finally and irrevocably. Through the thick forest of anger and hurt in his head, he couldn't and wouldn't see that the real betrayal was, of course, his father's.

There was another knock on the door, a cursory one this time, and Pippa came in without waiting for an answer.

'I thought you might like some help,' she said, plumping herself on the floor beside Grania.

Grania moved a pile of presents to make room for her. 'Thanks,' she said as graciously as she could. She'd been pleased to be on her own up here.

'Is this Caitlin's?' Pippa picked up an empty stocking. 'Tangerine at the bottom? Does everything have to be wrapped? Clattie always wrapped everything in ours.' She began cutting up wrapping paper. 'I hope we all have a good Christmas.

187

Clattie does want it to be like it always is.' Her eyes clouded. 'It can't quite be, of course, but we must all try to make it as jolly as possible, I think.'

'Everyone thinks that. We'll all do our best.' Grania rolled up a pair of boxer shorts in tissue paper and stuffed them into Kit's football sock. 'So what are you going to do after Christmas?'

Pippa stopped wrapping and sat back on her haunches. 'I'm staying here. Clattie needs me here so I've decided to look for some sort of office job near by.' Pippa made a wry face. 'Isn't that traditionally what the youngest unmarried daughter does? Stays at home to look after Mother?'

'I don't think she has to, not in this day and age.'

'I didn't mean to sound resentful.' Pippa looked worried. 'What I meant was, I don't have anything else to do. No career or lover or anything.'

'So you're definitely not going back to the community?'

'It didn't work out. I was older than most of the others and somehow the community just made me feel a bit of a failure.'

'Then it certainly isn't the place to be,' said Grania.

Pippa started stuffing her stocking with forceful jerky movements. 'I'm forty-three years old and what have I got to show for it? I've done nothing with my life.' She sighed gloomily. 'I haven't got a husband, or children; all my relationships have foundered sooner rather than later. I sometimes wonder what's the matter with me.'

'Absolutely nothing—'

'I mean, in seven years I shall be fifty.'

'Now you're sounding like Bella,' Grania said with a smile. 'She's dreading being fifty next year. Throwing HRT and ginseng down herself because she can't bear the idea of getting old and wrinkly—'

'I can't really see Bella as old and wrinkly, she's way too beautiful. Anyway, she's always treated her body like a temple. I don't see her accepting the idea of cellulite without a fight. Do you know?' Pippa stopped wrapping a bottle of bath oil. 'I really don't mind that bit, not at all. You can't stop old age, whatever

Bella thinks. No, I want being older to mean that I'm more gentle and receptive. That I'm content with what I've got instead of worrying about what I haven't.'

Grania nodded her head in agreement. 'A very good philosophy. Not easy to stick to, though.'

'Anyway,' Pippa's voice turned sprightly, 'I shall stay here and look after Clattie, certainly for the time being. And then if things change . . .' She smiled ruefully. 'I expect I'll find someone else to look after, don't you?'

'Where did you get that?' Caitlin came into the book room as Kit switched off his mobile phone.

'Um . . . off Ed. He's selling it to me cheap. He's got two.'

'Oh yeah?' Caitlin looked at him disbelievingly.

'Yes. I'm hoping I can pay him off with Clattie's Christmas cheque.'

'Who were you talking to?'

'Just a friend.'

Caitlin looked at him intently for a moment. Kit could almost see her brain working.

'You're not still hanging out with that Summer, are you?'

'No. No.'

Caitlin grinned and poked him.

'You so are. If you get caught . . .' She shook her head. 'Man, I wouldn't want to be you.'

'Don't say anything, will you?'

'What, and make Dad even more pissed off than he is already? Of course I won't.' She looked seriously at Kit. 'But do be careful, honestly. Dad is really upset at the moment and you can tell Mum is worried about him.'

When she had left the room, Kit pressed redial – he had to hear Summer's voice once more.

On Christmas afternoon Mark went into the book room to make a phone call on his mobile and found Kit on his, talking quietly. He looked up guiltily as his uncle came in and Mark, moving through the conservatory into the garden, wondered vaguely what his nephew was up to. He dialled a number.

'Happy Christmas, you.' Freddie sounded cheerful. 'Having a good time?'

'Nope. It's hell. Everyone is very tense.'

'Oh, we're having rather a good one here.'

Mark was not interested in Freddie's Christmas. 'Families! Who'd have them. Thank God I haven't got any children to fuck up. This is the longest three days of my life. I can't wait to get out.'

He didn't say that, even with the Gaffer no longer in the house, his sense of mastery and self-worth were slowly declining, as though the house itself were sucking power from him – just as his father had.

'Ralph is only just managing to remain civil to me,' Mark continued. 'Pippa is in overdrive, looking after us all. Grania sews, Clattie watches us anxiously, and my wife is behaving most oddly.'

He didn't tell Freddie that when they got back from midnight mass, Bella had, for once, instigated sex. Mark needed sex and had enjoyed it, but the face he saw on the pillow below him was Freddie's younger one, laughing up at him.

Bella had forced herself to make the effort with Mark in bed, and once they'd got started she was surprised and pleased to find that her body still worked and that she had not forgotten how to work Mark's body. It felt as though they were together again, sharing something just like they used to. Afterwards, with Mark still on top of her, their hearts pounding together, she said, 'When we leave here, let's go abroad for a week, somewhere nice, just the two of us. We could go on to Florence or something.'

'Not a hope. I need to put some work into Basil and I don't want to leave Palmers for that long.' Mark rolled off her. 'There'll be a dip after Christmas, everyone's too short of money to eat out. I want to get together with Greg and work out some promotional ideas, get the punters in. We're going to need them. I think now's the time to start an advertising push. I had this idea . . .'

Mark's voice droned on and, feeling spurned, Bella retreated into her head again and tried not to think of the future as a long, lonely line of nothing.

Clattie sat at her dressing table and wearily creamed off her make-up. Boxing Day was over and for that she was much relieved. She had watched the family soldier through the rituals of Christmas, each one an island, preoccupied with their own anxieties. Ralph had tried to take his father's place while still leaving a space for his memory, but there was no warmth emanating from him. Clattie had covertly observed him in church – he and Pippa the only two kneeling properly on their hassocks – and she had seen his set face and wondered what he was praying for this Christmas morning.

Clattie finished creaming her face and got into bed. She turned her head towards the photograph of Jack on the chest of drawers and wondered fancifully whether he was hovering somewhere above them, watching them all trying to pretend, just for Christmas, that something had not disintegrated with his death. Natural conversation had been made heavy and stilted by the unspoken presence of the taboo subjects . . . and what else? Clattie could feel the secrets kept between them all. Bella was quiet, seemingly only half here, Grania watchful, stoically sewing at every free moment as if to keep herself occupied and grounded. Mark was resentful with Ralph, tense and sullen. Even Kit and Caitlin were subdued and Pippa exhausted herself and the rest of them by running around trying to please. Clattie had waited apprehensively for the underlying discord between the family to come to a head, but everyone continued to circle warily round each other, self-contained and holding on tightly to their emotions.

Now, getting into bed and turning off her light, Clattie wished they all had the courage to spread their secrets on the floor for everyone to see and then somehow to start at the bottom again, slowly climbing up to some sort of harmony. Restless, she lay awake for most of the night, thinking about her own culpability.

Mark and Bella were the first to leave the next day. There was a feeling of relief that their enforced Christmas incarceration was now at an end.

The rest of them were having a cold lunch in the kitchen when the front door bell rang.

Pippa got up and went into the hall.

'Who's she talking to?' Ralph said, as they heard her greeting someone with surprise.

Pippa came back into the kitchen, ushering in a young woman carrying a small suitcase.

'This is Joyce, a sister in the community,' she announced. 'Isn't she kind? She's brought my car back.'

Clattie, her fork suspended in the air, recovered first. 'How very thoughtful. Would you like some lunch? You must be hungry after your journey.'

Joyce declined the offer with a smile as she went round the table shaking hands with everyone.

'I've suggested she stay the night.' Pippa's eyes had a wary look in them.

'Of course.' Clattie struggled to her feet. 'We'll need to put some clean sheets on the bed in the yellow room—'

'I'll do it.' Pippa indicated that her mother should sit. 'Come with me, Joyce.'

'Well, it's good we've got the car back,' Ralph said. 'But I don't like the look of her suitcase. She's obviously planning to stay.'

'She was one of Pippa's friends in the community,' Clattie pointed out. 'If Pippa wants her to stay, then of course she must.'

Ralph looked disturbed. 'I know what these sort of Christians are like. They don't like to let their disciples go, even one like my sister. She might want to stay until she's reconverted Pippa.'

He looked at his watch. 'We should go. I'll ring you, Clattie. Watch the bag lady. Don't let her stay more than one night – you might never get rid of her.'

'I'm quite able to control who comes and goes in my own house, Ralph,' Clattie said irritably.

Grania saw her husband raise his eyebrows and purse his lips as he got up from the table.

Titus and Jane spent New Year's Eve at home together. Jane loathed English New Year parties; she could never understand why people would want to turn out on a cold, foul night and kiss total strangers, fervently wishing them a happy New Year, in the full knowledge that they probably wouldn't meet again until the next New Year's Eve party. Alby and Summer, not sharing her view, had gone out in a flurry of scent and mobile phone calls from their friends.

Titus cooked pheasant and profiteroles and the two of them sat round the kitchen table.

'I must ring Mark tomorrow,' Titus said.

'And I should ring Clattie about going down to The Mill,' Jane said.

'I don't want to go,' Titus answered shortly.

'Why not?'

Titus poured more wine. 'I just don't. I don't think we should go there again. It's all changed. The Mill, Clattie, them, everything to do with the Gaffer has become more complicated now.'

Jane thought for a moment. 'Are you saying it was easier when it was a secret?'

'I didn't have to deal with it then. It was just as it had always been.'

'By not going down to see Clattie, you're *certainly* not dealing with it now.' Jane's voice was sharp. 'For pity's sake, Titus. The man is dead, the family myth has been exposed. You've got to get it sorted in your own head.'

'God, you can be so Australian sometimes,' Titus said unkindly. 'Why does it have to be sorted? Why do you think things always have to be taken out and dealt with? Some things are best left to lie.'

'God, you can be so English sometimes,' Jane responded. 'Uptight, self-deceiving, and that's just for starters. I can tell you're not prepared to let things lie. It's gnawing away at you. If you worked out exactly what you think about your family, you'd feel better about it.'

'I feel perfectly all right about it. Why can't we just forget any of them exist?'

'Just possibly,' Jane said crisply, 'because you've entered into a business arrangement with one of them.'

'Titus is becoming disagreeably persistent,' Mark said. 'He's left three messages on my answer machine and we've only been back at work a few days.'

'You can hardly blame him,' Freddie said, picking at the grapes in front of her. 'It's not unreasonable for him to want to know how his business is going.'

Bella was away for the night on company business, Freddie's husband was visiting his mother and Mark had cooked Freddie dinner at his house.

'Titus doesn't really want to get involved,' Mark was saying, as he worked the espresso machine. 'He just *thinks* he does. I'd better find him something harmless to do, I suppose, keep him off my back while I try and make the place work for us.'

Freddie, fidgeting with her glass, looked up. 'It's going okay, isn't it?'

'Ish. Post Christmas is a testing time. It needs to be doing better. And Basil,' Mark spoke tersely, 'is not good.' He was relieved to talk about it. He'd found keeping his increasing concern to himself a strain over Christmas. 'I haven't told Bella, but actually, between you and me, I'm a bit edgy. We were well down on Christmas bookings, and I've just had a salmonella scare. It wasn't salmonella, as it turned out – just a couple of guests allergic to something – but people lose trust so easily. Orders are still down and enquiries have dried up completely at the moment. The accountant's on my back, big time. I hate to say this, but thank God for Bella servicing my loans. I'd pretty much be looking at disaster without that.'

'Come on,' Freddie encouraged. 'This is always a bad time of year, you said so yourself. You can get the customers back – in both places.' She grinned, willing him to rouse himself. 'It just calls for a charm offensive mixed with a bit of your bullying skills. You're the master of that combination. I've seen you do it.'

Mark brought the coffee over and grinned back at her.

'Yes, you're right, it'll be okay. I've just got to work at it. I plan to make some serious money from this enterprise.'

'Money won't necessarily make you happy, you know.'

Mark looked at her as though she'd said something stupid. 'Of course money will make me happy, it makes everyone happy. With money I can do what I want, preferably before I get too old to enjoy it.'

'And what *do* you want to do?' Freddie asked. Mark looked blankly at her. 'I mean,' she went on, suddenly pettish with him, 'given that your whole life has been dedicated to the pursuit of money, what exactly do you want to do when you've got it?'

Mark looked sideways at his mistress who was rarely so sharp with him.

'Oh, I'll find things, don't worry. I'm not being greedy. I only want *enough* money—'

Freddie interrupted him. 'There is no such thing as enough money, Mark. When it comes to money, the goal posts are constantly moving. Trust me, I'm married to an economist. I know these things.'

'You don't understand. Money that you've made yourself gives you power to call the shots.' Mark looked at Freddie fiercely. 'I want to prove that I'm not an also-ran. I want to sit back and raise two fingers,' he spoke through gritted teeth, 'to my dear, dead father – show him I'm a chip off the old block after all.' He paused for a moment in thought. 'And I also wish

195

that one day my brother bitterly regrets that he gave me no support when I asked him for it. That's what I wish.'

'Do you know what my grandmother used to say to me?' Freddie said, standing up and taking Mark's hand. 'She used to say to me, "Careful what you wish for, little girl, for you shall surely have it." You should think about that. Anyway, right now, Mark, I wish that you would stop talking and take me upstairs to your bed.'

In the lightening hours of the dawn, Freddie woke up to see Mark standing at the window – shoulders drooped, a small paunch hanging over his boxer shorts – staring out, lost in thought. She studied him lazily from the bed and her first passing thought was why men never got fat legs no matter how fat their bellies became. Her second thought was how very downcast he looked and how unconfident he'd seemed the evening before. Somehow it made him seem much less attractive.

'Hello,' she said softly. As Mark turned round, she thought he suddenly looked terribly old.

Clattie felt that the strain of Christmas would not be at an end until she'd got over the hurdle of Jane and Titus's visit. She wasn't sure how Pippa would take to the idea of them at The Mill. Although able to talk about her father easily and naturally, the subject of Titus and his place in the family was never mentioned by her. Joyce had stayed for three days, sitting in the same chair every day like a pouter pigeon, in a moat of loose clothing, sewing her tapestry with dogged intensity. Her vapid conversation began to weigh heavily on Clattie. And also, it seemed, on Pippa.

'How long do you think Joyce is intending to stay?' Clattie asked curiously.

'I don't know,' Pippa said, making a guilty face. 'I haven't the heart to say anything to her. I've dropped a few hints but I think she's enjoying being back in a proper home and I know just how she feels.'

'Tell her to go and find her own proper home then,' Ralph had advised over the phone from London.

'Is she trying to get you to come back to the community?' Clattie asked Pippa.

'Not really. She's tried a bit, but I've told her categorically that's it's not right for me. I've made it clear that you need me, and I have to be here with you.'

Clattie felt exhausted by her responsibility to need Pippa.

In the end it was a telephone call from Meredith that sent Joyce scampering back to the community.

'Mrs Palmer?' He spoke formally when Clattie answered the telephone. 'I believe one of our sisters is with you.' Clattie was about to call Joyce when Meredith continued. 'We were sorry to lose Pippa. She has a lot to give but she must find the right place to give it. There is some place that will benefit from all she has to offer. There is somewhere for her to flourish, I know it, and I'm quite sure she'll find it one day.'

Clattie was surprised to find herself much comforted by Meredith's words.

Jane was tentative about her welcome at The Mill.

'I'm afraid Titus is tied up,' she said hesitantly when she telephoned Clattie, 'so it'll only be me and the children. We'll just come down for the day. Is that okay?'

Pippa was clearing out one of the garden sheds when Clattie broached the subject of Jane's arrival. She looked up at her mother over a pile of cardboard boxes, her face flushed and dusty.

'Who?'

'Jane, Alby and Summer are coming down for lunch tomorrow,' Clattie repeated patiently.

'Oh right. I think we've got some pork pie left or do you want me to make a hot meal? I could make a moussaka. What do you think?' Pippa wouldn't let her mother in. 'I'll just finish this. I'd better rustle up a pudding, I suppose. What about a big mincemeat pie or do you think we're all fed up with them?'

Pippa stayed working in the shed all day until a mild asthma attack brought her inside.

Watching Pippa with Jane, Alby and Summer when they arrived, Clattie saw her daughter take the middle way with them – not angry like Ralph, not accepting like Mark – but treating them cursorily, as though they were insignificant guests who were passing through. She prattled politely at them and then excused herself to cook the lunch.

Jane looked tired, Clattie thought, and she left her reading the newspaper on the sofa while she joined Summer and Alby for a walk round the village with Razor.

In the kitchen, Pippa heard Clattie and the others in the hall getting ready to go out. Clattie called to her and Pippa answered. 'Lunch in three-quarters of an hour.'

The front door banged and Pippa turned the radio on and concentrated on boiling sugar and grating lemons for the pudding. It was as she was leaning across the back of the Aga to pick up the old china vegetable dish that her hand caught the side of the saucepan with the sugar in it. The saucepan tipped and bubbling liquid fell on to her wrist. Pippa shrieked, stepped back and dropped the vegetable dish. It smashed against the front of the Aga and lay in large pieces at her feet. The design on the dish had been a hunting scene, yet the painting on each broken piece seemed, strangely, almost complete as she looked down at them spread over the floor.

Clutching her wrist, Pippa sank to her knees, her first thought to pick up the china and try to piece it together. Suddenly someone was crouching beside her.

'What's happened? Are you hurt?' Jane gently took Pippa's hand away from her wrist. 'Shit, that's not good. Come here.' She helped Pippa to her feet and drew her towards the sink.

'What happened?' Jane asked again as she held Pippa's hand under the tap.

Pippa felt the cold water ease the burn but she pulled away.

'Nothing, it was a silly accident. I'm making lemon toffee pudding and I spilt the sugar. It's fine, please, honestly.' She wrenched her arm away and moved towards the Aga. Her foot kicked against a piece of china.

'I've broken the dish,' Pippa wailed. 'It was the Gaffer's favourite. He loved it.' She knelt down and the tears began to stream down her cheeks. 'I've broken his dish,' she sobbed.

Jane, now beside her, began picking up the pieces. Pippa snatched them out of her hand.

'Leave them. Don't touch them. I'll do it,' she said sharply. 'Owww!' she clasped her wrist instinctively as the reddening burn flared up again and the pain stung her skin.

'Pippa.' Jane's voice rang out clearly. 'Go and put your wrist back under cold water. You can pick up the pieces later. You must cool the burn down or it'll blister.'

The cold water again made the pain subside and Pippa began to calm down.

'I'm so sorry, such a stupid thing to do and I'm making such a fuss.' She put on a polite voice. 'I'm fine now. Please do go back and—'

'Shut up, Pippa,' Jane said firmly but not unkindly.

'I loved this dish too,' Pippa said in her normal voice. 'The Gaffer used to tell me the story of the hunt and then I'd eat the peas that were in them.' She smiled for a moment. 'I hated peas. I still do.' She looked at Jane. 'I thought you'd all gone out.'

'No, I stayed and let Clattie have Alby and Summer to herself for a while.'

'Why?'

'Because they're fond of each other.'

Pippa was silent, her face blank. Then she looked down at the pieces of china, tears welling up again. 'How could I have been so clumsy? Such a special dish.'

'It was an accident. It could have happened to anyone.'

'But it happened to me. Are they really fond of Clattie?'

'Yes, of course. We all are.'

'Where's Titus?'

'He didn't want to come. He's . . .' Jane searched for the words. 'He's unhappy about the family thing. He feels excluded. Unwanted.'

'Why?'

'Because . . .' Jane hesitated. 'Because your father's death has made him see that he ought to confront things and he doesn't want to. He wants it to go back to what it was before.'

'So do I.' Pippa spoke with a heartfelt sigh.

'But it can't go back.' Jane spoke abruptly. 'That's the thing. None of us can go back and unsay things or unknow things.' She smiled. 'If you see what I mean.'

Pippa was silent.

'Titus feels guilty that he lied to our kids,' Jane went on. 'He also feels guilty because he didn't like his father very much.'

Pippa saw Jane watching her warily. She nodded. 'Mark didn't like him much either. The Gaffer was always horrible to him.'

The two women grinned at each other in sudden solidarity.

'Now I don't suppose Mark and Titus have had that conversation, do you?' Jane said.

'Aren't men stupid sometimes?' replied Pippa with a smile.

They finished cooking the meal together. Jane collected the pieces of the vegetable dish and put them on the table.

'They're all big pieces,' she said. 'We could stick them together.'

'No.' Pippa shook her head. 'Throw it away. I couldn't use it properly covered in superglue, no matter what the packet says.' She took a piece and turned it round in her hands. 'I remember it. I don't need to have it in front of me.' She handed the piece back to Jane and turned to fill a saucepan with water. 'The Gaffer was a great horseman you know. He was riding up until just last year.'

'I know,' Jane said quietly.

Pippa wheeled round and seemed to scrutinise Jane for a minute. Then she nodded her head slightly, as if inwardly con-

firming something to herself. 'Yes, of course you do. I know you
do.'

Kit sat bolt upright in his seat on the top of the bus. Every time
he leant back the pain shot down his arm.

'Better to have it on your arm than your shoulder. It'll be less
painful,' advised the tattooist who was a walking psychedelic
picture, studded and tattooed all over his body. But Summer
had been adamant – it had to be the shoulder. 'Well, better
than having it on some of the places I'm asked to do,' the tattooist had winked at them. 'Don't worry, it won't hurt much.'

The man had lied. It had stung badly at first and now it felt
bruised and was beginning to throb. Kit wondered if Summer
was suffering as much as he was.

When Kit had returned from skiing, he rather hoped that
Summer might have gone off the idea of a tattoo, but he found
that, in his absence, Summer was as keen as ever and had been
busy designing a dove motif for them both.

'We don't want anything naff like our names. I want it to be
stylish.' She appeared to have no fear of the operation.

'We want them sort of like Picasso's dove of peace,' she
explained to the tattooist, who'd looked at her blankly and held
out his hand. 'Just give me the picture and I'll copy it.'

And that was what he had done. When he had finished, he
showed Kit the results in the mirror, but it was bleeding and he
couldn't see it properly. Summer's was the same, but she had
managed to keep her vision through the gore.

'It's great,' she'd said, 'really great.'

Kit showed it to Ed, who examined it doubtfully. 'What's it
meant to be?'

'Picasso's dove.'

'Oh. Right. It looks a bit rough to me.'

'My parents would go ape-shit if they knew about this,' Kit
said.

Ed looked at him pityingly. 'You'd better not let it get infected

201

then. If you're lying in hospital dying of septicemia they're bound to want to know what caused it.'

'Fuck off,' Kit said good-humouredly. 'They're not going to find out. No one is at home.'

But Caitlin, with only a cursory knock on the door, came into his bedroom that evening while he was changing his shirt. He wheeled round when he heard her, 'what the fu—'

'Sorry, I didn't know you were here.'

'Get out, will you,' he shouted at her, keeping his back away from her. And anyway don't come into my room when I'm not here.'

'Excuse me. I only came to get my hair dryer back.' Kit saw her eyes shift towards the mirror.

'What's that?' Caitlin moved forward and turned him round. 'A tattoo? You? I thought you hated pain. What's it meant to be?'

'Picasso's dove.'

'His wasn't red and puffy, was it?'

'Oh, ha-ha, very funny – *not*. Don't say anything, will you?'

'No, I won't, but you'd better look after it properly.' Caitlin examined it closely. 'They go septic very easily. Why particularly Picasso's dove?'

'Summer designed it.'

'Ohhh.' Understanding dawned on his sister's face. 'I see. Has she got one too?'

'Yup.' Kit looked anxiously over his shoulder into the mirror. 'Only hers doesn't look quite so grungy as mine.'

Kit's tattoo and its origins were, in Ralph's mind, the final disintegration of the family solidarity. Only a few days before, he had approached Grania with a question to which logically he knew the answer, but which emotionally he refused to accept.

'You don't think . . .' he'd spoken slowly, willing her to give him the answer he wanted, 'that Gerry and Clattie are . . . more than just friendly?'

He'd been unable to shake off the vision of the two of them together. The way she talked about him when he wasn't there continually reverberated round his head.

'I think they're very fond of each other, yes, I do.' Ralph could see that Grania was choosing her words carefully to make it more palatable for him.

He was walking past the bathroom when he heard Kit yelp. Then he heard Caitlin.

'It's really crusty, you know. Hold still, I can't put this stuff on if you keep moving.'

'It hurts, it bloody hurts,' Ralph heard Kit say.

'Let's hope Summer doesn't ask you to have your penis pierced to prove your undying love then,' Caitlin was saying cheerfully. 'Now I bet that would *really* hurt.'

It took Ralph a couple of minutes to register what Caitlin had said. He stood beside the half-open door and watched her dabbing at Kit's shoulder. Something black was happening inside his head and he felt completely surrounded by treachery. He felt isolated, as though he were all alone, bobbing about anchorless in a rough sea. Mark with Titus, Clattie with Gerry and now could it be that even Kit had betrayed him with Summer? What had happened to this family? When had it become so out of control? What about the Gaffer, he wanted to screech at them all. Where was the loyalty to *him*?

Ralph went downstairs into his study and stood by the window. He looked across at the square in front of the house and watched two men up a tree sawing branches. Our family is a bit like those branches, he thought mournfully, just falling, one by one, off the main trunk that's stood there strongly for so many years.

'I met her a couple of times – by chance,' Kit said immediately when Ralph confronted him. 'I don't know her that well, honestly.' His eyes shifted focus.

'Don't lie. Whatever else you do, Kit, don't lie to me, please.'

The sadness in his father's voice was a hundred times worse than the anger Kit had expected. 'Yeah, okay. It's true, we have got it together. We've been seeing each other since Gaff's funeral.'

'And how did it come about, that you met again afterwards?'

'She turned up outside school one afternoon.'

'Umm,' Ralph snorted derisively. 'Just like her grandmother obviously. Can't leave a man alone.'

'No, it wasn't like that, Dad,' Kit responded hotly. 'We both wanted it. We get on, we like the same things.'

'And what about who she is? Did that occur to you? You know how we all feel about that family. How do you think Gaff would have felt about your behaviour?' Ralph obviously wanted answers from Kit, but he had none to give.

He shrugged. 'It's nothing to do with what other people feel. It's to do with us.' Kit could hear Summer in his head as he spoke; he could feel her and smell her – an unaccustomed defiance took him over.

He met his father's glare and spoke boldly. 'Dad, this family thing is not a big deal – not to us. It's history. Nothing to do with Summer and me.' Kit braced himself. 'And I don't want to split up with her just because of . . . everything. I'm not going to stop seeing her, because of how you feel, whatever you say.'

Kit held his breath but kept looking at his father, refusing to yield. Ralph dropped his eyes first and threw himself into an armchair.

'Go away, Kit – just go away.'

Kit crept out of the room, wishing that his father had shouted at him.

Grania knew that if Ralph found out that she had known about Kit and Summer, it would be the final Judas kiss for him. He would feel he had no one left in his corner, that he was alone in the battle he seemed so determined to fight. So when he told her about Kit and Summer, she didn't tell him that she already knew.

Clattie was taking down the Christmas decorations. Razor skidded around at her feet, snuffling at the piles of dry holly. There is something touchingly sad about Christmas decorations once Christmas is over, Clattie reflected, as she bagged up the discoloured tinsel. Bella once told her that her parents used to take their tree down with undisguised relief on Christmas Day evening and Clattie had been terribly shocked, but today, she felt herself in sympathy with Bella's parents. The moment Christmas day is over, the decorations become just a dusty and tarnished memory of a happy time – and this year, they weren't even that. Clattie was glad to see them go.

Pippa had taken a temporary clerical job in a solicitors' office in Tunbridge Wells and she was upstairs in her bedroom deciding what to wear for her first day at work. Doris had gone home and Clattie almost had the house to herself. It was, she realised, something that, in the months after Jack's death and before Pippa's arrival, she had slowly come to value: this peace, this solitude, this empty space that wasn't about to be fractured by someone's demands, someone's drama.

She lit one candle on the tree, as she always did, before she began carefully unhooking the bright, coloured baubles and packing them away in tissue. The familiar fear came upon her – that she would not be the one unpacking the Christmas decorations next year. But each following Advent, she was there, unpacking the boxes, remembering this feeling and smiling at her own foolishness.

Razor heard someone on the gravel path outside long before Clattie. He stood expectantly in the hall, ears pricked, and just as Clattie was stretching for the star at the top of the tree, the kitchen doorbell rang. The sudden noise in the quiet house and Razor's excited barking gave her a start and the chair on which she was standing wobbled. She lost her balance and flung a hand out to save herself, grasping the tree which tottered to the floor, ornaments smashing as the branches of the tree hit the fire guard.

'Bugger, bugger, bugger.' Clattie looked at the mess and stamped on the lighted candle. The doorbell rang again.

Pippa called down the stairs and Clattie shouted back. 'It's all right, I'll go.'

Gerry began speaking as she opened the door. 'I knew you were still up, the drawing-room light was on. I've bought some Twelfth Night cheer.' He waved a bottle of champagne, then stopped and looked at Clattie. 'What's the matter? Are you all right?'

'So stupid. I've tipped the tree over and some of the decorations have fallen off and now,' she looked abashed and gave a small smile, 'I feel it's some sort of sign or omen.'

Gerry grinned in relief. 'Only that you'll have to buy some new ones for next year. Come on, I'll help you clear up.'

'The tree must be dismantled by midnight, otherwise it's tomorrow and that's bad luck.'

'We'd better get on with it then. You get some glasses. Are you on your own?'

'Pippa is upstairs. I wanted to do this by myself.'

The two of them raised the tree and rescued the unbroken ornaments. Clattie sat in a chair wrapping them in tissue paper, while Gerry swept up the thin, tinkly, coloured glass and began taking off the decorations that remained on the tree's branches.

'Pippa starts work tomorrow then?'

Clattie nodded. 'It's only a temporary job. She's looking for something more interesting, apparently. Jane came down the other day and she and Pip were talking about Australia. I rather hoped it might inspire her to do a bit of travelling. It would be so good for her.' Clattie sighed. 'But I think it is she who needs to be here looking after me, rather than the other way round. Although it occurred to me this morning that my daughter has become the most balanced of my children over this. She appears to have mourned her father at last and is beginning to look to the future. She and Jane got on extremely well, and she seems perfectly happy about you being around. But the boys. I can't get through to either of them. Ralph is rigid with anger, some of it directed at me, I think, and he looks dreadfully worn. He and Mark hardly spoke over Christmas. Mark is very tense. Something's on his mind – he's very short with everyone. I have great sympathy for both my daughters-in-law at the moment. You know, sometimes I feel dreadfully constricted by my family.' Clattie smiled. 'Listen to me. I'm grumbling on just like an adolescent.'

Gerry took the last bit of tinsel off the tree and folded it into the box. 'There, all done. I'll take the tree out in a minute.' He bent and kissed Clattie on the forehead. 'Another drink?'

She held up her glass and Gerry replenished their drinks and sat down in the chair beside her.

'Talking of being adolescent,' he started with a smile, 'I was a bit adolescent in Norfolk over Christmas.' He began to speak seriously. 'I took myself off for long solitary walks and I thought about us. We are important, aren't we? Us?'

Clattie stared into her glass and nodded.

'Well then, I shall be honest with you, Clattie. I think it's time to leave your family to sort themselves out. They're all adults, middle-aged even, and you cannot keep feeling responsible for them for ever. You've got to let them go. This is *your* time now.' He half raised his glass as some sort of salute to her. 'And I want to be part of it.'

Clattie listened in silence while a bubble of outrage built up and then burst out of her, seemingly from nowhere.

'I can't believe you're telling me what to do, Gerry. You've never been a parent. Families are never "happy ever after". They're raw and gritty and they're always there. Inside you. You can't just relinquish responsibility for your children, no matter how old they are. It's a ridiculous idea. My children are part of me. I created them, I nurtured them. I may feel confined by them sometimes but that's how it is. And all the guilt.' Her voice rose. 'You don't know how guilty I feel. Every day. It never leaves me. What the children become is the parents' fault, it has to be. But how would you understand that?'

Clattie could see, through her anger, that she was hurting Gerry, but she couldn't stop; it was almost cathartic.

'You don't understand anything about families. You're not the one who has to watch the people you love hurting. You're so selfish, you've only got yourself to think about—'

'I thought you might like some help with the tre—' Pippa arrived in the room in her dressing gown, holding a cup of tea. Taking in the atmosphere and her mother's flushed face, she hovered uncertainly. 'Sorry . . .'

Gerry stood up. 'Don't worry,' he said coldly, 'I'm going.' He picked up the tree. 'I'll put this by the dustbin on my way out.'

He left the room silently and the ice in Clattie's empty glass rattled as her hand shook.

Mark was sitting in his office waiting for his accountant to call. In front of him was a pile of invoices. This had been a very bad week. When he began to do the figures properly, it appeared that Basil Catering accounts were much worse than he had anticipated and, judging by the final demands piled up on his desk, he was about to have difficulty getting credit from his suppliers. Having got rid of the chef and Caroline at Christmas, Mark was running the kitchens on his own and yesterday when he'd been cooking for one of the clients – just a small dinner party, the large jobs had dwindled to nothing in the post-Christmas slump – he remembered how much he used to enjoy creating dishes; he loved the humid bustle of a kitchen, the artistry, the final work of art laid out on a plate like a painting. He'd been a bloody good chef when he was younger; now he was doing it all on automatic pilot – no imagination there now; no flair, no magic. Just going through the motions . . . to keep the business going. To add to his problems, the figures from Palmers were on a disappointingly downward track – he needed to pay attention there as well, not just leave it to Greg. They had to get the punters in. Mark rubbed his eyes. Could he manage to keep juggling? Or was he too exhausted, in too deep to wade out of the mire? There was so much to do, and it was all down to him. He couldn't bear to talk to Bella. Even if he did swallow his pride, she was never there to listen to him. Recently she seemed removed – in some far-off place of her own. And when she looked at him, there was a remote look in her eyes. Freddie was really his only support and ally.

The telephone rang beside him. Mark picked it up quickly.

'Hi, it's Titus.'

'Oh. Oh. Right. Hello.' Mark didn't mean to sound dismissive.

'The menu's changed.'

'Menu?' Mark focused his thoughts and then he remembered. 'Oh yes, the menu. We were going to discuss it. Look, I'm sorry, mate, I'm flat out here so I left Greg and Chef to do it. It looked fine—'

'I wanted some input on that,' Titus interrupted.

'Yes, yes, I realise that.' Mark spoke wearily. He didn't need this at the moment. 'It was merely a time-saving measure this month.'

'Our directors' meeting is overdue too.' Titus spoke steadily. 'What about Thursday this week?'

'Look, Titus,' Mark tried the placatory tack. 'This week's difficult for me. I'm a bit short-handed at Basil; the chef's gone skiing. How about I give you a call at the beginning of next week? When I can see things a bit clearer.'

There was a pause at the other end of the phone, and then Titus spoke carefully. 'I'd really rather not leave it like that, Mark. We need a firm date. If not this week, at least the beginning of next.'

Mark could hear the obduracy in his partner's voice. He felt overwhelmed with hopeless lassitude and he had to get Titus off the phone, so that he could talk to his accountant. He shuffled the pile of invoices. *And* he needed to find a way of dealing with these.

'Whatever,' he said irritably. The man was becoming a nuisance. He sighed and flicked through his desk diary. 'I could do next Monday, early evening. I suppose. It's really the earliest I can do, I'm afraid.'

'Right, if that's *really* the earliest you can make,' Titus replied. 'Shall we say six-thirty at Palmers?'

'Okay.' Mark looked at his watch. 'Look, Titus, forgive me. I've got to get off the line. I'm waiting for an important call.'

Titus inferred, therefore, that his own call was not an important one.

Chapter Nine

*B*ut Mark and Titus never did hold their meeting on Monday because that was the day that Pippa had the morning off for a doctor's appointment.

Clattie had planned to go shopping, so she went with Pippa and waited in the surgery reception area for her.

Bored by the magazines on offer, Clattie watched the nicely laundered receptionists dealing with the queue of ill, sad, shocked and sometimes irritated patients, and wondered how they could remain so politely remote and so removed from the distress around them – they seemed as antiseptic as their surroundings.

Gerry had not been round since he left so abruptly that evening, and Clattie missed him dreadfully. Every day she meant to ring him, or to go round and see him; she'd even started writing a letter. Each time she put it off, it became harder and the gap between them wider. She wanted him to know that she had spoken out in a moment of heat and a feeling of inadequacy and she deeply regretted being so unkind to him – that none of this was his fault, only hers. For a brief, heady moment with Gerry, she had glimpsed a kind of freedom – nearly broken out of the tangle that was her family. But she'd been foolish and self-ish to imagine she deserved the sort of joy Gerry was offering her and the guilt had returned, doubly so, because she had deceived herself into thinking that she could find happiness, even while her children were in such confusion and turmoil.

Clattie had gone to church with Pippa the day before and tried to remember how to pray for forgiveness. At the end of the service Pippa was the first up to help serve the coffee at the back of the church. Clattie had watched her laughing with one of the team of priests and when Pippa introduced him as Simon, he had taken Clattie's hand and held it for a long time, saying, 'It's so nice to have Pippa back. She's such a valuable member of the congregation.'

Now one of the practice nurses swept past Clattie in the waiting room.

'Hello, Mrs Palmer. It must be such a help having Pippa home again. Lovely for you to have the company.'

Pippa, never the gentlest of drivers, crashed the gears and executed a ferocious three-point turn in the surgery drive and Clattie nervously put on her seat belt.

'I've got to take my prescription into Boots.' Pippa began to drive erratically towards the shopping centre. 'More creams that'll only work for a couple of months.' She sighed. 'You'd think we'd have got a cure for eczema by now, wouldn't you? If we can clone sheep, we should be able to stop itchy skin.' She took a left turn. 'I'm not going to that other chemist. I never think it really does proper medicines. Gaffer was like that, wasn't he? Do you remember how he only watched the BBC news? He didn't believe a commercial channel could get real news.'

She stretched out and twiddled with the radio as she accelerated down the road and, alarmed, Clattie offered to change the station for her. 'You concentrate on driving. What do you want?'

'Some sort of music.'

Clattie took off her seat belt and leant forward to move the radio through the stations.

'That'll do,' Pippa said, as a country singer came on and filled the car with his sobbing voice, mourning a lost love and a violent death.

Extraordinarily, given her driving, the accident was not Pippa's fault. As they were cruising through the shopping complex, a white van shot out of a left-hand side road and went straight into the wing of the car. Clattie's last thought, as she was violently slung towards the windscreen, was that at least she wouldn't have to listen to any more of that awful music.

Ralph rang Mark on Monday afternoon.

'Clattie and Pippa have had a car smash.' He sounded calm and in control. 'Pippa's fine, distraught of course, but Clattie was knocked unconscious and they think she may have broken her leg.'

'Christ, how did it happen? Is she all right?'

'She's recovered consciousness apparently, but they're not sure what other injuries she may have. I'm on my way down now. I'll see you there.' The phone went dead as Ralph hung up. There was no question, in his brother's mind, that Mark would not be there. This was another family crisis.

Mark looked at the pile of papers on his office desk. It was only a fleeting thought, arriving unexpectedly, unasked for and pushed back as soon as it emerged. But its insane appearance shook Mark to his core. He had shocked himself.

If Clattie had died, he could have got out of this financial mess.

Titus slammed down the phone with such venom, Jane feared for the instrument.

'Great. I ring up Mark to confirm our meeting tonight. No answer. I ring up Palmers to see if he's there and Greg tells me that he's gone down to The Mill. Clattie's been involved in an accident and Greg doesn't know when Mark'll be back. So,

212

obviously, no meeting. I reckon this is me being fobbed off. He wasn't keen to see me in the first place. And he didn't even have the courtesy to ring me himself to say the meeting was cancelled—'

'My God!' Jane interrupted Titus's tirade. 'Clattie. What happened? How is she?'

'She's in hospital, broken her leg, apparently. We'll have to rearrange the—'

Jane looked at her husband with disgust. 'Titus. Shut up. Try thinking about poor Clattie for a moment instead of Mark and that fucking restaurant. And, actually, if you're going to be pissed off, be pissed off that none of your siblings had the decency to ring you about Clattie's accident. That should tell you something about your arrogant family.'

Clattie had no head injuries, but she had broken her wrist and also her leg, which needed to be pinned. She would make a full recovery, but would be in hospital for at least ten days. Ralph, Mark and Pippa found being at The Mill on their own an uncomfortable and strange experience. There seemed to be a lack of focus, no heart to the house. It was as though there had been another death in the family.

'I went to the hospital. She's sitting up having supper,' Mark reported when he arrived. 'They're going to pin her leg tomorrow. She's remarkably cheerful. Worried about us, of course.'

They all found something to do. Ralph walked the dog, Mark poured drinks and Pippa prepared the supper.

'I'm afraid there isn't much food.' Her face crumpled slightly. 'We never got to the supermarket.'

Mark handed her a drink. 'She's going to be all right, Pip. Stop worrying.'

'It was my fault. I feel so awful.'

'You make the supper. It'll take your mind off things.'

'I could do pasta. Or, we've got masses of eggs. I'll do omelettes, shall I? Is that all right?'

'Whatever.' Mark threw himself into a chair and looked down

at his drink. He suddenly remembered Titus and the meeting. He half got up to go to the phone and then slumped back.

'Fuck it,' he muttered to himself. 'Greg'll tell him where I am.' He drained the glass. Being down here had given him a sudden feeling of relief – almost serenity – in the middle of the maelstrom that was beginning to build up around him in London.

'I'm afraid Clattie's going to be pretty incapacitated for some time,' Ralph said as they sat round the kitchen table, eating supper.

'I'll be here. I'll look after her. Does anyone want cheese?' Pippa got up.

'Sit down, Pippa,' Ralph said crossly. 'We're fine and we need to discuss this properly. You've got a job, you can't take on full-time nursing.'

'It's only a temporary job. I can give it up. Or . . .' Pippa gave him a weak smile, 'is it that you don't trust me now I've nearly killed her?'

'Don't be so ridiculous,' Ralph admonished her.

'She's only broken her leg,' Mark said, refilling his glass of wine. 'She'll be fine in a month or so. Completely back to normal.'

'She's seventy-five years old, Mark,' Ralph said. 'We've got to start thinking long term. She can't live here on her own. It's a big house and she might fall over at any time.'

'There's no evidence to show that you fall over more in a big house than in a small one,' Mark pointed out.

Ralph sighed. 'This is not a joke, Mark. I'm concerned about her, even if you're not.'

'I never said I wasn't. Of course I'm concerned.' The brothers faced each other, historical animosity rising up in them both.

Pippa jumped in between the two. 'But, I said, I'm here. I'll look after her, and she's got lots of friends.'

Ralph frowned. 'We can't rely on friends. This is the family's responsibility.' He looked at Pippa. 'I know you'll care for her, and for the time being that's great. But, realistically, you won't always be living here, will you? You might want to go off and do something quite different and it wouldn't be fair on Clattie to give her another change. No, as I say, we've got to think long term. Get something set up for her now that will give her a bit of security. And I'm quite certain that she shouldn't be living here alone, especially with all her memories of the Gaffer.'

Mark sat up, suddenly eager and alert. 'Do you mean sell The Mill?'

'You can't sell The Mill,' complained Pippa. 'It's our home.'

'It's about time you left home,' Mark said brutally.

'And what's that supposed to mean?' Brother and sister stared each other out.

'Stop it, you two.' Ralph picked up the wine bottle and poured them all another glass.

'Think about it, Pip. You can't commit yourself to looking after Clattie for the rest of your life. She will become more and more frail as she gets older. It would end up a full-time job. It's not fair on you. You've got your own life to lead.'

'I suppose.' Pippa looked thoughtful. 'Talking to Jane about Australia the other day made me realise how unadventurous I've been all my life.'

'Jane? Who's . . .?' Ralph answered his own question, and hurried on. 'Anyway, we've all got to do our bit for Clattie—'

'This house'll fetch a fair amount.' Mark talked over Ralph as he got up to collect the other bottle of wine from the sideboard. 'Good family house, big garden and commutable to London.'

Mark's progress round the dining room was unsteady.

Ralph watched him. 'Do we need the other bottle? I've had enough—'

'Maybe you have,' Mark said truculently, 'but I haven't. Family meetings always need a great deal of lubrication, don't you think?' He swept a flamboyant bow and sat down heavily in his chair.

'I don't believe any of us really want to see The Mill sold—'

'I'm not bothered.' Mark interrupted Ralph. 'It's served its purpose. Time to move on, I reckon. Let's release some of the Gaffer's money while it can do some good.'

Ralph raised his eyebrows. 'The house has so many happy memories for us,' he persevered.

Mark snorted derisively into his glass. Ignoring him, Ralph continued, 'There's no need to sell. I think the simplest solution is for Grania and me to move in here. We could convert a downstairs flat for Clattie quite easily. Self-contained, so that to begin with she doesn't feel too dependent. This way the family home stays in the family—'

'Oh-ho.' Mark smirked at Ralph. 'So, this is what it's all about, is it, big brother? Taking over your inheritance? After all, you're the eldest son. Oh no,' he slapped his hand to his head theatrically. 'I forgot, of course, it turns out you're not after all.'

'That's enough, Mark.' Ralph raised his voice. 'This is only about Clattie – nobody else. We're the family and *we*'re going to make the decisions.'

Pippa put her head in her hands. 'Please, please, don't quarrel.'

But Ralph and Mark were past listening to her.

'But don't be concerned, Mark,' Ralph's voice was icy. 'You'll get your fair share of whatever is going, if that's what you're worried about – and clearly it is.'

Mark pushed back his chair and rose to his feet. 'It probably wouldn't be enough, anyway.' His words were slurred. 'I need a bloody miracle, that's what I need.' He slammed the door as he left.

'What did he mean?' Pippa turned to Ralph, who shrugged his shoulders.

'I've no idea. I don't suppose he has either; he's had a little too much wine to be completely coherent.'

Brother and sister sat in silence.

'What does Grania think about you living here?' Pippa asked after a while.

Ralph took his time to answer.

'She'll do what's right for the family. Look, Pip, you need to think about the future. Everything's different now.'

'I know I do.' Pippa spoke robustly. 'Mark's quite right, it *is* time I left home. And if you do decide to come and live here, Clattie won't need me to look after her as well.'

Ralph rose to his feet and began clearing the plates. 'Well, we'll see. Anyway, first we have to think about Clattie's immediate needs. You don't have to think about giving up your job immediately because I shall suggest that she comes up to London to convalesce when she gets out of hospital. Grania's at home all day and she'll be happy to look after her. Time enough to think about the future when Clattie's back on her feet.'

But Clattie was thinking about the future now.

Gerry came to visit her in hospital two days after her operation. Through the glass partition of the ward, Clattie watched him stop and talk to a nurse and then turn as she pointed towards her bed. Their eyes met and he walked slowly into the ward, as though unsure of his welcome.

'I'm so glad you've come.' Clattie's face creased into a genuine smile of delight.

'Are you really?' Gerry still looked nervous.

'You don't know how much.'

He perched at the end of the bed, put a pile of books beside her and handed her a bag of tangerines.

'My wife always got constipated in hospital.' He produced a bottle of eau de cologne. 'And she also liked to smell nice.' Thoughtful presents.

'I'm so sor—' she started.

'I wanted—' he said at the same time.

They stopped and smiled at each other.

'Let me talk first,' commanded Clattie and she began to say all the things that she had been longing to say since the night of their quarrel. When she'd come to a stumbling halt, she looked at Gerry with brimming eyes. 'What a horrible old woman I'm becoming,' she said vehemently.

He took her hand and squeezed tightly. 'And that's nonsense.'

'And,' Clattie said, wiping the tears from her eyes, 'now Ralph is suggesting that he and Grania move into The Mill.'

'You mean, while you convalesce?'

'No,' Clattie wailed. 'For ever. He's talking about converting some of downstairs into a flat. No stairs, in case I fall down them, and he's probably got a disabled loo in mind, as well. They plan to look after me, you see, wipe my dribbling chin and make sure my clothes are clean.' Clattie stopped in horror. 'Oh God, Gerry, listen to me. This is what I meant . . . This is family. It just never goes away. That's what I was trying to tell you—'

'Hey, Clattie.' Gerry shuffled up the bed to sit beside her. He put his arm round her shoulders. 'That's what I wanted to say. I do understand, I really do. And I want you with your family, not without it. I never thought for a moment that I could have you without it.' He paused. 'What is it they talk about nowadays? Baggage, that's it. I want you and your baggage.' He smiled at her. 'We'll deal with it together.'

Clattie snuggled against his arm and felt herself fit into it.

'I have to be there for them always.' There was a note of desperation in her voice.

'I know your family mean well,' Gerry went on, 'and I know you love being with them. And I understand that you feel responsible for them. But you've got to realise that they're adults and not necessarily the adults you might want to live with for the rest of your life. And it's all right: you're *allowed* to feel that way. I don't think you need to have had children to work that one out. That's all I was trying to tell you.'

Clattie nodded. 'Yes, you're right, and I didn't mean to say those unjust things. I'm so sorry.'

Gerry patted her hand. 'It's all right. It's forgotten. All I'm doing is pointing out something you know already. First though, we need to get you well and on your feet. And I have a plan. I want you to come and convalesce with me. No disabled loos, I promise, and I wouldn't dream of wiping your chin—'

'Don't be silly. I can't impose like that—'

'No, *you* don't be silly. You know you can impose on me. You know how I feel about you and I'm sick of the hole-in-the-corner relationship that we're carrying on at the moment. You and I have been behaving very stupidly.' Clattie was silent and Gerry peered at her anxiously. 'Is it that you'd rather not come and stay with me when you leave here?'

'I can't think of anything I'd like better,' she said simply.

'That's what you'll do then and if your family are horrified by the idea, we'll face them together, you and I. And as for the future . . .?' He petered out.

'We'll see.' Clattie stiffened her back and sat up straight. Now, cocooned safely in hospital, away from the epicentre of her family's drama, she was beginning at last to feel calm, relieved. Her reconciliation with Gerry, the commitment between them, made her feel that her previous life was being packed away in a case, just needing the lid to be put on and fastened down.

'But there's something I must do first,' she said determinedly. 'Something I should have done months ago, when this all started.'

Kit rang Summer.

'Dad knows,' he announced. 'It was really weird, he just sat there. I thought he'd go into one, but he hasn't said anything more about us, so I suppose it's okay with him now.'

Summer, sitting in the college canteen, absorbed the information. 'Great,' she said coolly.

Kit sounded excited down the phone. 'Yeah, it's good, isn't it? No more hiding around, pretending. And Mum says it's fine for you to come round. Anyway, Dad's commuting to The Mill quite a lot at the moment.'

'Great.' Summer eyed the boy walking towards her with two cups of coffee and smiled at him. 'My brother,' she mouthed, pointing at her phone. 'Gotta go,' she said to Kit. 'I've got a lecture. I'll ring you later.'

Kit clicked off his phone and looked at Ed who was standing beside him at the bus stop.

'What's the matter with her then? She sounded really off. I thought she'd be pleased.'

'Very hard to please, girls,' Ed observed. 'My dad says it's their hormones and that they never learn to handle them properly.'

Ralph drove down to see his mother in hospital after work. He came across Gerry in the car park, unlocking a battered Morris Traveller. He greeted Ralph cordially.

'Great improvement today,' he said. 'She's looking much better and the physiotherapist's been round to see her.'

Ralph was surprised to see Clattie's dog in the back of the car. Gerry followed his glance.

'I have Razor during the day and take him back in the evening as company for Pippa, when you're not here. Didn't she say?'

Ralph shook his head, holding on to his vexation. He had not been down for a couple of days and he felt shut out by an arrangement not made by him.

'Pippa's out all day,' Gerry went on, 'and I like the excuse for a good daily walk.' He opened the car door and Razor leapt out of the seat, launching himself on to Gerry, licking him noisily.

'It's very kind of you,' Ralph said frostily. As he strode towards the hospital, he heard Gerry call something out to him, but chose to ignore it. So he was not expecting to find anyone at Clattie's bedside and he didn't immediately register who the two people were that rose to their feet as he arrived.

'Darling, how lovely.' Clattie lifted her face to be kissed. 'Jane and Summer have come all this way to see me. Isn't that kind?'

Ralph nodded perfunctorily towards the two women and turned back to Clattie. 'I've been talking to the ward sister. She says you can come home in a few days so I thought—'

'Hello, Uncle Ralph.' He was suddenly aware of Summer standing beside him, balanced, with her legs slightly apart like a gladiator facing an opponent.

Discomfited by this challenge, Ralph muttered shortly, 'Hello.' He looked over her head at Jane. 'I'm sorry, I'd like to talk to my mother alone, if you don't mind. I wonder—'

'Ralph.' Clattie frowned at him.

'Yes, we were just going.' Jane gathered up her large colourful basket. 'We don't want to intrude.' Her voice was laden with sarcasm.

Clattie held out her arms in silence for Summer and Jane to kiss her and Ralph experienced an almost physical sickness as he watched the overt affection between the three of them. When they'd left the ward, Clattie lay back on the pillow and looked at Ralph in silent condemnation.

'Anyway,' Ralph said, 'the ward sister agrees with me that you simply can't be on your own when you come—'

'Ralph.' Clattie pointed to the chair beside her. 'Come and sit down, I need to talk to you. I've made my own arrangements. Gerry and I have decided that I'm going back to his house when I leave here.'

'I don't think that is at all suitable,' Ralph said immediately, with a dismissive wave of his hand. 'Absolutely not. Grania and I are expecting you to come to London until you're more mobile and after that we'll have to see. It's all been arranged.'

'Ralph.' Clattie struggled to sit up further, her face stern, eyes sharp. 'I'm quite capable of arranging myself, thank you. And I want to stay with Gerry for the time being.'

'Does Pippa know about this?'

'Not yet.'

'She'll be very upset.'

'I don't see why. Any more than if I came to you to convalesce.'

'She's offered to give up her job and look after you.'

'It's time she *stopped* looking after people,' Clattie said crisply. 'No, I've made my decision and it's non-negotiable. What looking after I need – which, I may say, Ralph, is not as much as you would have it – will be done by Gerry.'

'You should be with your family,' Ralph burst out. 'We should be looking after you, not some man we don't know very well.'

'Don't know very well?' Clattie exploded, eyes now blazing.

'*You* don't know him very well, I grant you, but I do and that's what counts. I'd be grateful if you would credit me with some intelligence and stop treating me like some dithery old fool. I'm staying with Gerry when I come out of hospital because that is where I want to be and that's an end to it.' Ralph was silent. Clattie's outburst had bewildered him and left him feeling uncharacteristically humiliated.

Clattie, breathing heavily, spoke resolutely. 'I'm sorry, darling. I just feel it's time for me to do what I want.'

Ralph remained silent.

'Did you know that Summer is Kit's girlfriend?' he asked eventually, in a low voice.

'No. No. I didn't.' Clattie tipped her head as though thinking through this development. 'That's curious. Nice, though, that they're friends.'

'Nice?' Ralph's voice rose to a quiet roar in indignation. 'That family are like weevils, they get everywhere. Poor Gaffer, he must have had a dreadful time trying to get away from Titus and his mother – parasites the both of them, that's what they are – and now the children are the same. I don't know why you put up with them for so long. You and the Gaffer were much too kind to them, quite unnecessarily. Most men would have refused to have anything to do with an illegitimate son born in such manipulated circumstances—'

'Ralph.' Clattie squeezed his hand. She spoke quietly but firmly, commanding his attention. 'The people you rant and rage at are utterly blameless in all this. Titus, Jane, their family. How can it be their fault? What have they done except be who they are? It doesn't make sense. It's my fault. It's your father's fault—'

'My father's? No, that's rubbish. There's no proof that Titus was the Gaffer's son. He didn't even name Titus as his son in the will. That poisonous woman deceived him and took advantage of the fact that he was an honourable man. She obviously lied in a bid to get the man she loved. Unfortunately for her, he didn't love her, he loved you.'

222

Clattie silently let Ralph wind down.

'No, it wasn't like that, Ralph, I'm afraid. Not at all.'

She wanted to explain. She'd already planned her words, but while Ralph had been speaking her resolve had, all of a sudden, been swamped by exhaustion and she was struggling to finish what she had started. She sat silently for a moment, head bowed, her fingers fiddling with the sheet, then she looked up at Ralph, a determined expression on her face.

'Darling, I want you to go back to The Mill and look in the little drawer at the back of my desk. You'll find two bundles of letters there. They are your father and Shirley's letters to each other and I want you to read them. I'm sorry. I've been a coward all my life and I'm being a coward now, but I just can't do the explaining. I'm so tired.' She flopped back against her pillows, her eyes swimming and deep lines etched on her face. 'I was keeping the letters for Titus,' she murmured quietly, 'but I kept putting off giving them to him – a question of pride.' She gave a weak smile. 'Go on, darling, go now. Please read them. It's the only way you will really understand. Please do it. Just you though, not Pippa at the moment. Read them this evening. Promise?'

Ralph opened the first bundle of letters when Pippa had gone to bed. He sat in the drawing room of The Mill until dawn broke.

Jack had loved Shirley.

I can never never love any woman as I love you. You fill the whole of my head and the whole of my heart every minute of the day and night, my dearest, darling girl.

And Shirley had loved Jack.

Last night I slept with your handkerchief spread out on my pillow. I'm completely foolish, I know, but I think of you all the time. I want you to see the work I am doing, it's so good and it's all because of you, my darling Jack.

Ralph read all the letters of love and passion and then he opened the second bundle. Shirley to Jack:

So, convention has managed to do what we always thought was impossible. It's perfectly true I would not be a suitable army wife, but together we could have turned you into an artisan, couldn't we? You just needed the courage but it turns out that you're a coward, emotionally craven. Suitability has been the destruction of what we had and you have managed to cut me out with a coldness I never knew you were capable of. I wish I could be as big a bastard as you, but all I can do is destroy every painting that reminds me of you and then weep you out of my heart. Only one great love in any lifetime, Jack, and you were mine. I think I was yours too, but you're too arrogant to admit it. I don't want to see or hear from you again.

But then there was a letter from Jack to Shirley, dated a few months later.

I have found a little wife who will do me very well. She is very young, kind and terribly pretty, but not at all artistic, wild or passionate, so she will never remind me of you. But there is never a day when I don't think of you and love you with my whole heart. Enclosed is the wedding invitation. I need you to be there, one last time. Will you come?

At around two in the morning, Ralph got up and, followed by Razor, walked round the walled garden, stretching his cramped legs and trying to make sense of what he had been reading. He couldn't shake himself free of the feeling that he was reading fiction, a made-up story about complete strangers. Back in the house, he poured himself another large whisky and settled down by the dying fire to read the rest of the bundle.

Jack wrote to Shirley after the wedding.

You were right, of course. One should never accept second best and last afternoon back in your flat was a reminder of how best you are. We can't let each other go again, it would be more than I could bear.

An angry Shirley to Jack dated eighteen months later.

You are a monster, Jack. You can't treat people's hearts in such a cavalier manner. You want everything but you're making us all unhappy. You made your decision when you married your sweet wife and now she's given you a legitimate son so it's time for me to bow out. I never meant to let you back into my life but you always were my great weakness. At least from that weakness came Titus and I gave him your name because I was proud he was your son. But he belongs to me. He's my present from you and now your punishment from me because I refuse to let you see him any more. One day when he's old enough to understand I shall tell him about his father and then he can decide on his relationship with you, but till then you don't exist for us and you've got to live with that. So you stay with your wife and son and have a safe life. I loved you so much, but it's over, well and truly this time. Leave us both alone. We don't want anything from you and I never want to see you again.

A brief note from Jack to Shirley.

You once called me too arrogant to admit you were the love of my life. You maligned me. I have never and never will love anyone as I have loved you. There will not be a day when I don't think of you and my son Titus.

The final letter, also from Shirley, was written in shaky writing.

Monica will take Titus and look after him, but, please, one last request: will you keep him in your life? I know I said I never wanted you to see him – I was angry and hurt – and we have managed very well without you up till now. But things have changed and he will need you. He has no other family besides Monica and I want him to know that his parents once loved each other. Your wife has put up with a lot from you but I hope she will understand this request – as one mother to another. I lie in my bed all day just remembering the times we had together before you spoilt it. It could have been so different, but I suppose I can't help but be grateful for what we did have. Goodbye, my love.

As Ralph was bundling up the letters, a small scrap of paper fell to the floor.

I am sending you back your letters to Shirley, I found them under her bed and I think you should have them to remind you what a bloody bastard you are. I shall be in touch shortly about Titus.
Monica.

Ralph visited Clattie in the morning on his way back to London.

In a halting voice full of heartbreaking sadness, Clattie began to spill out the truth. Ralph listened, as his mother told him that she had been cowardly and proud because she didn't want her own children to know that their father loved another woman more than he loved her – that she couldn't have borne their pity.

'The truth is,' Clattie said, 'although I think your father grew to be quite fond of me, I could never be Shirley. He couldn't love me as he loved her. I could never get rid of Shirley. She was always there in his head and his heart. Even after she died.'

Ralph looked up. 'Why did you accept Titus . . . and become so fond of him?' he added bitterly.

'He was such a little boy and had no family apart from

Monica and Will.' Clattie smiled distantly. 'And the irony is that Monica and I got to like each other. We became good friends. She understood and accepted how I felt about Shirley and I knew what she thought of Jack – how much she hated him. We used to meet often. I'd go up to London and we'd have lunch or go to the theatre – your father hated the theatre. He would have been furious if he'd known who I was seeing and I never told him, even after she died. That was my secret.'

Clattie went on talking, spelling out the truth, destroying Ralph's memories. She told him that his father was a thoughtless, selfish, singleminded, ambitious and very misguided man, but that his whole life had been coloured by his great love for Shirley. He was utterly, utterly obsessed and he never forgave himself for letting her go.

'I knew when he married me that it wasn't me he really wanted.' Clattie spoke calmly, her eyes far away. 'But he was too scared to marry her: she was too unconventional, too strong, and he planned to go places in the army. Of course, it was unfortunate that he found it necessary to leave the army shortly after we were married—'

'I thought it was you who persuaded him to leave the army,' Ralph interrupted.

'No,' Clattie said. 'It was the army that decided to dispense with your father's services. He stopped thinking straight for a while when Shirley finally sent him packing. There was a drunken evening in the mess and some unwanted attention on a young woman who complained to his commanding officer. I didn't want to know about it. You must have been about eighteen months and Titus just over two at the time, and we came to live here and he started the business. It was some months later, shortly after Mark was born, that Shirley died and Jack was devastated, completely broken and . . .' Clattie hesitated and then said in a low voice, 'very, very angry with me because I was the one alive. It was a dreadful time.' She shuddered. 'You were his only solace. He'd spend hours with you, teaching you how to ride, taking you with him everywhere he went. He couldn't bear to be with me or with Mark. It wasn't logical, but he resented Mark and wouldn't take any interest in him. He just always connected his birth with Shirley's death. Their relationship never recovered.'

Ralph nodded his head slowly, something connecting in his head. 'Yes. Oh yes. Poor Mark.' He sat quietly. 'I believed,' he said at last, 'that my father was a good man, but I was wrong. He was a bully.'

'I'm sorry, darling. I know how much you admired the Gaffer and how much you loved each other.'

Ralph looked steadily at his mother. 'Does Titus know how much the Gaffer loved his mother?'

Clattie shook her head. 'Jack kept only one promise to Shirley. He stayed in contact with Titus but he never spoke of her in front of him, let alone tell him that his mother was the one woman he had really loved.'

'But *I* could have told him.' Clattie was insistent, as though she wanted her own culpability laid out once and for all. 'Titus didn't love his father, because he never knew the truth. We kept it from him for all those years.' Clattie sounded desperate. 'When Jack died I should have told him, but I didn't. I hid behind the excuse that it wasn't my secret and your father had always been so . . .' she searched for the right word, 'intractable.'

'Were you frightened of him?' Ralph's question came as a shock.

'No,' she answered slowly. Then abruptly. 'I wasn't frightened, I was pathetic.'

Mother and son sat silently together.

'The important thing for you to remember is that none of this changes how much he loved you,' Clattie said eventually. 'Your relationship with the Gaffer was your own. As indeed was mine.' She sat up straighter and her voice lightened. 'I've always been second best but maybe now, with Gerry, I have a chance to be first best.' She smiled, but there was a glint of steel in her blue eyes. 'And I'm going to take it. I want an uncomplicated relationship with someone who loves me because I'm me, and who

228

will never make me feel that I'm constantly being unfavourably compared to someone else. I'll always be there for you and Mark and Pippa, you know that, but I want to be at peace with my own life now. You wouldn't begrudge me that, would you?'

And, now, Ralph did not begrudge that at all.

When Ralph came home, Grania was at the computer struggling with an essay on medieval literature. Her first thought was that he had been in an accident. He stood by the door, silently looking at her, great black shadows under his eyes, and his mouth set in a tight thin line.

Grania rose to her feet. 'What's happened? What are you doing here? Why aren't you at work?' And again, now shaking his arm to make him register her. 'Ralph, what's happened?'

He looked down at her and said with infinite sadness, 'Grania, I love you. I've never loved anyone as much as I love you.'

Grania felt her heart flip over. An unexpected thought came into her head. Could there be a *but* waiting for her round the corner?

'I'm not a bully, am I?' Ralph waited for her answer.

Grania shook her head. 'No, what—'

'I'm not like my father.' He interrupted her urgently, as though she might try to gainsay him. 'I'm not like my father. I don't want to be like him and I'm not. I mustn't be.'

Grania took his hand and found it cold and shaking in hers. He allowed her to lead him to a chair. 'I always wanted my children to respect me just as I respected my father,' he said in a low voice. 'But I was wrong because respect can be lost. I want my children to know everything about me. I want them to love me – as the person I really am.'

And then he told Grania the truth about his father.

Chapter Ten

Jane had just received a letter from her brother in Australia when Titus came in from his meeting with Mark. The letter had filled her head with colours – blues, greens and yellows – and she yearned for the sun, the sea and the freedom of her homeland. She had dragged herself back from the playgroup through cold fog that grated in her throat and she longed to be warm again, walking barefoot on a beach with the soft silver sand trickling through her toes. Titus banging the front door shattered her reverie.

'That's it. That man is definitely trying to sideline me.' He was talking as he walked through the hall. He came into the kitchen and threw his keys on to the dresser. 'Last Monday the restaurant area was closed for a private party – did I know anything about that? No, nothing. And, guess what? It was a friend of Mark's—'

'Good to fill the restaurant, I would have thought.' Jane put down the letter and her dream and went to switch on the kettle.

'Of course, that's what Mark said. Monday's a quiet day . . . but that's not the point. Why wasn't I consulted? And, another thing. We're a waitress down apparently so of course I suggested Alby.'

'Why? He's got a job he likes at the pub.'

'Well, he might prefer to work in a proper restaurant. Anyway, he could have kept his eye on things for me.'

Jane's eyes narrowed. 'Titus.' She spoke sharply. 'Just keep a grip on reality would you—'

'That's the thing, Jane. I'm only just beginning to see reality.' Titus paced the room, his body taut and angry. 'The reality is that Mark does not want me around in Palmers. He doesn't want my son working there. And why doesn't he?' He banged a cupboard door as he passed it. 'That's what I want to know. There's something odd going on, I know there is. The figures are very bad, well down on our forecast, but we don't seem to be doing anything about it. Apparently Mark's been tied up with his other poxy interests. I expect they're making money—'

'As *you* would be,' Jane interrupted crisply, 'if you concentrated a little more on Palmer's Restoration.'

Titus ignored her, rolling on a wave of wronged sensibilities.

'He puts off meeting me because of Clattie, but he does have time to meet Greg apparently. He says it's about things like hand-drying machines and window cleaning – not in my jurisdiction under our agreement and fair enough, if that *is* what they talk about. But I don't trust that Greg. He's got some sort of finger in this pie. I'm going to watch them, both of them, and see what they're really up to—'

'Oh please.' Jane thumped the kettle down angrily. 'Stop being so bloody paranoid, Titus. It's boring. His mother has had an accident, he's probably been visiting her every day. Just think about it. Mark is thoughtless, arrogant and tactless, we know that, but why would he bother to scam you? What would be the point?'

'There's sure to be one and I bet it's something to do with us being part of the family—'

'Excuse me.' Jane spoke sweetly but her lips were set and her eyes flashed. 'Did you not assure me a few months ago that neither Mark nor you ever mixed family with business?'

Titus shrugged. 'I was obviously wrong in Mark's case, wasn't I? This must be what it's about – unless the man's a crook, of course.' Titus poured himself a cup of tea, picked up his post and went to the kitchen door.

'I've told him I'm going to watch him. I know there's something going on.'

When she heard the door of the workshop bang behind Titus, Jane sat down at the kitchen table and tears rolled down her cheeks and smudged her brother's letter.

'Now the man's put his accusations down on paper.' Mark threw the letter on to his desk.

Freddie stared moodily into her glass. She had come round to the Basil offices with a bottle of wine to be met by a raging Mark. She was fed up. They hadn't had sex for weeks and Mark's conversation revolved entirely around money and now, it seemed, Titus and the restaurant.

'Listen to this,' Mark read aloud. '"I may be forced to take action to prevent your other interests jeopardising the success of Palmers." He's cross because I postponed the meeting due to Clattie.' He began ticking off the grievances on his fingers. 'He's upset about the takings – as we all are – and he wanted his son to come and be a waiter.'

'And?' Freddie was bored.

'I said no. Only because we've got enough male waiters at the moment. We need a girl to balance up the staff, to please the male punters. It makes sense. Nothing to do with not wanting his son. I just don't know what to do with the man.'

'You decided to go into business with him,' Freddie pointed out.

'Yes, and now I'm wondering just why I did. Bloody little bastard. And that's what he is, after all, nothing but my father's bastard. And,' Mark picked up a piece of paper and waved it at her, 'look at this. Another cancellation of a Basil order, a regular

232

one too. And this one comes from someone living very close to Titus. What do you make of that?' He looked at her triumphantly.

'What am I meant to make of it?' Freddie asked wearily.

'He's putting the boot in already, isn't he?'

'Why on earth should he?'

'Because he doesn't want Basil to be solvent if the restaurant isn't. Fat chance of that at the moment. He thinks I'm screwing him, and he's returning the favour. The people in the office next door found a cockroach in the yard two days ago and then yesterday I get a spot check from the food inspectors. Coincidence? I don't think so.'

'You've lost me.'

'It's obvious, isn't it? Titus introduces vermin and then calls the inspectors. He's trying to grind me down.'

Freddie was tempted to wonder out loud whether Mark wasn't doing just that himself.

'You're getting paranoid,' she said instead. 'Of course it's a coincidence. No one just plants cockroaches. You're being silly. And how many clients do you have living in south London? So this one happens to have the same post code as Titus. Come on, Mark. You want to be careful, you're in such a panic, you're falling out with everyone—'

'You don't understand, Freddie.' Mark spoke as though he was in pain. 'I'm in real trouble here. Two of Basil's suppliers have withdrawn my credit. I can't pay them what I owe. I'm trying to keep that afloat and doing the work myself. I don't have the hours in the day to work on Palmers. We need to sort out some proper promotions, do a bit of cost-cutting. Frankly, if Palmers is going to survive, it must have a further injection of cash.'

'What about your wife?'

'Bella? She's already servicing the loans. I can't ask her. Anyway, I never see her; she's always at her office or in the gym, at the moment. I'm not telling her about Basil. She's so competitive and such a success herself, she'd just rub my nose in it.' He shuddered. 'God, she'd have a field day with me.' He sighed. 'She doesn't understand me.'

Freddie laughed. 'Oh come on, Mark. You can think of a better line than that.'

Mark smiled then.

"Yes, I know. But it's true.'

'Why don't you make it up with your brother . . .' Freddie stopped as she recognised the possible confusion in her words '. . . with Ralph?' she amended. 'He could probably help you out—'

'No chance,' Mark scoffed. 'Ralph never backs down, over anything. He's much too proud.'

'Runs in the family then,' Freddie muttered. 'Okay, not Ralph, but why alienate Titus—'

'He's alienated himself.'

'Communicate with him, Mark. Tell him about Basil. Get him on side. Involve him properly. I've never understood why you don't, anyway. He seems a perfectly reasonable man.'

'Well, you've always fancied him.' Mark sounded truculent.

Freddie sighed heavily. 'Oh don't be ridiculous, Mark. I'm just suggesting that maybe he might have some ideas for making Palmers work better. For a start, you could suggest that perhaps he could hold off the rent demand until business picks up. It's in his interest to make the place work.'

'I don't want to go grovelling to him.'

Freddie rolled her eyes. 'It's not grovelling, Mark, he's your partner.'

'But he's also my brother and I reckon he's on some personal quest to get me.'

Freddie stood up. 'You're being boring, Mark. And completely illogical. Stop panicking and get a grip on the situation. I've never seen you like this. I'm going home to find some decent conversation.'

Mark's head was bent over his glass and she looked down at his bald patch. It seemed to be getting bigger. He raised his head.

'No. Stay a bit longer. Please.' He rose to his feet and made a half-hearted attempt on her breasts. 'Please stay.'

Freddie stared into his tired face and suddenly felt very sorry for him.

'No, come on, let's go home.' She disentangled herself and waited while he put on his coat. Outside the office, she put her arms round him and looked him in the eye.

'Try and think clearly, Mark,' she said gently. 'You can sort this out. Stop behaving like a loser, because you're not one. Not the Mark I know and sleep with, anyway.' She smiled up at him.

Bella, driving back from the gym, had paused outside the Basil offices debating whether to offer Mark a lift home. She watched as Freddie kissed him.

Kit took an unwilling Summer back to his house.

'We'll call in on the way to the cinema,' he said.

'What do I want to schlep all the way to Camberwell for when we can see a film round here?' she grumbled.

'Come with us, Ed, do us a favour,' Kit had pleaded to his friend in the morning. 'You want to see the film, you said you did and if you came home with us, it would make things easier. It's the first time she's been there.'

'I thought you said your dad was cool about Summer,' protested Ed.

'Cool?' Kit made a face at Ed. 'When exactly has my dad ever been cool about anything? He's accepted that there *is* Summer, but that's all. He still looks way grim about the whole family thing, so it would be easier if we looked like a group. I'll pay for your ticket and I'll buy all the drinks,' Kit offered desperately.

Ed had thought about it.

'Okay, I'll come,' he said, 'but I want a large popcorn as well.'

Summer was surprised at how warmly she was greeted by Grania – as though she was a treasured friend of the family.

'How's your mother?' Grania asked, as if she really cared.

Ralph came home while they were eating pizza round the kitchen table.

'Hello,' he said with surprise and acknowledged them all politely.

'Hello, Uncle Ralph,' Summer said, with the same challenging look she had given him in the hospital.

Ed stopped eating and watched Ralph's reaction.

'Hello, Summer.' Ralph appeared to be speaking carefully.

'You've got a lovely house,' Summer continued. 'Thank you for letting me come.'

Kit nudged Summer, not sure if she was being sarcastic. 'Shut up and eat your pizza,' he mumbled.

'I'm only being polite,' Summer said.

'They're off to the cinema in a minute,' Grania jumped in, 'via several large pizzas.'

She handed Ralph a drink. 'Come on, let's leave them to it.'

'What are you going to see?' asked Ralph, still looking at Summer.

'*Nil by Mouth*.' Her lips twitched. 'It's about dysfunctional families.'

Ralph and Summer stared at each other and the glimmer of a smile crossed Ralph's face.

Spontaneously and without thinking, Summer returned the smile. A connection passed imperceptibly between them.

'You definitely have Palmer blood running through your veins,' observed Ralph.

'That's good, is it?' Summer asked defiantly.

Again Ralph smiled, a sadder, softer smile this time. 'Like the curate's egg. In parts.'

Summer didn't understand what he meant.

After the cinema, Summer left Kit and Ed in the pub.

'She was keen to go.' Kit bent over the pool table and potted the white ball. 'Shit,' he muttered. 'I tell you, she's going off me.'

Ed took over and deftly notched up a high score. 'You know how you can always tell. She's put me off enough times lately and with really lame excuses. I've got work to do – like Summer ever works.'

Ed was sympathetic. 'She could be having hassle at home with the olds.'

'No. The thing is, no one seems to mind any more – you saw Dad this evening – we're free to do anything. But like, now she's not interested.'

'Maybe the excitement's worn off,' Ed suggested. 'Maybe she's the kind of chick who's into rucks.'

'No. I think she's got someone else.'

'I always said she wasn't in your league – no way,' Ed said cheerfully, as he potted the last ball.

'Of course she's in my league. She's my cousin, she's family.'

'Well, that's weird to start with.'

'You were the one who said it was okay to shag a cousin,' Kit pointed out crossly.

'Shag yes, but not get heavy over it. I mean, man, cousins. Don't cousins make funny babies together?'

Kit went home depressed. Sometimes Ed was a bit much to take.

A few days later, Summer met Kit out of school and slipped her arm into his.

'Let's go and grab a coffee,' Summer said. 'We need to talk.'

'Do we?' Kit said miserably.

'Yeah, and you've got to listen to me.'

So Kit listened while Summer told him that she was moving on to someone from college who was a little older than Kit and a wicked bass player.

'We get on really well and . . . you know, it just happened,' she said, looking straight into Kit's eyes with her usual honesty that at this moment he was finding hard to take. 'I really, really like you, Kit,' she said earnestly, 'and I want us to be friends as well as cousins, but you and me . . . as an item, that's got to be over.'

Kit stared at his bottle of lager and was surprised to find that the blackness inside that he had expected was not materialising. Instead there was this glimmer of a feeling that he slowly began to recognise as release.

'I suppose we were getting a bit intense,' he muttered.

'We knew it wasn't going to go on for ever. It was fun though, wasn't it?' She grinned at him. 'And we got a tattoo out of it.'

The two of them slowly began to rebuild a bridge in place of the one that Summer had just destroyed.

Kit had to ask. 'Was it the family thing?'

Summer looked thoughtful and then made a face. 'Sort of. I know it's always been there, but, I don't know, seeing your dad with Clattie in hospital. All that aggro, and then going round to yours, it all seemed a bit large, if you know what I mean.'

Kit nodded.

'We can still be friends though, can't we?' Summer asked anxiously. 'I mean, we have to be, don't we – we're family.'

Titus and Jane were sitting either side of the breakfast table. To Jane it seemed a very big table – a great big space that symbolised the gulf that was opening up between them.

'What a cheek!' Titus exploded suddenly.

'What?' Jane asked coolly.

'Ralph. A letter from Ralph now. Suggesting he and I meet. It looks as though I've been called into head office.'

Jane read the letter.

'It does not. He wants to talk to you. Maybe,' Jane rolled her eyes, 'just maybe he's hoping to heal the family rifts. Or would that be too normal for you to cope with?'

'I don't think so.' Titus was scornful. 'No, I tell you what it is. Mark has told Ralph that I've been bugging him about the restaurant and I bet the two of them have cooked up a deal to buy me out. That's what it is, the toe rags. Big brother coming along to save little brother. They're bringing in the big guns. Pay me off. They all think throwing money at a problem is the only way to solve it. They see everything in terms of money.'

Jane looked at her husband as though he was a very bad smell under her nose.

'Just like you do nowadays,' she observed with venom in her voice. 'Money and what's due to you, that's what this is all about.'

'It's you that minds about the money,' Titus responded furiously. 'You wanted the money to go home—'

'Yes, I did, I really did,' Jane interrupted heatedly. 'And it wouldn't have been so bad tying up all the Australian money in the restaurant, if you only enjoyed the sodding thing.'

'Haven't been given a chance to, have I?'

Jane sighed. 'Shit. Not this one again, Titus. You've absolutely no proof that Mark is turning you over. You've just got completely psychotic about it.'

'No, I've worked it all out.' Titus began fiddling with the breakfast things. Jane watched him rearrange the china and the cutlery into straight lines as he talked. 'There is something funny going on. Tymar. It was Mark's idea to call it that: Take Your Money And Run.'

Jane winced.

'It was a joke, but of course, now I realise it isn't a joke at all,' Titus continued. 'He did want to take my money and run. He didn't have the money to do a restaurant himself because he didn't get any money from the will. He needed to get his hands on my inheritance. That's what this is about. He never wanted me to be involved at all, it was just necessity. And, of course,' he added, 'he probably thought he was killing two birds with one stone; finance his dream and grind the family bastard into the mud—'

Jane picked up a milk bottle and hurled it on to the floor. The noise of the shattering glass brought Titus to a halt. She turned on him in a fury that neither of them had ever experienced before.

'That's it, Titus. I've had enough. I said all along business and brothers was a bad combination. Would you listen? Would you hell! Oh, no, completely separate, you said. But look at you

239

now. Completely obsessed. In the space of a few months you have become someone I just don't know and really don't *want* to know any more. You wanted this bloody restaurant, you wanted to go in with Mark. You promised me it was all cool and I believed you. I thought you should have the opportunity to do something that you longed to do. I understood that you'd got bored and needed a new challenge. But now the whole enterprise has turned into a bloody mess. Has it not occurred to you that perhaps this business venture which was going to make us so rich has in fact turned out to be a failure? And maybe it isn't even anyone's specific fault? And, by the way, are you too caught up in your conspiracy theory to realise that at the moment we're rather short of money? You've let your business ride through all this restaurant shit. We're struggling to live on my salary—'

'The rent's due,' Titus said in a subdued voice.

'Overdue, by my reckoning,' Jane pointed out. 'But you won't do anything about it, no doubt, because all you do is sit about here in a pique, brooding about this plot against you, and thinking of ways of getting the better of Mark. You're like a little boy who's had his favourite toy stolen by a bigger boy. You're greedy for all the big money you think you're being done out of. That's a murky gene pool you come from, Titus Palmer. You and Mark and Ralph. You're all the same, despite your different conditioning. Your dark side just took longer to come out. You're all proud, arrogant and greedy. Money, money, money,' Jane bent towards Titus and made a rubbing gesture with her hands, 'that's what's important, isn't it, when it comes down to it? Money and, of course, pride. Making sure no one even sniffs around what you think is rightfully yours. I don't like your family any more than you do, but do you know what? I don't like you at the moment either.'

Jane at last had shouted herself to silence. Titus looked too stunned to move. He stared at her, speechless.

Tears began to roll down Jane's cheeks as she threw herself into a chair.

'I'm sorry, Titus. That's it. I've had enough.' She spoke calmly, but there was no doubt about the determination in her voice. 'I have to get out of this situation. I'm going to have to leave for a while. This mess that you've created has gone too far and it's fucked us up. I've talked to Mum and she's lending me some cash and I'm going home to Australia for a bit, which is where we should have gone when your father died.' Jane, now sobbing, huge gasping sobs, stood up and made for the door. 'As for you,' she turned back to look at him scornfully, 'you can stay here and continue turning into your brothers.'

Mark walked home, trying to think clearly, as Freddie had suggested, but he was no nearer finding a solution. There was no sign of Bella in the house. 'Still at work being successful,' he said out loud and bitterly in the kitchen, as he opened a bottle of wine. He was rootling in the fridge for some supper ingredients when Bella came home. He heard the front door slam and, moments later, she appeared at the kitchen door. The two of them stared at each other.

Bella had watched Freddie disentangle herself from Mark's embrace outside the Basil offices. She'd seen Freddie drive away and Mark start walking towards home, too deep in thought to register her car. Long after he had disappeared round the corner she continued to sit, shaking and shocked, until her savage anger had subsided and was replaced by cool, clear determination.

'Hello.' Mark shut the fridge door. 'I'm looking for some supper. I expect you need a drink. You've had a long day – and a very lucrative one, too, I'm sure.'

Bella gave him a careful look. 'Not particularly. What's the matter with you?'

'Oh, nothing that Titus's immediate disappearance wouldn't improve.'

'Mark,' Bella said in a chilly voice. 'Is there something you'd like to tell me?'

'No. Well, yes there is, actually. I've worked Titus out.' He poured out the wine and handed her a glass. 'He thinks it's pay-back time. I've realised that he's convinced he's missing out on something – like he did when he was growing up. It's the family thing. He resents us, thinks we owe him something. Should be the other way round though. He owes us. He's got all the Gaffer's money. We just get what Clattie hasn't used up when she dies, and, believe me, that's not going to be enough. He's taken away our inheritance. Ralph was right when he called him an incubus – that's what he is. He's slowly and purposefully destroying our lives.'

Bella could see her husband's mouth move as he spoke, but she ceased hearing the words. She could only think of the way Frances had held Mark as though he belonged to her. He disgusted her and she felt strong.

'Get out, Mark,' she said in a loud voice that rose as she spoke. 'You're a sad bastard. You're completely self-obsessed. Everyone owes you, don't they? Poor victim.' She put on a whiny voice. 'Poor little Markie, whose father never loved him. Poor little Markie, who wasn't the favoured elder brother. You think you're so much cleverer than the rest of the family, don't you? You want to be like your father. You want his approval – even from beyond the grave. You're still fighting the same old battles you've been fighting since you were a little boy, but now you've made an almighty cock-up.'

Mark made to interrupt, but Bella could not have stopped even if she'd wanted to. She wasn't just tired of Mark, she was tired of everything – the effort of being Bella was suddenly too much for her. The future was looming ahead of her, empty, loveless and dull, but she was determined to *take* the future rather than have it handed to her by Mark.

'Oh yes, I know Basil's in trouble and that you're worried about the restaurant. But I only know because I made it my business to find out. You didn't tell me . . .' she fixed her eyes on Mark, 'because you've been too busy weeping on your mistress's shoulder. I'm sure she listens to your troubles, gives you the things I can't any more. You think I want what you want and, yes, I used to. But hey, guess what, unlike you, I'm a woman, so I can change. I don't go on fighting the same battles. And I'm tired of this one, really tired of it. So,' she looked triumphantly at her husband, 'get out. Go to Frances. Let *her* listen to your whining.'

'At least Freddie understands and she loves me.' Mark sounded defiant.

'Good. And if she really loves you that much she can underwrite you in the future.'

Mark, standing by the table, was silent. Bella wondered if he had taken in what she had said. She pushed him to one side as she moved across to the sink to fill a plastic water bottle.

'I mean it, Mark. Tomorrow I'm cancelling the loan repayments. That's a promise. Ten per cent of the profits? Of that place? The way you're going there won't be any, so I'm well out of the agreement. You and your precious *Freddie*,' she spat out the name, 'can sort out your mess together and I hope you both rot in hell. Just fuck off, Mark. And if you ever do grow into a human being, don't bother coming back. You're not any human being I want to be with. I'd rather be on my own.'

She picked up her sports bag from the corner of the kitchen and stuffed the bottle into it.

'I'm going to the gym and you're not to be here when I get back.' She flipped her hand in a dismissive gesture as she passed him, knocking over his glass. Wine poured on to the floor. 'Just piss off out of my life.'

Unflinching, Mark sat still and he didn't even move as the front door banged behind his wife.

Ralph was putting his life in order – making his peace. He drove down to The Mill to take Clattie out of hospital. In some way he felt that driving Clattie to Gerry's house was a concrete sign of his acceptance of their relationship and an acknowledgement of his part in her unhappiness. He sat in an armchair in Clattie's bedroom while Pippa collected their mother's clothes and packed them into two bags.

'Summer was at our house the other day. She's a nice girl.'

'She is,' agreed Pippa vaguely.

'You know, Pip,' Ralph started hesitantly, 'it's perfectly possible that Clattie might stay with Gerry even when she's better.'

'I know.'

'You do?'

Pippa sat down and began folding a jersey on her lap.

'Ralph,' she said with the slightest of patient sighs. 'Of course I do. I know Gerry and Clattie are fond of each other and I also know that the Gaffer and Clattie didn't get on.'

Ralph looked at her with surprise and Pippa went on as though explaining something to a dull child. 'You forget I lived here for at least ten years after you and Mark left home. I saw them together, heard them. They never really talked, you know, and you could tell that quite often Clattie really irritated the Gaffer. I always thought it was up to me to keep them together.' She gave a deprecating smile as though acknowledging her foolishness.

Ralph had a sudden thought. 'You didn't know that the Gaffer loved another woman all along, did you?'

'No, of course not.'

Then Ralph told her about the letters. She seemed quite unperturbed.

'I did know that the Gaffer was always horrid to Mark most of his life,' she said vehemently, 'and I hated that. I loved my father. He was good to me, he spoilt me and no child can resist that. I felt safe with him and we enjoyed doing the same things, but I sort of knew, inside me somewhere, that he probably wasn't a very nice man.'

'I never saw it,' Ralph said sadly.

'No, you wouldn't have,' she said shrewdly. 'You're male and you were the eldest. You didn't need to see anything.'

Pippa began refolding the jersey. 'I know everyone thinks I don't notice things, but actually I do. I just trained myself to pretend not to see things I didn't like. I learnt to do it when I was a child and had to listen to the Gaffer being demanding and irritable with Clattie. It was a type of defence mechanism, I

244

suppose. You see, I wanted perfect parents who loved each other and who loved all their children the same. I wanted a storybook father like the one you thought you had. But I knew he wasn't like that, so I learnt to pretend.' She almost chuckled. 'I can pretend that black is white if I want to, but it doesn't mean that I don't know the truth really.'

Ralph stood up and began zipping up one of the bags.

'I wonder when my family will stop surprising me.'

'When you stop asking too much from them,' Pippa answered unexpectedly.

They met in a quiet, unassuming wine bar, well away from either man's home territory. Ralph was already sitting at a table when Titus arrived and the two of them shook hands tentatively.

'Drink?' Ralph asked. Titus asked for mineral water. He wanted to keep a clear head to listen to whatever deal Ralph was going to offer him.

'I appreciate you coming,' Ralph began formally. He bent down to his briefcase on the floor, brought out a large brown envelope and placed it carefully on the table. 'This is for you.'

Titus picked it up, his mind already on the amount of notes that must be in there. He found the fact that the pay-off should be made in cash particularly offensive.

'They're letters,' Ralph said and watched as Titus drew out the bundles and turned them over in his hands. 'They're your mother and my father's letters to each other. Clattie gave them to me to read. She would have sent them to you, but I wanted to bring them myself.'

Titus slowly began putting the letters back into the envelope. The unexpectedness of seeing his mother's handwriting disturbed him and he wanted to put them out of sight until he felt more prepared.

'Thank you,' he said dully.

'I expect you've known all along that your mother and our father were always very much in love. I've only just found that out.'

Titus's head shot up and he looked steadily at Ralph.

'I'm afraid that's not true.' He spoke confidently. 'Not at all. The man treated my mother abominably. My aunt Monica knew the truth. That's why she was always so angry with him.'

'He loved your mother more than any other woman in his life.' Ralph spoke in a low voice. 'He did treat your mother badly but,' he gestured towards the letters, 'if you read those, you'll see how much he loved her. He treated my mother just as badly. Their marriage was just a pretence.'

Titus sat in silence, absorbing the information. He took a sip of water and then began speaking in a quiet monotone.

'The Gaffer never spoke about her, you know. He refused to have her name mentioned. As a child, even as an adult I hated him for that. Then he made me lie to my kids for him. Just to keep his secret. I've never understood why he wanted to see me. But maybe,' he gestured towards the envelope, 'if he really did love her—'

'Oh he loved her all right.'

'I never loved him,' Titus said sadly. 'I didn't even like him.'

'You've got some common ground with Mark then,' Ralph said grimly. 'He came in for a very bad time from our father simply because he was born as your mother was dying.' He stopped and said with difficulty, 'I'm afraid our father was selfish and manipulative.'

Titus looked at Ralph and for the first time saw the hurt and mortification on his brother's face.

'This must be pretty shitty for you,' he said.

'I seem to have been the only one in the family who never saw the Gaffer as he really was. For God's sake, even Pippa knew we didn't have the perfect family, but me – I wish he was alive now. I'd tell him what a bastard he was—'

'Makes a change from calling me one then.' Titus grinned. Ralph did not respond to Titus's flash of levity.

'I wanted to bring you these letters myself,' he continued, 'because I owe you and your family an apology. Not only was I very rude to you all, but some of the things I've been privately thinking and saying about you . . .' He shook his head. 'I felt threatened. I felt that the security of our family was being attacked and, if I'm being honest, I was jealous too. I resented Clattie being so fond of you all. And then when Pippa and Mark seemed to accept you and your family and then Kit and Summer,' Ralph looked at Titus and shrugged his shoulders, 'I felt this violent anger that you had appeared to destroy my precious family. I blamed you for what I now know were my father's sins. I was crass and I'm very ashamed of myself.'

'All my life I've envied you, Mark and Pippa,' Titus said when Ralph had come to a halt. 'You had proper parents. I had an absent father who treated me as some sort of possession that he had a duty to. You had The Mill. I loved that house. You had Clattie. I loved Aunt Monica and Uncle Will but I would love to have been part of a proper family, with brothers and sisters. I was never allowed to think of you as brothers and sister. Aunt Monica would never allow any discussion about you. She lied to me by omission.'

'This whole family is built on a foundation of lies,' burst out Ralph. 'It's all lies.'

'Alby was very angry with me for lying to him and he was hurt and upset. But I did it against my better judgement. I was wrong but I went along with it.' Titus paused and looked at Ralph. 'We were all lied to because our parents thought it was the right thing to do at the time. I suppose all children judge their parents but they do it in retrospect. Unfortunately, it seems that it's no guarantee that they don't make similar mistakes when they become parents.'

Titus studied his half-brother across the table, his fingers fiddling with the brown envelope. Ralph stared back at him. The shared pain between them was almost tangible.

Ralph broke the silence. He swigged the rest of his water and stood up.

'I'll leave you to read the letters. I'm sure you don't want me around. I just needed to make some sort of peace with you. I'm

247

ashamed of my behaviour and sorry seems a singularly ineffective word.' He held out his hand hesitantly.

Titus ignored Ralph's hand. He looked up at him and said with a soft smile, 'I think I'd like a proper drink now – would you stay and have one with me?'

Chapter Eleven

*F*reddie's basement flat was lit up and soft light shone through the curtains as Mark looked down from the street.

When Bella had banged out of the house Mark had immediately felt maligned and hurt. He'd sat down and finished the bottle of wine. Where had all her anger come from so suddenly? And so unreasonably. Hot defiance rapidly took the place of his injured feelings and, as he threw some clothes into a small suitcase, he experienced a heady feeling of freedom that he felt he needed to share at once with Freddie. Her mobile was on answer, so he left a message and rang for a minicab. Her flat looked warm and welcoming and he was already feeling her arms around him, tender, sympathetic Freddie. He realised that he had only been waiting for Bella to make the first move. He had been noble and patient, staying with her, waiting for her to be the one to break their marriage. Now he could see no obstacles in the way of Freddie and him sharing the rest of their lives together. There was one obstacle, however, that Mark, in his adrenalin rush had forgotten, and that was Freddie's husband Peter.

Who opened the door to Mark.

'Hello.' He greeted his visitor cordially.

Mark tried to look business-like and shook Peter's hand vigorously.

'Mark. Mark Palmer of Palmers restaurant. Freddie? Is she in?'

'No, I'm sorry, she's not here. I'm expecting her back in about half an hour.' He hesitated. 'Is it important? Do you want to wait?'

Mark had not bargained for his future being out. The impetus that had carried him thus far drained out of him.

'No, no, thank you,' he said calmly. 'She said she had some lighting catalogues she'd lend me. I was just passing. Thought I might pick them up. I'll ring tomorrow. Thank you so much.' He wrung Peter's hand as if the man had already given Mark permission to take his wife away.

Peter closed the door and Mark climbed back up the basement steps. Leaning against the railings at the top, he began to plan his and Freddie's new life. With her by his side he would be secure and happy and everyone else could go and screw themselves. She was so young, so positive, so full of life and, what was more, she really loved him. Perhaps she could have a baby. Mark stood in the shadow of a large bush overhanging the pavement and smiled at the idea of being a father. He would be rather a good father – not like the Gaffer – in fact they might have two children. They could inherit his chain of restaurants . . .

A car drove up and parked near by and Mark moved forward to peer into it. Freddie, head bent, was rummaging in her bag on the passenger seat.

He wrenched open the driver's door. 'She's chucked me out. It's all over.'

Freddie recoiled from Mark's hot breath and fought down the panic that was rising up in her. Mark here, outside her flat and with a suitcase. This was not good. 'Why has she chucked you out?' she asked warily.

'I don't know. It doesn't matter, I'm free.' Mark flashed a beatific smile and said loudly, 'We can be together now.'

Freddie's heart flipped over.

'Be quiet and get in the car,' she commanded.

Mark threw his suitcase in the back and slid into the front seat. Freddie drove round the block and parked the car in another street.

'Now look,' she spoke slowly and clearly. 'I'm sure Bella doesn't mean it really. It was probably a fit of temper and tomorrow you will make it up and everything will be as it was.'

'Oh no, she meant it. Thank God. *Told* me to come to you, in fact. Says we should be together. There was something about her being able to change . . .' Mark waved his hand dismissively. 'You know what women are like at her age, full of shit about the meaning of their life. Anyway the thing is, here I am.'

'It's time you weren't. You've got to go home, Mark.'

'Oh, I can't,' he said. 'I've left my key there. I've left everything. I want you and me to start a new life together as we planned.'

'We never planned anything, Mark.' She sensed that he wasn't hearing what she was saying. She shook his arm. 'Listen to me, Mark—'

Mark nodded his head. 'No, you're right. It's too late to talk now. I shall go to the office and bed down there. Then tomorrow we'll discuss the future.'

'Too right we will,' muttered Freddie.

Mark slept on the sofa in his office. He woke up cold, cramped and with a memory of being rather reckless the previous night. He made for the front door to breathe some fresh air. Outside he met the postman and he walked back to his desk, opening his letters as he went.

He wasn't looking at the envelopes as he opened them, so the letter from the Inland Revenue came as a crashing shock. A tax inspection. Mark thumped down into his chair, threw back his head and closed his eyes.

'I hope your door wasn't wide open all night.' Freddie arrived in front of his desk.

'There's nothing much to steal here,' he replied, his eyes still closed.

'Uncomfortable night?' Mark could hear the laughter in her voice. He opened his eyes.

'I'm sorry about last night. I did try and ring you first. I shouldn't have come round.' He held out his arms for her but she sidestepped him.

'No, you shouldn't have. That was breaking the rules.' There was no laughter in her voice now.

'I wasn't thinking. I wanted to celebrate my freedom.' Mark waved the letter still in his hand. 'But look what's happened this morning. The bastard's put the tax man on to me now. He's determined to see me lose everything.'

'What on earth does he gain by putting the tax inspectors on to you? Anyway, you haven't done anything wrong.'

'Except fuck up two businesses. And have you ever known a tax investigation that doesn't involve paying money into the Treasury?'

Freddie shrugged carelessly. 'I've never known a tax investigation.'

'No, well. You need to have a proper job for one of those.' Mark grinned at Freddie but her face didn't crack at the familiar tease. 'That was a joke,' he added.

'Not very funny.' Freddie's lips curled. 'If you stopped wallowing in self-pity, you might be able to see things as they really are. You and Titus both have your own agendas; you think Titus is out to get you and he thinks you're fiddling him. The Palmer family certainly goes in for over-active imaginations. It's time you both grew up and stopped letting family issues get in the way—'

'This has nothing to do with family.' Mark thumped the desk with his fist.

'Oh get real, Mark. Of course it does. Most things go back to family. Everyone's stuck with their bloodline in some way,

252

whether they like it or not. It's all to do with inheritance—'

'Inheritance,' Mark shouted. 'I can tell you about inheritance—'

'I'm not necessarily talking about money.' Freddie stood facing Mark, resting her hands on the desk. 'Now look, Mark—'

'This is some sort of revenge he wants to exact on me—'

'Mark.' Freddie raised her voice. 'I've come to say something and it's got nothing to do with your family or your business. Listen to me, Mark, and hear what I'm saying.'

Mark suddenly knew what she was going to say. He wouldn't let her finish.

'But I thought you loved me. I know I shouldn't have been there but I meant what I said last night. She's chucked me out. We can be together now.'

'We can't, Mark. That's not how this sort of relationship works, you know that. Bloody hell, you were the one who told me the very first time we went to bed together that you'd never leave your wife. We agreed – just fun and fucking.'

'Things change.'

'No, they don't. Not in this case. Neither of us were in this for a life commitment; I never wanted to spend the rest of my life with you. You were my dumb blonde and I was yours. A divertissement, a distraction, a bit of fun, that's what you were for me. I was the same for you. But lately it's stopped being fun, don't you think? And once this sort of relationship gets stale, it loses all its purpose so . . .' She put her head on one side and waited for Mark to speak.

Mark sat nonchalantly back in his chair.

'You'll miss me.'

'Possibly I will – for a while.' She spoke evenly. 'But I really believe this has run its course for us both.'

'Have you found someone else?'

Freddie laughed at him.

'You sound like a teenager.'

Mark was conciliatory.

'Okay, I've said I'm sorry about last night,' he began in a

reasonable voice. 'I got a bit carried away – I was happy, for God's sake – but that's no reason to stop you and me, is it? Why finish something that works for us both?'

'Mark, it's not working for me.' Freddie spoke gently, trying to make him understand. 'You don't make me laugh any more. For the last couple of months I've been a convenient quick shag and an understanding ear to listen to your business problems and family dramas.'

'I'm so sorry if I've bored you.' Mark was sarcastic and defensive now that he realised Freddie was serious.

'You haven't. Well, only recently.' She smiled at him affectionately. 'You're not as awful as you seem. You never have been, I know that. But who else does? Sort it out, Mark. I mean everything: Titus, your father, your failing businesses, Bella.'

Bella. Business. Something clicked inside Mark's head. Something he remembered with awful clarity, that Bella had said last night. No more loan servicing, no more agreement.

Mark stretched his arm across the desk and clutched on to Freddie's hand.

'You don't understand,' he said desperately. 'You can't leave me—'

Freddie took his face between her hands, stopping him from speaking.

'I can, Mark, and I'm going to. I don't regret you, not at all; it was fun and it was exciting, like . . . I don't know . . . permanently sliding down the banisters. I'm very fond of you and the sex was brilliant, but I've had enough now. And so have you really, I think you'll find, when you start thinking straight.' She gave him a soft kiss on his lips and left the office.

Sitting at his desk, Mark felt alone and vulnerable, and wondered if he had the energy to fight for his survival.

Grania looked at Ralph anxiously when he came back from meeting Titus.

'You've been a long time. How did it go?'

Ralph moved across the kitchen to switch on the kettle.

'He's a nice man,' he said simply. 'A better man than me, I feel, at the moment.'

Grania held out her arms and gave him a hug. 'You're a lovely man. I've always known that.'

Ralph rested in her embrace and then broke away.

'I think there's a problem between Mark and Titus. He wouldn't talk about it.' He reached for the tea caddy.

'And between Bella and Mark apparently.' Grania went to the fridge and brought out the milk. 'Bella rang this afternoon. She sounded awful. She's chucked him out. He's been having an affair, a proper one this time, she says. And Bella reckons that Basil and Palmers are fast going down the drain.'

Ralph rubbed his eyes. 'Oh Christ. When is this mess ever going to end? You shore up one leak in this family and then the shit oozes out somewhere else. I suppose I'd better try getting through to Mark.'

'I think Bella expects you to blame her,' Grania said. 'Letting down the family and all that.'

Ralph laughed mirthlessly. 'I think we've covered that area without Bella's help, don't you?'

Pippa, in London to meet a schoolfriend, was staying the night at Camberwell. Grania invited Bella to supper and was surprised by the alacrity of her acceptance.

'I could invite Titus and Jane?' Grania ventured to Ralph. He shook his head. 'Probably a bit too soon I think, especially with Bella at the moment.'

Pippa arrived in ebullient spirits with Razor waddling behind her.

'What's that thing doing here?' Ralph enquired as he greeted his sister.

'He comes everywhere with me now.'

'I thought you were allergic to him.'

'We've bonded since Clattie's accident. We wheeze together.' She bent down and patted the dog and then sneezed.

255

'Hardly a match made in heaven,' Ralph observed with amusement.

Kit was out for the evening, so it was just Grania, Ralph, Pippa and Bella who sat down to supper. Bella was pale and composed.

'I've taken up riding again,' Pippa announced as she heaped beans on to her plate. 'Simon and I try and go every weekend. There're some good stables at Malden.'

'Who's Simon?'

'Just someone from the church. He's part of the church ministry. I called on Jane this afternoon, by the way. I went to see her playgroup because I've been asked to run the Junior Church.'

'What's a Junior Church?' Ralph asked.

'Sunday school to you.'

'God,' grumbled Ralph. 'It sounds like the army.'

'How's Mark?' Pippa turned to Bella who'd been quiet, almost silent, since she'd arrived.

'I don't know,' she said quietly. 'He and I are not living together any more. He left a week ago.'

Pippa looked horrified. 'Oh no. Why? When? God, I'm so sorry. I've been rabbiting on about me and . . . What's happened? Does Clattie know? How terrible. I'm so awfully sorry. God, that's dreadful.'

Bella pushed back her chair. 'Excuse me,' she mumbled and rushed out of the room.

Grania waited a few minutes and then followed her, leaving Ralph and Pippa at the table.

Bella was in the kitchen, sitting on the back doorstep, drawing heavily on a cigarette. She dashed her hand across her eyes as Grania approached.

'Sorry. I'm not good at this.'

Grania sat down and put her arms round her. Bella almost shrugged her off.

'What?'

'Crying.'

'You don't have to have a fag outside, you know. In a crisis we allow smoking in the kitchen.'

'I need the fresh air.'

'Do you know where Mark's living?'

'Officially with some friends of ours, although Lizzie says he's not there much. Probably off with her. I imagine she's dumped her husband. Bitch. And she's a fool. He's bound to find someone else younger, sooner or later. It's congenital with him – and he's getting older so he'll just get worse.'

Bella threw down her cigarette and ground the stub viciously into the step. 'I miss him, Grania. He's a pretty crappy husband, but he's all I've got now. I'm lonely without him, you know.'

'You've got a career, you've got friends.' Grania felt inadequate in the face of such misery from Bella.

'No, I haven't. Not proper friends. They're only work friends. If I stopped working, they'd soon disappear. I've been bloody lonely this week. I wish I'd stocked up a larder with proper people that would always be there for me.' Bella stopped and a ghost of a smile flickered round her lips. 'I bet you never thought you'd hear me sound so wet.' She grimaced. 'I'm feeling very sorry for myself. Let's go back and finish supper and give me another drink, for God's sake, before I have a complete personality change.'

The rest of the evening was subdued, almost sombre. Ralph told Bella about the letters.

'Mark never told me,' she said.

'He doesn't know yet. I haven't been able to get hold of him. He won't answer his phone or return any calls.'

'I don't know whether it will make Mark feel better or not,' Pippa mused out loud.

'Probably not.' Bella spoke briskly. 'He's so enraged about Titus and that bloody restaurant, it'll just compound his anger and paranoia.'

'Jane said that Titus is the same.' Pippa picked at the cheeseboard. 'He's obsessed, apparently, convinced that Mark is double-crossing him.'

Grania poured more coffee. 'I really think it's only men that could get themselves into this truly awful mess—'

'I never had you down as a champion of women, Grania.' Bella looked at her sister-in-law.

'I'm not necessarily.' Grania glanced at her husband. 'It's obvious, if Titus and Mark could talk to each other, they'd sort it out, but then communication is not a strong male trait, is it?'

'So you think you women would have sorted this situation by now, do you?' Ralph asked her confrontationally.

'We wouldn't have let it get this far,' Bella said fiercely. 'We're not so full of shit.' She began ticking off the list on her fingers. 'Women are not so pig-headed, not so proud; we're not scared of being seen to get things wrong; we're not so afraid of talking about real things . . . I know I'm generalising,' she added, with a genuine smile this time, 'but there is an element of truth in what I'm saying.'

'Maybe it's because women don't mind so much about their image,' Pippa suggested.

'Ah, there you've got me, I'm afraid,' Bella said flippantly. 'I have to admit to being a bit of an image merchant. But I do think,' she went on more seriously, 'men can be so blinkered. They can only concentrate on one thing at a time, and when they get an idea in their head they just won't let it go.'

'You mean they lose all reason,' Grania said, smiling across at her husband.

Ralph held up his hands in submission.

'You could be right, I suppose,' he said with a sigh. 'Look what Clattie had to do to make me see round the corner.'

There was sadness in Bella's eyes as she said pensively, 'Kit and Summer friends, Pippa visiting Jane and you lunching with Titus. So now it's Mark who's the pariah.'

Ralph telephoned Mark's mobile and for once it was answered. He could hear the background sound of traffic through the phone.

'I hear things aren't going so well,' Ralph started cautiously.

'Now I wonder where you got that from,' answered Mark unpleasantly.

'I wanted to know if there was anything I could do—'

'Bit late to start offering your support now. I needed it last summer, if you remember. If you'd come through then, I'd never have got involved with the little shit.'

'We really need to talk,' Ralph persisted against the increasing traffic noise. 'There are some things I want to explain to you. Family business.'

'Family?' Mark sounded outraged. 'What family is that then? I don't want anything to do with family. Not this one. You're all a waste of space as far as I'm concerned.'

'I don't think—'

'Oh piss off!' Mark yelled violently down the phone. 'You and our maggoty half-brother who has put me in all this shit. Just fuck off all of you.' He turned off his phone.

Humiliated by his brother's concern and offers of help, Mark wrote to Titus acknowledging that the rent was due, but suggesting a three-month rent-free period to allow the restaurant to recoup the heavy losses it had sustained since Christmas. He set out a series of objectives and future ideas that he was sure would turn the fortunes of Palmers. His letter was brimming with a bravado that came from an uncomfortable feeling of being cornered.

His parents' letters sat in their envelope on his desk in the workshop and every day Titus took them out, sometimes to read, sometimes just to hold them in his hands. They didn't, he was beginning to recognise, solve anything. They didn't need to. He felt quite removed from the story that was unfolding as he read. And as he read, the past began to fade away for him. The Gaffer was as he was – who he loved and how he behaved was all becoming very unimportant. Titus understood now how much worse this was for the other Palmers and for Clattie; he had always seen himself as the victim – this belief had become part

259

of his history – but now he understood that actually he had never had any expectations. It was not the trust in *his* family that had been shattered.

Slowly, over a drink followed by lunch, Titus and Ralph had begun to learn about each other. Conversation was cautious to begin with – as though neither man wanted to stretch the relationship too far, too soon. Piece by piece, the two of them gently unravelled their childhoods, keeping the words light and the issues unemotional. As they were leaving, Ralph asked after the restaurant. Avoiding his eye, Titus answered abruptly, 'I don't know. Mark is not very communicative at the moment.'

Ralph had seemed to recognise the message in Titus's voice and had changed the subject.

'I like your Summer,' he'd said instead. 'She's got the Palmer spirit in her, I think.'

When Titus had got home, he'd wanted to talk to Jane about Ralph, but she had been fierce with him.

'Did he have a solution about the restaurant?' she'd asked. 'No? Then I don't want to hear about him. I don't want to hear about any of them until you've sorted it.'

Later he asked her if she would like to read the letters and she said regretfully, 'No Titus, I'm sorry, not at the moment. They'll just get in the way.'

So now he spent every day in his workshop working, he felt, through some sort of penance. As Jane had pointed out, business had fallen off and his workload was light so Titus was filling his time by making a rocking chair for her – for Jane who was enclosed and silent as if, in her head, she was already on the other side of the world. Summer and Alby were also remote and Titus felt surrounded by the whole family's wordless condemnation.

He tried to reach Jane.

'It's not the restaurant that's the problem,' he pleaded, 'it's Mark.'

Jane looked at him pityingly.

'It's neither,' she said. 'It's you. You've changed.'

260

Then one day, emptying a chest of drawers that needed repairing in Summer's bedroom, Titus came across a bundle of photographs. They were pictures of a summer holiday they'd had when the children were small. They had rented a tiny cottage in Devon with hard beds, plastic furniture and an overwhelming smell of gas. It was the only place they could afford and it had rained for the whole week. Titus sat on the floor and leafed through the pictures of the four of them laughing, in thick clothes on rainy beaches. Nothing, it came to him clearly at that moment, was worth jeopardising his family for. So, feeling as though he were packing away his dream, he wrote to Mark suggesting that Mark buy his share of Tymar, pointing out that his part in the restaurant company had not turned out to be quite as he'd expected. Titus would continue to own and control the freehold of the building, but he would like nothing more to do with Palmers restaurant. Titus didn't tell Jane about the letter. She was too unapproachable at the moment.

Their letters crossed. Mark read Titus's and screwed it into a ball and shied it at the wall opposite. 'Not a hope in hell, brother dear,' he said angrily to the empty office around him.

Titus read Mark's letter and his heart sank. The message was clear. Mark would not have the money to buy him out. Impasse. Now what? He looked across at Jane, who these days never asked him who his letters were from, and he wondered how he could get out of the mess into which he had manoeuvred them.

Clattie and Gerry sat by the fire, reading. Clattie sighed, put down her book and took up a knitting needle.

'This wretched itching,' she scolded at her leg as she dug the needle down the side of the plaster cast.

Gerry looked up. 'Only one more week, then it'll be off.'

'I can't wait.' She removed her spectacles and folded them neatly on top of her book. 'Gerry, I've made a decision.'

Gerry closed his book. 'I know you have.'

Clattie frowned. 'How do you know?'

'Because after Pippa came to see you yesterday, you were very quiet, then your face began to clear – you looked ironed out.'

'Gerry, you're a dear man. You're quite right. It seems that Ralph and Titus were only *part* of this family's turbulence. I haven't darned up the other holes that are there apparently—'

'Are you sure it's up to you to do the darning?'

'No,' admitted Clattie, fiddling with her spectacles. 'It's not. I know I can't. But I can do something that might help. I'm going to sell The Mill and give the money to my children.'

Gerry was silent.

'Money doesn't solve much in the long run, you know,' he said eventually. 'In fact, it seems to me, it's been one of the causes of your family's troubles. Of course,' he added humbly, 'I'm only speaking as an outsider.'

Clattie stretched out her hand as if to bridge the space between them.

'No, Gerry, you're not an outsider.'

Gerry reached across, and taking her hand he stroked it.

'Mark's in financial trouble,' Clattie went on. 'Pippa wants to move out of The Mill and get her own place, and Ralph, well, he of them all, needs to put The Mill behind him. He needs to break the family pattern.'

'And you?' Gerry asked gently.

Clattie looked round at the cottage sitting room and thought how secure the smallness of it made her feel, as though she had at last found the shell that fitted her properly.

'I want to be here. Where it's all complete and where I can just be.'

Titus rang Mark's mobile phone for three days before he got hold of him.

It was late and Mark was drinking with Greg in the restaurant bar after the customers and kitchen staff had left. He answered the phone without thinking.

'We need to talk,' Titus urged Mark.

'Nothing to say.'

'I want out.'

'Tough. I can't buy you out. I can't even find your sodding rent.'

Titus's voice remained steady.

'We've got to have a meeting with our accountants. We need some proper advice here. I'm not prepared to sit back and watch my investment shoot down the pan, just because you can't be bothered to put some hard graft into the place.'

The injustice of Titus's remark cut into Mark and he began to shout. 'I'm doing my best to survive here. And if you'd stop putting the squeezers on me, I might have a chance—'

'What? What are you talking about?'

'Oh right. So of course you had nothing to do with cancelled catering orders, spot checks by health inspectors and now a tax inquiry?'

'I don't know what you're talking about, Mark.'

'As if. You want to get back at me. You think I'm shafting you. I tell you, if I was, Palmers would be in a much healthier state than it is now. You don't have a clue how to run a restaurant. If I'd had the money from the Gaffer that was my right,' Mark hissed out the words, 'believe me, I wouldn't have even passed the time of day with you—'

There was a moment's silence on the other end of the phone.

'You really are a slippery bastard, aren't you?' Titus's voice was cold.

'Actually, Titus,' Mark drawled nastily, 'correct me if I'm wrong, but aren't you the bastard in this family?' He snapped off his phone.

'I need another drink,' he said, getting up unsteadily to fill up his glass from the optic. 'Another beer?'

Greg shook his head. 'No, I'm going home. I'm on early tomorrow.' He studied Mark anxiously. 'I think you should go home too.'

'Wherever that is,' Mark muttered.

'Are you okay?'

263

'Oh never better,' Mark said sarcastically.

'I think it'll pick up here.' Greg sounded encouraging. 'We've just got to give it time.'

'Haven't got much of that left. I'm finished, unless, of course, you'd like to buy me out. Though I'm afraid you'd be stuck with a partner who'd shaft you as soon as look at you.'

Mark's speech was slurred and his movements uncoordinated as he waved his glass at Greg.

'Tell you what. I'll *give* you my share—'

'No thanks. Come on, mate, I think we should get out of here.' Greg got up and tried to take Mark's arm. 'I'll give you a lift.'

Mark shrugged off Greg's arm and said more coherently. 'You go. Go on, get home, you've had a long day. I'll lock up.'

Greg hesitated.

'Go on, man,' Mark shouted. 'Bugger off home, or don't you trust me to lock up my own restaurant?'

Greg raised his eyebrows silently as he turned off most of the lights and made for the door.

'Are you sure I can't give you a lift?' he tried one last time. Mark shook his head. 'Will you be all right?'

'Why shouldn't I be?'

'I'll see you in the morning then?'

'Whatever,' Mark mumbled into his drink.

Left alone, Mark tottered behind the bar and clumsily took the vodka bottle from its optic, pouring the liquid into a pint glass and taking a long drink. He walked round his restaurant, bumping into tables and chairs, occasionally touching the walls in caressing gestures.

He sat back at the table and it occurred to him foggily that he was suddenly very hungry. He lurched into the kitchen, now cleared and silent: tea towels hanging on the airer, saucepans neatly stacked, plates and dishes in clean piles. Opening one of the large fridges, he peered myopically at the contents packed neatly inside and fumbled at the plastic boxes. He found a neatly packaged loaf of pâté, and tearing it open he crammed it into his mouth.

Casting his eyes round the kitchen, Mark noticed the deep-fat fryer full of congealed oil sitting beside the cooker. Chips. That's what he wanted. Chips. He lit a gas ring and put the fryer on top of it, turning on the overhead fan as he walked to the cold cupboard looking for potatoes. On the way, he forgot why he was going there and he looked back at the cooker with a frown. The tea towels on the airer near the fan were waving in the breeze it created, and the noise of the motor seemed very loud without the kitchen full of shouting, steamy chefs. He was still very hungry. Mark stood for a moment thoughtfully, watching the fryer before finding two potatoes and a loaf of bread in one of the cupboards.

Gobbling the bread, he moved back into the restaurant and poured himself another drink from the bar. He was sure he had a vodka bottle somewhere and where was Greg? He lurched towards the table. He was going to cook supper for Greg, or was it for Freddie? No, not for her, not any more. She was against him, she was a traitor. Just like all the others, she'd upped and left him to sort everything out. But he was cooking supper for someone, he was sure of that.

Putting the two potatoes carefully on the table, Mark picked up his phone and clumsily pressed a pre-dial number. His eyes were watery and his body felt heavy as he slumped on to a chair. He was very tired: tired of the whole thing . . . tired of the whole world, in fact. He rested his head on his hands.

In the kitchen the oil in the deep-fat fryer became so hot it caught light. The tea towels ignited and all the residue of fat in the fan above the cooker burst into noisy flames.

Jane heard the telephone; the ringing sound seemed to come in waves as she struggled upwards through layers of sleep and battled with the duvet to release her arm. When she picked up the receiver she could hear heavy breathing and she was about to cut off when she heard a muddled voice.

'Supper . . . making chips . . . come along, all together now . . . inviting you . . . chips.'

Jane recognised Mark's voice and she shook Titus awake with one hand while speaking down the phone.

'Mark? Is that you? Mark. Are you okay? It's Jane here.' There was silence at the end of the telephone. 'Titus, I think it's Mark on the phone. He sounds completely pissed and he appears to be inviting us to chips.'

Titus propped himself up on his elbow. 'Tell him to fuck off then,' and he lay down, covering his head with a pillow.

Jane looked at her watch – quarter to two. 'Mark, it's the middle of the night. Where are you?'

'Restauranty . . . it's mine restauranty . . . Come for chips.' Mark started to cough. 'S'ot, very hot, smoky . . . smoke.' The phone went dead.

'Titus.' Jane removed the pillow from her husband's head and shook him violently. 'I think Mark's at Palmers and something's wrong. He sounds as though he's ill. Something's wrong, I know it is.'

'He's what's wrong.' Titus turned over.

'Wake up. Blast you, wake up. You'll have to go and find out if he's okay. Go *on*.'

Stumbling out of bed and on to his feet, Titus pulled on his clothes and looked balefully at Jane.

'I'm doing this just to shut you up,' he grumbled. 'As far as I'm concerned that man can roast in hell.'

Opposite the restaurant, Milly Woods woke up her husband. She had the baby in her arms.

'Wake up, Paul. Fire, there's a fire somewhere near. I can smell it. Quick.'

Paul shot upright and was out of bed running round the house in an instant. He returned to the bedroom and found Milly by the window.

'It's not us,' he said.

'No, look.' She pointed across to the restaurant.

The blinds were down over the large windows but he could see smoke pouring out from the back of the building.

Milly shifted the baby on to her other arm.

'I think you should go and check.'

Slippers flapping on his feet, Paul ran across the road and began banging on the door. Expecting them to be locked, he pushed, almost falling in as they opened. Smoke was seeping through the kitchen doors, wreathing in circles along the ceiling of the restaurant and curling along the floor. Mark sat slumped at a table in the middle. He raised his head as Paul arrived at his side.

'Chips? Titus . . . coming too.' His head slumped back into his arms.

Paul took Mark's arm. 'Hey. Come on, let's get out of here.' He tried to drag Mark off the chair, but Mark lay heavily across the table. The smoke was slowly thickening around them. Seeing the mobile phone on the table, Paul put it in his dressing-gown pocket and half carrying, half pulling, he got the now inert Mark to the door and out into the street. Propping him up against the litter bin on the pavement, Paul took the mobile out of his pocket and dialled 999.

Titus saw the two figures outside the restaurant as he drove up. Three fire engines thundered up behind him as he got out of the car. Firemen began pouring out of the vehicles.

'What the hell . . .?' he said to Paul.

'I think the kitchen's on fire.' Paul pointed the firemen towards the restaurant and then turned to Titus. 'I found him slumped inside.' A brief smile flickered across his face. 'I think it's the drink that's rendered him insensible rather than the smoke.'

A fire officer knelt beside Mark and examined him briefly.

'He looks okay. An ambulance is on its way. Are you all right with him?'

The two men nodded and Titus crouched down beside Mark.

'Mark, Mark, it's Titus. Are you all right?' Mark opened one eye and looked at Titus blearily. 'Perfectly, thank you,' he said with dignity and began to cough. A crowd of neighbours was beginning to assemble around the drama. Someone brought a chair, another some water and between them, Titus and Paul hauled Mark on to the chair and made him drink the water.

'What were you doing in there at this hour?' Titus asked.

Mark slowly began to focus. 'I don't know,' he said in a puzzled voice. 'I was having a drink with Greg.' Suddenly alarmed, he looked towards the restaurant. 'He's not in there, is he?'

'You were alone when I found you,' Paul answered.

Mark looked up at him. 'You found me?'

Paul nodded and Mark held out his hand. 'Thank you very much. Very good of you,' he said in a polite voice that was only slightly blurry at the edges.

Paul shook Mark's hand without enthusiasm, handed Titus Mark's mobile, which was still in his hand, and then moved away towards the gaggle of people bunched on the pavement watching the fire fighters.

Titus and Mark were left set apart from both the spectators and the action.

They gazed in silence at the hosepipes snaking in through the door, the firemen rushing in and out. The lights inside had blown and the restaurant was dark apart from the flickering of the firemen's torches. The smoke seemed to be coming thicker and the smell of burning greater.

'When Ralph and I were little,' Mark said quietly but quite lucidly, 'and we were quarrelling over a toy, Clattie would say "If you two don't stop quarrelling you'll break it and then neither of you will have it."'

Side by side and in silence, the two men continued to watch their toy going up in flames.

Chapter Twelve

*T*he woody thud of the croquet balls against the mallets could be heard from inside the drawing room. Alby, Caitlin, Kit and Summer were on the lawn in the warm April sunshine. It was the weekend of the anniversary of the Gaffer's death and the whole of the Palmer family was gathered at The Mill for a final Sunday lunch.

For Clattie, coming back had been like visiting a deserted film set. After the smallness and the warmth of Gerry's cottage, the old house seemed already to be empty of the Palmer family, as though it was in cold storage waiting for the new family to come and draw back the curtains to let in the sun. She had already begun to pack up, to label the few things that she wanted to take with her. Now it was time for the children to decide what they wanted from the house. It had been Ralph who suggested that Titus and his family were invited to join them.

'I think we should all be together,' he had announced clearly and no one had argued.

There was, however, a small argument about to break out in the garden.

'That was a crap roquet,' Summer was shouting across the lawn to Kit. 'Look where you've put me. We're meant to be partners.'

'I've got a plan,' retorted Kit.

'Run with it, Summer,' called Alby. 'You know Gaff always said that men can see the angles better.'

'Look.' Kit moved towards Summer's ball. 'Now your ball's in the flower bed, we can put it two mallet lengths on to the lawn. House rules.'

'No, it's only one mallet length if we're all equal players,' Caitlin argued. 'And it doesn't count if you hit into the flower bed on purpose. Isn't that right, Alby?'

'I'm fed up with playing, anyway.' Kit threw down his mallet. The four of them looked at each other and then laughed.

'Gaff always used to say croquet's just like Monopoly. It brings out the worst in everyone,' Caitlin said.

'He still liked us to play it, though,' Alby said. 'He was always so pleased when you played well.'

'And he was a good teacher,' said Caitlin. 'He really took time to explain things.'

'I climbed on to the dovecote roof once,' Kit joined in. 'He was furious, but then the next day he climbed up with me and showed me how you can see six villages from there. I was scared of him sometimes though. When I was really young,' he added quickly.

'I wasn't at all,' Summer said.

'That's because he spoilt you rotten,' Alby interrupted. 'You were always his favourite.' He petered out as he realised what he was saying. The silence between the four was an acknowledgement that there were still things being said that sat uncomfortably between them.

'I loved him so much.' Summer broke the silence. 'I still wish I'd known when he was alive that he was our grandfather too.' She sat down at the garden table and picked up her drink. 'Who's going to have the croquet set, anyway? In this great share-out.'

'We are, I think.' Kit joined her at the table. 'We've got a lawn almost big enough. We can play while you're staying with us.'

Summer lifted her arms above her head and stretched luxuriously.

'Four months and then I'll be in Australia. A whole year off before art school. Wicked.' She looked at Kit. 'You're cool about me staying with you until I go?'

'Course.' Kit was casual. 'Why shouldn't I be? You were right to pull the plug on us,' he added bravely. 'I was pretty gutted at first, but then I sort of got it together. Like it's much better to be cousins. Cousins are always around.'

'Just think, this time last year,' Caitlin said to Alby as they collected up the croquet stuff, 'we'd just found out about you lot.' She shuddered. 'That was awful. My poor Dad.'

'Poor everyone, I say.' Alby spoke matter-of-factly. 'And what's really weird is your dad – of all people – offering to have Summer to stay till she comes out to Australia. I mean, when you think what he felt about us—'

'The family thing's really important to Dad.'

'Yeah, but he didn't think of us as family. Remember? Something must have happened to change his mind.' Alby sighed. 'And I don't suppose they'll ever tell us what. They'll keep it a secret or they'll lie to us about it if we ever ask. I swear to God, I'm never, never going to lie to my kids if I have any.'

'I bet that's what everyone says before they have kids,' said Caitlin.

Titus was in the drawing room and he found it strangely comforting that he was alone – it made him feel like family rather than a guest.

He sat on the sofa and idly watched the croquet game in the garden through the long windows. He thought of this time last year; this same room full of people mourning the old man who, by his dying, had created so much instability in a family that had thought itself invulnerable.

271

Since the fire, this last month had seemed to pass in a series of meetings, negotiations and ultimatums that had Titus feeling as though something heavy had rolled over him, leaving him flattened and empty.

Titus had rung Bella on the night of the fire and she had taken control, sweeping into the hospital, taking Mark home and emerging three days later with a proposition for Titus. She planned to sell her business and buy his fifty per cent of the company.

'This is nothing to do with Mark,' she'd declared at their first meeting. 'You sell to me, not to Mark.'

With the help of lawyers and accountants, the two of them thrashed out a deal. In the event, Bella could only manage half of Titus's original investment and she suggested the remaining half should be considered a loan with Titus receiving interest at three per cent over base rate.

Titus and his accountant held out for an added percentage of the profits.

'It's only fair, after all,' Titus said to Jane after the first meeting. 'My money has been tied up for nine months. I deserve some recognition of that and he set the bloody place on fire. It's through his negligence the insurers aren't paying out in full for the new kitchen.'

Jane had looked at him in disgust. 'You still don't get it, do you?'

'I'm just trying to get the best deal for *us*,' he'd argued.

Jane had backed off. 'No, count me out, Titus. I want no part of it—'

'What's happened to us, Janey?' Titus had interrupted her.

'Money happened.'

'I only wanted it for us.'

'Is the money or your family more important?' Jane had asked dispassionately.

'You. You, of course,' Titus had repeated.

'Well, work it out, Titus. Get out of the restaurant company. Once and for all.' Jane had smiled at him then and said more gently, 'You'd better take the money and run, hadn't you?'

And that was what he'd done. He'd taken the money and dropped the claim for profit percentage. Now The Mill was to be sold for more than anyone had expected, Mark was going to pay the outstanding loan from his share of the sale and then Titus would be completely rid of Palmers restaurant. He felt relieved, yet saddened by his loss, and to begin with this extended holiday to Australia seemed to Titus to be a kind of running away from his failure and also from his future. It had felt like a dereliction of duty, although he couldn't quite place where his duty lay any more.

But in the last week a proposition from his architect friend, Geoff Turner, had changed Titus's perspective into something more positive. While they were in Australia, he and Jane would discuss – as they now could again – the possibilities of Titus's closing Palmer's Restoration and joining Geoff's design company.

Titus put his head into his hands and imagined the future; slowly rebuilding his hurt pride, putting all the anger and resentment behind him and being a family again with Jane and their children . . . and with the *other* Palmers.

He heard someone come into the room and he looked up. Ralph was standing in front of him, holding the hunting horn and the silver flask from the hall table.

'I know you said you didn't want anything from here, but Clattie said your children always enjoyed playing with these when they were small. Please have them,' he urged. 'Take them for Summer and Alby.'

He watched as Titus took the horn and flask from him and laid them in his lap.

'Thanks. They'll like that. And thank you too for having Summer to stay. We really appreciate it.'

'Our pleasure.' Ralph sat down in an armchair and smiled at Titus. 'That's what families are for.'

Grania had been sorting out sheets in the linen cupboard

upstairs. She took a heap of bed linen and piled it on the chest at the top of the stairs. Crossing the landing, she saw Bella sitting on the balcony, smoking a cigarette.

'Bella, there're some more sheets and pillowcases going if you want.'

Bella turned round and gave her sister-in-law a scornful look. 'What on earth do I want more bed linen for?'

'I just thought you might. Jane's having some and the rest is going to auction.'

Grania came on to the balcony and leant over the railings and watched the croquet players on the lawn below. At the end of the garden, the white pigeons sat in rows on the dovecote roof. She pointed at them.

'There's one with a few grey feathers in it.'

Bella looked across. 'Oh yes. Now why does that remind me of Titus?'

'Oh Bella.' Grania sounded reproving. Since Mark had come back, Bella had regained her brittle superiority and, in a curious way, Grania decided, she preferred Bella to be the way she'd always been. It seemed to keep things more in place, more normal.

'Someone should wring its neck,' observed Bella, 'before the whole flock becomes tainted.'

'I don't know,' Grania said meditatively. 'Why should it be slaughtered just because it's different? Poor thing, it's not its fault, is it?' She turned round to find Bella grinning at her.

'What?'

Bella shrugged. 'I was just listening to you wittering on about pigeons. It was *pigeons* you were talking about, wasn't it?'

Grania smiled back. 'Of course.'

A current of warmth passed between the two women, one that had never been there before and was gone almost as soon as it appeared.

Grania sighed. 'I'll miss this place.'

'I thought you were going off on your country idyll?'

'Eventually. When Kit's finished his exams. I expect we'll have

274

to find a version of this house somewhere. Ralph won't be able to help himself.'

The two women continued to gaze over the garden.

'How's Mark?' asked Grania.

'He's okay.' Bella stubbed her cigarette out on the decking. 'Ours isn't a marriage made in heaven, never has been. But I think we'll make good business partners. You know, Mark may have lost the spin recently but he's still a top chef and I've got plans.' Her eyes lit up. 'We'll have a relaunch and Palmers will rise like a phoenix from the ashes. We're going to turn the place round and make a fortune. Show Titus how to do it. And one day,' her eyes lit up with avarice, 'I'll get the freehold off the dreary little man, just watch me.'

Going into the dining room to decant the wine, Mark found Jane laying the table.

'I'm sorry,' he found himself saying as he hesitated at the door.

Jane put down the pile of forks on the table and looked straight at him. 'Sorry for coming in here or sorry for something else?'

Mark was silent for a moment, then he walked forward and rested his hands on the back of his father's chair.

'Actually, yes, I'm sorry about everything.'

'You don't like Titus, do you? You never did.' Jane spoke calmly.

Mark replied in the same quiet voice. 'I know that's what you both think, but that's not strictly true. At the beginning I thought Titus and I got on rather well but, in the end, we both realised we had nothing in common—'

'Oh, but you did.' Jane's eyes blazed. 'You stupid men. You did have something in common. You both hated your father. You both felt done down by him. Both jealous, resentful. But that was too much to acknowledge, too much for you to talk about together, wasn't it? Too soppy? Too likely to make you both vulnerable? And, of course, it would have been muddling up the compartments – the pigeon holes in which you keep all the different bits of your life. Business, family, emotional stuff. You both thought you could keep it all in separate boxes. Well, now you know you can't, don't you?' Jane turned back to the table in disgust.

Mark looked down at his hands on the mahogany chair back. The Gaffer's chair suddenly seemed small and insignificant – no different from the others in the dining room.

'Yes,' he said in a low voice. 'Everything you say is absolutely right.'

'I'm going to have a party in the flat as soon as I've decorated it,' Pippa said. 'I want you all to come.' She looked across the lunch table at Jane and Titus. 'Oh, but you won't be here. I shall just have to have another when you get back. Simon is making me a grand dining-room table so I can have proper Sunday lunches with everyone.' She gestured with her hand and knocked over a glass of wine. 'Oh, I'm sorry. I'll go and get a cloth.'

'I suppose she's safe to live alone, is she?' asked Ralph. 'It seems to me there's a pretty fair chance she'll set fire to the place within a week.'

There was a deathly pause round the table.

'You mean like her brother did,' Mark said, his face bleak.

Ralph winced. 'I'm sorry, Mark. I didn't think.'

'She's not going far,' Clattie broke in. 'I can keep an eye on her. She's got all her friends at the church and this Simon seems to be around a lot. She'll be fine.'

Pippa came back and mopped the table. Clattie motioned her to her seat and cleared her throat.

Looking across at her, Mark remembered a year ago – Clattie's strained face as she stood in front of them in the drawing room to tell them about Titus. Now Titus was here with Jane and Summer and Alby – all of them an undoubted part of the Palmer family. And that was, he realised now, perfectly all right. He caught Titus's eye and the two men looked at each other. Unobtrusively, Mark nodded at Titus and with a glimmer of a smile Titus nodded back at him.

'I'd like to propose a toast.' Clattie stood up and spoke resolutely. 'I think we should drink to all the people who have coloured our lives, in whatever way, and who are no longer with us. I want us to let them go and together move forward from here. I give you the toast of "Absent Friends".'

HOPING FOR HOPE

Lucy Clare

'Emotionally convincing debut novel'
The Times

When Liddy Claver visits her doctor a few days before her
fiftieth birthday, she assumes she is menopausal. But
instead, her doctor has some astonishing news for her: she
is thirty weeks pregnant. Liddy is shocked, but not as
shocked as her husband Martin is going to be. Liddy and
Martin haven't had sex for five years.

Liddy learns that Martin has also been unfaithful, and she
hopes that being honest with each other might bring them
back together. But when Liddy gives birth to a baby
daughter, Hope, it is a child that her husband wants
nothing to do with, and equally problematically, that their
three grown-up children – Laura, Miranda and Alex –
each feel should be theirs to bring up . . .

Compassionate and compelling, Lucy Clare's debut novel
is an emotive page-turner par excellence. It is a story about
families – about hoping for understanding, hoping for
support, but above all, about hoping for Hope.

'A story written with tender humour'
Sunday Mirror

Fiction
ISBN 0 7515 3157 X

You can now order superb titles directly from Time Warner Paperbacks:

☐	Hoping for Hope	Lucy Clare	£5.99
☐	A Risk Worth Taking	Robin Pilcher	£6.99
☐	The Greek Villa	Judith Gould	£6.99
☐	Wild Weekend	Celia Brayfield	£6.99

The prices shown above are correct at time of going to press. However, the publishers reserve the right to increase prices on covers from those previously advertised without prior notice.

timewarner
paperbacks

TIME WARNER PAPERBACKS
P.O. Box 121, Kettering, Northants NN14 4ZQ
Tel: 01832 737525, Fax: 01832 733076
Email: aspenhouse@FSBDial.co.uk

POST AND PACKING:
Payments can be made as follows: cheque, postal order (payable to Time Warner Paperbacks) or by credit cards. Do not send cash or currency.

All U.K. Orders   **FREE OF CHARGE**
E.E.C. & Overseas   25% of order value

Name (Block Letters) _____

Address _____

_____

Post/zip code: _____

☐ Please keep me in touch with future Time Warner publications

☐ I enclose my remittance £ _____

☐ I wish to pay by Visa/Access/Mastercard/Eurocard

Card Expiry Date

_____